A VERY PRIVATE WAR

By the same author

YOU CAN'T SEE ROUND CORNERS

THE LONG SHADOW

JUST LET ME BE

THE SUNDOWNERS

THE CLIMATE OF COURAGE

JUSTIN BAYARD

THE GREEN HELMET

BACK OF SUNSET

NORTH FROM THURSDAY

THE COUNTRY OF MARRIAGE

FORESTS OF THE NIGHT

A FLIGHT OF CHARIOTS

THE FALL OF AN EAGLE

THE PULSE OF DANGER

THE HIGH COMMISSIONER

THE LONG PURSUIT

SEASON OF DOUBT

REMEMBER JACK HOXIE

HELGA'S WEB

THE LIBERATORS

THE NINTH MARQUESS

RANSOM

PETER'S PENCE

THE SAFE HOUSE

A SOUND OF LIGHTNING

HIGH ROAD TO CHINA

VORTEX

THE BEAUFORT SISTERS

A VERY PRIVATE WAR

Jon Cleary

William Morrow and Company, Inc.
New York 1980

Originally published in Great Britain in 1980 by William Collins
Publishers Pty Ltd

Library of Congress Cataloging in Publication Data

Cleary, Jon, 1917-
  A very private war.

    1. World War, 1939-1945—Fiction. I. Title.
PZ3.C58Ve   1980   [PR9619.3.C54]   823   80-12006
ISBN 0-688-03648-1

Printed in the United States of America

  2   3   4   5   6   7   8   9   10

For Vanessa

AUTHOR'S PREFACE

This is a work of fiction. Though it deals with the field work of an actual organization, no character in the book is meant to represent anyone who served with the Coastwatchers. They were all heroes who need nothing from me to colour their exploits.

There is no Taluka airstrip on New Britain. However, the method of camouflage described in the story was used to hide the construction of an airstrip at Lambeti plantation on Munda Point on the island of New Georgia. U.S. reconnaissance photo interpreters eventually detected the camouflage.

I was helped by some excellent advice from Mr W. H. Brooksbank, Mr Reg Evans and Mr Peter Figgis, all of whom were with the Coastwatching Service. Mr John Mackenzie, historian with the Australian Navy Office, and Mr Bob Piper, of the RAAF Historical Section, provided valuable information. I could not even have begun the book without first absorbing the background supplied by Eric Feldt's *The Coastwatchers* and Walter Lord's *Lonely Vigil*. A chapter heading in Mr Lord's book gave me my title.

Chapter One

I

Cornelius Mullane was playing catch with Buka, the latter's strong right arm thumping the ball into Mullane's battered old baseball mitt, when Frank Vokes came chug-chug-chugging across the bay in his launch to say that the Japanese were coming at last.

"It's more than a patrol this time, Con! A supply boat and four barges – looks like they're coming down to stay. They've just passed Murota, so they should be here in an hour at the outside."

Frank Vokes had an excess of energy, was never still; he was tiring to watch and sometimes tiring. He had a long angular face, the sort Mullane had come to think of as an Australian face. But unlike the wary, prove-it-to-me-mate countenance of most of the Australians Mullane had met, Vokes' was wide open with curiosity at the world. He also had a wide open mouth; he was the most garrulous man Mullane had ever met. He was twenty-two years old, the assistant manager of the Burns Philp plantation across the bay and he was the last person Mullane would have voluntarily chosen as company in the weeks or months ahead.

"You all ready to go, Con? Geez, I'm raring to go, you know what I mean? All these months sitting on our bums – "

"I've never seen you sitting down all the time I've known you." He turned round to give an order to Buka, then jumped as a shot went off right behind him. "What the – !"

"Sorry, mate." Vokes picked up his .303 Lee-Enfield from where it had fallen by his foot; a bullet had scored a mark across the toe of his boot. "I dropped it. I suppose I'd better warn you – I think I'm, what do they call it, accident-prone?

7

You wouldn't read about the things that happen to me. I must be the only bloke in the world who's ever been attacked by a *dove*."

Mullane restrained himself from asking about the vicious dove. He feared he was going to learn more about Vokes than he really wanted to know about any man. Though they had both been Coastwatchers for the past six months, each time they had had to flee their plantations and head for the mountains when a Japanese patrol had appeared, each of them had gone to his own hideout. But orders had come in on their radios last week that from now on they were to operate as a team.

Mullane sighed. "Let's keep the accidents to a minimum, shall we? One a day at the most."

Vokes grinned. "I wouldn't bet on it. But I'll try."

"Okay, Buka. Get the boys rounded up." He was always glad that Buka spoke and understood English. Mullane loved language and languages and the infant talk of pidgin always irritated him. "Tell Bingiti to hide Mr Vokes' boat with mine – Who the hell, may I ask, is *that*?"

"What?" Vokes looked back down the beach. "Oh, *her*. That's Ruth Riddle. You know, the NMP, the native medical practitioner, from down at Malapio. She came up the day before yesterday. They'd had a visit from a patrol at Gasmata and she went bush, then decided she'd better come up here. Said she thought she'd be safer with us – "

"With *us*? She's not coming with us!"

"Con – we can't leave her here! You know what the Nips would do to her, a good sort like her. I know she's got a touch of the tar-brush in her, but she's not like these boong girls – "

"She's not coming with us," said Mullane adamantly.

Vokes looked as if he were about to explode into argument, then abruptly he shrugged. "Right, you tell her then. I'm not going to have her on my bloody conscience."

Ruth Riddle took the lid off her medical box, stood up and waited as the tall American came down to the beach with Vokes and stared angrily at her. "Miss Riddle, I don't want you to think this is personal – "

She laughed, a pleasant gurgle. "Mr Mullane, I've been

hearing that preface ever since I came back from my medical training in Fiji two years ago. It's always personal, Mr Mullane, so please don't beat about the bush."

"Ruthie – " Vokes had an Australian habit of adding *ie* to everyone's name; Mullane was waiting to be called Connie, whereupon he was going to deck Vokesie. "I haven't had time to tell Con that you're going to be a great help up there in the hills. I mean who knows when, how many times, we're going to need medical attention? Having you on hand – "

"Frank, *please.*"

Mullane held up a silencing hand, but did not take his eyes off Ruth Riddle. He was surprised at how good-looking she was; not all the mixed bloods, the *locals* as the white Islanders called them, looked like Dorothy Lamour in her sarong. She was no taller than any of the native women here on the plantation, but she carried herself very straight and looked taller. He wondered if her carriage had some defiance in it, a challenge to the white men and women who would never accept her as an equal. But he was just as impressed by her voice and the fact that she had used the word *preface.* It was a word he had never heard Vokes, the man of a million words, use.

"My dear young lady, I'd preface my remarks to the Virgin Mary in the same way. Where we are going is no place for a woman."

"I'm not your dear young lady, Mr Mullane. I try to be a lady occasionally, but if it doesn't come naturally to me – " She let out something that was half-sigh, half-snarl. "Damn it, do you think *this* is going to be a safe place for a woman like me?"

Mullane pulled at his black beard in exasperation. He had grown the beard only in the past three months when he had spent some time in the hills avoiding a Japanese patrol that had come down to Kiogo. He was a handsome man, his looks spoiled only by a certain sadness and cynicism in the dark blue eyes; but he was a charitable man who did not lay his moods on other people. He knew he was not being charitable right now and it irked him.

"Just a minute, Con." Vokes was standing still for a moment, arms akimbo. "So far there's been no argument about who's going to be boss on this job. But I got word in the night before last – "

"I was tuned in, too. You're now a sub-lieutenant in the Royal Australian Navy. You want me to salute?"

Vokes started waving his arms. "No, I don't! But if it comes down to a fine point, a naval bloke's got to have the edge over a civilian. Especially, if you don't mind me mentioning it, a *foreign* civilian. How does that strike you? I don't suppose a Yank ever thinks of himself as a foreigner."

"Occasionally," said Mullane, thinking of Tokyo and how foreign he had always felt there, even in the dark alone with Mieko. But that had been five years ago and now this was August 1942 and here on this island in the South Pacific he had lost any sense of being a foreigner. True, till last December and Pearl Harbor, he had also lost a good deal of the sense of being an American.

"Well – " said Vokes uncomfortably, not sure of how a naval officer should act; he had expected more argument from Mullane on that point. "Well, I say she comes with us. That's settled, then. Right?" He sounded more wishful than adamant.

Mullane looked out across the wide bay to the distant point where the Japanese would soon appear. The sea and the sky, though at times they could be stormy, always suggested to him the peace he had come seeking here. And had found up till early last February when the first Japanese patrols had come prying their way down the coast. There had been peaceful days since then, but the calm had always been fragile. He had always known that the Japanese would come back to Kiogo to stay.

Blomfield, the RAN lieutenant, had told him that when he had flown in here by Catalina just before the first Japanese patrol had appeared. "We can't hold any part of New Britain, Mullane. They took Rabaul as if we'd handed it to them on a plate. Don't quote me, but they can take New Guinea just as easily if they want to press on."

"I gather it was a rout in Rabaul. Some of the troops passed through here on their way out."

"A bloody shambles. Never had a hope. That's why we're

advising everyone who wants to leave the island to do so now. But if you want to stay, we can't *order* you out – "

"I do want to stay, Lieutenant."

Blomfield believed in the blunt approach; if he had been in charge of a ship he would just as soon have rammed the enemy as shelled him. "I'm looking for volunteers. For the Coastwatchers. It's a bit unfortunate you're an American – "

"I'm sorry about that." Mullane wondered if Australia had ever produced any diplomats.

"I only meant we could commission you if you were an Aussie. Might help if the Nips caught up with you. The Geneva Convention, all that sort of thing. If they should capture you as a civilian, they could shoot you as a spy."

"Couldn't the U.S. Navy commission me?" If that should happen, he wondered what his brother Liam, sitting at his desk in the Navy Department in Washington, would think of it.

"I suppose so. Don't know how the USN works." Somehow Blomfield's tone suggested a double meaning. After the disaster of Pearl Harbor, he wondered how any navy that could be caught napping like that could work at all. "Well, are you willing? I mean, if you're staying on – "

"I'm willing," Mullane said after a long moment.

He already knew of the Islands Coastwatching Service which had been developed as part of the Intelligence arm of the RAN. Manned by volunteers drawn from British Colonial officers, planters like himself, traders and missionaries, the network of stations stretched in a 2500-mile arc from New Guinea down to the New Hebrides, with headquarters back at Townsville in northern Queensland. The Coastwatchers were under strict orders not to fight unless absolutely necessary to save their own lives; they were to avoid contact with the enemy at all times. They were the eyes of the forces defending Australia and the islands to the north and north-east of the continent; small though their ranks were and meagre their resources, they had become invaluable in the desperate defensive campaign now being fought by the Allied forces. They were spies, possibly the loneliest spies, subjected to the most uncomfortable conditions, of anyone working behind enemy lines in the whole world-wide war. It gave Mullane a certain sardonic amusement that he should be volunteering to spy again, particularly since his last effort had been in circumstances where he could go home every night to the comfort of his home and the arms of his wife. But he did not mention that to Blomfield.

"I'm willing." Committing himself, he felt a sudden fierceness which he managed to hide. He did not want to have to explain to Blomfield why he felt more a sense of vengeance than of patriotism.

And now the Japanese were coming again to Kiogo and he and Vokes were all ready to go. He would have to accept the girl's presence whether he liked it or not.

"Okay. But you're Frank's responsibility, not mine."

"I'm nobody's responsibility but my own, Mr Mullane. You learn that when you're a local."

He grasped the strap of her medical box, took it firmly from her. "Frank, get an extra boy. I've got a couple standing by as reserves."

Vokes took the box, almost dropped it, grinned at his clumsiness and went up through the coconut groves to where Buka had marshalled the natives who were to act as carriers.

Ruth Riddle looked after him, then up at Mullane. "He must have forgotten that he out-ranked you. Or do you see yourself as the natural leader?"

"Let's say he bows to my greater age. Thirty-eight is very elderly to someone Frank's age."

"Mine, too. Lead on, Dad."

A mocking woman: just what he needed. Then he heard Vokes shout: "Con! They're just off the point now!"

Mullane had only time to glimpse the ship and barges appearing round the distant point, when there was another shout and immediately following it the roar of an approaching plane. He swung round, saw the Zero coming in low above the mangrove swamps at the southern end of the bay. He shouted "Down!" and dropped flat. It only struck him later that he did not look to see if everyone obeyed him; if self-preservation was the idea, he was a leader who set a natural example. Vokes and Ruth Riddle fell down, but most of the natives, some bewildered, some excited, remained standing. The bullets zipped down through the trees and found targets.

The plane went over, just a swift dark roar that flattened the tops of the trees, sent a coconut falling, like a dud bomb, and was gone as swiftly as it had come. Mullane stood up, saw it curve out over the bay in a beautiful moving arc, waggle its wings at the oncoming ship and barges, then head for the Burns Philp plantation. Vokes' natives were going to get the same treatment.

Then he heard the moaning and the weeping and the solitary scream of anguish. A young woman was crouched over a child, hugging it to her bosom; an elderly man and two women lay still on the ground in attitudes of sleep. Mullane moved quickly, but Ruth Riddle was ahead of him, shouting for someone to bring her medical kit. The villagers, stunned by the abrupt appearance of the plane, sent further into shock by what they saw it had done, moved slowly and stiffly, like clockwork figures whose springs had run down. Then suddenly they sprang to life, converged on the wounded and dead, began to wail and shout.

"Get back!"

Mullane bellowed and shouted, trying by brute force to impose some sort of order on the panic that was taking hold of the natives. Bingiti, the village headman, came running down from the main house and Mullane yelled at him to help restore calm. Later he would remember that he had sounded anything but calm himself. Trembling with anger and shock at this needless strafing of the natives, he was like a psychopath trying to quieten an asylum. Even in the heat of the moment he was certain that the pilot could not have seen him and Frank Vokes. The plane had come in too quickly and unexpectedly, its guns already firing at the moment of its appearance over the trees.

Mullane's rough methods worked; the natives quietened, stood back. Ruth was on her knees beside the young woman and child; then she looked up at Mullane and shook her head. The woman began to wail again; but Ruth had already moved on to the other fallen villagers. Mullane looked for Vokes, saw him getting the carriers back into line.

"I'm taking them out, Con." Vokes looked shaken; he sounded like a stranger, cryptic and low-voiced. "You coming?"

Mullane glanced back at Ruth working on the wounded. "You get going. Leave me one carrier. We'll catch up with you."

Buka shouted an order for the carriers to pick up the packs and gear. Twelve of the natives were required to carry the various parts of the radio transmitter and receiver. The transceiver itself was packed in three metal boxes, but there were car batteries required to operate it and a seventy-pound petrol engine that would be used to recharge the batteries; Mullane had wondered if the Japanese had developed something lighter and easier to carry than this Type 3BZ that he and Vokes would have to cart around the hills. The remaining six natives were packing bedding and tents and food.

But the carriers were not moving. They stood irresolute, still in line but with their heads turned towards the villagers congregated around those who had been hit. Then one of them broke from the line, ran towards the group; immediately the others followed him. Buka yelled after them, but they ignored him.

Vokes looked helplessly at Mullane. "They're your boys. They're not going to take any notice of me – "

Mullane wanted to shout at the boys to come back into line; but he couldn't. This wasn't their war; he had no right of command now. If they wanted to stay here on the plantation and take their chances with the Japanese, or even just flee into the jungle, he could not blame them. The white man had brought enough misery to this part of the Pacific: disease, exploitation, even religious conscience. He could not order the natives to bear the worst misery of all, other men's war.

Buka, anger oozing from him in a sheen of sweat, loomed up beside Mullane. An ex-police sergeant, he believed only in simple methods of authority. "I break their bloody heads, boss – "

"No, Buka. We won't do it that way." He crossed to Bingiti, who was trying to comfort the young woman who had lost her child. Mullane saw now that it was the headman's own daughter.

14

"Bingiti, I need your help!"

The old man's gullied face had a look of reproach that Mullane had never seen before. "Is this what you are going to bring to my people? Why should we help you now?"

"Con – for Christ's sake!" Vokes' shout had a note of panic in it. "One of the barges is coming across the bay!"

Mullane glanced quickly out at the bay, then back at Bingiti. "We didn't bring this to you," he said in dialect, speaking carefully, trying to sound convincing but knowing he was lying. "The white man didn't start this war – "

"The men in that boat – " Bingiti nodded out at the barge, now only a mile away. "They don't have skins like ours."

There was no argument to that: this was a different sort of colour bar to that which he had known at home. He and all the Europeans like him were lumped together with the Japanese in the eyes of this old man.

"Bingiti, those men will treat you worse than we ever did – "

He hoped that was true; though he did not want it to happen. Bingiti would never understand any explanation of what the Japanese had done in the rape of Nanking, for instance; but perhaps the old man remembered tales of what the black-birders, the white slavers who had kidnapped natives to work on the sugar plantations in Queensland in the last century, had done. The crimes of other generations suddenly hung round his neck like a heavy chain.

"We'll come back, Bingiti, but we'll need your help. Then things will be like they used to be – "

The old man just stared at him: he had no words to answer Mullane but the answer was there in the sad, cataract-scarred eyes. Things would never be like they used to be, not as they were before the white men had come to the Islands.

Then Ruth came up, spoke directly to Bingiti. "I have helped your wounded, old man. They will be all right. But if any should get sick, send a message and I shall come back."

The old man nodded, gratitude softening his look. "Do you have to go with the white bosses?"

Ruth did not look at Mullane. "I must. The men who are coming here would not let me stay. They would do things to me – "

Bingiti nodded again, understanding what she meant; but he showed no sign that he knew his wife and daughter might also be raped. "Go, then."

"Con!" Vokes was struggling with two of the metal boxes. "Let's go, for God's sake!"

Mullane looked at all the gear still lying where the carriers had dropped it. Then all at once he had an idea: cold, calculating, completely alien to the way he had treated these natives in the past.

"Bingiti, if the Japanese see all those boxes and packs they will know that white men have been here. And they will punish you till you tell them where we can be found. But we may not be easy to find and they will go on punishing you."

Bingiti looked hard at him, recognizing the blackmail. "You are not the man I respected."

"I can't afford to be. Not if you refuse to help me."

The old man looked out towards the bay; the barge was clearly visible. Suddenly he shouted to the carriers, his voice a harsh croak. The young men looked at him, some of them bewildered, others glaring resentfully. But he was their headman and after a moment's hesitation, muttering among themselves, they moved up to the line of baggage, picked it up and waited sullenly for Buka to give them the order to move off.

Mullane picked up his own gear and his Thompson submachine-gun. It had been left behind by a fleeing Australian soldier with just enough ammunition for Mullane to have to use it sparingly. He put out his hand but Bingiti ignored it, looked instead at Ruth.

"If we need you, will you come back and help us?"

Ruth did not look at Mullane: he was the white man, outside this circle of two. "I'll come back, old man." Then at last she did look at Mullane, said in English, "We'd better go. We've caused enough misery as it is."

That's the white in her, Mullane thought. And wondered whose side she would be on as their small war, up there in the hills, wore on.

16

"Closer? You want us to move *closer* to King's Cross?"

"If it's possible. We need earlier warning. We have lost contact with Charlie Edward Charlie and Don Robert May."

Mullane sat back, switching off the crackling receiver. NYY, Nellie York York, was his own code signal; CEC and DRM were stations down on the northern end of Bougainville. King's Cross was the code name for Rabaul; and headquarters at Townsville, through the relay at Port Moresby in New Guinea, was asking him to move closer to the town. Where there could be as many as 50,000 Japanese in occupation.

"They're out of their flaming heads," said Vokes. "How close do they want us to go? Who do they think we are, the Invisible bloody Man?"

Though for months he had felt as remote from the war as if he were in a neutral South American country, Mullane had charted the conquests and aims of the Japanese here in the South-west Pacific. His work in Japan had given him an appreciation of strategy and it had not been difficult to guess at their intentions. The Solomon Islands – Bougainville, Guadalcanal and a dozen others – lay 700 miles to the south of New Britain, a chain that, if occupied, could be used to throttle the supply line from the United States down to New Guinea and Australia. The Solomons had to be held.

What neither Mullane nor Vokes knew was that a major task force of American ships and Marines was on its way to land at Guadalcanal. The Japanese, already in force on that island, were building an airstrip near a place called Lunga; the airstrip was to become the keystone of the defences of whichever side held the island. Within the next twenty-four hours the American invasion was to succeed; but that was only to be the beginning of the Guadalcanal campaign, one of the most bitter of the Pacific war. Within hours of the American landing, the Japanese would be regrouping for a major counter-attack. The base for the counter-attack, for its planning, its supplies, the marshalling of its ships and troops, its squadron upon squadron of bombers, was Rabaul, hundreds of miles from the soon-to-be-besieged Guadalcanal but only fifty miles or so from where Mullane and Vokes now were.

There had been a sharp shower of rain and water still dripped from the trees; it hung in beads round the brim of Vokes' slouch hat. The camp site, a wide ledge backed by a cave whose entrance was covered by bushes, was just a mat of muddy grass. Cloud had come in to obscure the bay, now five miles away and below them; up the slope behind them the mountain seemed to have slid down below its cloud cover to threaten them. Mullane had the feeling, both physically and mentally, that their world had suddenly become small and fragile.

"We have to find out first if we're going to be able to move on at all." He looked pensively at the radio. He was 1000 miles from headquarters in Townsville and he could only deal with them through Moresby. Maximum range of the 3BZ radio was 400 miles on voice and 600 miles on Morse key; and all contact had had to be kept to a minimum so that the enemy could not get a bearing on their whereabouts. The conditions were anything but ideal for argument and debate. "Those boys still aren't enthusiastic."

Some of the carriers were sitting, others standing; but none of them was lying down. That was significant: they were all too tense to stretch themselves out and rest properly. It had been a fast, back-breaking, leg-crumpling climb up from Kiogo; Mullane had been constantly looking back for the pursuing Japanese he had expected. But Bingiti had either convinced them there had been no Europeans at Kiogo for months or they were content to take their own time, confident they had himself and Vokes trapped. In the meantime the safest course was to move on from this post. If the carriers were willing to continue . . .

"I'd leave them to Buka," said Vokes. "He'll belt them into line."

"That's not going to do it. If we're going to belt them, why shouldn't they go back to Kiogo and let the Japs do the same?"

"What are you going to try then? Diplomacy? Soft-soaping a boong is about as effective as putting the hard word on a lesbian. I met one once, woke up too late I'd spent money on her for nothing."

"You obviously have more experience than I'd credited you with."

"Biggest shock I ever had. A female homo!" Vokes shook his head in wonder.

"Well, I can't see any other way of getting these fellers to co-operate *without* soft-soaping them. I may need to upgrade the brand of soap – How much money do you have?"

"About two quid, that's all. I paid off all my blokes just before I came across to your place. What about you?"

Mullane shook his head and raindrops fell from the peak of the faded baseball cap he wore. It was one of the few clues to his past that he ever showed in public, a valued relic; but no one, not even Vokes, had ever asked him what the interlocked letters NY stood for. If anyone had ever guessed that the cap was that of a New York Yankee the fact had never been mentioned.

"I've got about a fiver. The cheque for my last copra shipment is probably still in the post office at Rabaul. Well, seven pounds – that's not going to last long." The pay for a plantation worker was ten shillings a month. "Not if we have to keep some in reserve for further bribery."

"You reckon we're going to have to do much bribing?"

"I think we may be just about to enter a jungle Tammany Hall. We'll be buying votes like every politician I know back home. If the Japs start leaning on the natives – " He could never bring himself to call them boongs, just as he had never thought of the coloured boys working in the locker-rooms back home as coons and dingoes. "There's no reason why they should show any loyalty to us. There's one natural law about war – if it's not your war you learn very quickly to live with the side that's the winner. And they may find they can live very easily with the Japs."

"Not from what I've heard."

"How would you know?" he said sharply. "You don't know anything about the Japanese."

"How do you know so much then?"

"I once lived in Japan," he said, giving away more than he had intended but having to defend the ghost of Mieko and all the decent Japanese he had known and worked with.

He got up, showing his back to the suddenly curious Vokes, and went along to the main group. Ruth Riddle, sitting on her medical box, looked up at him but said nothing as he passed her. She had kept up with the fast pace of their climb, but now she was exhausted. Mullane had not gone near her to ask her how she was, afraid of sounding condescending after he had been so adamant that she should not accompany them.

"How do the boys feel, Buka?"

The big man looked contemptuously at his fellow workers. "They say they go no farther, boss. They worried about what happening back at Kiogo."

"Aren't you worried?"

Buka hesitated, then nodded. The natives on this part of the coast were not a handsome lot and Buka was less handsome than most. His face could have been a relief map of the district where he came from: a mountain of a nose jutted out from deep ravines furrowing his cheeks, a crater of a mouth showed betel-stained teeth, his eyes were the colour of muddy creeks, a jungle of beard covered his lower jaw. His temper could be just as volcanic as some of the mountains to the east of where they now stood.

"Yes, boss. But my woman understands why I come with you."

"Thanks, Buka," said Mullane simply; then walked across to one of the young men. "What's the matter, Mariba?"

The young man looked up from under sullen brows. Normally he would have sprung to his feet when the boss spoke to him but this afternoon he sat stolidly, as if anchoring himself to the ground through his buttocks.

"We want to go back," he said in pidgin. "This new feller just come, he might be killing our families."

Mullane knew that could be true, though it would be bad tactics on the part of the Japanese. "If I send someone back to see what's happening, will you stay till he comes back?"

Mariba glanced right and left at the other carriers, then

looked up insolently at Mullane. "Maybe."

Suddenly Mullane wanted to boot the black son-of-a-bitch up the ass. *Steady, Mullane!* He came of an intolerant family and he had had to learn tolerance, almost as he had learned languages. Now it seemed that he was dropping back to being a natural McArdle like a man lapsing into his rough native tongue. He had discarded the family name when he had come here to the Islands, taking his mother's maiden name, but he had not been able to discard the family. Or anyway its influences.

"Listen, Mariba – "

Then he made the first recruiting speech he had ever made or was likely to make. It was not based on patriotism; it was mostly lies and guesses; it was not far off some wartime propaganda, but he didn't know that. He emphasized the self-interest angle and even in his own ears sounded more convincing then.

"Those men down in Kiogo won't treat you as well as the white man has. You must help us drive them out, send them back to their own country. I looked after you well, didn't I?"

Mariba looked at his companions, all of whom stared back expressionlessly. Christ Almighty, Mullane thought, this is like recruiting mercenaries in Amish country.

"You know the boss looked after you!" Buka bellowed, and Mullane had to wave a restraining hand in that direction.

Finally he ran out of argument. He was exhausted. He had been talking in pidgin and, fluent in six other languages, he had always found it tiring and difficult. But the strength, if not the substance, of his argument appeared to have had its effect. Mariba at last stood up, moved over to the other natives and they congealed into a muttering huddle.

Only then did Mullane look towards Ruth Riddle, who had been listening to every word. "You put a nice case, Mr Mullane. If ever I commit murder, I'll ask you to defend me. Were you a lawyer before you came out here?"

"My father was. He read torts to us instead of the Bible."

For the first time she smiled at him. It was a beautiful smile, altering the whole character of her face; the cautious defiance that had spoiled it disappeared, as if a disguising caul had been removed. Only tiredness made the smile fade away, though he was pleased to see the earlier expression didn't replace it.

"You're going to need more than a legal mind to get us out of this. I heard what your headquarters are asking you to do. Are you going to say yes to them?"

"If we do it will mean we'll have to make other plans for you."

"Not necessarily," she said, but he had no time to press that argument with her.

Mariba came stalking back, the other carriers behind him. Buka glared at the younger men, but they ignored him. Mariba said, "We go with you, boss, if two of us can go back to Kiogo to see if our families are safe. If they are, we come back and carry your things for you."

Mullane nodded, relieved. "You and Rama can go at once. But be careful – do not let the Japanese see you."

"One more thing, boss. We want more pay."

Mullane felt rather than saw Vokes come up beside him. He could also feel Vokes' shock at this new phase of rebellion; and out of the corner of his eye he saw Buka swelling up with temper. "How much do you want, Mariba?"

Mariba held up two fingers. "Two times what you pay us down on the plantation."

"Bloody danger money!" Vokes was incredulous. "Holy Jesus, what next will they ask for?"

"Pension funds," said Mullane, but he didn't feel as flippant as he sounded. He and Vokes were speaking softly in English: "How far will seven pounds go?"

"I feel like the bloke in the old saying – if it cost only a quid to go round the world, I couldn't get out of sight. I think you've got to jump on these bastards right from the start, Con, tell 'em where they get off – " Vokes was winding himself up again, arms flailing, tongue beginning to flap as words rushed to spout out of him.

"Okay, *okay*." Mullane dammed the flood before it could get properly started. He turned back to Mariba. "You'll get double your money, but only at the end of our journey and only if you give me no more trouble."

Mariba looked at the other carriers. He was new to rebellion; he was not sure how far he could go. At last he nodded. He has a lot to learn about bargaining, Mullane thought with relief. "We agree, boss. Now Rama and I will go down to Kiogo."

"No." Buka stepped forward; his big feet came down so hard in the mud that they splashed Mullane's boots. "I go with Rama, boss."

Mullane was about to say no when he recognized that Buka was trying to tell him something: *Mariba could not be trusted.* The younger man glared resentfully at Buka, but he knew enough not to argue. Buka would just knock him to the ground in front of the other young men.

Mullane nodded. "You and Rama go, Buka. Be careful. And be back before dark."

Buka and Rama, the latter a boy of eighteen, went off immediately. It only struck Mullane when they had disappeared that there had been no discussion as to what Buka and Rama should do if they should find that tragedy had struck at Kiogo. A massacre, perhaps. He had defended the Japanese to Vokes, but the Japanese he had known in Japan were not the same men who were in the army. He wondered if all nations changed their character when they put on a uniform.

He went back to the radio, followed by Vokes and Ruth. "How are you going to pay them double, Mr Mullane? I heard you say how much you had."

He sighed, annoyed that she should be so alert. "If ever you do commit murder, Miss Riddle, you won't need me to defend you. I'm sure you'll have every point covered."

"You haven't answered my question."

"I don't have the actual cash, if that's what you mean. I'll have to write IOUs."

"Which you may or may not honour, depending on whether you survive. The natives always get the dirty end of the stick, don't they?"

"Not while you're around, I'm sure." What to do with such a woman? He remembered Mieko, who had never queried anything he had ever done, who had been content as a good

Japanese wife to accept his decisions as always being right. "My dear young lady – "

"Balls," said the dear young lady and Vokes' eyebrows went up.

"You insisted on bringing her," Mullane said to Vokes. "Why don't I hear a word of support from you?"

Vokes grinned and shrugged. "I never was any good with girls. I told you about the hard luck I had with the lesbo."

Ruth looked at him then. "Good God!" she said and went off.

"Women!" said Vokes, but it was more a confession of his own ignorance of them than a judgement.

"What's that you have there?"

Vokes held up the telescopic sight he had been polishing. "I joined the rifle club while I was in Rabaul. They suggested I get one of these, otherwise I was never going to find the target. I forgot to tell you – I'm short-sighted, too."

Mullane shook his head. "What other talents do you have to be a Coastwatcher?"

Vokes grinned. "Persistence. I'm the most persistent bugger you're likely to meet. I may be tangle-footed and short-sighted and undiplomatic – "

"That too?"

Mullane kept Moresby and Townsville waiting till Buka and Rama returned; if they would return, though he was certain that no matter what happened Buka would come back to report. He stayed off the air because he did not want to give the Japanese more opportunities than was necessary to pick up his signal. It was another two-and-a-half hours before Buka and Rama came panting up the track.

"We watch careful, boss." Buka was exhausted but stood at attention; now they had left the plantation he had become a police sergeant again. He is the only one of us with enthusiasm for this, Mullane thought. "They treat our families well. Some of our men smile at them," he said with contempt.

And why not? From what Mullane had read there had been smiles from some Frenchmen for the conquering Germans in 1940. Collaboration was only another means of survival. "Don't be too harsh on them, Buka. They have to live with the enemy. We don't." He could feel Ruth standing in judgement behind him, but he did not look in her direction. Instead he glanced at Mariba, who had come up to stand close by. "Do you come with us now, Mariba?"

Mariba drew in a deep breath and Mullane, pessimism already seeping into him, waited for a refusal. But the young native said, "We go with you, boss. For two times money."

He held up two fingers again. Mullane suddenly wanted to laugh: it looked like an obscene gesture of defiance. Churchill had used the same salute with yet another meaning; victory was a long way off, though, and he doubted that Mariba really cared one way or another. "Okay, Mariba. You will be paid double when we return to Kiogo."

He waited for Ruth to ask the sardonic question, but it was Mariba himself who got in first; "When that going to be, boss?"

"Soon," said Mullane and turned at once to Buka. "We move off in ten minutes. As soon as I've spoken to headquarters."

Buka splashed mud again as his foot stamped. "Sir!"

"Stone the crows," said Vokes as Buka, pushing Mariba ahead of him, went marching across to the other carriers. "Who does he think he is – a Grenadier Guard?"

"Don't laugh at him. He may be the only one around here who's on our side."

"If that's aimed at me," said Ruth, moving away, "you may well be right."

Mullane turned his back on her, sat down beside the radio, waited for the hiss that said the set was working. Moresby came in almost immediately, but it seemed to him that he had had to wait several minutes. He was becoming edgy, something foreign to him. "Message to be relayed to Townsville. We'll move on as ordered."

The answer came, sounding far too laconic for his sensitive ear: "Jolly good. Good luck. Keep in touch."

"Oh, we'll do that," he said sarcastically. "Over and out."

"And up them for the rent!" said Vokes with quiet venom. "Wouldn't they stuff you? I could hear them sipping their pink gins as they said that."

Mullane pulled down the aerial from the tree where he had slung it, began to repack the radio.

"Well, here we go." Once again he felt the sense of commitment; it might be suicidal, but all at once he was aching for the opportunity to strike at the Japanese. There was still the debt to be repaid to Mieko . . . "Which is the best track for Rabaul?"

Chapter Two

They camped that night on a ridge above a river. The natives put up some shelters made from huge taro leaves; Mullane and Vokes had their own small tents. Mullane, after some ungallant hesitation, approached Ruth.

"You may use my tent."

"No, thanks. I've slept out in the open before this."

He didn't argue. "Do you have a mosquito net?"

"Yes. Did you bring your atebrin with you?" She sounded professional, like a starched hospital matron.

"I have three months' supply. I think I may be safer against the mosquito's bite than against yours. Have you any antidote for your bite?"

"A little understanding helps. Good night."

There was no door to her taro-leaf shelter, but he felt something had been shut in his face. He went back to his tent, crawled in under his net and slept while fears and doubts crept through his mind like rats.

In the morning he went down to the river bank to wash. He had just stripped off his shirt when he saw the movement farther along. Ruth, naked above her trousers, was washing her breasts and arms. She looked up, saw him, but made no attempt to hurriedly cover herself.

She picked up a towel, began to dry herself. "I came down early before the boys were awake. The mission where I grew up taught me to be modest. It's a handicap at times."

He wondered whether he should turn away or be casual. He decided to be the latter, as if the sight of beautiful dark-cream breasts was something he saw every day. "You should be more careful of the crocodiles."

She looked up and down the swift-flowing river. "They like calmer water than this."

She pulled on her shirt, tucked it into her trousers. He noticed she had not put on her brassiere and he found that as disturbing as the sight of her bare breasts. He felt like some callow youth starting to look at a woman and see more than was exposed.

"Don't worry, Mr Mullane," she said sweetly: almost too sweetly, as if she were reading his mind. "I can take care of myself."

Then he heard the low-flying aircraft. He looked up towards the ridge and saw the natives come out from beneath their shelters and he yelled at them to get back under cover. His and Vokes' tents were under the screen of a raintree and, being the same green as the surrounding foliage, he hoped they would be undetectable. He dropped down beneath a bush, saw Ruth do the same farther along the bank. She lay on her back and it seemed to him even at a distance that she looked relaxed. Or anyway resigned.

The slow-flying observation plane came over the ridge; it swung back and forth in the sky like a giant playful bird. It made several circles, then it suddenly swung down towards the river. For a moment Mullane thought he had been spotted, but the plane went on, following the river down to the sea. Mullane and Ruth stood up and up on the ridge everyone came out from under their cover.

"You reckon he saw us?" Vokes shouted.

"I don't know. He could have seen us and not let on. We'll have breakfast, then get going."

He waited for Ruth, then climbed the hill with her, once taking her hand to help her up the track. If any intimacy had been about to develop between them down on the river bank, it was gone now with the appearance of the enemy plane.

"I'll get on to Moresby," he said when they joined Vokes. "We're going to need an air-drop for more supplies."

When the order had come that they should move east towards Rabaul it had meant that the supply cache, built up over several months, had lost its usefulness. When they had moved out yesterday afternoon the carriers had been able to pack only a fraction of what had been stored in the cave in the hillside. The rest had been left: a hundred cases of tinned food, bags of rice, cases of kerosene, drums of petrol. And twenty cases of Chivas Regal, his one extravagance. All he had brought with him were two bottles of the good stuff, carrying them himself, not trusting them to the sometimes careless carriers.

Moresby came in at once on the radio. "We'll want supplies. Enough for – " He hesitated, wondering how long he and Vokes would be expected to stay here on the island. "A month?"

Townsville, through Moresby, didn't contradict him. "A month's supplies. Where will you be?"

He looked at his map, chose a spot, wrote out the coded co-ordinates, spelled them out and gave the coded name for the time of the requested drop. "One more thing. We'll want some money. A hundred pounds. Two hundred, if the war effort can afford it."

"We'll do what we can. We'll have to ask Paymaster to authorize it."

"Tell him I'll send a personal cheque. Over and out."

Half an hour later he led the party down towards the river. Twice they heard planes and they all stopped abruptly, standing like tree stumps among the tall trunks of the trees themselves; but these were fast-moving aircraft and their sound died away almost immediately, leaving Mullane wondering who was going to be bombed or shot up in the next hour or so. The party moved on, slipping and sliding on the narrow track Buka had found, looking for a way across the river.

Then Mullane called a halt and he, Vokes and Buka moved forward to the edge of the stream. Lawyer vines and red D'Albertis creeper hung down like frayed fishermen's nets from the trees; they looked through a screen at the narrow, swift-flowing river. It would take some minutes for all the party to cross, loaded as the carriers would be, and they had to be certain there were no Japanese patrols in the vicinity.

On the opposite bank half a dozen herons walked in single file, like First Communicants, towards the altar of a fallen tree. The image was Mullane's and he wondered why he should all at once be thinking of the Church he had left long ago; maybe he was going to start praying again, as his religious mother had always exhorted him to do. Whatever their image in his mind, the birds were a sure sign that this part of the river was un-inhabited.

"We'll cross here. Try and find us a safe spot, Buka."

Buka was a strong swimmer with no fear of the water. He strode through the curtain of creepers, the herons on the op-posite bank taking off as soon as he appeared. He went straight into the water without bothering to remove either his shirt or his *lap-lap*. But the water caught him and he had to start swimming at once. He was swept downstream and he had gone fifty yards before he managed to struggle ashore. He came back, shaking water from himself like a huge dog. Mullane and the others were now out on the bank waiting for him.

"No good, boss. Better go further up."

"Wait!" Vokes grabbed Mullane's arm. "There's someone coming down on the other side!"

There was no time to hide. They had moved down away from the track and now they were trapped on the few yards of bank between the river and the wall of jungle behind them. Even in that moment Mullane knew how much he had to learn. If they got out of this he must not let themselves be so exposed again.

The track on the other side of the river ran along behind a tall screen of wild sugarcane. Mullane could see movement through the tangle of stalks; but something told him this was not a Japanese patrol. Not unless the leader had taken to wear-ing all-white. Then the newcomers came out on to an open stretch of bank.

"Stone the crows!" said Vokes, who had given up swearing when he was close to Ruth. "Where the hell have *they* come from? There's no mission within miles of us."

The small procession halted and looked across at Mullane's party in equal surprise. An elderly priest, dressed in a white cassock and carrying a white umbrella, led the group. Behind him was a nun, in black habit, and three small native boys, aged about ten or twelve, each of them carrying a bundle on his head. The priest and the nun each carried a small suitcase.

"Have you just crossed the river?" Mullane yelled.

The priest nodded and gestured upstream. He said something, then turned to the nun. Her shout was even louder than Mullane's. "About a hundred yards up – there's some stones you can't be missing!"

Ten minutes later Mullane and the others joined the small mission group.

"Good morning, sir," said the priest in a stiffly formal manner that was out of place in the circumstances. Had Stanley and Livingstone been like this? Mullane wondered. The priest's voice was heavily accented. "Allow me to introduce myself. I am the Bishop of Waku, Bishop von Scheer. This is Sister Brigid from the Talio mission in my diocese, and these three rather weary little boys are Matthew, Mark and Luke. Sister Brigid named them," he added with a tired but pleasant smile.

Mullane introduced himself and Vokes and Ruth. "You've come all the way from Waku?" That was 200 miles west of here. "What are you doing up this way, Bishop? I thought everyone had been evacuated from your end of the island."

"The good sister and I decided to stay. We thought the Church could be neutral. Then – " His soft guttural voice withered away and he turned his head, gazing down the river but not seeing anything.

"We left before the Japanese got to us," said Sister Brigid; the brogue was as thick as Kerry cream on her tongue. "His Reverence has some ideas that, begging his forgiveness, he should be forgetting, yes. I've been arguing with him all these months – "

"She is a splendid one for argument," said the Bishop, turning back to them. "Very Irish."

"Months?" said Mullane. "You've spent months wandering around the island?"

"Glory be to God, no!" Sister Brigid had appointed herself the Bishop's spokeswoman. It was difficult to tell how old she was, to know whether it was age or the rigors of life here in the Tropics that had marked her face. She had shrewd blue eyes, faded a little by too-bright sun and perhaps the occasional doubt of the promise of heaven, and a wide mouth that Mullane saw, with growing disquiet, was as mobile as Vokes'. "We found ourselves a nice village down the coast, nice, yes. We hid every time the Japanese would be coming down, going into the jungle while the Bishop, begging his forgiveness, would be making up his mind about what's troubling him. I've been praying to the good Lord to give him guidance – "

Mullane had to dam the flood. "Frank, move everyone on. I'd like a word with the Bishop."

When the others had moved on along the bank he said to Scheer, "Why are you wearing your cassock? Don't you have any other clothes? You're a bit conspicuous if you're trying to dodge the Japs."

"I was preparing to say Mass when the Japanese came the last time. We had to leave in a hurry. I was fortunate to be able to bring even this with me." He looked up into the white dome of his umbrella. "I am very sensitive to the sun. I chose the wrong territory to be a missionary. Unfortunately all the souls that need to be saved seem to be in hot climes."

"The good Lord, as Sister Brigid calls Him, probably had his reasons. Now would you care to tell me what's on your mind? I have reasons of my own for asking."

Bishop von Scheer sighed. There was a worldly look to his thin handsome face that years among the sun-baked lost souls had not dimmed; sometimes he wished he had stayed among the lost souls of Munich or Augsburg. He had come to the wrong part of the world looking for his own salvation.

"I am debating with myself whether I should return to Germany. I am at the moment an enemy alien. Do you wish to arrest me?"

"I don't think I have any powers of arrest. You're a long way from Germany. How do you propose to return there?"

"God, give me guidance," Scheer said in German.

"Maybe God is like the Church," Mullane said in German. "Trying to be neutral."

"You speak German so well. But why should I be surprised? A man should never be surprised at whom he meets in the Islands." Then he reverted to English, as if that were safer, made him less of an enemy alien: "I am thinking of surrendering to the Japanese in Rabaul. From there I hope they may repatriate me to Germany."

Mullane had to ask the obvious question: "Are you a Nazi

32

sympathizer, Bishop?"

Scheer shook his head. "I know nothing of Nazism other than what I've read. I have not been home for fourteen years. When I was last in Germany Herr Doctor Stresemann was still trying to save the Fatherland from economic chaos. Herr Hitler still had to make his name. I am not a Nazi, Mr Mullane. All Herr Hitler and I have in common is a passion for Wagner. To offset that I am trying to develop a liking for Mozart, but I find him a little light for my taste."

"Perhaps you should stick to liturgical music." So far Mullane had no sympathy or any other feeling towards Scheer. "How did you get this far east?"

"We had a small motor launch. But we lost it last night – it ran aground on a reef at the entrance to this river and sank. We were fortunate to get ashore. I'm afraid we shall have to walk the rest of the way to Rabaul."

"Are you planning to take Sister Brigid and those kids into Rabaul with you?"

"I'm hoping the Japanese will repatriate her, too. The Irish are neutral – or are supposed to be. One finds it difficult to imagine the Irish being neutral about anything. The trouble is, Sister Brigid doesn't want to leave the island at all. She is so intent on saving souls."

Downstream Sister Brigid was not missing an opportunity. "You're a local, aren't you, my dear?" she said with Irish tact. "Were you brought up on a mission?"

"Yes," said Ruth. "A Methodist mission."

Sister Brigid didn't flinch. "Well, it's some sort of start towards salvation. What about you, my boy?"

"I'm a Mason," said Vokes. "Or my father was."

This was stony ground, if ever she'd seen it. "Glory be to God, you poor lad. You hear that, Your Reverence? We've got a Mason."

"I don't think you should be playing the evangelist just now, Sister." Scheer looked ruefully at Mullane as the two men joined the party.

"I'll pray for you," Sister Brigid told Vokes, who then looked bewildered and worried, as if prayers were something he'd rather avoid.

The sun was high above the trees now and it was warm and humid here in the narrow valley. Japanese patrols had a habit of following rivers, where the tracks were flatter.

"We're heading towards Rabaul, Bishop," said Mullane. "I think you better join us."

There was a note in the American's voice that made the German look at him sharply. "That sounded more like an order than an invitation, Mr Mullane."

"I've just decided I do have the power to arrest you. At least till my headquarters tells me what to do with you."

"Arrest His Reverence! Glory be to God, what will you be doing next?"

"Calm down, Sister. Mr Vokes and I have a job to do and we don't want it fouled up by someone who may be more committed to the other side than he thinks he is. Even some Popes were belligerents. Leo the Ninth, I think, was one."

Sister Brigid was prepared to be another belligerent, but Mullane cut her short. "Let's get going. Keep an eye on the Bishop and Sister Brigid, Frank."

Vokes was reluctant and embarrassed. "What do I do?"

"Just imagine they've invaded a Masonic temple. You come up front with me, Miss Riddle."

"Am I under arrest, too?"

"Ah, if only I had some grounds for it . . ."

"I once stabbed a man who was trying to rape me. A district officer who'd had too much to drink. He thought of arresting me for intended castration, then decided I might talk too much in court."

"Rape never crossed my mind. But I fear trying to seduce you might be just as dangerous. What happened to the district officer?"

"I stitched up his wound, dressed it and went home."

Mullane smiled. "Miss Riddle, you're what my mother used to call a caution. You're also a goddam nuisance."

"So are the Bishop and the nun, aren't they?"

They were walking in single file along the narrow overgrown track. He looked back over his shoulder at her. "Especially the Bishop. A man with divided loyalties is more dangerous than the totally committed man. At least you're not

34

trapped into trusting the committed one."

"Does that mean you'd like to trust the Bishop?"

He gave no other answer than a shrug of his broad shoulders. She gazed at his back as he walked ahead of her; he was well-made, every inch of him. She was a physical woman who responded to the physical side of men; had she been totally white she might have been promiscuous. But she had gone against the grain of her sexual nature because she had not wanted to be thought as easy as men expected her to be. Too many white men took it for granted that all mixed-blood women were easy. The drunken district officer was the only one who bore any lasting scars of her contradiction of that; but there had been other men. It had angered her and frustrated her, too, that one or two of the men had had real attraction for her, but she had known that none of them would ever consider marrying her. Several white men had proposed, but they had always been like her, not quite acceptable to the closed European society.

She had never known her father. He had been the skipper of a trading schooner and he had left the Islands and gone back to Sydney as soon as he had learned he was to become a father. Six years old when her mother, half-Chinese, half-Polynesian, had died of blackwater fever, she had been reared and educated by a Methodist missionary couple. They had sent her to Fiji to be trained in medicine, promising to do their best to have her transferred from there to Sydney University to have her fully trained as a doctor. But Sydney had rejected her, saying she was not up to its standards; she was not quite sure what standards they were applying, but even as a child she had been accustomed to such rebuffs. She had graduated from the school in Fiji as a Native Medical Practitioner; professionally it was as high as anyone of her class could expect to go in the Islands. Socially it got her nowhere. She had not yet accepted the fact that her life's work, and her happiness, lay in treating the natives. She had left the Solomons and come to New Britain hoping for a new start. She was still ambitious, still wanted to be white.

Intent on her thoughts, she walked straight into Mullane's back as he pulled up sharply, arm in the air.

35

"Watch it!" His voice was low; he didn't turn round. "Pass the word back to be quiet!"

They had come to a fork in the track; one path continued on along the river bank, the other swung left up a slope. But it was not the choice of tracks that had halted Mullane. He stood tense, ears strained; he had heard a sound that brought back memories. Then he heard it clearly, a cheerful whistling; he recognized the tune, the merry marching beat of "Ai Koku Koshin Kyoku".

He pointed up the left-hand track, waving the rest of the party to hurry on ahead of him. They responded at once, even the Bishop and Sister Brigid. They all stumbled up the track; the natives slipped easily into the bush on either side, but the Europeans were awkward.

Vokes stopped by Mullane. "One of the kids is back there! He stopped for a leak."

Mullane swore softly, looked urgently back along the track, then pushed Vokes ahead of him. "Let's hope he has the sense to stay in the bushes. Move!"

He unslung his Thompson gun as he slid down beneath a bush. He had no intention of ambushing the Japanese patrol. The code name for the Coastwatching Service was Ferdinand, named after Munro Leaf's pacifist bull; orders were always to run rather than to fight; the killing of a Japanese soldier would only provoke a search-and-kill operation by the enemy. The best spies were the unsuspected ones: that had been his guiding principle in Japan.

The patrol came into view less than fifty yards away, five men walking jauntily along the river bank, all of them whistling, absolutely sure that they were in safe territory. Then abruptly the leader, a corporal, stopped whistling; the other whistles died away in discord behind him. The patrol halted, guns seeming to fall off their shoulders into the firing position. Oh Christ no! Mullane thought, don't shoot the kid!

The boy (Matthew? Mark? Luke?) came along the bank, the oilcloth-wrapped bundle balanced precariously on his head. He was bent over beneath the weight of the bundle; he was only fifteen yards from the Japanese before he saw them. He pulled up sharply; the bundle wobbled, then fell from his head. He looked about wildly and Mullane could imagine the whimper of fear that came from the small open mouth.

Sister Brigid stirred, rising on one knee; but Mullane, lying beside her, roughly pulled her down. She looked at him with furious rebellion, but he shook his head and kept his grip on her arm. A leech dropped from a bush on to his bare forearm, but he dared not move to brush it off. The patrol had fanned out and two of the soldiers were now at the bottom of the path that came up this slope.

The corporal was interrogating the boy, but Mullane was too far away to hear what was being said. All he could see was that the frightened boy was giving no answer, just staring with dumb fear at the soldiers. The corporal slapped the boy across the ear; it took all Mullane's strength to hold Sister Brigid down. Then one of the soldiers at the bottom of the track suddenly pointed at his feet, then gestured excitedly up the slope.

"Jesus!" said Mullane; it was a prayer as much as an expletive. The Japanese had seen the bootmarks of himself and the other Europeans in the mud of the track.

He was on his feet and out of the bushes on the run, the Thompson held tightly against his ribs, as the Japanese swung their guns in his direction. He plunged down the track towards them, gun pumping. The two soldiers at the bottom of the slope went down without firing a shot, one dropping quickly, the other following in slow-motion as if reluctant to die. The corporal and the other two soldiers on the river bank got off some shots but they went over Mullane's head. Then his own burst of fire hit them; they fell against each other in the one heap. And behind them the native boy stared at Mullane, then slowly slumped in the mud. He sat for a moment, then fell face forward at Mullane's feet as the latter reached him.

There was a scream from up the slope. Then Sister Brigid, habit flapping, looking like a huge berserk bird, came flying down the track. She dropped on her knees, grabbed the boy and cradled him to her, moaning – *just like the native woman back at Kiogo*, Mullane thought. Then she looked up at him and he was shocked at the hatred in the face dedicated to charity.

"You murderer!"

Everyone had now come down to the river bank. Buka and the other natives hung back, but Vokes, Ruth and the Bishop crowded forward as if to hide this bitter scene between Mullane and the nun.

"Let me look at him." Ruth had to prise the boy out of Sister Brigid's arms. "Which one is it?"

"Matthew." The nun shook her head in grief, the tears coursing down her cheeks. "Murdered!"

"For Christ's sake!" Mullane suddenly exploded; guilt blew out of him as anger. "I didn't murder him! It was an accident. He was just *there* – I had to kill the Japs before they killed us!"

"Why would they have killed us?" the Bishop asked quietly.

Not you and the others maybe, thought Mullane, but certainly Vokes and me. Although he could not even be certain of that; he could only feel it in his bones and every fibre of his body. He had acted from instinct as he had plunged forward out of hiding; there had been no time to think of any alternative. The one thing that had stuck in his eye as he had taken a last swift look around had been the radio in its three metal boxes. The Japs would have wanted no more evidence than that to kill him and Vokes on the spot.

"Bishop – " He tried to make his own voice as quiet as that of the German. "Mr Vokes and I are, technically speaking, spies."

"They'd have killed us all right," said Vokes. "They've already done it to a couple of other Coastwatchers. I'm sorry, but Mr Mullane and I have to look out for ourselves. We've got a job to do."

Sister Brigid stood up, leaving Ruth to lay the dead boy out on the ground. She had recovered from her hysteria, but there was no forgiveness in her face as she looked at Mullane.

"Sister – " Mullane kept a tight rein on himself. He was just realizing what he had done. For the first time in his life he had killed a man. Five men and a small boy: a massacre. He didn't look down at the bodies, but he would always remember the look on Matthew's face in the moment before the boy died. Suddenly he wanted to weep.

Then Buka, the native with the practical experience of war

among the tribes, stepped forward. "Better move, boss. What you want me to do with them dead fellers?"

"Tie rocks to them and drop them in the river," said Vokes. "The crocs will take care of them."

There was a gasp from Sister Brigid; Ruth and the Bishop looked at him in amazement. Even Mullane was surprised at the callous practicality of the Australian; but what he had suggested was commonsense. No evidence must be left that the patrol had been ambushed. That would only result in this part of the country crawling with vengeful Japanese patrols.

"Do that, Buka. But collect their guns and ammunition first."

"Do you want to look at their paybooks or papers?" Vokes said.

"What's the point? Townsville isn't going to be interested in that sort of information, not right now. No, get rid of them as fast as you can."

But Sister Brigid stood over the corpse of the dead boy. "You're not going to put Matthew in the river like that!"

Who needs the Japs? Mullane thought. He had an enemy right here in his own camp. "Okay, take him up the hill and bury him. He'll have a Christian burial, if that's what's worrying you. Frank, get the boys to bury him somewhere off in the bush, so the Japs can't find the grave. Buka and I will catch up with you."

Vokes at once marshalled the carriers into line, picked up the dead boy himself and started up the slope. Sister Brigid, after a final angry glare at Mullane, fell in behind him. Scheer and Ruth were the last to move off.

"You must forgive Sister Brigid," said Scheer. "She has very narrow standards."

"They'll have to broaden if she wants to stay with us." Mullane was in no mood for forgiveness; he had to forgive himself for the death of Matthew before he could make concessions to the nun. "Otherwise she's likely to find herself under arrest, too."

"Then I'd appreciate it, Mr Mullane," said the Bishop stiffly, "if you would contact your headquarters as soon as possible and have us evacuated. I should prefer to be interned rather than continue as we are."

He had come down the track from their hiding place with his umbrella closed. Now he snapped it open, raised it in front of him, shutting out Mullane, turned round and went stalking up the slope. It seemed to Mullane that under the mud-stained white cassock the feet were moving with a hint of goose-step.

Ruth said, "If it's any consolation I think you did the right thing. The only thing possible."

He looked at her in surprise, but had enough grace left in him to nod his head in thanks. "I hope so."

He looked down at the dead Japanese, now laid out side by side like lumber logs ready to be tossed into the river. Buka and the four carriers helping him, one of them Mariba, had worked quickly; rocks had been tied to the soldiers' feet with creepers. Mullane wondered how long the crocodiles would take to do *their* work; the bodies might not attract the crocs up here to the swifter water.

The shirt of the corporal was open to the waist; the good-luck sash he wore was clearly visible, marked with his blood. Mullane thought, you poor bastard. He had come all this way in the Emperor's cause to finish up in an unnamed river as food for the crocodiles. All that for $2.50 a month, no more than Mullane paid his plantation workers.

"Push them in, Buka."

The dead men were rolled into the river, sinking at once beneath the swiftly running water. The corporal was last to go. His eyes were still open; at the last moment before he slipped beneath the surface it seemed that he looked back at Mullane. Where had he come from? Tokyo, Osaka, Hiroshima? Or from some rice farm in Shikoku? Suddenly Mullane felt a nostalgia for the land that had given him Mieko, felt sorry for the dead men who would not be returning there. He had killed them, but somehow the killing had done nothing for the vengeance he felt. Something bigger was needed . . .

"What about the guns, boss?"

Mullane hesitated. He could see Mariba and the carriers eyeing the weapons expectantly; but he could not trust them with firearms. They had never learned to use them and they might wound or even kill themselves; and if they did learn to use them they might try to kill him. He picked up the four grenades that had been taken from the soldiers' belts and shoved them into his pack.

"Keep a rifle for yourself, Buka, and all the ammunition." Buka had learned to use a gun as a police boy. "Throw the rest in the river."

Buka almost danced with delight; he now had all the status he wanted. He scooped up four of the guns, threw them one by one out into the river as he would hurl a spear. Mariba and the other carriers watched him sullenly and enviously. Then he slung the last rifle, a 6.5 mm, over his shoulder, picked up the ammunition pouches and jumped to attention.

"Ready, sir!"

Ruth succeeded in·hiding her smile; she saw how seriously Mullane took his boss-boy. She waited till the five natives had moved ahead of them up the track, then said, "If there's no one else, at least he's loyal to you."

"That's something. Not everyone has it."

"No," she said; then reached for his arm. "There's a leech there, let me burn it off."

He had forgotten the leech, indeed hadn't felt it in the welter of other sensations that had been coursing through him during the past five minutes. He stood silently while she took a box of matches from her pocket, lit one and held the tiny flame to the leech.

"He doesn't want to let go. You must have rich blood."

"Pure Irish. But don't tell Sister Brigid." He was aware of her closeness, of the unfettered breasts under her shirt. He wondered what she would think of him if he asked her to wear her brassière. He, the man of the world who had been on touching terms with some of the finest bosoms on Broadway. Apricot Bloom and all the other girls would think he had been bitten by religion.

The leech dropped into the mud. She spat on the spot where it had clung to Mullane's arm. "I can put some antiseptic on it."

"No. I'm sure you have good antiseptic spit."

She looked up at him. "You're a bastard, Mr Mullane."

"I don't make an effort to be," he said.

They walked up the track, he feeling suddenly on the

41

defensive, she beginning to feel her interest in him growing. They came to a spot where the track flattened out for a few yards; the rest of the party was gathered there. Vokes came out of the bush with Sister Brigid and two of the carriers, one of the latter carrying the spade that Mullane always had on hand. He had not expected it to be used to dig a grave. Or at least not so soon.

"Where's the boy buried?"

He followed Vokes into the bush, saw the small mound covered with leaves and branches. And the small cross, just two large twigs tied together, erected above it. He pulled out the cross and tossed it away.

Behind him Sister Brigid said with quiet savagery, "You promised him a Christian burial!"

"Did you bury him with prayers?"

"The Bishop said them."

"Then he's had his Christian burial." He leaned tiredly against a tree, looked at the tense, belligerent nun. "Sister Brigid in other circumstances I'd see that Matthew had a proper funeral and a decent grave. I'd pay for a headstone, engrave any prayer you liked to name on it – I owe him at least that. But I'm afraid that here –." He waved a weary hand, a small circling motion that still managed to take in the bush around them, the hills towering above them, the island that was no longer safe for them. "Here, I'm afraid, Matthew has to be buried unmarked. He won't miss the cross. I don't think dead souls ever come back to see what monuments have been erected to their memory. And I have a lot of live souls I still have to care for. You should be applying yourself to them."

"Don't expect me to pray for yours, Mr Mullane."

She went back through the bush to join the party. Mullane looked at Vokes. "She's human, anyway. I used to wonder if nuns were lucky enough to have all our failings."

"I'll be glad when we've got rid of her and the Bishop. Missionaries always make me uncomfortable. Even Masonic ones."

"I didn't know there were any."

"You should hear my old man. He's worse than the Pope."

They marched for another hour, climbing all the time up the

42

track away from the river, the coast and the Japanese. At last Mullane called a halt and everyone sank down with what seemed one great sigh of relief. Mullane gave himself and Vokes five minutes to recover, then they set to work to assemble the radio. So far he and Vokes had been of no use to the Coast-watching Service; they had reported nothing. Even now he was reporting nothing, only making a further request.

He knew he was beyond voice range of Moresby now; the signal had been very weak this morning. He encoded a message for transmission by Morse key, then tapped it out: *Have German bishop Irish nun wish evacuation urgentest Advise.*

"What about Ruth?" Vokes said.

"We'll get rid of her, too, when the time comes. But one argument at a time, eh?"

The reply came in: *Advise no ship or aircraft immediately available. Suggest you co-opt your guests. Other rendezvous as arranged.*

"Co-opt our guests? What the hell do they think we're doing here, holding a prayer meeting?" Vokes bounced up and down.

"Well, we're stuck with them for a while. But at least the supply drop is on. If we're going to have to feed another four mouths maybe we should have asked for more rations."

Mullane leaned back against the tree beneath which he sat. He looked up and down the track at – his charges? He guessed so. He was still a civilian and Vokes had the service rank; but Vokes hadn't mentioned it again and seemed content to let him assume all the authority and responsibility. He had, in effect, been preparing for this war for years, far longer than any of those squatting and lying beside this jungle track, and now he was unprepared for what was being asked of him.

How the hell did I get here? he asked himself.

II

It had been a long roundabout journey, begun in the big house on East Avenue in Rochester, upstate New York. That had been another age then, another world; looking back it was difficult to believe he had belonged to it, even if only as an infant. A Roosevelt had been President then, too: Theodore, called

Teddy by everyone; not Franklin, whom no one would call Frankie, except perhaps Vokes. Tolstoy and Mark Twain had still been alive; people danced and marched to Sousa tunes. Women wore shirtwaisters and straw boaters in summer; automobiles were beginning to take over from horses and the McArdle family owned a Peerless. Patrick McArdle, his father, had had an interest in automobiles ever since he had assisted George B. Selden, a fellow Rochester citizen, in filing a hopeful patent as the inventor of the gasoline automobile.

The McArdle house had not been the biggest on East Avenue but it had not been out of place among its neighbours. Like them it had stood back on sloping lawns from the elm-lined street; the McArdles had as neighbours the Sibleys, the Macombers and George B. Eastman, all pillars of Rochester. Life had been easy and uncomplicated and families recorded memories of it with the cameras made for them by Mr Eastman. In retrospect a golden haze coloured everything, though Mullane was sure now that that had not been true: maybe it had been the sepia tint of the photographs. But, even though only a small child, he had belonged to that no-longer-believable world.

Patrick and Mary McArdle had had five children, Cornelius the middle of three boys and two girls. His older brothers, Liam and John, had gone to school at Hotchkiss because Patrick, more social-minded than religious, had not been able to find a Catholic school that came up to the image of himself as a successful lawyer. Then in 1915 a Catholic school, Canterbury, catering to those Catholics who had made it right up there with the wealthy Protestants, opened in Connecticut and Cornelius had been sent there. In 1921 he had gone to Yale to study law; it had been taken for granted that he would eventually go into the family firm. But Con, as he was now called, had had other ideas. The others sparkled round him and he had remained dimly lit in the family centre, affection from his parents sometimes landing heavily on him as an afterthought on their part. He was not dull: at school and college he had had a better record than either of his brothers. But at Yale he had begun to lose interest in law and the future planned for him. He had begun to learn languages, finding to his surprise and delight

44

that he had an almost perfect ear and the ability to think in any language he took up. He also found that he was a better pitcher than anyone else on the Yale ball team or in the Ivy League. When he told his parents at Commencement that he had received an offer from the New York Yankees and was going to accept it, his mother had fainted and his father had looked as if he were about to have a stroke. He had given smelling salts to his mother, shaken his father's limp hand and gone off to join the Yankees.

He had spent only half a season in the Yankees' farm club before he was promoted to the major league. A southpaw, he had a fast ball that cut back at the last moment into a right-handed batter. Another Ivy League graduate, Moe Berg, played in later years for the Chicago White Sox and when the two would face each other, McArdle on the mound and Berg at bat, less educated, less couth citizens in the bleachers would start to whistle *Doing the Varsity Drag*. Babe Ruth, who never gave any hint that he had been to school at all, was the national hero and ball-players who used words such as *ubiquitous* and weren't *sanguine* about their team's prospects were suspect. Ring Lardner and Heywood Broun each did a column on Con McArdle's ways with words, but fans gave up halfway down the columns and turned over to Damon Runyon, who spoke and wrote true American.

He had gone to Japan for the first time in 1933 with the Exhibition All Stars . . .

"Con! Aircraft!"

He sat up, coming back to the present. Vokes was on his feet, pointing to the south-east. A dark ragged cloud of planes was moving across the sky. He grabbed his binoculars and started to count. "Get on the radio! I'll give you the number in a moment."

Vokes sent it out in clear in Morse: *42 Bombers heading south.* Acknowledgement came in from Moresby at once. The message would now go through its relay; Vokes' warning would start a chain reaction. Somewhere down south US Navy ships and planes would start preparing for the arrival of the Japanese bombers.

"Where are they going?" Ruth asked. "Guadalcanal?"

"I doubt it. It's a fourteen-hundred-mile flight there and back. They'd have taken off earlier if they were going there. They like to be home before dark."

"What do you do now?"

"Wait and count them again when they come back. Then we let headquarters know how many are missing."

"The profit and loss of war," said Scheer. "It is so simple when one has to count only aeroplanes. I remember – " Again the quiet voice trailed off. The Bishop's thoughts and voice did not seem able to keep pace with each other. Mullane wondered how inconclusive his sermons were. Scheer had the look and sound of a man who no longer had any confidence in his own evangelism.

Mullane pressed him, just as quietly: "You remember what?"

Scheer, beneath his umbrella, blinked: against the sun or against a too-bright memory? The shade of the umbrella seemed to make him look frailer than he was.

"I was at Verdun in the last war. I've read since that a million men died there. How does one count so many dead?"

"War!" said Sister Brigid, though as belligerent as any general.

"I don't know," Mullane confessed. "That's one relief of this job. They don't ask us to count the dead. Only the planes they die in."

Vokes stood up, looking uncomfortable. Talk of the dead disturbed him; it reminded him that his own death was inevitable, an unhealthy thought for a young man. "I think we better get going, Con."

But when Mullane went to sign off, Moresby held him. In simple code it relayed a message from Townsville: *Imperative you move into King's Cross area. More detailed information troops ships urgently needed.*

Mullane sat back on his haunches. He and Vokes were alone; the others had moved away. "I think things are going to get much tougher. We're not all going to be able to push on into Rabaul."

Vokes' open face closed up with suspicion. "What are you trying to say, mate?"

46

"I think only one of us should go into Rabaul. You can take Ruth and the others down to the coast and wait for a sub to come in – "

"You can get stuffed, mate." Mullane had expected such an answer; he was only surprised that Vokes said it so quietly and pithily.

"Frank, you said yourself we can't dump Ruth – "

"I don't care about her and the others." Vokes knew that was untrue; there was just something that he cared more about. "I didn't stay on here to play bloody nursemaid to some idiots who didn't know enough to get in out of the rain when they had the chance – "

Mullane knew he was referring more to the Bishop and Sister Brigid than to Ruth; but he wondered at the bitterness in Vokes' still-soft voice. "Frank, I'm the one who's got to go on – these are my boys, they won't take any notice of you – "

"No." Vokes shook his head stubbornly.

"For Christ's sake, what's eating you?"

Vokes looked for a moment as if he were not going to answer. Then, still squatting, looking down at the ground in front of him, he said, "My old man fought in the last war. He's the greatest bloody Old Soldier who ever bored a young bloke like me to tears. He wouldn't talk to me a couple of years ago when I didn't rush out and join up when war first broke out. The last letter I had just before the Nips took Rabaul, he asked me how long I was going to keep running away. The only thing he didn't do was send me a white feather."

"Frank, how is he ever going to know what you're doing up here? The Coastwatchers aren't going to tell your father what you're doing, that you're some sort of secret hero – "

"I'll tell him myself at the end of the war. No argument, Con. If you go into Rabaul, I'm going with you."

And Mullane knew it was useless to continue the argument. At last he shrugged. "Okay. But that still leaves us with Ruth and the others."

"Yes." But Vokes offered no solution to that problem.

They started off again, still climbing. As if it were her natural position now, Ruth fell in behind Mullane again.

"Why did you mention Guadalcanal?" he said.

"I was born there."

"How do you feel about the Japs taking it?"

"I never thought of it as home."

She said no more and he did not press her. But he wondered if women like her ever thought of anywhere as home. He did, at least, have Rochester to go back to.

At the first bend in the track the Bishop was waiting for him. "Mr Mullane, did you mention my request to your headquarters? About my surrendering to internment?"

"They don't want you, not yet. We're stuck with each other, Bishop."

Scheer looked up the track that wound through the thick rain forest. The mountains lay ahead of them like barricades. He shook his head, exhausted in spirit as well as body. "If I refused to move on, just lay down to die, would that be suicide, Mr Mullane?"

"I'm not your confessor, Bishop. Don't burden me with that, too." Ruth had walked on and he and Scheer were alone on the track. "I was in Germany in 1935. I don't think it's your Germany any longer. You would never be happy back there."

The Bishop smiled. "Are you trying to recruit me to your side?"

Mullane smiled in reply. "All I'm trying to do is ask you to stay alive and not be a pain in the neck to me."

"I'll pray for the strength," said the Bishop.

Five hours later they were on another tree-clad ridge. Below them lay another river, a glint of silver-green among trees, not inviting, somehow menacing. There was a stillness to the jungle-covered hills that had always made Mullane feel ill at ease, had him waiting for something to happen. In his younger days, once the ball season was finished, he had gone hunting in the Maine woods; there among the birch, spruce and pines he had unwound, feeling the stillness of those woods almost as a balm. But not here: here storms could blow up and shake and sometimes fell the trees, but one was always left with the impression that the winds had gone on defeated. The mountains and jungles resumed their pregnant stillness; the cries and passage of birds through it were only colour notes to heighten the effect of the green silence. This was as close, he felt, to the primeval as one could expect to find: time had only just begun to tick here. He had the sudden premonition now that, no matter how long the war went on on this island, the tree-tangled hills would be the only winner.

Everyone, including the carriers, was exhausted by the long climb. But Mullane allowed them only fifteen minutes' rest, then set them to work building the watching post. He had kept the party on the march till he had found this spot. It was at the end of a narrow, steep-sided minor ridge that ran out from the main ridge they had been traversing. Jungle covered the side slopes and rain trees formed an arch over the crest; the ridge ended in a sheer cliff that dropped away for several hundred feet. The view was magnificent: Mullane estimated they could see ten miles of coastline in either direction. If he and Vokes got out of Rabaul this would be an ideal haven to return to.

He was giving orders as to what he wanted done when he stopped in mid-sentence, listened, then stepped out to the edge of the trees, raised his binoculars and found the returning bombers with his first aiming of the glasses.

"How many?" said Vokes beside him. "A good score?"

"Thirty-eight. That means they lost only four." He sounded disappointed; he dreamed of the impossible, a clear sky with no returning planes at all. "I'll set the radio. And I'll check the drop is still on tomorrow night."

"Are we far from the drop zone?"

Mullane took out a map. The maps he and Vokes had been given were more guesswork than proper surveys. They were based on old German charts brought up to date by some rather inadequate aerial surveying. He had given headquarters some co-ordinates but they were no more than a rough guide. "Try somewhere up beyond that rock outcrop. We can light our guide fires behind those trees and maybe they won't be seen down on the coast."

Vokes went off with one of the natives. Though he was still afraid of the Australian's talkativeness, Mullane was impressed by his willingness.

Vokes was back in an hour and a half. "I had to look around a bit, Con. That spot you picked was a bloody great slope, it would have been like trying to catch stuff on a slippery dip. I found a clearing farther up, but it means a pretty grim climb for the boys."

"We'll worry about that when it comes. Let's get everything set up here first."

Vokes looked around him. "The place is getting pretty bloody crowded. Why two huts?"

"You and I share the big one with the radio and the Bishop. Miss Riddle and Sister Brigid are in the other one."

Vokes grinned. "I'll share with Ruthie and you can have Sister Brigid."

"Don't complicate things by entertaining your crotch. Try and emulate the Bishop, keep your thoughts spiritual."

"I'll try. But my John Thomas seems to have a mind of its own. You've been up here – what, four, five years? If it's not too personal, what have you done to get the dirty water off your chest? I tell you, sometimes it's taken me all my time to keep my hands off of the native girls, they kept getting whiter every time I looked at them. I once went to a Chinese brothel in Rabaul – "

"Frank, sex as a subject bores me. I'm all for the actual indulgence in it, but talking about it reduces me to impotence. Your night in a Chinese brothel is not something I'd pay to see – whether your position was north-south or east-west – "

Vokes grinned again; he seemed impervious to rebuff. "Ah, they're not built like that at all. You should know that, if you lived in Japan – " Then he saw the sudden stiffness in Mullane's face. "I said something out of place?"

"Yes," said Mullane. "Now how about moving some of the gear into our hut?"

This time Vokes was rebuffed; or was more sensitive than Mullane had suspected. "Sure, Con. I'm sorry. No offence."

Mullane nodded, abruptly oblivious of Vokes as he thought of Mieko and the love-making they had had together. She had been a remarkable lover, far better than any of the girls he had known back home; her whole time with him, short though it had been, had been devoted to his pleasure and comfort. He would never find another girl like her and though the sex urge was far from dead in him he had never gone looking for another woman; if someone had told him in his free and easy days as a ballplayer and playboy that he would remain celibate for almost five years he would have told them that only a drastic operation could enforce such a condition. It disturbed him somewhat, especially in the circumstances, that he had once or twice looked at Ruth with less than spiritual thoughts.

By late afternoon the camp was complete. Two natives had been sent out on a foraging expedition and returned with the news that they had found an abandoned native garden where there were yams and taro. It had been a surprise to Mullane, when he had first arrived on the island, to find that the jungle provided very little in the way of food. It was a green desert that could taunt a starving man with its own lushness. Living off the country was not possible in these island jungles; game was scarce and the plants and roots that could be eaten were barely life-sustaining. Even the natives relied on cultivated food and some of them, the lucky ones, had come to have a taste for the white man's food in cans.

Mullane hoped that tomorrow night's plane would have no trouble in finding the drop zone.

III

In the Townsville headquarters of the Coastwatchers Roger Blomfield stared at the map of New Britain tacked on the wall opposite him. Each of the walls of his small office was papered with maps, all of them freckled with coloured pins. He felt a certain guilt that men whose lives were in constant danger should be represented by no more than a pin with a coloured head; he remembered that when he had been at school there was nothing worse that one could say about someone else than that he was a pinhead. The way things had been going in the past few months he wished for nothing more than that he could remove all the pins and leave the maps unmarked. But he knew with sickening dread, that it would be months, possibly years, before those maps would again be as bland and non-threatening as they had been in the days of peace.

Lieutenant-Commander David Lowell put his head in the doorway. "Anything new on Mullane and Vokes?"

Blomfield gestured at the copy of the message that had come

up from the radio room. "They've got company. A German bishop, a nun and some local girl, a medical aide."

"Jesus!" Lowell came into the office and sat down heavily. He was a plump, balding man with sparse black hair standing up in horns on either side of his head; he had big lugubrious eyes and a wide mouth that never seemed to be without his patched and chipped pipe sticking out of one corner of it. He looked like an old owl who had all the answers and was miserable at what he had learned. "That complicates things. Does AIB know about this?"

AIB was Allied Intelligence Bureau, a GHQ organization that was only a few months old and still feeling its way. Lowell was the USN liaison officer with the Coastwatchers and, like Blomfield, was suspicious of any new outfit that still wasn't sure how the war was to be won.

"They wouldn't be interested. All they want is for Mullane and Vokes to walk into Rabaul, pinch the Jap's order-of-battle and walk out. It must sound easy to them. I don't think one of the bastards has ever set foot on New Britain."

"Things are rough all over and getting worse by the bloody minute." Lowell had picked up *bloody* from the Australians he worked with, but it sounded like a foreign adjective on his diffident tongue. Other people's slang, he guessed, *was* a foreign language and he wished he could cure himself of the habit of trying to be so much one of the Aussies. But relations between the Australians and Americans in general were still strained and he was determined not to add to the strain. Before the war was over he'd be a fair dinkum, up-you-for-the-rent Aussie even if it meant flattening his tongue to paper thinness. Which was the way he thought most Australians sounded, including Blomfield. "Christ knows what's going to happen on Guadalcanal, the way things are going."

"I hate to say it, but I think AIB are right. Mullane and Vokes have got to get into Rabaul and find out what's going on."

"What's aerial recce been showing?"

"Practically bugger-all. There's been cloud cover all over the northern end of the Gazelle Peninsula for the past week. Joe Parnell up on New Ireland reported in a week ago that there was some ship movement at night, but he couldn't be precise how much. We haven't heard from him since."

Lowell looked up at the maps. "How long before you take *his* pin down?"

"We give them two weeks." Blomfield opened a drawer in his desk, took out an old tobacco tin. Five pins rattled loosely in it. "These are blokes we've lost contact with. Charlie Helidon, for instance. We haven't heard from him for over three months. I just keep hoping he'll turn up on the air one day and I can put his pin back on the map."

Lowell sucked on his empty pipe. "Let's hope you don't have to take down Mullane and Vokes' pins. In the meantime, what are you going to do about those people they're stuck with?"

"I'm hoping you can dig me up a spare sub to go in and bring them out."

"Fat bloody chance. I couldn't even get you a sub to go in and bring out Mullane and Vokes."

Blomfield put the tin of pins back in his desk, slammed the drawer shut. "I wonder what it's like to lose a war?"

IV

The next day seemed interminable to Mullane and he found himself unable to relax. He tried reading, taking a copy of Thucydides from his haversack; he had developed an interest in military history during his work in Japan. But today the Peloponnesian War held no interest for him; he had his own war, small and private. At five o'clock he went on the air to Moresby.

The others congregated around him. The radio, even though restricted to military messages, was their one link with the outside world. It was a world, Mullane guessed, for which the priest and the nun had little affinity; and a world which Ruth barely knew if at all. Yet it suggested a security for which they all longed, no matter how secretly.

Moresby confirmed that the supply drop would take place. Then it began to tap out a long message. Vokes decoded it as Mullane passed it to him.

At last the key stopped clicking. There was silence for a while till Vokes finished decoding. Then he sat back and looked at

Mullane. "They're still on our backs. It's Rabaul or nothing."

For the moment Ruth and the others might not have been there: Mullane saw only himself and Vokes and the carriers they would need to take with them. It was Ruth who intruded, breaking up the Coastwatchers' tiny world of men only.

"What do they want you to do? Or aren't we supposed to know?"

"They want us to go right into Rabaul, inside the Jap perimeter and come back with a report of what's going on there. Something big is happening but they're not quite sure what."

"How far do they want you to go?"

"As far as Simpson Harbour, I guess. As close as possible.'

"You can't go that far! Not two white men – "

"Can't you send a couple of the boys?" Sister Brigid did not want to help, but she was unable to stay out of any conversation within the perimeter of her own hearing. "They wouldn't be noticed."

"How the heck would a boy know what's going on?" said Vokes. "He wouldn't know one sort of plane from another, one ship from another. He can't count beyond ten. What would he come back with? Lots of machines that fly, lots of big canoes, lots of men. We could make up that sort of information without going anywhere near Rabaul and back at headquarters they wouldn't know the difference."

The Bishop had been the only silent one so far, but now he said quietly, "I take it, Mr Mullane, that you are going to go in then."

Mullane glanced at Vokes, saw no denial or even hesitation in the younger man's face, and nodded. "Yes, we're going in."

"What happens to us?"

"If they don't send a submarine in in the next day or two, I'm afraid we're going to have to leave you. All of you," he said, looking at Ruth.

"You'll just abandon us?" said Sister Brigid.

"I never pressed you to join us."

"Then you don't want us, it's plain."

"I didn't say that," said Mullane and wished at once that he had sounded more convincing.

54

There was silence again, then Sister Brigid abruptly stood up and walked away. "I'll be getting supper."

"You should treat her more gently," said Ruth. "You don't know, she may have lost much more than you or I."

Then she too went off, leaving Mullane feeling awkward and, suddenly and surprisingly, cruel.

"Sister Brigid *was* a good woman once," said Scheer gently. "I've known her a long time. But the last six months haven't treated her kindly. I think she is at the end of her strength. Spiritually as well as physically. One doubts God's goodness at times. Even – " Once again his voice trailed off.

Leaving Vokes to close up the radio, Mullane and Scheer walked out of the shade of the trees, stood on the ledge of rock that formed the lip of the cliff. The sun had already gone down behind the mountains to the west of them; sun-shot clouds flared up like the tail of some golden bird-of-paradise. A long way out at sea Mullane could see a ship; it was difficult to tell which way it was heading, it seemed fixed by distance, another island not on the map. He felt it was pointless going on the air to report it. The war seemed, as it had so many times in the past months, so remote from him.

"So the generals want you to risk your life even more than you are doing now?" Scheer took out a clay pipe, began to fill it from a worn and stained leather pouch. It was the first time Mullane had seen him smoke and he wondered where Scheer got his tobacco from. The German held up the pouch. "All I have left. I have been limiting myself to one pipe a week. You don't smoke?"

Mullane shook his head. Then abruptly he got up, went back to his hut and returned with a bottle of Chivas Regal and two mugs. He held up the bottle and the Bishop nodded.

"Splendid stuff. My father's favourite drink. All through the war, *my* war – or rather, his and mine – all through it, he still managed to get his supply of whisky from Scotland. I never found out how." He raised his mug in salute, sipped the whisky. He nodded his head in appreciation, took a puff on his pipe, then said, "My father was a general."

Mullane recognized that the German felt a sudden need to talk: to confess? "If he is still alive he must be pleased with the way things have gone," he said in German.

Scheer was grateful for the use of his own language, though he was not quite sure whether the American meant to be sarcastic or not. Even the most fluent linguists often missed the nuances.

"He died in the year Herr Hitler became Chancellor. Perhaps it was just as well. My father was a born elitist. He could never have hidden his contempt for some of the men who now surround Herr Hitler." He could not bring himself to say *der Fuehrer*; perhaps it was a measure of his doubts. "Like all generals, he had no respect for politicians. Especially politicians who think of themselves as military strategists."

"He wouldn't have liked Winston Churchill then."

"I wonder what the English generals think of him?" He puffed on his pipe. Speaking German and the taste of the whisky had given a new strength to his tongue; his voice no longer showed its tendency to fade away. "But then I once told my father that war should not be left to the generals. That is a popular cynicism now, but it still has a grain of commonsense to it."

"Cynicism often is just commonsense."

The Bishop nodded and smiled. "But you can't expect me as a churchman to preach that. My father despised cynics, yet in his own blind way he was an absolute cynic. I once asked him did all the casualties at Verdun trouble him and he said no. One had to take the broad view, he said, otherwise wars would never be won."

"What did he say when you lost?"

"Oh, he would never admit that the generals lost the war. They were stabbed in the back by the rest of the country. Your generals will say the same when you lose this war."

"You think we're going to lose?" Mullane had been relaxed; glad of the opportunity to talk without argument; but now he abruptly resented the German's arrogance.

But Scheer was not arrogant; he had left all that at home years ago, if he had ever been that way at all. "Mr Mullane," he said in English, "the war is almost three years old and what victories have you had? We Germans – " *Ah, there it was. I can never think of myself as anything else.* "We Germans and the Japanese have been preparing for this war for years. Your side

56

is still not prepared."

True, thought Mullane; but could not admit it. He wondered what the generals thought as they sat before their maps down in Australia. He doubted that any of them had made the specific order that he and Vokes should try to enter Rabaul; that would have been dreamed up by someone lower down the pecking order. It would, however, go some way towards helping him avenge Mieko . . .

Darkness fell an hour later and the supply plane, a Hudson bomber, came two hours later, on time almost to the minute. Mullane, Vokes and all the carriers had been up in the drop zone for an hour. The night air in the mountains was cool and the natives, all of them coastal boys and accustomed to the warm sea air, were restless and complaining.

Mullane was relieved when the plane arrived on time. Cloud had obscured the moon and he had begun to worry that the plane might not be able to come down close enough to see the guide fires. He looked at his watch by the light of his flashlight; two minutes later he heard the sound of the plane as it came in from the sea. It was too far to the east.

"Light the fires!"

The heaps of firewood, soaked with precious kerosene from their meagre supply, burst into flame at once. And at that moment it began to rain; water fell out of the sky in a deluge. The fires began to sputter and die; Mullane could no longer hear the plane. He yelled at Vokes for another can of kerosene.

Dimly against the flickering flames of a dying fire he saw Vokes running towards him, can in hand. Then the Australian stumbled; his clumsy foot, always looking for a protruding root, had found one. He plunged forward, the can shooting out of his hand. Mullane rushed towards it, picked it up; but he was too late. The top of the can was open, kerosene had spilled out. He wanted to swing the can at Vokes' head as the latter scrambled to his feet.

"Christ, I'm sorry, Con – !"

Mullane shoved him out of the way, ran towards the dying fire. There was still some kerosene in the can; he up-ended it and the tiny flickering flames flared up. He yelled for more wood.

"We'll have to make do with one fire! Keep feeding this one!"

"He'll never see it!"

"He's got to!"

"He can come back tomorrow night – "

But there was no guarantee of that. The plane would certainly come again; it was understood that the RAAF planes were the lifeblood of any Coastwatcher. But these supply drops were no daily milk run; they could only be made when planes were available. And the type of aircraft that was slow-flying enough to do this job and had enough range was limited; there were dozens of posts to be supplied, bombing raids to be made, patrols to be carried out. It could be a week or even a month before another supply drop could be laid on.

Then just as abruptly as it had started the rain stopped. But the clouds did not break open to reveal the moon; the night was still a black world. It was quiet again, however: Mullane could hear water running somewhere over rocks; the flames of the struggling fire crackled weakly. Then he heard the plane somewhere overhead; it sounded too high, as if the pilot were trying to avoid crashing into the cloud-wrapped mountains. Vokes somehow coaxed a burst of flame from the single fire; it flared up like a giant exploding orchid. And the cloud opened up for a moment, a ragged hole through which the moon stared like a cold marble eye.

Mullane heard the plane coming down again, engines growing louder. "Run! Get under the trees!"

For if the plane crew started dropping supplies there was no chance that he and the others were going to see what would come tumbling through the low clouds. Some of the stuff would come down by parachute; but most of it would be double-packed in jute bags or metal containers. A bag of rice or sugar falling on one's head from several hundred feet was just as lethal as any bomb. Mullane raced for the shelter of the trees and the others followed him.

Vokes was last under the trees and the first sack landed almost at his heels, as if the crew above had been aiming at him. No one could see the aircraft; they could only hear the roar of its engines as it swung up and came back in again. The fire was blazing now, lighting up the clearing; but it did nothing to mark out the clearing for the pilot of the Hudson. The bomber came over, lower this time as if trying to blow the clouds away with its propellers; Mullane heard the deafening roar of the engines and for a horrifying moment thought the plane was going to crash into the mountainside; it would not be the first time such a thing had happened on these drops. Then four more bags came crashing down through the trees in quick succession; there was a yell from one of the carriers as he was hit by a falling branch. The Hudson roared up and away, the pilot gunning the engines as if he suddenly realized he had to climb steeply to avoid running into the mountain.

"Stay where you are!" Mullane shouted. "There's more to come!"

The plane came twice more, sending sacks hurtling down out of the darkness into the trees and, once, into the drop zone. Then it came back for what Mullane guessed must be its final run; he had counted the number of sacks that had been dropped and he knew there was not much more to come. These would be the containers attached to parachutes; in them would be medicine, spare parts for the radio, perhaps even a bottle or two of whisky. The plane roared overhead and out of the clouds, their underside lit by the glow of the fire, appeared five parachutes, looking like giant pink puff-balls. Four of the parachutes held containers; the fifth, smaller than the others, held a leather Gladstone bag beneath it. Mullane, busy sending the natives out to collect the four large containers, two of which floated into the trees and were caught in the upper branches, did not see the smaller parachute till it was too late.

It floated gently across the drop zone, the bag dangling beneath it, and straight into the now blazing fire. The bag burst open at once and pieces of paper sprayed out, caught fire and added to the blaze.

By the time Mullane realized what had been in the bag, the money, all £200 of it, was just ashes.

Chapter Three

"Goddamit! It was the only goddam thing right on target!"

"They're never going to believe it," said Vokes. "Two hundred quid up in smoke, just like that!"

"Do the boys know what happened?" asked Ruth.

"No, fortunately. Con saw what happened and got them busy collecting the rest of the stuff before they could cotton on. I can still see it, like in a slow motion dream, you know what I mean? I could have chased it and caught it if I'd woken up what was in the bag. What else was in it, I wonder? It was stuffed full, that was why it busted open when it hit – "

"There was a bottle of something in it," said Mullane. "A bottle of whisky, maybe. There's a warning there somewhere – "

It was next morning and the three of them were having breakfast. Bishop Scheer and Sister Brigid, with young Luke and Mark, were at prayers; the chant of the Rosary came as a soft murmur from halfway along the ridge. The prayers, Scheer had suggested, were for the success of the drop.

It had taken them four hours to bring everything down to the camp. It had not been easy working in the darkness, but Mullane had wanted everything out of the drop zone before daylight, in case the Japanese had heard last night's plane and would send over a scout plane. The fire had been put out, earth thrown over it and leafy branches strewn on top to make it look from the air like a huge bush. The few trees that had been in the clearing and had been chopped down had been dragged into the jungle and the stumps of them smeared with mud to make them look like old rotting trunks. Finally a section of fence, which Mullane had had the natives weave together while they had been waiting, was run round part of the drop zone. It was a rough-and-ready camouflage, but Mullane hoped that from the air the zone would look like an abandoned native garden. He might need to use the same zone again in the future.

Now it was seven o'clock on a morning clear and shining as new glass. "What are you going to do with Yali?" Ruth said. "With that arm he's not much use. He should be sent home."

One of the carriers, a boy of eighteen, had broken his arm when he had fallen during the climb down last night.

"I don't know that I can trust him not to tell the Japs where we are," said Mullane. "He's Mariba's cousin and Mariba still wants to cause trouble. I threatened to kick him in the behind twice last night for loafing on the job."

"Would you have kicked him?"

Mullane saw the look of exasperation on Vokes' face but he ignored it. "A good solid boot is always a handy weapon. It works wonders on a bare behind."

Ruth was beginning to suspect that Mullane occasionally kidded her. She had been kidded before by other men, but that had all been part of their sexual approach to her and she had been able to handle it. But if Mullane's tongue was in his cheek it seemed to be for a more serious purpose.

"Yali is a weak character," said Mullane, pouring honey on one of the scones that the cook-boy had made in the bush oven Vokes had built. Mullane had discovered that Vokes, for all his faults, had a talent for improvisation – "It's an Aussie knack," Vokes had said. "Everything back home is second-hand. Even our navy is something the Poms gave us. If we couldn't improvise, the country would come to a standstill." The oven had been made from two kerosene tins and these scones for breakfast were the first product of it.

"Yali will do whatever Mariba tells him to. And when Mariba finds out we don't have any money to pay them, he's going to be hard to handle. I'll need something more than the threat of a boot in his behind. If we send Yali back to Kiogo, Mariba could just walk off with him and take most of the other boys as well."

The prayers along the ridge had finished and Scheer and Sister Brigid came back to the huts, bringing their breakfast with them. But the nun did not come to sit with Mullane and the others. She walked past the group without a word, seeming a stranger because the voluble tongue was silent, and went on to join Luke and Mark.

Mullane made no comment, but he caught the Bishop's eye and the latter said, "She will be all right soon. One just has to be patient with her."

Ruth got over the awkward moment by putting the conversation back on the track where it had been a minute or two beforehand. "But if you've had some of these boys working for you for four or five years, surely they wouldn't want to betray you? Not if you've been a good boss."

"I don't think I could blame any of them if they went over to the Japs. All they'd be doing would be choosing one foreigner as their boss over another. It's their privilege, if you can call it that."

"Then why don't you let them go?"

"Because I'm more concerned for my own neck than I am for their privileges. In this jurisdiction it's called Mullane's Law. I just promulgated it."

"I second that," said Vokes.

"Then it will be called the Mullane-Vokes Law," said Mullane graciously; then he looked back at Ruth. "So I'm afraid Yali has to stay here."

Ruth hesitated, then nodded. She was concerned for her own neck and she knew that Mullane had implied that she and the others were included in his Law. "All right, he can help me. A one-armed assistant won't be any worse than some I've had."

Later Mullane and Vokes sat down in front of the radio. "Have you made up your mind?" said Vokes. "I mean about when we head for Rabaul?"

"What do you think?"

"I didn't tell you last night – " Vokes gave careful attention to wiping clean the battery leads. "In one of those containers they dropped there was my naval cap and badges of rank."

"Why aren't you wearing them?"

Vokes grinned, suddenly at ease again. "I might put up the badges, just in case. But the cap – you wouldn't believe it. It's a seven-and-three-quarters. I take a size seven. The Nips would laugh themselves silly if ever they caught me in it."

"Well, keep it handy. You can tell them your head's shrunk while you've been up here in the hills. All set?"

The radio began to hum, whistle and crackle as it warmed up. A scramble of voices came and went as if they were being pumped through bellows; they were American voices, probably Marine or Navy pilots talking to their carriers. They would be somewhere north of the Solomons, part of the defence force that wanted to know what major threat there was for them in Rabaul.

Mullane sent out the first message to Moresby for relay to Townsville. It reported the safe drop of the supplies but mentioned the fate of the money. The reply was quick: *Bad luck about money. Go over to Champion.*

"This is going to be bloody slow," said Vokes, taking out a second code book. *Playfair* was the normal code used by the Coastwatchers: easy to send and to receive, it was also easy to break. But *Champion* was a new and much more difficult code. "I haven't had any practice on this one."

"You take over the key. I'll do the coding and decoding."

The message, when he had finally decoded it, was the longest he had ever received: *Suspect major activity soon regarding Guadalcanal. No word from CEC or DRM, suspect captured. Urgent you deliver Rabaul capacity aircraft, ships, troops. Expect information 48 hours.*

"They'll be bloody lucky," said Vokes, switching off the set. "Shit a brick, do they think all we have to do is stroll in there?"

Mullane coded a message, handed it to Vokes. "Send that."

"What's it say?" Vokes was still struggling to master the new code.

"Will need money first to pay carriers. Advise availability."

Vokes grinned. "That'll upset the bastards."

But someone at Moresby or Townsville must have anticipated them: the bastards were on the ball. The answer came back immediately: *Six hundred pounds in safe in bush half-mile up-river from Noku. In bush east bank. Leave chit in safe.*

"Funny buggers," said Vokes. "Leave chit in safe!"

"In bush on east bank – we could spend hours looking for it!"

"Sometimes I wonder about those no-hopers back at HQ – " But Vokes, for all his complaining, knew that most of the men in Townsville knew more about life up here than he did.

"Noku's probably occupied by the Japs now." Noku was another Burns Philp plantation several miles up the coast. "Who was the manager there?"

"Jack Kayser. He had to get out very early in the piece. There's a Chinese running the place now, Lee Chin. He's under some sort of parole from the Nips."

"Whose side would he be on?"

Vokes shrugged. "Anyone's. He was born on the island. He'd be like the boongs, I guess. Go with the winning side. Don't know that I'd blame him."

He was a little surprised at his own magnanimity. He might not have his father's rabid patriotism, but he had inherited all his xenophobia. Anyone who wasn't white, especially any yellow Asiatic, had to be suspect. He wondered if some of Mullane's broadmindedness was rubbing off on him. Though the Yank was perhaps too broadminded. He had not forgotten that Mullane had had a good word for the Nips, or anyway for some of them.

Mullane looked out across the green spill of jungle to the placid sea. Sunlight struck the small waves; it was as if a vast school of golden dolphins were at play. The party was safe here; or comparatively so. He could feel the strong temptation to stay put. But he knew he never could.

"Okay, we'll start off tomorrow for Rabaul. But first we've got to get that money down at Noku. Otherwise the boys are going to walk off and you and Buka and I are going to have to play at being carriers. Would that safe down there in the bushes be a combination job?"

"No, it's probably the same as we had on our plantation. An old-fashioned key job. But where's the key?"

"Lee Chin might still have it."

"What do we do – go right into Noku and ask him?"

Mullane smiled, though he was in no mood for humour. "I think that's exactly what we'll have to do. I may as well get started now. Then I can get down to Noku by dark and go in there tonight."

Vokes hesitated only a moment before he said, "I think I'd better go, Con. I'll wear my cap and badges of rank. Just in case."

"No, you're the senior man. You stay here and run the post."

"Bull." Vokes grinned with embarrassment; he knew he'd never be able to put up the badges on his shoulders. "Let's toss."

Mullane took out his wallet, took from it a silver dollar. "My lucky coin. Heads I go, tails you go."

But it had not been his lucky coin last time he had tossed it.

II

"I know we're asking a lot," his brother Liam had said. "But you could be in a better position than our own men in the embassy in Tokyo."

They were in Liam's office in the Navy building on Constitution Avenue in Washington. Mullane then had still had his old identity: Cornelius McArdle. He and Liam had never been close and he had been surprised when his brother had called and asked him to come down to Washington.

"I hear you've taken a coaching job in Japan. We haven't seen much of each other these past few years. Come down and spend a night with Margaret and me. Let me know what train you'll be on and I'll have a car pick you up."

McArdle had been about to decline, then decided that would be churlish. It was winter, January of 1936, and he had nothing to do for the next month before he left by train for San Francisco and then ship to Yokohama. He was, technically, unemployed and at leisure; though perhaps the other twelve and a half million unemployed in the country just then might not have considered him a welfare brother. He had played his last season with the Yankees at a salary of $30,000 and in September said good-bye to Lou Gehrig, Lefty Gomez, Joe DiMaggio and the others; there were down-and-outs across the country who would have considered themselves rich to be in such company even if they had only drawn nickels and dimes as a wage for the season. He had signed in October for almost the same salary to coach the Tokyo Athletics, where he was due to report 1 March. A couple of days in Washington with Liam and his wife would be no hardship. And it would please his father when he called to tell him where he had been. Mary McArdle had died two years ago, but Patrick had stayed on in the big old house in Rochester, shutting out the world that no longer bore any resemblance to the world he and Mary had enjoyed for so long.

The grey Navy Chevrolet picked up McArdle at the station. "The Assistant Secretary wants to see you in his office first, sir. We're to go straight there. Excuse me staring, sir. I saw you pitch against the Cubs back in 1932 in the World Series. I'm from Chicago. You beat us four to nothing."

McArdle smiled. "I didn't help the Yankees very much. 1932 wasn't one of my best years."

Last season had also not been one of his best; in fact it had been the worst in the eleven seasons he had played. But the Navy driver was too polite to mention that. "Here we are, sir. Good luck in Japan, sir. Can't imagine them playing baseball, all them little guys."

When Liam, after what seemed genuine delight in their re-union, told him why he had asked him to come to Washington, Con decided that his luck would be better if he stayed in the United States. "Spy? You want me to *spy*?"

"I haven't used that word, old chap." Liam had always been something of a stuffed shirt; likeable but stuffed, nonetheless. He had come down from the family firm to Washington in 1934 at the invitation of the President and after twelve months had stepped into the office of Assistant Secretary for the Navy; it was tipped that eventually he would be Secretary. Con, six years later, would wonder what had gone wrong with Liam's career that, having left the government for three years, he had come back still as Assistant Secretary. But that was all in the future on that January afternoon in 1936.

"Intelligence is what we're after. Just between you and me, we don't have a co-ordinated intelligence service. Our British friends put us down among the banana republics in that respect. But they have their problems with Hitler and his ambitions in Europe. Our problem is Japan. Do you take much interest in world affairs?"

"No," said Con, feeling all at once naive and frivolous-minded. "I went to Europe last fall and I saw some things there I didn't like. A Nazi rally in Berlin, for instance – it was frightening. But, I better be honest with you, I don't read all the news that's fit to print in the *New York Times*."

"What do you read?"

"The sports pages and the gossip columns. And Hemingway, Dos Passos, Molière, Aldous Huxley – I have a very catholic taste except that I don't seem to read any Catholic writers. Unless you include Cervantes. I've just finished *Don Quixote*."

Liam was impressed; he didn't read such authors himself. "At least baseball hasn't coarsened your intellect too much."

"On the contrary, it sharpened it. Baseball is full of Don Quixotes, most of them managers. I'll let you know if the analogy is true after I've had a season as manager in Tokyo. I've never had any experience with Japanese windmills."

"I'd be happier if you could let me know a few other things about Japan. The President is very worried about how things are going over there. They walked out of the Naval Conference in London last week, virtually told us to go to hell when we suggested a 5-5-3 ratio in naval power for Britain, us and them. They're going to build up their navy to their own needs. We're not quite sure what those needs are. But if we can find out what sort of ships they're planning to build, what sort of training they are putting their personnel through, then we can start to build a picture of where Japan might be heading."

"You don't think they're going to stop in China?" Suddenly the job in Tokyo began to lose some of its appeal.

Liam shook his head. "There are two factions in Japan, we know that much. The Navy is conservative and, we think, would like to keep their area of influence pretty close to home. But there are two schools of thought, the Strike-North faction and the Strike-South crowd. The Strike-North lot wouldn't need too much co-operation from the Navy, since their aim is to strike across Manchuria towards Russia. But the Strike-South crowd want to take the whole of South-east Asia under their wing, all the British and French and Dutch colonies. For that they would need a much bigger navy than Japan has at present."

"But why ask me? An amateur."

"Because the professionals, our attachés at the embassy, are watched day and night by the *kempei*, the Jap secret police. They won't be watching you. If you succeed in raising the standard of their baseball – and I believe they are becoming as crazy about the game as we Americans – "

"Not you, old chap."

Liam had the grace to smile. "No, not me. But if the Japs take to worshipping you as we worshipped Babe Ruth, then the *kempei* would never dare to harass you."

"I'm going out there to be a manager, not a player. Managers are never worshipped, not even in Japan." He gazed out the window at the grey cheerless day. It was a depressing day, not one for generating a mood for making decisions. "You're asking an awful lot, Liam. I don't think I've ever given a thought to 'My Country, 'tis of thee' . . ."

"It's time you did." Liam managed not to sound pompously patriotic; there was real concern in his face. "We're in a minority, a very small one, but there are some of us in this town who feel that, the way Japan is going, we'll be at war with her eventually. Next year, five years, ten years – I don't know. But some time, certainly. And we should be prepared."

"I've never had any training in this sort of thing. I wouldn't know what to look for."

"We can give you a crash course. Our Intelligence men will brief you. They were the ones who suggested I should approach you."

"I'll think about it. How long do I have to make up my mind?"

"Tomorrow?" Liam smiled, his whole stuffed-shirt image falling away from him, at Con's look of amazement. "Rushing you, eh? But you're leaving for Japan within the month, aren't you? Come on, let's go home. Your nephews want to meet a baseball hero."

Liam lived in Georgetown in a large rented house suited to an Assistant Secretary. His wife Margaret was an attractive woman who had to watch her weight and sometimes forgot to look at the scales; Con felt warmer towards her than he did towards his brother. They had two sons, aged 12 and 14, who could not hide their disappointment that their uncle looked less like a ballplayer than a diplomat. The Sulka clothes were not what they had expected.

"You're better dressed than Dad," said Tom, the younger. "Baseballers should look all rumpled, sort of."

"You look like Robert Montgomery," said Roger, the elder.

"There's nothing wrong with looking like a film star," said their mother. "It obviously does you no harm with the ladies, from what I read in Walter Winchell. You seem to have a different girl every month. Who was Apricot Bloom, for heaven's sake?"

"A Jewish chorus girl." Her real name had been Annie Pilsudski and she had been a Polish Catholic.

"Wow, dating a chorus girl!" said Roger. "You'll never get to do that in government, Dad."

"Thank heavens," said Margaret.

Next morning Liam came into the guest room. "Well, old chap? Did you sleep on it?"

Con, a late riser, a habit developed from dating chorus girls, was sitting up in bed tossing a silver dollar. "Babe Ruth gave me this. Said it was his lucky coin. I found out later he had dozens of lucky coins. But this one has done well by me."

"What have you tossed for? The choice of Apricot Bloom or some other girl?"

Con smiled. "You're closer to the truth than you meant to be." He spun the coin idly. "Heads I work for you in Japan, tails I don't."

"It's a hell of a way to serve your country. On the toss of a coin."

"You should read more history, old chap. And you're a music lover – did you know that Haydn sometimes rolled dice to make a choice among possible chord and key combinations?"

"There's a difference between composing a symphony and serving one's country."

"Well, that's the way it's going to be, Liam. I don't know what they do to spies in peacetime. They may chop off my head, slap me into jail or just kick me out of the country."

"There'll be no danger."

"You can't be sure of that. I could finish up a loser. You've

69

given me so little to base a decision on, it's difficult to make a rational decision. So we'll have to let my lucky coin decide."

He spun the coin, caught it, slapped it on his wrist, looked at it ruefully.

"Heads. Maybe it's not lucky any more."

III

Vokes said, "Well, what is it? Heads or tails?"

"Heads," said Mullane. "I go."

Then Buka came running along the ridge and pulled up panting in the doorway of the hut. "Boss – Jap soldiers down on track!"

"They must have heard the plane last night! Start packing!"

Mullane grabbed his Thompson gun and went running back along the ridge to the main track. On the way he passed Ruth and the others, snapped at them to be ready to move on at a moment's notice. When they reached the main track Buka, to Mullane's surprise, turned right instead of left.

"This way, boss!"

So the Japanese weren't coming up the track from the west, the one that Mullane and the party had traversed. He followed Buka east, pulled up abruptly as Buka waved him to a stop. The trees here thinned out, gave way to a tumble of huge limestone rocks that must have slid down the mountain perhaps centuries ago; there was no sign of their slide down through the thick jungle above them, but the rocks did not look as if they had been exposed on the slope at this point. They had been arrested here on their way down to the river in the narrow valley far below. Grey on their upper half, lichen-covered on their underside, they suggested a family of huge pachyderms that had died and turned to stone on this narrow ledge.

Buka, standing close to the largest rock, pointed down. "There, boss. I come along here look for gardens, maybe. Then I hear dogs barking – "

"Dogs?"

Then Mullane, who had caught a glimpse of movement through the trees far below, heard the barking of the dogs and a chill ran through him. There was something terrifying about being hunted by dogs; it reduced one to an animal level. He felt a fear he had never experienced before; the dogs' barking had a baying note to it, almost as if they had caught his and Buka's scent. Once, driving south through Georgia to spring training in Florida, he had passed a prison camp and a few miles farther on had seen a line of prison guards, with dogs on leashes, strung out across a field as they advanced on a thick wood of pines. He had stopped the car and at once heard the baying of the hounds on the crisp morning air. A dread had crept into his mind and he had looked out on the scene with horrified eyes, identifying himself with the unseen escaper hiding in the woods. Suddenly the guards had started to run, dragged along by the dogs. He had started up the car and driven off at speed, not wanting to see the climax of the manhunt. In his ears for days afterwards there had been the echo of the dogs' baying, the bugles of horror.

"They coming up here, boss. How we going to stop them? Jump on them, like you done back at the river?"

Mullane could catch only occasional glimpses of the Japanese as they moved up the jungle track from the river. Once they came out into an open stretch and he made a quick count: there were at least thirty of them. That would be too many for just three guns to ambush. He leaned back against the huge boulder behind him, his heels slipped in the mud and he sat down with a thump. Buka started to help him to his feet, but he waved him away. He looked in under the boulder, then scrambled to his feet.

"Get back to camp – quick! Bring the shovels and some of the boys. Tell Boss Vokes to get packed – we're moving on!"

Buka ran back towards the camp. Down below the dogs' barking was amplified by the funnel of the narrow valley through which the Japanese were climbing. Clouds rolled down off the mountains, abruptly cutting off the sun; Mullane stood in a sombre light that further depressed him. The Japanese would be up here on this ridge in less than half an hour at the rate they were moving.

He began to move among the boulders, picking out the ones which would be easiest to move. Buka and two of the carriers were back in a few minutes and Mullane at once pointed to two of the largest rocks, one behind the other.

The two natives looked puzzled; then Buka thumped one of them across the shoulders with the barrel of his rifle. They began digging furiously into the muddy soil on the downward side of the lower boulder. Once or twice they looked up anxiously at the huge mass looming over them, but Buka kept them at their task. Then Mullane called a halt, put them on to digging away beneath the higher rock. All the time he kept an eye on the jungle below, marking a spot on the track where, if the Japanese crossed it in time, they would be safe from the plunging rocks. That is, if he and Buka and the two natives managed to move the rocks at all . . .

Vokes came running along the track. "We're all ready, Con. Do I move them along this way?"

"Bring everyone up, but keep them back there out of the way. I'll need another half a dozen boys. Send 'em up with axes."

Vokes went running back towards the camp. The clouds all at once swung away, sliding across the face of the mountain like a grey lateral landslide, and the sun came out in a brilliant burst of light. And from down the steep slope of the narrow valley there came shouts as the Japanese caught sight of Mullane.

He dropped to one knee, making a smaller target of himself in case they started shooting. The baying of the dogs had increased; the movement through the trees flickered more quickly as the Japanese began to run up the track. They had seen the danger that lay ahead of them but they had decided to press on rather than turn back to safety. In another five minutes they would be beyond the point which Mullane had marked as the line through which the boulders would fall.

Vokes and half a dozen of the carriers, all with axes or machetes, were back in a minute. Mullane set them to work to chop down thick poles; under the sting of his tongue they all worked feverishly. The first poles were cut and ready; he yelled for them to be shoved under the upper boulder. A quick look had told him that the Japanese, slipping and sliding in the mud of the steep track below, were less than two hundred yards from his target point.

"Heave!"

Four of the natives lifted their shoulders against the poles. Mariba was one of them; for a moment he paused and looked hard at Mullane, then he lent his support to the other carriers' efforts. Faces strained, muscles standing out in ridges through their walnut-dark skin, they pushed against the huge boulder. It teetered on its base, then settled back. Vokes swore at the natives, jumped in amongst them with a pole of his own.

Mullane, tense, head swivelling as he tried to watch both the stubbornly immovable rock and the now frantically climbing Japanese, saw the odds going against his party. The enemy were going to make it to safety, come on up the track with their dogs. All of a sudden he dropped his gun, picked up a spade and started furiously to shovel mud away from beneath the boulder. Then a chip flew off the rock right beside him and a moment later he heard the sound of the shot. Another bullet slapped into the mud beside him, and another and another.

"Look out, Con!" Vokes' yell of warning was more a scream.

Mullane slipped in the mud, fell flat on his back, looked up and saw the huge mass of rock begin to totter. He heard the whine of a ricocheting bullet; he knew he was going to be either shot or crushed to death. Desperately he tried to crawl away; his feet and knees slipped in the treacherous mud. Then a big black hand reached out, grabbed him by the back of his shirt; Buka hauled him to safety as the boulder rolled past within inches of his legs. It hit the larger boulder in front of it. The rocks were still for a moment, one pressed hard against the other; Vokes hurled himself against them, as if he were going into a rugby ruck. The front boulder gave, began to roll. The two massive rocks, each weighing several tons, fell over the lip of the ridge and went crashing down on to the trees on the slope below.

Mullane, still lying in the mud, trembling from his narrow escape, lifted his head and looked over the rim of the ledge. The effect he had hoped for was happening. The boulders had hit two of the largest trees, 150-foot *erimas*, snapping them off close to their bases; a chain reaction started at once. Trees leaned down the slope; the image, on a larger scale, was of grass bending beneath a wind. Then the trees tore loose from their roots and a green surf of trees and undergrowth began to

73

cascade down the steep slope of the valley. The huge boulders rode the cascade like giant grey surf-balls; mud began to fly up in a dark spume. The avalanche went down the mountainside, carrying everything before it. Mullane saw the Japanese suddenly stop, turn and begin to run back down the track; but now they were running straight down the path of the avalanche. The dogs, let loose, stood terror-stricken as the huge swathe of trees, rocks and mud came down on them. It swept over the target point Mullane had marked, taking everything with it: trees, dogs, the Japanese. It plunged on down, terrible in its unstoppable fury; then there was a flash of bright splinters of light as it hit the river and a moment later there was silence. But for the whimpering of a dog (or a man?) somewhere on the edge of the destruction.

Mullane hauled himself to his feet as Vokes said, "Jesus Christ – what a way to die!"

Mullane, sweating, covered in mud, waited for the trembling in his legs to subside. He was learning something about himself: his recovery rate from emotional shock was improving. He could already feel everything settling in him, an emotional ballast that would keep him on an even keel and the right bearing.

He nodded to Buka. "Thanks, Buka. You saved my life then."

The big man showed a flash of teeth: his emotional ballast seemed never to shift. "Not want to see you squashed flat, boss. You be no use that way."

It was a cheeky retort, but Mullane knew Buka did not mean it that way. The bond between the two men had deepened since the trek had begun; but Buka would not take advantage of it. Mullane said gruffly, "Better get the boys moving. We want to be long gone from here before any more Japs come poking around. As soon as word gets back to their camp about that – " he waved an arm at the havoc down the valley " – they'll have a scout plane over here."

The rest of the party had now come up the track. Ruth said, "What about all those supplies? Do we have to leave them again?"

"I'm afraid so. How much did you manage to get packed?"

"Not much. The boys hid most of it in the bush. I brought this." She handed him his remaining bottle of Scotch.

He took it, decided a nip would do him good and had one. "Thank you, Miss Riddle. You're an understanding woman."

Sister Brigid had gone inquisitively to the rim of the ledge, looked over and then blessed herself. Now she turned back, made a conscious effort to sound co-operative and business-like.

"You need so many boys to carry your radio and batteries and that engine. If you are going to abandon us, Mr Mullane, why not leave us here with the supplies? At least then we shouldn't starve. Not for a while, anyway."

"The Japs will be up here in a day at the outside. I'm not – *abandoning* you to be picked up by them. We'll leave you in a safer place."

Sister Brigid picked up her skirts and went off down the track. She could feel herself at the end of her tether; she had no reserves left. She was going through the menopause, but she would admit it to no one, not even Miss Riddle; confession was good for the soul but there were limits. Prayer was all she had left to sustain her and lately she had, to her horror, begun to wonder at the efficacy of it. On the mission her days and her life had been full and prayer had been only in praise of God and not for her own ends.

The party moved off and once again Ruth fell in with Mullane. "I don't know what you were before you came out here, but you certainly were never a diplomat. Not with women."

"I played baseball. They didn't understand the word diplomacy in that ambience."

Ambience: it was a word she had never heard before. "When did you get your education? Before or after you played base-ball?"

"Before, during and after."

"Your education in women still has a long way to go."

"You're no diplomat yourself."

"I've told every man I ever liked the truth about himself."

"The truth about himself from your point of view, of course."

"Of course. There's no objectivity between the sexes. But Sister Brigid is different – you don't seem to treat her as a woman."

Then up ahead Vokes called an abrupt halt. The line shrank, everyone bumping into the man in front of him, like carriages in a suddenly-braked train. One native fell over and his companions laughed at him, the laughter petering out into giggling as it ran back down the line to Mullane and Ruth. As he hurried up the track it struck Mullane that there was less tension among the natives than among the whites. They were still not fully committed, they could walk off at any moment.

His sudden fear was confirmed as soon as he reached Vokes. "It's Mariba, Con. The bugger's acting up again. He's dumped his load and wants to know when they're going to be paid."

Mariba stood sullenly beside the metal box, containing part of the radio, which he had been carrying. Yali, his cousin, broken arm in a sling, stood beside him and four other carriers had congealed into a group just behind them. Rebellion was as plain on their faces as the betel-stain on their lips; even as Mullane looked at them, Mariba shot a gob of red spittle into the mud of the tracks. Mullane knew that that particular spit was an insult, not just part of the betel-chewing habit.

"I've threatened to kick him up the arse – "

"I don't think that's going to do any good, Frank. Too many asses. I think he's got most of them on his side." Then he said to Mariba in pidgin, "I told you you'd get your pay."

"We want it now, boss. No pay, we finish, go home."

Behind the sullen native Mullane could see the growing rebellion in the other dark faces. Buka, his own face contorted with anger, said, "Let me take this feller into bush, boss – "

Ah, for the good old days: Mullane was sure that method had worked in the past. But not now: Mariba and his fellow workers knew they now had a choice of masters. "No, they'll get their pay, Buka. But not today – today's Thursday. Mariba knows damn well they don't get paid till Friday."

"Good thinking," said Vokes out of the corner of his mouth.

I'm just glad Ruth Riddle, the workers' friend, can't hear me. She would be sure to accuse him of further exploitation, of bosses' casuistry. "You will be paid tomorrow, Mariba. I promise you."

"Where you get the money, boss?" Mariba had always been one of the more sullen boys, but he had never shown this much shrewdness before. Mullane, for one moment of fantasy, wished him on the Japanese, wondered how they would deal with his radicalism. Probably chop his head off.

"I shall get the money tonight," he said and wondered what would happen to Vokes and the others if he did not return from Noku.

IV

They trekked for another four hours. Mariba and his fellow unionists, as Vokes called them, had had a short conference and decided to continue. But they left no doubt that if they were not paid tomorrow they would turn round and go back to Kiogo. They expected the boss to produce or else.

Low clouds rolled down off the mountains and for the last three hours of the trek the party walked through a thin grey mist that chilled everyone as soon as they halted. At last they came to a ridge above another river. Mullane could not see the river through the mist but he could hear the roar of a waterfall. He took out his map, but the markings on it were unrelated to the tiny grey world in which he stood.

"That *should* be the Noku River we can hear, but I'm not sure. I'll have to follow it down to the coast and hope I come to Noku. We'll camp here."

It was a good spot for a camp, a flattening-out of the ridge under a canopy of mixed trees: walnut, a few pandanus palms, some rain trees. The trees were dripping moisture and the undergrowth was dank and rotten-smelling; but one couldn't have everything. Tenements, Mullane told himself unconvincingly, were often more secure than mansions. All the comfortable spots were down on the coast, right beside the Japs.

"How far do you reckon we are from Rabaul?" Vokes asked.

"If that map is correct, about sixty miles, maybe less. But

we're not going to get in there and out again in forty-eight hours." He did not allow himself to think how much depended on him and Vokes. He knew that battles in the past had swung on the efforts of one man, but he could not bring himself to entertain the conceit that he and Vokes could be so important. "I still have to get that money. And we still have to find a place where we can leave Ruth and the others."

"Christ Almighty – " Vokes wished he could think of some way of helping them, but his mind was blank. All he could console himself with was the thought that the others had managed to survive before he and Mullane had met them and their luck might continue till he and Mullane could get back from Rabaul.

The camp was set up. The mist thickened and the air was like a cold damp rag against the cheek; it was just the sort of weather to bring out any latent fever in the party. Mullane kept getting up and moving about from group to group, as much to stretch his aching limbs as anything else; his joints had stiffened and he wondered if he was at last going to feel age creeping up on him. The Bishop sat huddled in his cassock and when Mullane spoke to him *his* limbs seemed to creak as he stood up.

"I'm afraid I have no enthusiasm for discomfort. Job would have had little patience with me."

Sister Brigid, looking like a waterlogged crow, sat beneath a leaf shelter with Luke and Mark, occasionally speaking to them in a low voice. Mullane avoided her, unsure of how she would react if he asked for a truce. He did not attempt to think what she would be like tomorrow when he and Vokes left them. He had noticed that she seemed to have retreated completely from the party, not even exchanging a word with Scheer or Ruth.

Ruth was doling out food to the cook-boy, having appointed herself in charge of the rations. "I'm putting a bit extra in the pot."

"Can we spare it?" Mullane asked.

"I think it's needed. Everyone's pretty cold and down-in-the-mouth. And I think it might have a soothing effect on your rebels. There's a lot of truth in that saying about the way to a man's heart is through his stomach."

"I don't believe Mariba has a heart." Then he looked at her through the beads of water falling from the peak of his cap. She wore a floppy canvas hat that also dripped water. "Do you think I have one?"

"Oh, everyone has one, Mr Mullane. Not all of them are as black as yours."

"Keep it up, Miss Riddle. As a man-hater you're batting a thousand."

"That's good, I take it?" She reached into a sack, held out a handful of yams to the cook-boy. "An extra helping for the boss."

In the late afternoon it began to rain, a steady heavy drizzle that was like a visible manifestation of the misery everyone felt. The world was reduced, shrunk to a few square yards by the monotonous downpour; no one was in the mood for talk and there was no sound but the drum-drum of rain on the tents, the shelters and the thick soupy mud. Mullane began to chafe at the thought of how he and Vokes were being delayed from going into Rabaul.

A leech had somehow got inside the top of his sock and he was applying a lighted match to the swollen worm-like creature on his ankle.

"Don't put it out." Vokes took the match as the leech fell off Mullane's ankle. "I've got one of the bastards on my right tit."

"Is he after blood or milk?"

Then they heard the plane. It was somewhere immediately above them, flying low but invisible in the thick clouds. It flew over the camp, engines roaring; then the engines took on a louder, more desperate note as the pilot suddenly gunned them. The sound rose to a crescendo; the sudden booming crash was an unexpected climax. The hiss and drumming of the rain came back, but it could have been a hollow silence.

"That wasn't one of ours!" Vokes wrung his fingers as the match burned them; the leech fell into a fold of his shirt and he brushed it off. "He's come down pretty close – "

"It was probably one of their bombers trying to find his way home to Rabaul."

"Do we go looking for him?"

79

"Not in this rain. When it clears up – "

The camp had come alive with the sound of the crash. Everyone came out from under their shelter, stood in the rain in listening attitudes, as if waiting for an echo. The natives chattered among themselves; then as if no longer interested, broke up their groups and went back out of the rain. But the Europeans remained in the open, Ruth crowding with the Bishop under his umbrella. Mullane guessed it was the closest Scheer had been to a woman in forty years, but the Bishop did not look uncomfortable.

"That was a Japanese plane, wasn't it?" said Scheer. "It wasn't one of yours."

Still the enemy alien, Mullane thought; and nodded. "Frank and I will go up and take a look as soon as the rain lifts."

"There may be some injured." Sister Brigid, standing alone in the drizzle, spoke for the first time directly to Mullane. "Miss Riddle and I had better come with you. The Bishop, too. He was a doctor once, you know."

Mullane looked hard at Scheer and said in German, "You didn't tell me that."

"There was no reason to, Herr Mullane. I was a doctor in the German army. I gave it all up when I joined the Church. I am too out of practice to be of any use to you."

"Can't you two speak English?" said Vokes irritably. Like most Australians he was no linguist and he resented people who hid behind another language.

Mullane ignored him, said in English, "None of you will come with us. If there are any survivors, there could be some shooting. You'll all stay here with Buka and the boys. You'll be in charge, Buka."

At first Buka looked surprised that he should be put in charge of Europeans, then abruptly he nodded and seemed to gain inches in stature. He stamped his feet. "Yes, sir!"

"No kicking anyone in the behind, that's all."

"No, sir!" But it seemed that he was looking around for Mariba.

Then the rain suddenly stopped and the clouds started to lift. Mullane and Vokes set off at once to climb the mountain towards where they thought the crash had occurred. They took with them three of the more reliable natives.

The climb was a difficult one, made even more difficult because they were not quite sure where they were heading. There was no point where they could stand back and look up the mountainside to see if the jungle covering had been scarred by the crashing plane. They struggled up through vines that tried to lasso them, chopped their way through bushes that tore at them like a thousand iron fingernails, sank up to their knees in mud and leaf-mould that had the smell of death.

They climbed for almost an hour, though they had covered less than a mile through the thick jungle, and then Vokes, in the lead, suddenly gave a yell. Mullane began to hurry, struggling up to join Vokes on a narrow shoulder that jutted out from the main slope.

Below them, in a dip, the trees had been snapped off as if by a giant berserk lumberjack; yellow jagged stumps stuck up out of the green bushes and mud. A twisted mass of metal, hardly recognizable as a plane at first glance, had plunged into the mountainside, bringing the last trees it had demolished down on top of it.

"It's a Kawanisi," said Vokes. "A bit out of his territory."

The big flying-boat was identifiable only by its raised tail, the only section of the aircraft that remained intact. As far as Mullane could see there had been no fire. There was no sign of any movement in or around the plane.

Vokes looked up at the darkening sky. "We're not going to get back to camp before dark. And there looks to be more rain on the way."

"Let's see who was aboard."

They slid down the side of the dip, came up under the high tail of the flying-boat; it towered above them like some prehistoric bird, wings spread but unable to fly. Even above the smell of mud and undergrowth Mullane caught a whiff of petrol and oil. He told the three carriers to stand back and he and Vokes, moving in from opposite sides of the fuselage, each with his gun at the ready, stepped gingerly and awkwardly over the chaos of metal and fallen trees up towards the forward section.

Or what remained of the forward section. The rest of the aircraft had concertina-ed in on it, the whole fuselage breaking up as it had driven into the trees and mud. Mullane crouched down, peered through the gathering gloom into the wreckage, saw the four bodies (or what had been bodies) wrapped like red meat in the tangle of metal. He had no idea how many crew a Kawanisi carried, but four seemed a reasonable number for such an aircraft. He peered through the wreckage at Vokes on the other side.

"Four dead. You found any more?"

"I've got one here in the mud. A live one."

Mullane scrambled back round the plane, clambered up to where Vokes stood beside a stripped-off wing. Lying in the mud, one arm trapped under some wreckage, the other lying awkwardly and uselessly beside him, was a Japanese. He stared up at Mullane and Vokes, moved his body desperately and painfully; but he had no hand to clutch at the pistol in the holster at his waist. Then he grunted, lay back and waited for them to kill him.

"We might as well put him out of his misery," said Vokes; but hoped Mullane would do it. "It's the practical thing to do."

"I think we'd do better to keep him alive," said Mullane. "He out-ranks even you, Frank. He's a lieutenant-general."

Chapter Four

I

Mullane reached down and took the pistol from the holster. Then he said in Japanese, "I want your name, rank and number, sir."

There was just the faintest flicker of surprise in the eyes of Nara Kijomi at being addressed in his own language. He moved slightly, felt a wave of nausea at the agonizing pain in his shattered arm; but he did his best to keep his face expressionless. "I do not answer to civilians."

"My friend here is a Navy officer."

"He has no uniform. I refuse to recognize him."

"You are being unnecessarily stubborn, General." Mullane bent over again, searched in the Japanese's pockets, straightened up with some papers in his hand. He glanced at them, then at Vokes. "Meet Lieutenant-General Nara. He won't talk to me because I'm a civilian and he refuses to talk to you until you get into uniform. You got your badges of rank?"

"They're back at the camp with my cap. I'll get all dolled up for him tomorrow. A bloody general! What the hell are we going to do with him?"

On the western slopes of the mountain they stood in the last silver-green light of day; the eastern sky above the mountain was already dark with cloud and night. Birds, frightened away by the crashing plane, had come back and were settling in the trees; mosquitoes came looking for blood, from the living or the dead. A drizzle of rain began to fall, promising a chill night.

"We'd never get him down the mountain in the dark. Get the boys to put up some sort of shelter. I'll try and get him out from under this mess."

General Nara watched the American take the gold watch

from his broken and bloody wrist. Mullane saw the look in the Japanese's eyes, smiled and slipped the watch into the latter's pocket.

"I'm not a looter, General."

Nara was not grateful for the care with which Mullane extricated him from the wreckage. He wished he were dead; he knew he was dead anyway in the eyes of those back in Tokyo. He would have blown his brains out an hour ago if he had been able to reach his pistol; it would not have had the traditional dignity of *hara-kiri*, but in his own mind it would have been an honourable exit. Now he saw nothing but ignominy ahead of him.

It was dark by the time they were all ready to settle down. Mullane and Vokes had brought no food with them other than some biscuits and chocolate from last night's drop; they shared these, with some water from their canteens, with the three carriers. Then Mullane sat down beside the injured Japanese. The natives had hacked away a section of the wing with their machetes and it had been set up as a lean-to shelter. It was only enough to keep the rain off Mullane and Nara; Vokes and the natives were in other improvised shelters. Mullane switched on his flashlight.

"You better eat some of this chocolate, General. We've found some rations packs in the plane, but I think we'll keep those. Chocolate is very sustaining and, whether you like it or not, we're going to keep you alive." He turned the beam of his torch on Nara's arm. "We have a doctor and a nurse back at our camp. They'll look after you."

"I would prefer that you killed me."

Mullane laughed softly. "General, you don't really expect me to do that. Do the pearl divers of Toba throw away a treasure when they find it?"

Despite his pain and his depression Nara smiled. "You have an imagination. One doesn't think of Americans as imaginative."

"You'll revise that opinion, General, before this war is over." But Mullane wondered. So far the war, or anyway the military machine, had not thrown up any imaginative geniuses.

After a while General Nara dropped off into a troubled sleep.

84

Mullane himself slept only fitfully. Mosquitoes, on their way to the corpses in the front of the plane, stopped off for an appetizer. The rain had stopped, but the damp night air had its own soaking effect. Leeches, round-the-clock workers, came up out of the mud and three times Mullane had to light matches and burn them off; once he turned the flashlight on Nara's arm and saw the small mist of mosquitoes hovering over it. There were bloodsuckers everywhere in a war.

He woke everyone at first light, gave them all a biscuit and a piece of chocolate each. "Get the boys to make up a stretcher, Frank. I'm going to have another look through the plane."

"What for?"

Mullane nodded at the now unconscious Nara. "With a general on board there's a chance he had some papers with him."

He searched for twenty minutes, going over every inch of the wreckage; he found nothing other than the air crew's flight papers. Finally, puzzled and frustrated, he climbed up to where Vokes and the carriers stood waiting with General Nara lying on a rough stretcher at their feet.

"Not a goddam thing. Maybe the Japs have given up fighting the war with paper."

"That'll upset our blokes if ever they find out. They might have to follow suit."

If Nara could have heard them he would have smiled at their frustration but been equally puzzled. Neither he nor Mullane was to know that his brief-case, flung out of the flying-boat with a host of other things when the crash had occurred, had landed in a small swamphole and sank from sight into the watery mud. So are battles lost and won because the terrain is always part of war.

Nara stirred once or twice during the rough passage down through the jungle but did not recover full consciousness. The descent was so steep that they had to bind him to the stretcher with vines. When they finally reached the camp the five stretcher-bearers, though they had shared the work amongst them, looked almost as exhausted as the man they carried.

"He's all yours." Mullane slumped down in the mud, put his back against a tree. "I want him kept alive. If he comes round, don't put anything near him, a knife or anything like that. He'll commit suicide at the first opportunity."

"What makes you think all Japanese want to commit *hara-kiri*?" said Sister Brigid.

Mullane gave her a weary look. "This one is a general, Sister. He belongs to a class that considers suicide a matter of honour. Don't start putting a Christian image on him. Just help the Bishop and Miss Riddle to fix him up. Buka?"

The big man loomed over him, stamped his feet hard, splashing the boss with mud. Mullane looked down resignedly at the fresh dark blobs merging into his sodden trousers.

"Buka, don't splash me with so much respect. Just get me, Boss Vokes and the boys some breakfast. An extra helping for the boys."

Buka raised a foot for another stamp of respect, suddenly grinned, spun round and went away, yelling for the cook-boy. Mullane remained sitting in the mud, oblivious of its cold wetness. No one from the old days would have recognized him as the elegant figure he had once been. He was taking on, day by day, a coating of jungle. He scratched his face through his beard and allowed himself to dream for a moment of a hot bath and a masseur, or preferably a masseuse, working on him afterwards.

While he was eating breakfast of rice and powdered milk, followed by toasted scones and honey, Ruth came up to him. She squatted down beside him, careful not to sit in the mud. He noticed that she squatted native-fashion and did it as easily as if she had been doing it all her life. "You'd better let me clean up those scratches of yours."

He hesitated, then peeled off his shirt. She examined him frankly. "Nice muscles. You're well preserved."

"For thirty-eight, you mean? Some of us older men do manage not to decay before our time."

She began to clean the scratches. He was aware of her closeness, of the smell of a woman, something he had almost forgotten and which she was bringing back with disturbing regularity. She, too, was very aware of him, but she had something more immediately important on her mind.

"That Jap's arm is in a bad way. The Bishop and I have been arguing about it."

"What's your opinion?"

"That it should come off."

Mullane all at once began to wonder when he and Vokes could start for Rabaul. Were all these obstacles omens to warn him that the expedition was impossible? "Is he likely to die if you don't do something about it?"

"He could. It could turn gangrenous."

"He could also die of shock, couldn't he?"

"You mean from the amputation? Yes."

"Do you have the equipment? Any sort of anaesthetic?"

"A small bottle of ether, that's all. It might not be enough if the operation proved a long one." She looked away from him, biting her lip. "I hate to admit this, but I don't think I'm competent to do an operation like this. I wouldn't have said it if the Bishop hadn't said he was once an army doctor – he probably did things like this in his war. It's not just a matter of sawing off the damaged part of the arm. There are blood vessels, a flap to be sewn back over the stump – I'm afraid I'd botch the job."

He stood up, pulled on his shirt. He felt stiff and weary, in spirit as much as body; he was like Scheer, though for the moment he was too concerned with himself for comparisons. "It's your decision, yours and the Bishop's. I just want the General kept alive, that's all. Until I can get a plane or sub in here to take him off my hands."

Ruth gazed at him, wondering what made him tick. It seemed to her that Frank Vokes' dedication to the war was simple and obvious: he just wanted to be on the winning side. But something else was firing this American, something that waxed and waned as if he were driven by an ebb and flow of memories. It seemed that he *wanted* to go into Rabaul, that he had to throw himself against as many Japanese as he could find. That he had to commit his own *hara-kiri* as some matter of honour.

"If you have to wait to have him taken off the island, what happens about you going into Rabaul?"

87

"It will have to be delayed, I guess."

"Good," she said and went off.

He was surprised at the emphasis in her voice, for the hint of concern for him. But he could not let himself think of *that*: he already had enough problems.

The morning was fine and he could now see the river running down to the coast from the still-hidden waterfall; down at the mouth of the river a plantation was clearly visible. He was within sight of Noku. But he knew they could not stay here. It was too close to the site of the crashed plane and within hours search patrols would be combing every square foot of this area. He gave the order for everything to be packed for immediate moving on. But first he had to report his and Vokes' catch.

While Vokes set up the radio he worked on coding the message. He used the *Champion* code, but he did not use Nara's name or rank.

"The Japs might have cracked the code, in which case they'd know he's still alive and we have him. What's an alternative to lieutenant-general that they'd understand down in Townsville?"

Vokes was fiddling with the radio. "The batteries are running low. Maybe I'd better re-charge them."

"There isn't time. Well? Have you any ideas for a code-name for the General?"

Vokes thought for a moment while he worriedly listened to the faint static on the radio. "How about Top Jockey? Peter Blomfield would understand that. He told me when he was up here that he's a dead keen punter, does all his money on the horses. Do they have horse racing in Japan?"

"Virtually none, as far as I can remember. They had one or two thoroughbred studs, someone once told me, but racing never caught on."

"Then they wouldn't know what Top Jockey meant."

So the message went out that they were entertaining a top jockey from another racecourse who might be able to give some hints on current track form. The reply came back and it seemed to Mullane that the Morse key at the other end was stuttering with disbelief: *Hope we understand you correctly. Visiting jockey most welcome. When pick him up?*

They had not been able to promise any evacuation means for Ruth and the others; but a Japanese general was another matter. It figured: Mullane was learning the flexibility of military priorities. However it did mean he could send the other three off with Nara. But he would have to keep the Japanese alive to guarantee that the Catalina or submarine would come in.

"Con," said Vokes, staring down towards the coast, "I think we're going to have visitors before we can get rid of him."

Mullane picked up his binoculars. A light destroyer had appeared round the eastern point of the shallow bay; two patrol boats and three landing barges followed it. While he was still looking at the small flotilla edging its way in towards the shore he heard the drone of aircraft. Automatically he yelled for everyone to take cover under the trees; then he looked up through the green overhang and saw the two slow-flying scout planes come over the top of the mountain. They were followed almost immediately by a Kawanisi flying-boat.

"Holy Jesus!" Vokes fumbled awkwardly as he hastily began to pack the radio. "It's busier than Pitt Street on Friday night!"

Mullane shouted again for everyone to remain still and under cover. He sat down on one of the battery boxes, kept his face down as one of the scout planes cruised by no more than five hundred feet above the top branches of the trees. Several birds took off in frightened flight, whirling away down the mountain-side like clumps of leaves blown away by the gusts from the plane's propeller. The plane climbed up the slope of the mountain; Mullane knew that in less than a minute it could cover the distance that had occupied him and Vokes and the carriers for an hour. It was only a matter of a short time before the crashed flying-boat must be discovered.

"That puts the kybosh on us moving on." Vokes was sitting crouched beside the radio. As always he was having difficulty in keeping still and he sat with his energetic hands clasped between the vice of his knees. "Those scout planes will have to go home to refuel, but the Kawanisi can hang around for hours."

"We sit and take our chances. Once we started moving we'd stand out like a Fourth of July parade. Hello – ?"

They heard the buzz of the scout plane as it came speeding

down the side of the mountain towards the coast. It went down the narrow valley of the river. Mullane, checking that the flying-boat and the other scout plane had remained up above the mountain, moved out to where he could pick up the coast through his glasses. He saw the scout plane fly out over the plantation towards the destroyer, circle the ship and waggle its wings, then it headed back up the river, climbing through the gorge and going straight up the mountain, where the flying-boat and the other plane were now circling above yesterday's wreck. He could imagine some officer on the destroyer taking a bearing on the line of flight of the returning scout plane.

Down at Noku the landing barges were already nosing into the beach; it was impossible to count the number of soldiers scrambling ashore but there must have been a hundred and fifty of them. Mullane began moving his binoculars back up the river, examining everything closely.

"There are two tracks that they'll probably follow. One comes up the river and disappears somewhere in that gorge, then comes out about half a mile along the slope here. It probably joins the track we've been following. The other way comes up right below us, but it looks pretty steep and they could decide not to try it."

"What do we do, then? Sit here and trust to luck?"

"That's about it. If we moved on along this track, if we went singly so that we shouldn't be too obvious, they'd still pick up our bootmarks. Unless you feel like walking two or three miles barefoot?"

"Nothing doing. With my luck I'd pick up every bloody thorn and jigger lying around loose. I vote we sit it out and trust to luck. Maybe Sister Brigid can get to work on her rosary beads."

Mullane got up and moved cautiously back to where the rest of the party sat silent and worried. Even the carriers looked worried, he noted with some satisfaction. That meant they still had some doubts about which side they preferred to be on.

"You're going to have to be very patient. We're going to sit tight and hope the Japs don't come near us. It means no moving around, maybe for four or five hours. I hope patience is one of your virtues."

He waited for something aggressively honest from Sister Brigid, but she said nothing. She had gone back into her shell again, looked sick and sullen.

"We can but try." The Bishop's cassock was now a muddy grey, the umbrella a limp tattered crook; if he had ever taken vows of poverty he had at last now achieved the reality, or anyway the look of it. "But don't expect too much, Mr Mullane."

"Imagine you're in retreat, try some meditation," said Mullane. "How's your patience, Miss Riddle?"

"Shall I come and sit with you and we can test each other's?" She did not want to spend the next few hours sitting with the Bishop and Sister Brigid. She was as muddied and bedraggled as the priest and the nun; but she was young and hadn't lost hope and that made all the difference. That, thought Mullane, and the fact that her shirt was tighter than the Bishop's cassock and better filled. "What are you smiling at?"

"I was thinking of a young lady named Apricot Bloom. She wasn't unlike you." He couldn't remember a single facet of Apricot's nature, but he did remember her bosom, which had bounced delightfully through *Anything Goes* and half a dozen other musical comedies.

"Apricot Bloom? You're pulling my leg."

Sister Brigid watched the exchange between them with a suspicious, disapproving eye, but Scheer smiled the smile of a priest who hadn't forgotten he was a man. Mullane winked at him and passed on to tell the natives to stay out of sight.

"Boss?" Mariba didn't stand up, but he did pause from splitting the piece of sugarcane he held in his big hands. "When we going to be paid? It's tomorrow now. You promised."

Jesus, this son-of-a-bitch is going to test my patience more than sitting out the Japs. "I have to go and get the money, Mariba. I can't do that till the Japanese have gone. But if you want you can go down there and ask the Japs for it. I'll tell you where to find it."

It was a calculated risk, a bluff. Mariba looked up at him, then bit into the stick of sugarcane and chewed on it. He turned his head and looked away at his fellow carriers; his

91

attitude was as insolent as it could be. Mullane heard a growl behind him and he looked round. Buka, eyes wild with anger, was ready to jump on the rebel.

"We wait," Mariba said at last.

You bet your sweet ass you will. He knew now that Mariba and those siding with him were not yet ready to go down and join the Japanese.

Mullane motioned for Buka to follow him along the track. When they were out of earshot of Mariba he said, "Buka, belting him isn't going to do any good."

Buka's hand itched at the buckle of the old police belt he wore round the top of his *lap-lap*. "Let me try, boss. I give that young bugger some hurry-up."

"He'd be gone before you got half a dozen licks in at him, and he'd take Yali and some of the other boys with him." Mariba might not go down to join the Japs but he could go bush.

Buka said no more, but his expression said enough. Mullane doubted that he himself would live long enough ever to see these natives gain their independence, but if ever they did he wondered who would rule them, the autocrat like Buka or the radical like Mariba. Both were simple men, but they would breed heirs who would not be so unsophisticated. But that was all in the future and in the meantime they had the choice of two masters, himself and Vokes or the Japanese.

He moved past Buka and looked down at the man who could be the top Japanese on the island, albeit with no power right now. "How are you feeling, General?"

Nara, exhausted by pain and loss of blood, made no reply. The physical side of him was grateful to the priest and the two women who had attended to his arm; he saw no merit in the unnecessary bearing of pain. But the mental and emotional side longed for death and wished that they would leave him alone here in the jungle to die. He thought of his father, who had also been a general and was retired now; the old man who sat in his austere house on the *tatami* floor, disdaining even a pillow, his whole being dedicated to the bushido code as outlined in the *Hagakure*, the code that exalted a meaningful death above a meaningless life. Nara Iwani, his son was certain, would have found a way to die honourably long before this.

"You know what's happening." Mullane jerked his head; from high above the mountain there came the faint drone of the circling aircraft. "They've found your flying-boat. But they're not going to find you, General. I promise you that."

"What will you do?" Nara's voice was weak. "Kill me and bury me?"

"I detect a note of hope in your voice." They were speaking in Japanese; the language had a bitter taste on Mullane's tongue. "Men like you are the only ones I know who talk optimistically of death."

"What about your priest?"

But Nara was too weak to continue the argument and he turned his head away, not waiting for Mullane's answer, and listened to the distant invisible planes. He had been on his way to Rabaul to take command of the force that was to land in the Solomons within the week. The previous commander had been repatriated ill and he had been a hasty substitution. Even if he were rescued today he would be in no fit state to take command. The war, it seemed, was over for him and life itself might as well finish.

Mullane went back to join Vokes, who was watching the river mouth. "They're coming up on the other side of the river, Con. What happens when they find His Nibs isn't up there in the wreck? They're going to spread out all over this mountain like a bloody rash."

Mullane had no immediate answer. He was finding that the art of war was not learned in one or two easy lessons; military history had been his hobby for several years now, but all his reading seemed to have taught him nothing about tactics on the small, day-to-day scale. The art of survival was a different matter; that was a question of instinct. But the present situation was more than just a matter of survival. The presence of General Nara had raised it to another level.

Then the two scout planes came buzzing down the mountain, flew out over the destroyer, waggled their wings and turned east, soon disappearing round the shallow point. "They've gone back to refuel," said Vokes.

Mullane was still scanning the river. "There's a track goes

up from the river on the other side. It's under cover most of the way – you've got to look hard to pick it out. Those scout planes could pick it up if they were down low, but I think the Kawanisi could miss it. Get everybody ready to move. We'll go down in small groups, no more than four at a time. I'll go first and take the General with me – I'll need two of the strongest boys to carry his stretcher."

"Where are we heading for?"

"I don't know – exactly. I'll find us a place to ford the river. When we cross the Japs' tracks on the other side everyone has to take his boots off, the women included. Then get Buka and the boys to cover our tracks. They'll know what to do."

Vokes got everyone prepared to move while Mullane continued to watch the Japanese moving steadily up the path on the far side of the river. They came and went under the cover of trees, moving in the one long, tightly-bunched line; they obviously felt safe from any attack. Mullane was glad for who he was and what he was. A professional soldier might not have been able to resist the opportunity to try to ambush the enemy.

The last of the Japanese passed a point Mullane had mentally marked on the river. Beyond that they would be out of sight below the gorge cliff; the path down through the jungle on this side would equally be out of sight of the Japanese. The only danger lay in the risk of being seen from the cruising flying-boat.

"Okay, start moving at hundred-yard intervals. Keep as much under the trees as you can. And Bishop – could you do without the shelter of your umbrella?"

"Of course." Scheer folded the target disc of his umbrella, which he had put up without thinking. But he was wondering if this was not the moment to make his decision, to attract the attention of the Japanese and hand himself over to them. But he also wondered if the American would shoot him before that could happen. He had detected a certain determination, perhaps even a ruthlessness growing in Mullane even in the past twenty-four hours.

Mullane signalled to the two natives who were to carry General Nara on his stretcher. One of them was Mariba, chosen not only for his strength but because Mullane wanted to keep a close eye on him. The two carriers picked up the lightweight Nara.

"This is going to be uncomfortable and painful, General," said Mullane. "Try for a little *Satori*. It may help you overcome it."

"Soldiers do not need Zen." He had always been too practical to concern himself with religion and philosophies. He had always been successful up till now and, unlike most of the military class, had had little time for Zen; religion was for failures who needed any comfort they could get. "The sound of one hand clapping is like the sound of the bullet that kills you. You never believe either of them."

"I do believe, General, that you want to stay alive."

And Mullane saw that he had offended Nara: the truth of what he had said was there in the Japanese's eyes, like a cast of which he was ashamed.

The first part of the descent was not easy. The path below the flat site of the camp was no more than a mud slide. Mullane went down first, on his backside, heels dug in. Nara, strapped by vines to his stretcher, was then lowered by a long vine rope. It took only five minutes to negotiate that section, but to Mullane, standing out in the open, alert to the flying-boat up above the mountain, it seemed much longer. Then the two carriers were down at the bottom of the slope beside him, had taken up the stretcher and they moved on down under the cover of the trees.

It took half an hour of slipping, sliding, cat-footed descent before Mullane was down to the level of the river. He left the two carriers with Nara while he searched for a place to cross the river. It was much swifter-flowing than he had expected; but it meant there was little chance of any crocodiles being this far upstream. The roar of the waterfall came at him out of the mouth of the gorge, obliterating all other sound; there was no way of knowing now where any of the Japanese might be. At any moment he might look up and see a group of them standing on the other side of the river, rifles aimed and the silent fusillade already on its way. He thought of Nara and the sound of the bullet that you never hear and never believe.

Then he saw the rocks and the rough vine bridge slung above them, each end tied to a large tree. The waterfall, a tumbling white column that never left the perpendicular, falling straight down a cliff-face, was only a few yards up from the bridge. The rope span trembled in a shimmering mist of spray, looking as insubstantial as the strands of a spider's web. There was no other way across the river and it had to be risked.

It was another twenty minutes before the rest of the party had arrived. The roar of the waterfall ruled out any conversation; he could only tell them what he had in mind by gestures. The bridge was no more than a thick vine-rope slung between the two trees, with two thinner ropes stretched across as hand-grips and connected to the foot-rope at intervals by some vines. One would have to walk splay-footed across it and it was going to be as difficult, even allowing for the hand-ropes, as attempting to walk the slack-wire in a circus act. For the waterfall seemed to create its own wind in the deep bowl of the gorge and the bridge swayed back and forth through the spray.

The mist whirled all round the bottom of the gorge, a perpetual rain that had turned the rocks at the edge of the river to black glass. Mullane, wet through, feeling the chill of the gloom down here at the bottom of the gorge, handed his Thompson gun to Ruth, gesturing that he would come back for it. Then he took the end of the stretcher, put the poles on his shoulders, nodded for Mariba to do the same.

He put a tentative foot on the main rope, grasped the hand-ropes and eased his way out from the rocks. Now he was on the bridge he could not see the other side; he was walking through a grey cloud of water. Then suddenly the sun came over the rim of the gorge; the grey turned to white and then colours sparkled like floating gems. He was walking through rainbows and he felt light-headed; the rope swayed beneath his probing feet, adding to the feeling. The waterfall thundered beside and above him; the roar of it was like a physical battering. Almost inch by inch he worked his way forward, walking downhill on a slippery path of rope only as thick as his wrist, till he was at the middle of the bridge. Here he was only a foot or so above the white boil of water; he caught an occasional glimpse of jagged rocks seeming to rise up like attacking sharks. Then he felt the stretcher begin to rock on his shoulders.

Nara, still tied to the stretcher, was trying to hurl himself into the river. Mullane let go of the hand-rope, clutched one of the poles. He could not look back to see what Mariba was doing; he was too busy trying to stay on the swaying bridge. He could feel his forearm beginning to ache with the strain of holding the stretcher-pole; he looked with streaming, despairing eyes through the spray at the thin swaying rope stretching uphill ahead of him. He began to climb, feeling cramp take hold in his feet as he tried to curl his toes, to turn them into prehensile claws inside his boots. The fierceness of his grip on the pole was causing cramp in his hand; but he couldn't let go. He wanted to scream with the pain; silent obscenities bubbled into the water running down into his open mouth. The rocking suddenly stopped, as if Nara had abruptly become exhausted (or had decided he did not want to die); Mullane let go of the stretcher-pole, eased the cramp out of his hand and took hold of the hand-rope again. But there was still the cramp in his feet. Slowly, agonizingly, like some ancient monster learning to walk, he crawled up out of the thick mist and on to the rocks at the far side of the river. He sat down at once, slipped the stretcher from his shoulders without any care as to whether Nara might be hurt, aware only of his own pain. He grabbed his toes and bent his feet; slowly the cramp eased. He felt no better when he saw Mariba sitting on a rock and smiling contemptuously at him.

He stood up, moving his feet inside his boots, looked down at Nara. The Japanese's eyes were closed; but that could have been because of the spray falling on his face. Mullane gestured for Mariba to stay with Nara, then he took a grip on the hand-rope and started back down the sloping track of the bridge.

Another twenty minutes was lost in getting everyone across the bridge. Mullane, now back on the east side of the river with Nara and Mariba, watched anxiously as the carriers, burdened with the radio and the supplies, appeared out of the mist. He counted them all, checked on what each of them had carried across and wondered what Vokes, the last to cross, had chosen to do with the charging engine.

Then he saw the Australian and Silas, the last of the carriers,

97

the engine slung on poles between them, coming up out of the mist. Vokes was bent over like an arthritic old man; he had taken on too much. Silas was in front, moving steadily up the rope; behind him Vokes struggled to keep up. Then, when they were no more than fifteen feet from where Mullane stood, Vokes missed his footing. He slipped off the foot-rope, hung suspended from the hand-ropes.

The poles supporting the engine slipped down till the engine rested against his face and chest, threatening to take him with it into the cauldron of water below. Silas was clinging desperately to the hand-ropes, screaming silently for help. He had a hand on one of the poles, but his arm was being pulled back over his shoulder. Mullane plunged towards him, almost running down the slope of the foot-rope; how he managed to keep his own footing he would never know. He grabbed hold of the pole that had slipped off Silas's other shoulder, but even as he did so, felt the weight of the engine, he knew the situation was hopeless. On the sloping, swaying bridge they could get no purchase to strain against the heavy weight; they were going to lose the engine and maybe Vokes too. Mullane could see the agony on Vokes' streaming face as the engine pushed down on him; the Australian could hold on only a few moments more. Mullane let go of the pole, swung past Silas, making the bridge sway even more, and somehow clambered over Vokes.

He turned round, facing up the slope of the rope again. He took hold of one of the poles cutting its way into Vokes' shoulder, held desperately with the other hand to a hand-rope. He automatically shouted, forgetting that Vokes could not hear him in the thunder of the waterfall. Then he kicked the Australian in the back. Vokes looked up and at once got the message. As Mullane took the strain of the pole, Vokes dropped his shoulder and swung out on the hand-rope. The bridge swayed alarmingly; Mullane felt himself swing through an arc as if on a child's swing. Silas spun round, no longer able to keep his hold on the other end of the pole. For just an instant Mullane was supporting the whole weight of the engine; then he let go. It dropped into the white boil of water and was gone from sight in the blink of an eye. Even in that moment Mullane felt a sickening loss, knew their position had become even more desperate. Without the engine to recharge the batteries they would soon be totally out of communication with Moresby and Townsville.

Vokes groped his way back on to the foot-rope, stood bent over as he gasped for breath. The three men stood suspended in the mist in attitudes of exhaustion and utter dejection; then slowly they climbed up the rope and on to the solidity of the glistening black rocks. The party stood there in a tight drenched group waiting for Mullane to lead them on.

The weight of responsibility was suddenly more than that of the engine that had almost dragged him into the river.

II

The path away from the waterfall led back along the gorge, then swung up steeply to join the path that went up the mountain. The mud of the main track was a blurred pattern of bootprints where the large enemy party had trekked through. Mullane, who had come ahead on his own, stood on a hummock of flattened grass and looked at the bootprints. There was no sign of any Japanese either up or down the main track; they evidently felt there was no need to post sentries along the way. But Mullane did not feel safe. The roar of the waterfall still came out of the gorge behind him. The Japanese could come at him and his party from either direction, up or down the track, and there would be no warning of their approach.

On the opposite side of the main track a narrow path, obviously little used, ran through ferns and bushes into the jungle. Mullane waved to Buka to join him, then sent the big native up the main track to the first bend. He called up Silas, now recovered from his ordeal on the bridge, and sent him down to stand scout at the first bend in the opposite direction. Then it was time to bring the others on.

They crossed the main track as carefully as possible, stepping across sideways so that their feet fell into the Japanese bootprints; the Europeans were made to take their shoes off. Then Mullane told Ruth to put her shoes back on and step back into the mud of the track. She understood at once what was wanted; her flat-heeled shoes were no larger than the average Japanese boot. She stepped into the prints of the native feet, turned them into a passable imitation of the line of bootprints that ran up the main track. Then Mullane, still barefooted, lifted her out of the mud and set her on the grass beside the side track up which the rest of the party had already disappeared. For just a moment he was aware of the softness of her; he had forgotten how slim and fragile a woman could seem in one's arms. Then he let her go, not looking at her, though she looked up amused at him. He gave a short low whistle and Buka and Silas came running back to him, keeping to the grass on the side of the main track.

"Cover it, Buka."

He pulled on his boots, went on along the side path, knowing that the two natives would know how to cover the new tracks that led off here into the jungle. The one advantage he and Vokes had over the Japanese was that they had had a longer education in what little the jungle had to offer. One benefit was that the jungle could swallow up a man or men as swiftly and cleanly as a deep green swamp.

The party, despite the urgency of their position, could only move slowly along the narrow winding track under the thick overhang of trees. The track began to drop and down here at this lower level the humidity almost choked one; it seemed to Mullane that even his lungs were sweating. To Bishop Scheer, imagination turning to fantasy as exhaustion made him light-headed, it was like walking through a great green cathedral whose walls had contracted to frame just a narrow aisle; he dreamed, almost but not quite wide awake, of the churches of his youth, at Naumburg and Magdeburg. Sister Brigid saw only the mud beneath her feet as she trudged on, muttering to herself in prayer. Ruth, more exhausted than she would admit to Mullane or anyone else, saw only a blur of greenness, felt only the chafing of her soaked shoes on her aching feet. General Nara, succumbing to the pain of his arm, had lapsed into a semi-coma and saw and felt nothing.

They were coming out on to a stretch where the trees thinned out above the track when they heard the flying-boat. It came in a swoop down the side of the mountain and went on to Noku, taking its sound with it. On a signal from Mullane, young Luke clambered up a tall tree, looked out towards the sea and the destroyer still standing offshore. He came down to report that the big bird had flown out over the big canoe, turned that way (gesturing to his left) and flown away.

"He's gone back to Kavieng or Rabaul, wherever he came from," said Vokes. "That means we're safe from the air anyway."

"For a while," said Mullane, pessimism itching him as much as his sweat. "They're not going to give up looking for the General. Generals are expendable, like all other soldiers, but they like to see the bones."

It was after midday before Mullane called a halt. He had found no track leading up to the ridges and now they were getting into swamp country. The narrow track was soggy and the trees on either side had begun to alter their character. The air, thick and stifling, smelled of brackish sea-water swamp. Everyone's legs were covered in leeches; the only one who had escaped was General Nara, high and safe on his stretcher. Mullane, passing around two boxes of his precious matches, gave the order that everyone was to cleanse himself of the leeches first.

"Then we'll see about food. No fires, so it'll have to be something cold. You dole it out, Miss Riddle. Where are you going, Sister Brigid?"

The nun, face strained and shining with sweat, gave him a look full of resentment. She was on the verge of hating this man; she had to hate someone. Her whole life was being taken away from her; she could not be angry at God and so far she had not been close enough to a Japanese to hate him; all she felt for the wounded general was pity for the agony he was undergoing. Oh Lord, she prayed, forgive me my sins! For she knew now that the only fire that could keep her going was anger. And Mullane was the only convenient target: it was his own fault, she told herself, for continually offering himself.

"I am going into the bushes, Mr Mullane. My legs are covered in leeches. I will not expose them to anyone's gaze."

Mullane, weary and ready for anger himself, was about to make a sarcastic remark. Then he recognized the despair in the whimpering voice; with a sense of shock he realized the nun was on the verge of tears. Controlling himself, he nodded and did his best to sound kindly.

"Do that, Sister. Take your time."

She looked at him in surprise, the Irish ran out of her and she had nothing to say. She turned away and crept into the bushes, blinded by tears, unaware of the thorns that caught at her habit and tried to hold her back. Mullane looked after, found himself admiring her, an attitude that would have left the nun helpless if she had known.

He sat down beside Vokes, rolled up his trousers and began to burn off the leeches. "We're in a mess."

"I know." Vokes had not mentioned the loss of the engine since they had left the gorge. There was a cut and a bruise on his face where the engine had hit him, and a large black bruise on his chest. He could still feel the engine pressing against him, like the pain of guilt. "I'm sorry about what happened, Con. I told you I was accident-prone, bloody bumble-footed. I ought to've let one of the boys carry it across with Silas. But I didn't trust Rama, I thought I could do better myself – "

"Forget it." He bent carefully to burn off the last blood-glutted leech. "Frank, in future don't try to do too much. You don't have to prove anything to me."

"Who the bloody hell was trying to prove anything? You just said it wasn't my fault. Christ, you give me the shits, Mullane! You're so bloody superior – "

"Do you realize what you've done? We're supposed to be Coastwatchers – spies, information gatherers, call us what you like. But we might just as well be blind and dumb for all the use we're going to be if we can't get our messages out! They won't even know what's happened to us – "

"If you'd let me re-charge the batteries this morning, at least they'd work till we got *that* message through!"

"I'd have let you re-charge them if I'd known you were going to lose the goddam engine – "

Then Mullane became aware of Nara, lying on his stretcher nearby, watching them carefully. A stranger to the Japanese might have thought the thin bony face was impassive; but Mullane had learned to read expressions in the almond-shaped eyes. Nara's eyes showed his satisfaction at what he was witnessing, blazing dissension in the enemy camp.

Vokes, too, had remarked the Japanese's interest in their argument. "What the bloody hell are you staring at, you Nip bastard?"

"Not a bastard, Mr Vokes," said Nara in slightly lisping English. "I think my ancestry might prove much more honourable and legitimate than yours. I saw you Australians in Singapore – you all seem to regard each other as bastards."

"How would son-of-a-bitch suit you, General?" But Mullane was grateful for the Japanese's intrusion, unwilling though it had been. He forced a smile, trying, as much as anything else, to push away with it Vokes' unexpected antagonism. But maybe he had asked for it: maybe he *was* bloody superior.

Nara smiled, showing slightly prominent teeth that were remarkably white. They were his one vanity, his one attractive physical feature; at the military academy he had been known as The Smiling One, but he had never resented his fellow cadets' jokes. His smile had always won him attention from the geishas. And, his wife had told him, it had been the feature that had won her heart when, strangers to each other, they had first met as betrothed partners.

"I don't think you would have called my mother a bitch if you had met her, Mr Mullane."

Mullane accepted the rebuke: he had learned to respect one's parents in the Japanese way. "I apologize, General. Where did you learn to speak English so well?"

"At Sandhurst and West Point. I did courses there when I was a young man."

"Stone the bloody crows!" Vokes spat in disgust. "You Yanks and the bloody Poms taught these bastards how to fight this war!"

"I don't think so." Mullane hadn't taken his eyes off Nara. He remembered this man now, he had actually put his name into a report he had sent to Washington. "You learned all about fighting wars in China, didn't you?"

It was Nara's turn to look carefully at the man opposite him. "You know I was in Manchukuo? You are well informed for someone so far from the scene."

Vokes watched the two men. His argument with Mullane was already forgotten; it had been like a boil bursting, frus-

103

tration and anger at himself as well as at Mullane erupting out of him. But he was not one to harbour resentment and, in his wary interest in the Japanese lying on the stretcher, he had quickly forgotten how close he had been to throwing a punch at Mullane. He would have done so in another minute or so, even though he guessed the Yank would have flattened him at once.

"Where's Manchukuo?" he asked.

"It was the name Japan gave to Manchuria after they'd invaded it in 1932 and set it up as a puppet state. Right, General?"

Nara made no reply. He had never been proud of what had happened in China and Manchuria and he dreaded the American's next question. It came, as he expected it would.

"You were also at the rape of Nanking, weren't you?"

"Just what did you do when you lived in Japan, Mr Mullane? Did you work for the American government?"

Mullane shrugged; what did it matter now? "In a way. I can't remember your division at Nanking – "

"I was on the staff of General Matsui. I was not involved in the rape, as you call it." But that was what it had been and semantics would never alter the fact.

"Rape?" said Vokes. "Nan King? Who was she?"

War, for Vokes, had started only two years ago when Australia had lined up with Britain against Germany. He had thought it a stupid gesture, typical of the Pom-loving Prime Minister Menzies and the death-or-glory veterans like his old man, most of whom were too old to enlist anyway. Like the great majority of his generation in Australia he had had no interest in any war before September 1939. They were just something you read about in school: Caesar's conquest of Gaul and Britain, the Hundred Years War, the Great War. He and his contemporaries had been taught virtually nothing about any American war, either that of Independence or that between the States; as for South America, as far as he knew that continent had lived in peace since the times of the Conquistadores. He had been ignorant, beyond a glance at the headlines, of the wars in Ethiopia, Spain and China in the 1930s. He had been an Isolationist without knowing it.

Mullane and Nara exchanged smiles, made conspirators for the moment by Vokes' ignorance. "Nanking was a city, Frank, where General Nara's countrymen put a big black blot on their country's honour. They murdered over two hundred thousand men and raped twenty thousand women, all in the name of war."

"Jesus!" Vokes was unable to comprehend such figures of disaster.

"You are very pat with your figures, Mr Mullane."

"I was a baseball player once. It's a game that's built on figures. Aggregates, averages, percentages – figures are a national obsession with us, General. Twenty per cent of the population of Nanking was killed, or rather murdered, by General Matsui's divisions. If you were on his staff, as far as I'm concerned you were involved in the rape and murdering. You can see the effect on Mr Vokes of what I've just told him. I think if he had the choice he'd murder you."

"He is welcome," said Nara and looked at Vokes. "A bullet would satisfy my honour and your revenge, Mr Vokes."

The Australian waved an angry, helpless hand. "Revenge? I wasn't there at Nanking. Maybe we should take you down to Noku and hand you over to the Chinaman there."

"Whatever you say, Mr Vokes. I am not particular about my executioner."

Vokes looked helplessly at Mullane. "What the hell do you do with a bugger like that?"

"I think we'll keep him alive," said Mullane and smiled at Nara. He reminded him of some of the older men he had known in Tokyo and he began to wonder if he could kill Nara if he had to. "I think you are a man of honour, General. You may even have some guilt about what happened at Nanking."

"Only guilt for others, Mr Mullane." Nara was surprised at his own confession; at the military academy he had been taught that no man betrayed his colleagues. Even when the soldiers in the ranks had gone back to Japan and started to talk about Nanking, about the virtual orders to rape and kill given by their officers, about the examples set by the junior officers, he had kept silent, loyal to his own class. "I feel no guilt for myself."

Then Ruth suddenly appeared. "Where's Sister Brigid?"

On that instant they heard the half-scream, half-shout for help. Despite their weariness Mullane and Vokes were on their feet and running at once. They ran back along the narrow path, plunged off into the scrub and almost immediately found themselves stumbling through water. Mangrove trees stretched away ahead of them, a grotesque *corps de ballet* with arms raised in attitudes that were both mocking and threatening. Hummocks rose out of the water topped by clumps of wild sugarcane, but the mangroves dominated the view ahead. A pale yellow light was reflected from the muddy waters as the sun struggled to filter down through the trees. Mullane and Vokes pulled up, searching frantically for a sign of Sister Brigid.

Mullane shouted, "Sister Brigid!"

Then they heard the cry again and, swinging round, saw the nun off to their left. She was backed up into a clump of sugarcane, pushing hard against it but held by the tight, thick wall of stalks. Moving steadily towards her, its grey-green scaly back just showing above the surface, gliding gently through the lilypads that lay on the water like pale green plates, was one of the largest crocodiles Mullane had ever seen. It looked almost graceful as it floated towards the nun, unhurried, weightless in the water, a grey-green log that was harmless. Then the upper snout came up out of the water.

Mullane had forgotten his gun, but Vokes had the Lee-Enfield. It went off right behind Mullane's ear, deafening him; but if the bullet hit the crocodile there was no sign that the huge saurian had felt it. Sister Brigid let out another scream, louder this time; she waved a frantic hand at the beast and Mullane saw that she was holding her rosary beads, like some charm trying to ward off evil. She turned and tried to claw her way into the sugarcane, but it continued to push her back. Mullane snatched up a dead branch and, without any clear thought of what he was going to do, stumbled through the water. But he was thinking clearly enough not to come in at the crocodile from the rear. He had seen how that huge tail could smash a canoe or a man to pulp.

Tripping over mangrove roots, dragging his feet through the mud beneath the water, he stumbled along like a drunken rioter, the thick branch held as a club above his head. The crocodile sensed him coming at it; the tail slashed in his direction and he fell rather than jumped to the side. He could see now how huge the crocodile was; it must have been close to twenty feet. But for all its size he knew that it could move faster than a man. Vokes' rifle went off again and this time the crocodile seemed to shudder; Mullane almost fell on it, hitting it across the snout with the heavy branch. But he was too late.

He would hear forever, a dreadful echo, the scream of Sister Brigid as the crocodile's jaws closed on her leg. She turned her head towards Mullane and under the black coif he saw the animal pain and terror in the contorted white face. She died with a pure primeval scream rather than a prayer, sliding away from Mullane as the crocodile pulled her out of the sugarcane and down into the brown waters already brightened by her blood.

Mullane beat frenziedly on the hard-scaled head but he might just as well have beaten at a rock. The giant tail slashed in a wide arc, sending up sprays of blood-flecked water; but the jaws did not let go of the dead nun. Vokes had come up and stood, legs wide apart, pumping bullet after bullet into the huge monster; but all his and Mullane's efforts were too late and the shooting and the bashing were futile expressions of anger and despair. The tail gave one last thrash at the water, then shivered and was still. The crocodile sank beneath the water, taking Sister Brigid with it.

The nun's black-clad arm stuck up out of the water, her hand still clutched in agony amidst her own blood that floated on the surface like a giant red flower. In the hand, like a last offering, were the rosary beads.

Mullane reached down, took the beads and, without thinking, put them in his pocket.

III

They did not bury Sister Brigid but left her there among the mangroves with the dead crocodile. Both Bishop Scheer and Ruth protested, but Mullane was adamant.

"Frank let off a whole magazine – the Japs could have heard those shots. I've got no idea how close they are and I'm not going to stay around to find out. I'm sorry, Bishop, but you'll have to say your prayers for Sister Brigid on the run. Please include my prayers with yours. I mean that."

Scheer was suffering from shock. The two small boys, Luke and Mark, were weeping and he held them against his bony hips, trying to comfort them: trying to be a father to them, a talent he had never really developed. Ruth stood off on her own, not weeping but with her face strained from the effort of keeping back her tears for the sad, unfortunate nun.

Mullane took the rosary beads from his pocket. "You better take these."

Scheer shook his head. "I have my own. Keep them, Mr Mullane."

"I gave up this sort of praying years ago."

"Then keep them as a good-luck charm."

"They didn't help Sister Brigid. I'm surprised at you, Bishop – I thought you'd be too sophisticated to believe in charms."

"I believe in omens. Perhaps I have been too long with these people – " He gestured at the natives standing along the track.

Mullane looked at the rosary beads, then shoved them into his pocket. They were unimportant; he would throw them away later. He still felt sick and weak at the manner of Sister Brigid's death. He had little idea what had made her go into the mangrove swamp; perhaps she had been looking for no more than privacy and had stumbled into the swamp. The crocodile could have stolen up on her and, panicking, she had stumbled deeper into the swamp instead of out of it. All at once he felt a deep guilt for what he had said to and thought of the poor, unhappy woman. Her life had been much more useful than his own and if she had finished up sour and dried-out, he guessed it had been because her usefulness had come to an end.

Vokes, even more shaken than Mullane, was marshalling the carriers into line again, doing everything he could to keep busy and stop thinking about what he had seen a few minutes ago. He had yet to take for granted that death, anyone's, including his own, was constantly on the cards in their present situation.

"Where are we heading, Con?"

"Back up into the hills. I'll feel safer there, and not just from the Japs."

It was ironic that Sister Brigid should have died as she had. New Britain, though it had some of the wildest mountain country in the world, did not present much danger in its tangled jungles. The forests harboured no big cats; the most dangerous animal would be the wild pig. It had very few venomous snakes, many less than New Guinea, the larger island to the west where the world's deadliest snake, the taipan, was always a threat. But New Britain did have crocodiles and Mullane cursed himself for his carelessness in having allowed the nun to go off alone in this swampy coastal tract. He was beginning to blame himself for her death, the sort of guilt brought on without any sense of logic.

Buka had been sent off at once to look for a path leading up into the hills and he came back saying there was a rough track some distance along the way they were following. Within five minutes the party was climbing it, moving up through a stand of tall *erimas*, then on through thick pandanus palms where they sometimes had to cut their way through creepers that had grown across the track. An hour's climbing brought them to a narrow ridge that jutted out like a broken shoulder from the mountain behind it.

Mullane's first task was to check on where the Japanese search parties now were. The track up had brought them back closer to the source of the Noku River. Through his binoculars he caught sight of movement through the trees; the Japanese were going back down to the beach at Noku. He felt a sense of relief that, for the time being, he and the party were safe.

Ruth organized a meal: bully beef, dry army biscuits and a small piece of chocolate washed down with water. Mullane did not talk to anyone during the meal; he had a lot on his mind and the others tacitly recognized it. Vokes felt he should be sharing some of the worry, but until Mullane asked him to do so he was prepared to let the American shoulder the lot. He was still distressed at the loss of the engine; he was not going to make a fool of himself again. Though he did not remark it himself, he was more silent than he had ever been in company before.

When Mullane stood up and walked out to the main vantage point on the ridge, Vokes hesitated, then went across to join him. His ankle had swollen slightly and he favoured it.

"You all right?" Mullane looked at him as he limped up.

"Yes. What's going on?" He hadn't meant to sound belligerent, but even in his own ears that was how it sounded.

Mullane was in no mood to continue any argument. He did his best to sound conciliatory: "Frank, what do you say we make this our permanent camp? If we can get Mariba and the boys back on our side, maybe we can send them back to the two supply dumps and bring it all up here."

"*If* you get them on our side – " Vokes, despite himself, still sounded contrary; but all his life his tongue had run loose. "We still have to pay them."

"If the Japs move out, I'll go down to Noku tonight."

"And if they don't?" He wanted to bite his snapping tongue.

Mullane's sigh of patience was a little exaggerated. "Frank, let's have a little optimism. Our whole survival on this island is based on *if*. If this, if that . . ."

Vokes had never been taught gracious manners; but he knew when he was being ungracious. "Okay, Con. You're the boss."

"I don't want to be the boss." That was untrue. He did want to be boss, because he knew he was the only one capable of taking charge. That, he supposed, was his damned sense of superiority coming out again.

"Con, for Christ's sake – " Vokes waved a hand, as if fighting his way out of a web. "Don't let's argue. You tell us what's got to be done. Buka and I will see that it's done."

Mullane all at once felt sorry for the boy. He recognized what Vokes wanted to say but couldn't: *Don't you see I was never meant to be a boss?* "Okay, this is what I have in mind . . ."

He and Vokes spent the rest of the afternoon taking turns watching the plantation down at Noku. Buka set the natives to work erecting huts beneath the shelter of trees well back on the ridge. Mullane set up the radio and tried to transmit, but the batteries were absolutely flat. At four o'clock Vokes called to him from the observation point out on the ridge.

"Con, they're pulling out!"

Through his binoculars Mullane saw the barges moving out

from the beach below the plantation. Offshore the destroyer was getting up steam; as the barges approached it, it began to move slowly ahead of them. In twenty minutes the small convoy had disappeared round the eastern headland.

"What do you reckon, Con? They all gone?"

"I won't know till I go down there. I may as well start now. I'll wait in the bush till it's dark, then go in and see what Lee Chin has to offer. I won't come back in the dark – I'll stay down there till first light."

"I go with you, boss." Buka had followed Mullane out to the end of the ridge.

"No, there's no point in risking two of us – "

"I think he should go with you," Vokes said quietly. "That gives us a fifty-fifty chance of one of you getting back to tell us what's happened if something goes wrong."

"There you go, being pessimistic again." But Mullane grinned and acknowledged the wisdom of Vokes' advice. Any message, even of disaster, was always better than to have the rest of them left worrying about what had happened to him. No news was not good news, not in a war. He wondered what Moresby and Townsville would be thinking when he and Vokes did not come on the air this evening.

He went back along the ridge to Ruth, asking for rations for himself and Buka. "I think you could have the cook-boy start a fire in that hollow back there, give everyone a hot meal. The fire probably won't be seen from down there at the plantation."

Ruth sent Luke and Mark off to get rations for the boss. She had taken on the responsibility of the two small boys, had kept them busy so that they would not have too much time to pine for Sister Brigid. "If you wait a while we can give you some hot rice and tinned milk."

"I don't want to waste any of this daylight."

She searched his face for some hint of what he felt about this danger he was going into. He looked weary but not afraid; but that was not to say he was fearless. She had seen the panic when the whites had fled this island last January; some of the men had looked as calm, as they boarded the evacuation ship, as if they were going out for a day's fishing. Then the ship's captain had tried to stop some of the men boarding the vessel, saying it was overloaded. In that moment all the calm masks crumbled and the men had become ugly with the fear of being left behind. They had stormed the small ship and in the end it had departed packed like a cattle barge. She knew it would hurt her to see even a hint of that ugly fear on Mullane's face.

"Good luck." She put frank pressure into her handshake; he could make what he liked of it. "If Lee Chin has any spare supplies down at Noku, ask him if we can have some."

"Do you know Lee Chin?"

"I delivered his wife's last baby. She's a local like me." Then she said, "Don't blame yourself for what happened to Sister Brigid."

"Does it show that much?"

She nodded. "It was on your face when you came out of the swamp to tell us what happened. Someone else may die before we get off this island – we've all got to be responsible for ourselves."

He put out a hand, touched hers; it was the first intimate approach he had made towards her. "I've always held myself responsible for someone else's death – I guess the feeling still persists."

He left her abruptly, almost as if shutting a door on their moment of intimacy, and went along to the Bishop. "I'm going down to Noku. Say a prayer or two for me."

"I shall do that, Mr Mullane. It is always better to pray for the living than for the dead. Even Sister Brigid believed that." He sighed, a sound that was almost a sob. "I'll miss her, even her complaints."

"She may be happier where she is. It was just a hell of a way to die."

"She probably is happier. She had no doubts at all that there is a heaven. But I should have insisted that she went out with Father Holtz and the other sisters. Father Holtz was my assistant and he didn't want to go, either. But he was a very sick man and he had no choice. Unfortunately, Sister Brigid insisted she had a choice and she stayed. Even bishops are powerless against a nun's determination." Then he abruptly changed the subject: "I have had another look at our Japanese guest."

"*Our* guest, Bishop? You've come down on our side then?"

"A slip of the tongue. A habit from one's past breeding – in the Church and before it. I thought you'd understand that, Mr Mullane. You have breeding."

Mullane smiled. "My mother and father would bless you for that. The Irish in America have never been accused of being well-bred. They breed well, but in the other sense. But what about our guest?"

"I agree with Miss Riddle now. I think his arm should be amputated."

Mullane looked at him hard. "Miss Riddle won't attempt it. Will you do it?"

Scheer turned away. He was standing in a patch of sunlight; he had not brought his umbrella with him and the bright glare assaulted him like an old enemy. The American had asked for prayers for himself; he wondered whom he could ask to pray for *him*.

"If it has to be . . . It is twenty-four years since I last touched a scalpel. Then, too, I was repairing a war wound." He held out his slim hands; he was surprised to see they were shaking a little. Old age, the chill of memories when young? Something trembled within him. "I'd hate to think that was all these hands were meant for. They have blessed people, too. But one never knows how successful a blessing is."

"Try the operation. But wait till I come back in the morning. Just one thing – "

"Yes?"

"If your patient asks you to let him die, remember whose side you're on. The Church won't allow euthanasia. Neither will I, not in this case."

"I'll do my best. But despite these – " he held up his hands " – everything will really be in the hands of the Lord."

"Then we can't lose, can we? From all the speeches I've heard, even the atheists among our leaders think the Lord is on our side. I mean *our* side, not Hitler's."

Mullane and Buka left the camp as the sun went down behind the western shoulder of the mountain. Vokes went part-way along the track with them, one hand in his pocket. When they came to where a branch track led down the slope through the jungle he took his hand from his pocket.

"My badges of rank, Con. You want to put them up, just in case?"

Mullane shook his head, touched by the gesture. "Thanks, Frank. But I don't think I could ever pass for a sub-lieutenant in the RAN, not even with this sailor's beard. I just don't have that rough panache that distinguishes you Aussies."

"Panache? Is that right?" He would look up the word if he lived long enough to see another dictionary; he wouldn't educate himself by asking. "Well, please yourself. Just don't get caught. Oh, and if you see Lee Chin ask him if he has a spare engine." Then, sober-faced: "Good luck, Con. You too, Buka. Look after yourselves."

He watched them go down the track, disappear into the wild sea of trees and vines. He was surprised to find himself sweating, even in the cool purple air of the evening.

IV

Blomfield looked at the two coloured pins stuck close together on the map. Without thinking, he pulled out the drawer of his desk, heard the pins rattle in the tobacco tin; then he realized what he had done and he angrily slammed the drawer shut. One day's silence didn't mean that Mullane and Vokes were lost.

Lowell, looking more worried than ever, came into the room and sat down heavily. "I wish I'd stayed home in Newport. I could've had a soft job there, in charge of security at the dockyard. No GHQ to worry about – "

"They on your back again?"

"There's a son-of-a-bitch down there, a bird colonel, keeps calling me every hour on the hour. What's the latest on Rabaul, what's the hold-up? The Air Force sent a B-52 over there this morning and it was shot down, but that didn't seem to upset him. He told me this afternoon he knows more about the situation in North Africa than he does about Rabaul, so I asked him why he didn't go and fight his fucking war in North Africa. I could be out of a job tomorrow. What's your good news?"

"None. Mullane, Vokes didn't come on the air either this morning or this evening."

"Would they have already started for Rabaul?"

"Not without telling us. What would they have done with this Jap they've got? No, if he is a top jockey, a general or someone close to that rank, they wouldn't just dump him and take off. He sounds too important. Have you got something that can go in and pick up this bloke whoever he is?"

"They've promised me a sub, but they'll only hold it for forty-eight hours – it has to go back on patrol in the Solomons. But until we hear from Mullane or Vokes, where the hell do we send it?"

"What's the latest sitrep on Guadalcanal?"

"Guarded optimism was the phrase I think they used. Which means any moment the shit can hit the fan, but they hope the fan will break down."

Chapter Five

I

"Japs in there, boss. Couldn't count 'em myself. Boy tell me six, eight, he dunno. He kept holding up different fingers, silly bugger."

Buka pulled on his shirt, hoisted his pack on his back. Wrapped just in his *lap-lap*, looking like any other native on the plantation he had left Mullane here in the bush by the river and gone quietly into Noku. He had been away less than twenty minutes, had now come back with the bad news.

"The boy you saw won't give us away to the Japs, will he?"

"He come from my village, boss. He knows I break his bloody neck he tells the Japs about us."

There was a faint lessening of the darkness as Buka smiled. The moon would not be up for another hour and the darkness here beneath the trees was that of a windowless dungeon. Buka, coming back up the track, had not been able to find Mullane and the latter had had to call softly to him, hoping his voice would not carry down to the plantation on the still night air.

Mullane busily rubbed citronella on himself; the mosquitoes did not need any moon to find their feast. A mosquito was caught in his beard and he crushed it with his fingers. "Where are the Japs? In the house?"

"They down on the beach, all sitting by fire. One feller walking up and down, he on guard."

"Lee Chin and his family in the house?"

"They in there."

Mullane put the cork back in the citronella bottle, buttoned his cuffs. "Okay, we wait till everyone's settled down for the night. Another couple of hours."

"Boss, you go to sleep. You pretty damn tired."

For a moment Mullane loved the invisible brown man. He put out a blind hand, found Buka's arm, pressed it. "Wake me when the moon comes up. That's all the sleep I'll need."

But it seemed that he had barely shut his eyes when Buka was shaking him awake. For a moment he was completely disorientated; then with a shudder he came fully awake. He had already killed men, but he was still a novice in the war game; he would have to sharpen his reflexes if he was to survive. He might once have been a natural athlete but he was not a natural animal, alert on the instant to his surroundings. Then his mind cleared and he was amused by the idea that a civilized man had to be trained to be a primitive.

The moon was up, a rheumy yellow eye slowly growing whiter as it climbed above the mountains. Mullane and Buka stepped out on to the track beside the river, moved cautiously down towards the plantation. They paused on the edge of the jungle, beside the rough picket fence that protected the vegetable garden from marauding pigs. The rows of coconut trees ran down ahead of them; Mullane noted with distaste that Lee Chin had not kept the cover crop trimmed down between the trees. There was a mat of thick vines and wild grass almost two feet deep; if he and Buka had to make a run for it on their way back it would be difficult. Something on the other side of the garden moved and he and Buka brought their guns up; then he saw the two goats, tied with long ropes to a coconut tree, move out into a patch of moonlight. Farther down he could make out two humps lying in the ground cover; then one of the humps moved and he saw the horns of a cow. Lee Chin and his family had one of the luxuries of life here on the island, fresh milk.

"Any dogs, Buka?"

"No, boss. Unless Japs got some."

He hadn't heard any dogs barking when the Japanese had been climbing the mountain; but that was not to say there were no dogs down on the beach. He could see the glow of the fire down by the water, but so far he and Buka were too far away to discern any sentry.

"I'll go into the house. You stay outside and watch the Japs down on the beach. Don't shoot, you hear me? *Don't shoot.*"

Buka held up his rifle; moonlight gleamed on the barrel. "What gun for, boss? Only six, eight fellers down there – I kill 'em all, no trouble."

"There'd be plenty of trouble afterwards. Just do what you're told – no shooting. Unless you absolutely have to," he added and saw the rifle barrel move, a mote of moonlight gleaming like a reflection from Buka's eye.

There was a path beaten by the bare feet of the plantation workers down through the ground cover to the drying sheds. Mullane and Buka ran silently down between the trees, through the black stripes of shadow laid across the blue-green of moonlight. Mullane could smell the copra in the sheds; he wondered whom Lee Chin could sell it to now. Over to their right he could see the huts of the workers, the faint glow of almost-dead fires in front of some of them. The main house was between him and Buka and the beach and so far they were safe from being sighted by a Japanese sentry.

They came to a shed with open sides and a corrugated-iron roof; Mullane saw the shape, like an angular beast, of the large petrol engine in the shadow of the shed. It was too big for there to be any hope of his carriers carting it back up into the hills, even supposing he could get it away from Lee Chin. But if the Japanese left here he might be able to bring the batteries down to Noku . . .

He pulled up, gestured for Buka to move round the corner of the house and watch the beach. The house was like all Islands dwellings, raised on pilings for coolness and to alleviate the dampness. Carefully, as silently as he could in the heavy boots he wore, he went up the back steps, opened the screen door and stepped in on to the veranda that ran right round the house. Now he had to find Lee Chin. If Jack Kayser, the late manager, had been like all other plantation owners or managers, he would have one of the front rooms as his bedroom, with a view of the beach and a chance of catching some of the breeze that blew in off the sea. If Lee Chin was like all other juniors who had been unexpectedly promoted to boss, he would have moved into the ex-boss's bed as well as his chair.

Mullane crept along the veranda towards the front of the house. He stopped abruptly, sinking back on his heels, bringing up the Thompson into the ready position. One part of his mind remarked how instinctively he had acted; he had had no training in killing but the instinct was there. A Japanese sentry was sitting on the front steps. Mullane saw the tiny glow of a match as the sentry lit a cigarette; that meant the Japanese was probably going to sit there another five minutes while he enjoyed his smoke. Mullane, a non-smoker all his life, fretted with impatience. He nodded with satisfaction as the Japanese hacked out a rough, sputum-loaded cough. The son-of-a-bitch should die from his habit, preferably now.

Inside the house a child began to cry. Mullane flattened himself against the wall as an oil lamp was turned up just inside the window by which he stood. The sentry stood up, came up to the top step; but Mullane had already slipped round the corner, hearing the floorboards creak beneath him, sounding in his ears like the demolition of the entire house.

He made no attempt this time to flatten himself against the wall; he dropped on one knee and held his gun ready to shoot as soon as the Japanese came round the corner. He could feel himself sweating, knew he was going to kill another man, felt regret and disgust and fear, but knew it had to be done. He heard movement within the house, the child's crying dying to a whimper; but he knew that when his gun went off the crying would turn to screaming. Lee Chin and his family were going to suffer, possibly be killed in the crossfire; oh, for the simple wars of simpler times, when armies met on a field as if in a stadium, when the *samurai* met like matched heavyweights. But there was nothing else for it: once he had shot the sentry he would have to plunge off the veranda and head for the beach and kill the Japanese there. Operation Ferdinand in this sector was turning into a series of small massacres.

Then he heard the scrape of boots on the steps and a moment later the cough of the sentry as he moved away down towards the beach. Mullane eased himself upright, feeling his joints creak; tension had frozen him like a cold wind. He lowered the Thompson; he had to force the hook out of his finger on the trigger. There was no itch in his finger as he knew there would have been in Buka's.

He returned to the rear of the house, tried the back door. It was locked, something he had not expected; locked doors were as rare as fireplaces in the houses in the Islands. Lee Chin must have no trust in the Japanese, though Mullane wondered what defence a plywood door would be against a fusillade of bullets. But at least it hinted that Lee Chin might still be neutral, not yet a Japanese ally.

Mullane knocked gently on the door, waited and knocked again. Then he heard the creaking of floorboards behind the door.

"Lee Chin," he whispered, bending over to speak through the keyhole and feeling slightly ridiculous doing so, a keyhole conspirator out of some French farce. "This is Mullane, from down at Kiogo. Let me in."

There was silence for a moment, then the sound of a key being turned. The door opened a few inches, but in the darkness under the veranda awning Mullane could see no face in the crack. He could feel himself being scrutinized; he stood perfectly still, his skin tightening. Then the door swung open and a dim hand beckoned him in.

He slipped into the house and the door was closed behind him. He could see nothing in the blackness in which he stood; then a hand groped for his arm and he was led along a short passage and into the front room that he guessed was the living-room. A pale reflection of the moonlight came through the window that faced the sea; gradually his eyes became accustomed to the darkness. He saw the dark silhouette of a thin man with a close-cropped or bald head.

"Lee Chin?"

"Yes. You are Mr Mullane? I wouldn't have recognized you."

Mullane was puzzled. "You know me?"

"I saw you once up in Rabaul, at Burns Philp's store. I worked there before I came here. You had no beard then." Lee Chin either had no teeth or had taken them out for the night; the room hissed with his whisper like a den of snakes. "What do you want, Mr Mullane?"

Then there was a yellow glow in the doorway of the room leading off this main room. A woman in a shift stood there, one arm cradling a baby, the other holding an oil lamp. Lee Chin stood revealed as a middle-aged man, bald and gaunt-faced; he wore only a long white singlet that barely covered his loins. Again Mullane had a sense of the ridiculous. Maybe there was an element of farce in all dangerous situations, though he could not imagine death's having a comic side.

Lee Chin hissed to his wife to put out the light. She lifted the globe to her face, blew out the small flame; Mullane caught a glimpse of a woman older and less attractive than Ruth. A local, but too dark ever to have any hope of being taken for anything but what she was, a native woman's daughter. With the blowing out of the lamp she seemed to disappear; when Mullane's eyes became accustomed to the darkness again she was no longer in the doorway. There was just the tiny whimpering of the baby in the darkness of the bedroom, devils it did not understand walking in its sleep.

"What do you want?" Lee Chin repeated. "The Japanese will kill us all if they know you are here."

Mullane could see him more clearly now. As if embarrassed by what the lamp had shown he now stood pulling his singlet down in front of him, a dim caricature of the old *September Morn* calendar pictures Mullane had known in his youth. Mullane felt the relief of silent amusement flooding through him and he began to relax.

"When Mr Kayser left here, Lee, he took the company's safe up-river and left it in the bush. I want the key to it."

"What for?"

"There's money in it. I'm authorized to take it. I want to pay my boys. We're up there in the hills and I have no money for them."

He wondered how much he could tell Lee Chin. The Chinese in the Islands were a community in and of themselves; they never attempted to mix with the Europeans or the natives. Most of them were traders, running their own stores; but some, like Lee Chin, had taken jobs with the plantation companies. They were nearly all Cantonese and, from what Mullane had heard, they all belonged to the Kuomintang, as if they dreamed of some day returning to China. But maybe Lee Chin did not dream of going home, was just like the natives, had no other ambition than to remain here and live with whoever ruled the Islands.

He had to take the risk: "Lee, I'm up there with Mr Vokes, from down at Tanga. We're Coastwatchers."

"I know Mr Vokes. He also works for Burns Philp, like me."

There was a note of pride in the Chinese's voice. Somehow Mullane had expected him to be self-contained, loyal only to himself. Good old Burns Philp: maybe its employees thought it was like belonging to the Church. Or the Masons.

"The Japs have taken over Tanga. What's happened here?"

"I am on parole. They come down every two weeks from Rabaul to check on me. Those men down there – " He nodded through the window. The fire on the beach flared up as the sentry tossed more wood on it. "They come looking for an aeroplane that crashed up in the hills."

Mullane didn't mention what he knew. "How long are they staying?"

"I don't know. I hope they go soon. My wife is frightened, very much afraid. So am I," he added and pulled his singlet further down in front of him, like a fearful virgin. "If I give you the money, Mr Mullane, please go quickly."

"I have no desire to stay – What did you say? *Give* me the money?"

"I have it here in the house, in the bedroom. When Mr Kayser left I went up and found the safe and opened it. I was afraid the boys would find it and try to open it, or throw it in the river. I am the book-keeper. Some day Burns Philp may ask me about the money."

Mullane silently sang the praises of a conscientious book-keeper. "I shall bear witness to your honesty and loyalty, Mr Lee. Now may I borrow the money and get the hell out of here?"

Lee went into the bedroom, still pulling the singlet down in front of him but exposing his bony buttocks like twin reflections of his bald head. There was some whispering in the bedroom, then the sound of something being scraped on the wooden floor; Mullane guessed that a box was being pulled out from under the bed. It seemed to him that Lee Chin was taking an interminable time to bring out the money. He looked out the window, saw the fire flare up down on the beach, then the sentry began to walk back up towards the house.

In the bedroom there was more whispering; then Lee Chin came back into the living-room. He wore a pair of shorts now, his singlet tucked into it. Mrs Lee had obviously told him to make himself respectable.

He held out a paper bag. "£608, Mr Mullane. Will you sign a receipt, please?"

Mullane took the paper bag, put a hand in it and felt the rolls of notes held together by rubber bands. Then he signed the receipt-book that Lee Chin held out to him. There was no light to see what he was signing, but this was the least of the trust he had to place in the Chinese. If Lee should give him away to the Japanese, then he would be dead and the receipt, whatever it was for, would be as useless as his own corpse.

"How are you paying your own boys?"

"I am not paying them. The Japanese will not allow it. Each time they come down here they bring Japanese money. They say it is the only money we are allowed to use, that we have to get used to it."

"Thank you for this money, Lee. I'll tell Burns Philp — " Then he remembered he could not tell Burns Philp or anyone else anything at all. "Lee, do you have a small engine, one I could send my boys down to get? I need it to recharge the batteries for our radio set."

"No, Mr Mullane. The Japanese took the small engine when they took my wireless. They said I did not need to know what was happening anywhere else. They left the big engine — "

"I saw it." Out in the front garden he could hear the sentry whistling softly to himself, keeping himself company. "What about the plantations further up the coast?"

"I don't know. But I think they would have taken their wirelesses, too. And their engines. They don't want us to know anything, Mr Mullane. Are we winning the war?" he asked plaintively.

"Not yet, Lee." In his own ears he sounded as hypocritical as all propagandists; but lying, he knew, was a legitimate weapon of war. Even against one's own side. "But we'll win, don't give up hope. Be patient."

"I'm Chinese," said Lee Chin.

.In the darkness Mullane smiled. "I apologize. We Americans haven't yet learned patience."

"Some day – " said Lee, but Mullane knew he was only being polite.

He stuffed the paper bag into his pack. "I won't be back, Lee. I don't want to endanger you and your family. You do the same for me and Mr Vokes."

"Of course. The Japanese know there are Coastwatchers up in the hills – I heard them asking the boys. They must have picked up your wireless signals – "

"Well, we have no wireless now – " But it seemed that their position was more perilous than he had thought. Perhaps the Japanese had already guessed that the Coastwatchers had got to General Nara . . . "I'd better go."

"Tell Burns Philp I am on their side." Not Australia's or America's or even China's.

"I'll do that. But first I have to find a radio – "

"There is a small engine up in the mountains."

Mullane stopped in the doorway that led to the rear hall. "Where?"

"There is a boy named Kutari – " That goddam social ladder, Mullane thought. Even Lee Chin, who would never be accepted as an equal by the Europeans, had his own place for the natives: they would always be *boys* to him. "He has his own village. He has what they call a cargo cult."

Mullane had never seen any evidence of a cargo cult in his time in New Britain, but he knew what it meant and the false promises it could bring to the natives. The false promises did not distinguish the cultism from the fantasies of more civilized societies: the lotteries, the racetrack betting, the numbers racket, the cure-all of political philosophies. Nor was it distinguished from other day-dreams by the fact that, too often, its leaders were nefarious and intent only on their own aggrandizement. The native named Kutari was only a brother under the demagoguery to the political bosses, Tweed, Crump, Pendergast, back home in the States. What made cargo cults tragically different was that almost invariably the primitive people who believed the promises lost even that which they had possessed when their Messiah came offering to exchange the future for the present.

"He has a petrol engine," said Lee. "He uses it to run his picture machine. My boys have told me about him."

"His picture machine?"

"Fill-ums. He shows his fill-ums to the people. They believe him when he says he will bring them a world like they see."

"Where did he get a movie projector? And the films?"

"I don't know. They say he worked as a house-boy for one of the plantation owners, one of the private men. When the man retired and went home to Brisbane, he took Kutari with him. Kutari lived there for some years, how many I do not know. Then he came back here and went up into the mountains to his own village."

In the bedroom the baby began to cry again; in a room back down the hall another child called out. Out in the garden the sentry's whistling had stopped.

"Please go, Mr Mullane!"

Mullane hurried out of the house, away from the family sounds into the moonlit night where the sentry walked with his rifle ready to kill. In his hurry he almost fell down the back steps, tried to keep his balance and stumbled into a large metal trash can. It went over with a loud clang. He spun round and dived into the blackness under the house as the sentry, rifle at the ready, came round the corner. Mullane heard him say in Japanese, "Who's there? Stop!" Then there was the sound of the rifle bolt being slammed back.

Mullane lay perfectly still in agony: he was lying on top of a small pile of broken coconut shells. Their jagged edges pressed into him like broad-bladed knives; but he dared not move. He saw the Japanese, one cautious step at a time, move from the corner of the house towards the back steps. Then beyond the sentry he saw Buka, silhouetted against a patch of moonlight, move out from behind a coconut palm and take aim with his rifle. Mullane had to shut his teeth from crying out: *Don't, Buka, don't!*

Then there was the creak of the screen door immediately above him being opened and Lee Chin said, "What's the matter?"

The sentry spun round, his gun up, said in Japanese, "Someone was out here – "

"I don't understand." Lee Chin was nervous; his toothless gums sucked on his words. He came down the steps, carefully like an old man; Mullane saw his thin legs silhouetted against the moonlight, looking like sticks that would break at any moment. He picked up the trash can, put the lid back on. "Pig. Wild pig."

"Pig?" The sentry repeated the word; then said in Japanese, "What's that?"

Lee Chin seemed nonplussed for a moment; then suddenly he snorted, a ridiculous sound. Christ Almighty, thought Mullane, lying on his bed of coconut nails, who was it said that war is the worst farce of all? Lee Chin snorted again, rattled the trash can.

Abruptly the sentry laughed, coughed, put down his rifle. Beyond him Mullane saw that Buka had disappeared again behind the trunk of the coconut palm. The Japanese said, "Oh, a pig? Good night, old man. Go back to bed."

Lee Chin went back up the steps on legs that still looked ready to fold beneath him. On the floorboards above him Mullane heard running feet and the voices of frightened children. The sentry stood, lit another cigarette, coughed again, then slung his rifle over his shoulder and went back round the corner of the house and down towards the beach. Mullane eased himself off the coconut shells, felt the blood running where they had punctured him. He hoped he would not bleed to death before daylight: that would be a touch of comedy he could not laugh at.

Painfully he slipped out from under the house, went in a crouching run up through the plantation groves. Buka slipped out from behind his tree, followed him. They skirted the edge of the jungle, found the track that led up beside the river and followed it. Except for the odd section that wound back into the edge of the jungle the track was in the open for most of the way, easy to follow in the bright pale-blue moonlight. Once they pulled up sharply as a log lying across the track turned into a crocodile and slid out of their way into the river. Mullane had a sickening memory of how Sister Brigid had died and he pulled up, unable for the moment to go on.

"All right, boss. He gone, ain't going to hurt us."

Mullane regathered his strength, moved on. Up ahead he could hear the thunder of the waterfall. He slowed to a walk, now and again putting his hand to his wounds to feel how wet they were with blood. Most of them seemed no more than deep scratches; but there were two savage gougings, one above his knee, the other between his lower ribs, that were going to cause him trouble. He would have to stop soon and dress them, somehow staunch the flow of blood.

Just short of the waterfall they found the track that led up the mountain. They began to climb, stumbling through the darkness as the trees shut out the moonlight. At last Mullane could go no farther. He sat down abruptly in the mud. Almost at once the mosquitoes arrived for the feast.

But at least he was safe from the crocodiles. He did not even think about the Japanese.

II

Daylight filtered down through the thick overhang, like an upside-down tide. Birds sang and screeched, like old men who had gratefully survived another night. Somewhere down the track there was grunting and heavy movement as some wild pigs went foraging. Then there was the sound of engines and somewhere over to the east a flock of bombers headed south. Mullane, coming out of a fitful sleep, hoped that some Coastwatcher south of him, somewhere down in the Solomons, would spot the planes and be able to warn the Americans on Guadalcanal. But if CEC and DRM, the two stations in the direct line of flight south, were still off the air, then there might be no warning at all.

He sat up carefully, felt the dressings Buka had applied in the dark to his two major wounds. The bleeding seemed to have stopped; at least he hadn't bled to death during the night. The dressing on his rib was a pad made from a strip of his own shirt;

it was held in place by a long strip torn from Buka's *lap-lap* and wound round his rib cage. The dressing above his knee was a pad that had been the right sleeve of his shirt; the bandage that held it in place was the left sleeve. He had used up all that was left of his citronella, but still the mosquitoes had feasted on him. He was a mass of bites and scratches, one giant walking, stinging sore.

Buka, his *lap-lap* reduced to indecent shortness, the end of his penis hanging down below it like a dark tassel, helped the boss to his feet. "You all right, boss? I go get boys to carry you."

Mullane wanted to smile at Buka's appearance, but he knew better; the big man, like all the natives, had a strict sense of modesty. The missionaries had taught him what to be ashamed of. "I'll be okay. We'll just take it easy, that's all. I don't want to start bleeding again."

But his leg wound started bleeding after only ten minutes' walking. He kept going, saying nothing to Buka, who was climbing the track ahead of him. Occasionally Buka would look back over his shoulder, but Mullane just nodded and pushed the big man on and wished for some of his stamina. Buka had spent his youth trekking over mountain trails like this with various patrol officers and his legs seemed to have lost none of the strength that he had had when he was a police boy.

By the time they climbed the final stretch and reached the camp, the pad on Mullane's leg was a dark sodden mess; the knee felt as pulpy as the pad looked. He sat down awkwardly, collapsing on to a mound of grass as Vokes and the others gathered around him.

"Geez, Con – " Vokes was full of concern; his arms were doing their windmill act again. "Did you run into trouble? Were you shot?"

Mullane lay back as Ruth unwrapped the bandage from his leg. "I was attacked by a pile of coconut shells. I'm convinced that this war is turning into a huge joke. You wouldn't believe the laughs I've had – "

"Shut up," said Ruth curtly. "Frank, get some hot water. And tell one of the boys to bring up my medical case."

Vokes hurried away, shouting ahead of him for the cook-boy to put a cook-pot of water on the fire. Buka, all at once conscious of his indecency, had gone off to put on a new *lap-lap*.

Ruth took the pad off Mullane's ribs. "Well, there's no bleeding there, but it's still ugly. What do you think, Bishop?"

"Am I being asked for a professional opinion?" But Scheer squatted down beside her. "I think you are doing a very good job, Miss Riddle. Do you have anything to stop any infection?"

"There's nothing left in my case. I wish I had some of those new sulfa drugs I've read about."

"Mr Mullane has some Scotch whisky. A little application of that might help."

"Over my dead body," said Mullane.

"If needs be," said Ruth and went away to get the bottle. When she came back she said, "There's another bottle in the hut. We may need that – "

Scheer saw the look on Mullane's face. "Don't worry. We shall keep enough for inner medicinal purposes."

It was some time before Vokes returned, he carrying the medical case and Silas carrying a bowl of hot water. Ruth dressed Mullane's wounds, applying the whisky externally and internally. Mullane sat up, smacked his lips as he sipped the Chivas Regal.

"Ah, if only Dr Lister had used that instead of carbolic acid!"

"We'd have had a world full of antiseptic drunks." Ruth put away her kit, washed her hands. "You're on light duties for a week."

"With all due respect, Miss Riddle, like hell I am."

"You're not starting out for Rabaul – I'll chop your other leg from underneath you if you try."

"We'll come to that. In the meantime I have another call to make."

"Where's that?" said Vokes.

Mullane told him and the others about Kutari and his cargo cult up in the mountains. "I don't know where it is, but maybe one of the boys does."

In the background Silas coughed, then said diffidently, "I know the place, boss. Plenty long climb."

Silas was the next oldest native to Buka, a wiry man in his late thirties with a face already that of an older man; disillusioned eyes looked out at the world through a coarse veil of wrinkles. He was loyal and hard-working and Mullane had never discovered the reason for his disillusion. And had never asked for fear that he would learn of another white man's crime.

"All right, we'll go first thing in the morning." He held up a hand as Ruth was about to speak. "I'll rest up all day today. You can pamper me."

Ruth tossed away the dirty water. "We'll be too busy for any of that. The Bishop is going to operate on the General."

Nara was somewhere out of sight, in one of the huts that had been erected under the trees; Mullane had forgotten all about him. It was a measure of his own exhaustion that he should have done so and for a moment he wondered if he would indeed be strong enough to make the journey to Kutari's village tomorrow. He was not heartened when once again he felt the burden of more than just injury and physical weakness.

"He's your patient," he said. "Do you have everything you need?"

Scheer smiled apologetically. "Not quite. We have no antiseptic."

Vokes said, "Let 'em have that other bottle of whisky, Con. Now we've got the cash to pay the boys, we can send 'em back to the main dump. They can bring you as much grog as you want – you can do without your nip for a day or two – "

"Frank, I'm not a drunk. Not yet, though certain people around here could drive me to drink. You can have the whisky, Bishop. Just don't be profligate with it." He looked at Ruth. "Just remember I'm the important patient around here."

"Then stay off your leg, you stupid bastard. Sorry, Bishop."

Scheer smiled. "You have the makings of a fine matron, Miss Riddle."

Later, when Mullane was resting in his hut, Vokes came to him. "Did you see those bombers this morning? Forty-four of them. This is a good site, Con. I think we ought to come back here after Rabaul."

"Since we're off the air, I guess Townsville thinks we're already on our way in there." He saw the look on Vokes' face and realized it sounded like another criticism. "Have you paid the boys?"

"I gave them double time, like you promised. But only up till today. Mariba tried his luck, wanting another week in advance, but I told him to bugger off. I'd like to get rid of him."

"While he's here we can keep an eye on him. If we let him go he could give us away to the Japs. Which raises a problem – " He had tried to rest his mind as well as his body, but it was like a restless animal in the cage of his skull. "You better go back with the boys to the dump. If we send them on their own, they could just keep on going all the way down to Kiogo. Especially now that they have their money."

Vokes nodded, silently pondered the problem. He was less voluble than he had been, though he was still bursting with words. But he had been listening to the conversations of Mullane, Scheer and General Nara and for the first time in his life had become embarrassed at all the banal words that poured out of him. He had been stricken by an awful trauma, that of the compulsive talker suddenly ashamed of his own voice.

"You could stay here and I could go up and see that bloke Kutari. We could send Buka back with the boys to get the supplies. He'd keep 'em in line."

The proposition had its points; but it had one major drawback. Vokes knew nothing at all about cargo cultism and, from what Mullane had read and heard, a cargo cult leader had to be treated with the utmost diplomacy. To treat him otherwise, and Vokes as much a diplomat as he was a golden-voiced aesthete, would only prove part of the cult leader's point. Which was that the white men thought they owned the world and it was they who prevented all the good things of the cargo from reaching their rightful heirs, the dark people of the Islands. Mullane had no idea what sort of man Kutari was, but he was certain that Vokes was not the man to deal with him.

"How's your ankle?"

"Right as rain. It was only a slight sprain. Ruth worked on it last night with compresses."

"Then I think you better go back for the supplies. Buka can look after things here."

"What about the General? And the Bishop? Those two are a

131

real problem, don't you reckon?"

"The General isn't going to be for a day or two, not till he gets over his operation. How's it going?"

"They're nearly ready to start. I offered to help, but I tripped arse-over-Charlie and nearly scalded Ruth with a basin of hot water. She told me to bugger off. I'm glad in a way – I think I'd pass out if I had to watch."

Mullane eased himself to his feet. "I think I better get over there. They may need some help."

"I wish I could be more help, Con – but I know I'd keel over. All I could do was make some clamps for them – I did it last night after you'd gone down to Noku. Ruth told me what she wanted and I fixed her up with some clamps by taking the spring clips off the battery leads and mucking around with them."

Mullane marvelled at him. "You're full of surprises, Frank."

Vokes grinned with embarrassment. "I told you, us Aussies are the greatest improvisers you'll ever find. I just hope the bloody things work," he added soberly.

Ruth met them when they were halfway to the hut where the operation was to take place. "I want blood," she said flatly. "What blood group are you, Frank?"

"Group O. Geez, how much do you want?"

"As much as you can stand to lose. I've already taken some from Buka. Fortunately he still has his police dog-tags and he's an O, too." She looked at Mullane. "You've already lost enough, otherwise I'd be sucking some from you, too."

"I'm an AB. How does the General feel at the thought of having all that black and white blood mixed in with his?"

"He's past caring. What are you doing on that leg of yours?"

"I'm about to come and stand-by – or sit-by – in case you need some help. Frank tells me he keels at the sight of blood."

She hesitated, then nodded. "We'll need help. You can be the anaesthetist."

The operation began an hour later. Outside the hut two cook-pots boiled above a fire, sterilizing the instruments. Inside the hut Nara's stretcher had been raised on to two rough hurdles put up by the natives. Ruth had mixed up a saline solution and it was in a bottle hung by a piece of rope from a cross-beam of the hut; from another beam hung a bottle of blood; the bottles looked suspiciously like jam jars and Mullane wondered where Ruth had got them. Scheer, for his part, just looked at what was to be his theatre and shook his head in wonder. When he had last operated, in the shattered house on the outskirts of Sedan, he had worked in very inadequate conditions. But never in anything as primitive as this.

He had spoken to Nara in the morning, preparing him for the amputation. He remembered from experience of long ago that emotional shock could kill a man as much as the actual cutting off of a limb; the amputee had to be prepared psychologically for the loss of a part of his body that had been so useful to him. Nara had listened stolidly and without expression and the Bishop had been thankful for the Japanese's stoicism.

"I'll pray for you, General. Also for skill in my own hands."

"Pray for yourself, Bishop," said Nara politely. "I do not need your prayers."

Well, the Bishop thought now as he waited for Mullane to apply the ether, we'll see who needs the prayers. He was ashamed to find that he was praying more for himself than for the General.

Mullane sat on a roughly constructed stool at the head of the rough operating table. Ruth had supplied him with a rubber mask ("It's mainly been used on native women having a bad time in childbirth") and he was slowly dripping ether through a cotton-wool pad attached to the mask's tube. Ruth had given him some brief instructions, but he knew it was going to be a trial-and-error task in determining how much anaesthetic he should give Nara. He could only hope there would be no error.

He kept his gaze concentrated on Nara's face as Scheer made the first incision in the badly mangled arm. He was not sure that he would not be like Vokes and faint dead away as soon as the blood started to run. He had a clean handkerchief tied round his lower face over his beard, but he could smell the ether and the blood and he wondered how long the operation was going to take and if he would last it out.

But gradually he began to take an interest in what was going on. A very tight tourniquet had been tied round Nara's upper arm; even so, when Scheer severed the brachial artery blood spurted. But Ruth snapped on one of Vokes' home-made clamps; the flow of blood was cut off at once. Scheer worked clumsily at first, but Ruth was cool, brisk and, Mullane noted, magnificently efficient.

Buka stood at the bottom end of the table supervising the slow drip of blood from the transfusion bottle. He never once looked at the table, but kept his gaze fixed on the bottle. Sweat was running on him like rain-water and it seemed to Mullane that the brown man's skin had taken on a tinge of grey.

Scheer's hands began to take on confidence, helped by Ruth's seeming confidence in him. They had started slowly but soon they were working as a team; it struck Mullane that this could not be the first amputation at which Ruth had assisted. Then it was time to cut the humerus bone just above the elbow.

Ruth looked at Mullane. "This isn't going to sound too nice. Better try and not listen."

"How does one do that?" At the other end of the table he saw Buka's eyes open wide in trepidation as Scheer picked up the butcher's hacksaw that had been borrowed from the cook-boy and had been sterilized in boiling water and Chivas Regal.

"You could sing."

Even at that moment he saw the laughter in her eyes above her mask. At first he thought she was joking, then he saw the sense of it. He had always had a good loud baritone, though he couldn't remember when he had last sung. Probably not since he had gone to parties with Apricot Bloom; he had once drowned out Ethel Merman and that hadn't been easy. He racked his brains for a song he remembered.

Then he began to sing 'The Riff Song' from *The Desert Song*. He and Buka stared at the beams above their heads while he belted out the song as he had heard Dennis King sing it; outside the hut the natives started up, wondering what madness had taken hold of the boss. One chorus, sung at full volume, was enough: Scheer was through the bone while the Riffs were still coming over the second sand dune.

Ruth dropped the severed arm into the native basket at her feet, then tapped Mullane on the arm and shouted, "Righto – no need for an encore!"

Scheer had been too intent on what he was doing to be distracted by the singing. He had been surprised at his own calm when he had sawed the arm; he had expected to have developed some squeamishness during his long absence from the operating table. Ruth had flinched as the hacksaw bit into the bone, but from then on she had been cool and controlled, holding the arm steady for him. Now he was sewing up the flap he had cut, turning the arm into a stump. He was pleased with the way it looked, but only time would tell how successful he had been.

At last he stepped back. He had taken off his cassock and worked in singlet and duck trousers; the latter were now streaked and splashed with blood. He looked nothing like a bishop; except, perhaps, one halfway through martyrdom. But for the moment he had another *persona*: he was a surgeon again and he had just performed an operation that would not have disgraced a doctor working in far better circumstances. He allowed himself a small dose of the sin of pride.

"Would you clean up for me, Miss Riddle?"

"With pleasure, Bishop. Congratulations." Ruth reached for the bottle of whisky. "With Mr Mullane's compliments."

Scheer smiled at Mullane, put the bottle to his lips. Bloodstained, in singlet and wrinkled trousers, the bottle to his mouth, he looked like any beachcomber recovering from a wild Saturday night in Rabaul. Then he handed the bottle to its owner.

"I think you could do with a nip or two yourself, Mr Mullane."

Buka, relieved by Ruth on the transfusion jar, had already gone outside, glad to escape. Mullane took the whisky, swallowed a large mouthful, then held it out to Ruth. She smiled, wiped the mouth of the bottle and took a swig. She coughed, then smiled again.

"I think we all deserved that." Then she looked at their patient, thin, shrunken, pale. "Let's hope he survives."

III

They had a hot meal that night: tinned meat and vegetables, rice and thinned-out condensed milk. The meal seemed to improve everyone's mood. Everyone, even the carriers, moved about with smiles and light talk amongst themselves, like holiday-makers on a camping trip. But occasionally Mullane wondered what was happening up in Rabaul and chafed at the delay in being able to get there. For all he and Vokes knew, preparations might be building up for the decisive battle of the Pacific war. But first he had to get their radio working and he had to have Nara taken off his hands. He had the sudden thought that perhaps more would be gained by letting the General die.

"I used to go on trips like this up into the Blue Mountains with the surf club," Vokes was saying. "That's about seventy or eighty miles inland from Sydney. I remember once I got lost in the Grose Valley. I was about seventeen, I think, and I thought I must be in the wildest country in the world. Stone the crows, how your ideas change, you know what I mean? If someone had told me I'd be stuck up here – "

The meal and the hot coffee had loosened Vokes' tongue again. He was ready to work his way through his pre-war youth; he would not confess it, but all at once he was homesick. He dreamed of the surf rolling in at Manly, of the beach parties on Saturday and Sunday nights, of the portable gramophone that was always getting sand in its works and of Frances Langford singing 'Let's Fall in Love'. And he remembered the girls who were willing but afraid to go all the way if you'd forgotten to pack your French letter along with the beer, the sausage rolls and the saveloys. He wondered if Saturday nights would be like that again when the war was over.

Then the mosquitoes, more regular than the bombers, came up out of the mud and the swamp-holes and the nightly tattoo of slapping hands began. Ruth made sure everyone took their atebrin tablets; she did not want to be faced with the extra chore of caring for someone who went down with a malaria attack. They had all been sitting out in the open on logs or their groundsheets; now they got up and started to move back towards their huts. Vokes looked at his watch and saw that it was only 7.30. If someone had told him he'd be going to bed at 7.30 on a Saturday night . . .

Mullane, still favouring his leg, touched Ruth's arm. "Would you walk me home, Miss Riddle?"

She moved closer to him and he put his arm on her shoulder. They had gone only a few steps when she said, "I think you are malingering, Mr Mullane. Or are you trying to take advantage of me?"

"Not in these circumstances, Miss Riddle." He took his arm from her shoulder. "You're right, I am malingering. I just wanted to talk to you. I have a proposition."

"Ah, Mr Mullane, you disappoint me." But she kept walking beside him as they went along the ridge, through the tree-dappled moonlight, to the hut where he and Vokes would sleep with the dead radio.

Vokes, about to follow the same path, hesitated and then turned back. He was surprised that Mullane wanted to do a line with Ruthie, but if that was what he wanted, good luck to him. He wouldn't mind a bit of the leg-over with her himself, especially since it was Saturday night.

Reaching the hut Mullane spread his groundsheet by a log and gestured to Ruth to sit down. He did it with a grace that stopped just short of parody; but, unaccustomed to such manners from the men she had known, she was not sure that he was not mocking her. Still eyeing him with cautious amusement she sat down. He lowered himself to the ground beside her, his injured leg stuck out in front of him.

"I hope you're not still thinking of going anywhere on that leg."

"I am, actually. That's what I wanted to talk to you about. Not the leg, but where I'm going. Can you use a pistol?"

"I've never used one. But I think I could if I had to."

"I'm sure you could. You're a very competent girl, Miss Riddle. I should not be suggesting what I'm about to suggest if I didn't think you were competent."

She looked around her, sure of herself now. "Saturday night, moonlight, tropic breezes – and all he wants to do is tell me I'm competent."

"A moment ago you said you were disappointed in me because I had a proposition to put to you."

"I think you're too experienced, Mr Mullane, to believe everything a girl says. Do I sound as if I'm flirting with you?"

"Heaven forfend, Miss Riddle."

She laughed. "Forfend! I think I'm safe. Men who use words like that don't proposition girls."

"Some day I'll tell you about Apricot Bloom, who never understood a word I said but it never worried her." It was years since he had had this sort of conversation, the smart-ass courting of a Yale man in his raccoon coat. He remembered other, later times: smoke-filled speakeasies. Bix Beiderbecke playing *Panama*, girls with names such as Apricot and Peaches . . . "But you're safe, Miss Riddle. What I'm proposing is that you, with Buka to back you up, take charge of the camp while Frank and I are away tomorrow. Frank will be gone a couple of days at least, but I'll be back tomorrow evening."

"I don't think you should go anywhere. Not on that leg."

"Miss Riddle – "

"Tell me, did you call Apricot Miss Bloom all the time? I don't think you'd be compromised if you called me Ruth. Just don't call me Ruthie, that's all."

He smiled, drew back the hand that was about to pat her knee of its own accord. It had its own tactile memory: silk stockings, warm firm flesh. Though he and Vokes did not know it, they were sharing the same memories, the Saturday nights of their youth. It seemed that all nights had been Saturday night. "Should I lay six measures of barley on you? Do you know your Bible?"

"I know the story of Ruth, if that's what you mean. I was brought up on a mission. But I didn't think you'd be a Bible man."

"I spent eleven years on the road with a ball team. In every hotel room there was a Gideon Bible. You find yourself reading anything and everything when you're trying to go to sleep in strange hotel rooms."

"Well, I don't think I'm much like Ruth in that book. And I'd rather call you Con than Boaz."

"I don't think Boaz suits me, despite my liking for whisky. Well, whatever you call me, Ruth, I'm going up the mountain tomorrow to look for that man Kutari. If he does have a working engine, we need it. I'll need someone to keep an eye on those left back here in camp."

"You think I can do that? What would you expect me to do – use your gun on the Bishop or the General?" She shook her head. "I wouldn't do it – Con. You forget – this isn't my war. It's personal with me, I'm only concerned for myself. I'm not going to hold a gun at anyone's head and tell him what side he should be on. If the Bishop wants to go home to Germany, why should I stop him? I'd go home myself if I had somewhere to go to."

"I wouldn't expect you to shoot him. I don't think I could cold-bloodedly shoot him myself – I like him too much. But so long as he's thinking of giving himself up to the Japs, he's a danger to us. To you, too. I don't think he'd deliberately give us away, but he could let slip where we are. There's no guarantee they wouldn't be a little rough on him. And if they came up here and found you, you'd either be raped by the soldiers who found you or you'd finish up in an officers' brothel in Rabaul. I'm sure they have one there. The Japanese are not puritanical when they go to war, not like the Americans and the Australians. They recognize their men have certain appetites."

"I'd use your gun on myself before I'd let that happen. I'm not puritanical, but there are limits." She was not afraid of any man alone, but the thought of being raped by a dozen of them terrified her.

"Well, let's hope you don't have to use the gun on either the Bishop or yourself. Incidentally, it's not my gun but General Nara's. I'll have a talk with Buka, tell him to look menacing all day – he's pretty good at that. Will you do it?"

She was silent for a while, looking sideways at his profile outlined against the distant moonlit sea. Down on the coast she could see the glow of a small fire on the beach at Noku, the red eye of the enemy, his and hers. At last she said, "I'll do it. But if you come back tomorrow evening and find the Bishop gone, you'll know why I let him go."

"I'll understand." He was studying her, looking at her now as a woman and not as a prospective camp guard. "Do you always put on perfume for dinner in the jungle?"

"No." She smiled without embarrassment. "I just felt like it tonight – to get the smell of the operation out of my nose as much as anything else. It's my last bottle, like your whisky."

He said cautiously, afraid of himself as much as of her. "You're a beautiful girl. I'm surprised you're not married."

"I could have been. Thanks – for the compliment, I mean. I think you'd be good-looking yourself behind that beard."

"When this is all over, maybe I'll show you the real Mullane."

She wondered what he would be like without the beard; then wondered what he would be like without clothes. She heard herself say, "Pull your pants down."

"Eh?" He let out a half-laugh in surprise.

"I'd better look at that leg of yours again before you go to bed."

He unbuttoned his trousers, slipped them down. "For a moment there I thought I was about to be bluntly seduced."

That had been in her mind, if only subconsciously. His shirt-tails hid his crotch and she could feel the temptation in her fingers to touch him. "I don't think you'd be up to it, Mr Mullane. I don't want two patients on my hands tomorrow morning."

He could feel the stirring in his crotch. "You better look at my leg, Miss Riddle."

Then, unwittingly, she killed whatever chance there might have been of their going any further. "Were you ever married?"

It was his turn to be silent. Then at last he said quietly, "Yes. I was married to a Japanese girl."

IV

He had met Mieko within two weeks of arriving in Japan in that early spring of 1936. He had been invited to a reception at the American embassy and had been introduced to a middle-aged Japanese, tall for his race, who spoke English with almost colloquial ease.

"I am Professor of Art at Imperial University." Tanaka Iwani was as elegantly dressed as McArdle, but in the English style. His family had money and he looked on his salary as a professor as a pittance, pin money that he sometimes neglected to collect for months on end. "I'm interested in European art. Perhaps we have something to learn from your culture. Though I shouldn't say that outside this delightful embassy."

"I'm not European, Professor Tanaka. I'm Irish-American, which inside this delightful embassy puts me just one grade higher than the barbarians. I also play baseball, which has no culture at all."

Then Tanaka led McArdle towards a group of women, three of them American and the fourth Japanese. "I should like you to meet my daughter Mieko."

He introduced the other three women, but McArdle barely saw them. He was fascinated by the Japanese girl. She was taller than the average girl he had seen since his arrival. She had her hair cut Western-style, in a bob with bangs across her unplucked eyebrows; except for her eyes, she reminded him of Louise Brooks, his favourite movie star of his younger days. She was dressed in a pale-blue silk kimono which, simply cut and less elaborate than he had been led to expect, did not look out of place amongst the long dresses of the other women. She was beautiful, with a natural beauty that owed nothing at all to the artificiality of the geisha tradition.

There was, however, a deference in her manner that the girls of New York had not prepared him for. She bowed her head when they were introduced; for a moment he felt like an American monarch. Later he would learn that her deference to men was out of respect for her father who, despite his modern Western sympathies, still believed in certain of the old traditions. One of them being that there was a proper place for women.

But Tanaka did not object when McArdle asked if he might call on Mieko. She spoke English, though not confidently; they had no subject in common other than an interest in each other. So they talked about themselves and, with no distractions, fell in love.

It had never occurred to McArdle that he would want to marry a girl without first having gone to bed with her. When he proposed she smiled. "What do you know about me? Much less than the other women in your life in New York."

"I haven't told you so much about them."

"I can guess. The chorus girls of Broadway seem little different from our geishas."

"It's a resemblance I hadn't noticed," he said, thinking of Apricot and Sunny and Blossom, the American geishas, and the *samurai* such as Dutch Schultz and Legs Diamond and Owney Madden. "I never really knew much about them. I never had conversations with them as I've had with you."

"I was not thinking of conversation." She touched his face gently with her fingers. "I'm a virgin, but not innocent. And sex is a very important part of marriage. My dear mother told me that before she died."

He looked around the room where they sat. He still found Japanese furnishings uncomfortable; his long legs were not meant for sitting on cushions and low stools. There were scrolls and paintings on the wall which Tanaka, with quiet pride, had told him were priceless works by Nõami, Motonobu and Sesson. This was her father's house, her father was in his study, and it was no place to seduce her. Because he was in love for the first time in his life or because of his surroundings, he was not sure which, he became a man whose intentions were strictly honourable. Mieko had that effect on him, something none of his previous girls had attempted or wanted.

"I should like to ask your father for your hand." The old-fashioned phrase did not sound out of place in this room.

She leaned forward and kissed him. "I have already told Father what his answer must be."

They were married six months to the day after they had met.

They rented a house on a quiet street in Shibuya, with trees in the high-walled compound and a section at the rear of the house set aside as a *kara-sansui* garden. McArdle, who had never so much as watered an indoor plant when he had lived in New York, now learned, under the tutelage of their gardener, to rake the sand and white gravel into patterns round the moss-covered rocks, creating images of islands in a white sea or of mountains soaring above a cloud-floor. He read Lafcadio Hearn, improved his Japanese till he was fluent in it, did all that he could to make Mieko feel that he was at home. His one exception was to buy several comfortable chairs in which he could relax his legs and spine into positions they had become accustomed to.

Each day during spring and summer he went to the ball park and put the Athletics through their paces. He towered above the players like a coach above a junior high school team. As manager-coach he had several assistants; but he was not left much free time. The owner of the team thought they were paying him well; they expected full value for their money. Everyone in Japan, it seemed, was working at full pace and to a purpose. Though the purpose was never publicly stated.

His first attempts at espionage were bumbling ones and he was fortunate to escape detection. He paid visits to the neighbourhood of various shipyards, surreptitiously took photographs that, to his inexpert eye, were virtually useless. But he sent them off anyhow, through his contact, the naval attaché at the embassy. They never met at the embassy; after his initial introduction there, when he had met Mieko, he went only once again, to the Fourth of July celebration. He and Kister, the attaché, met instead in various parks and temples where Western tourists, few though they were, were not out of place. They did not confine their meetings to Tokyo; Kister sometimes followed the Athletics as they moved on their schedule around the country. Mieko did not accompany McArdle on the out-of-town games and, subject to the calls of the team and its owners, he was free to meet Kister wherever the latter suggested.

Occasionally they met in the Tokyo Club, where the Europeans, especially the journalists, congregated each evening in the bar. It was at the club that McArdle met Johnson, an

American freelance journalist. They were no more than occasional drinking companions and then only for half an hour or so each time; McArdle would go home to the waiting Mieko, happy to do so, and Johnson would go out looking for girls at his favourite bar, Das Rheingold. It was Kister who warned him against Johnson.

"I'd stay away from him, Con." Kister had been turned out whole, without a blemish, from the Annapolis mould; even out of uniform he looked ready for a full-dress inspection. He was lean, crew-cut, crisp as a starched collar. "He's not American, he's German. We don't know what he's up to, but if the *kempei* are on to him they might start watching you."

From then on McArdle stayed away from the Tokyo Club and Johnson. It was no sacrifice; he was happy to spend all his non-working hours with Mieko. Their relationship was almost perfect; each found in the other the peace and comfort that is the basis of a happy marriage. Sex was an important part of it, but not all; and McArdle learned that it could be an expression of love and not just a rutting exercise. Apricot Bloom and the geishas of Broadway receded into dim memory.

Then, without telling her, he began to wonder how Mieko would fare when he took her back to the States. Because by now he knew that they would have to return to America in the next year or two. Japan, he was convinced, and he did not tell this to Mieko, was headed for war. The Japanese were building too many ships, too many planes, for a nation intent only on her own defence. The Strike-North and Strike-South factions were openly in conflict. Reports of their opposition to each other did not appear in *Asahi* or the other newspapers, but Kister had told McArdle that in diplomatic circles the aims and arguments of the opposing sides were common gossip. For the first time McArdle began to worry about Mieko's future. America, land of the free, had never really welcomed Orientals into its melting pot.

In the winter of 1936–7 he took her home to Rochester to meet his father and the rest of the family. Liam and Margaret had come up from Washington and for the first time since the death of their mother the whole family was together for Christmas. The house on East Avenue was bright with lights, banter and goodwill. The family, contrary to Con's expectations, had welcomed Mieko with genuine warmth.

But after Christmas dinner Liam had taken Con aside into their father's study. Stuffed with turkey and plum pudding, wrapped in cigar smoke, the glass of port beside him gleaming like an altar lamp in the glow from the desk light, Liam said, "There's going to be war, you know. Not soon but eventually."

"I'm glad you agree. I'd hate to think all my reports were being ignored."

"You've changed. You're more – *serious*. Concerned. I suppose you still have an interest in baseball, though?"

"It's a living. And it gives me a reason for staying on in Japan. But I have only a two-year contract."

"What will you do when it is up? Come back here? I could find you a job in Washington, if you wanted it. Except – " He sipped his port. From the living-room downstairs, where the rest of the family was gathered about the radio, there came the voice of Kate Smith singing a Christmas hymn.

"Except for Mieko?" Goodwill towards all men: except possible future enemies. "No, I don't think I'd like Washington. I'll find something to do in New York."

"It's a pity we couldn't use you in Washington. You have a very good analytical mind. All those years in baseball didn't entirely dull your intellect."

"It was keeping up with all those statistics. Have you any instructions for me when I get back to Japan?"

"No, just keep up the good work. I had dinner with the President last month. He asked how you were doing."

"As a spy?"

"No, he doesn't know about that. As a baseball manager. I was surprised to find he'd been a fan of yours. Said you threw a very intelligent pitch, whatever that means."

"It's a spitball you've given some thought to."

He and Mieko went back to Japan after two months' travelling by car round the States. She loved America, but hated New York; so he did not tell her that that was where he wanted them to live when he brought her to America. She had not demurred when he had told her he could not live permanently in Japan, that when his contract with the Athletics was finished he would have to return to his own country to make a living. She was content to be wherever he wanted to be.

They had been back in Japan a month when she told him she was pregnant. It was the first day of spring training; in the garden outside the first blossoms hung like faint pink explosions in the air. He kissed her, held her to him.

"Take care. I'll tell Asako to keep an eye on you." Asako was their cook-housekeeper, an elderly woman who had once been Mieko's nurse.

"Don't fuss. The doctor has told me I am built for having babies. You have always liked my hips."

But over the next couple of weeks he began to worry about taking Mieko and their child back to the States. They might have to settle in California, where there were a lot of Japanese; Mieko and their Eurasian child might not be so conspicuous there. On a Friday night he stopped in at the Tokyo Club, looking for Kister. The naval attaché was not there, but Johnson, looking a little the worse for drink, was sitting at the bar.

"My dear friend the baseballer. I'm surprised to see you here, my friend. I thought you would be at home consoling your wife."

"My wife?" McArdle, about to order a Scotch, waved the bartender away. "What about her?"

"You don't know? Ah, out there at the stadium you miss so much of what goes on. They took your wife in for questioning this afternoon. She and your cook."

"*They?* Who?"

"The *kempei*, everybody's friend, the secret police. Major Yorida is in charge of the investigation, I believe."

McArdle could feel himself trembling, everything in him turning to water. "How do you know all this?"

Johnson tapped his finger along his nose, smiled a drunk's secret smile. But he was not entirely drunk: intelligence still gleamed in his dark eyes. McArdle was sure now that the journalist was not an American and he wondered also if he was a journalist.

"I have contacts, McArdle. A good newspaperman always does. But perhaps I should not be talking to you. Who knows who is spying on us at this very moment?"

McArdle looked around him. It was still early and the bar was less than half-full. There were several Japanese present, but none of them seemed to be paying any attention to him and Johnson.

McArdle left the other man without further word, went out to his car and drove at a reckless pace home to Shibuya. The house was empty; but there was a police guard in the yard. He was in plain clothes, a short burly man who introduced himself as Lieutenant Fujisawa.

"You will remain here. Your wife will be returned to you in due course."

McArdle, anger mixing with his fear for the safety of Mieko, had to restrain himself from hitting the policeman. "You are mistaken, Lieutenant. I am not staying here while your people are doing God knows what to my wife. I am going to your head-quarters. You can come with me or you can try and stop me and I'll knock your head off!"

Fujisawa evidently did not carry a gun. He looked McArdle up and down, decided he was out-weighed, then bowed his head. "As you wish."

He sat impassive beside McArdle as the latter drove reck-lessly again through the dusk-gloomed streets to the Secret Police Headquarters just outside the north-east moat of the Imperial Palace. Once, when they were pulled up by traffic, Fujisawa said, "You have not asked directions. You are well informed on our whereabouts."

McArdle knew he might have made a mistake. But with straight-faced mockery he said, "Your headquarters was once pointed out to me when I took a guided tour. The gardens, the temples and other points of interest. Your headquarters was one of the points of interest."

It was almost dark when they reached the building. A guard stopped them at the front door when he saw McArdle, but Fujisawa waved him aside and they passed on into the main lobby, then down a corridor. The place looked so ordinary; McArdle was not sure what he had expected. Dungeons per-haps, and the sound of screams? But this looked no different from all the other institutions of bureaucracy that were scat-tered all over Tokyo.

McArdle was taken into a room and Fujisawa left him, closing the door. In five minutes, minutes that seemed to stretch interminably in McArdle's frantic mind, the door opened and a tall thin man, almost as tall as McArdle himself, came in. He wore a uniform with no insignia but his badges of rank.

"I am Major Yorida. I have some distressing news." It struck McArdle that neither Fujisawa nor this man had bothered to ask him if he spoke Japanese; they took it for granted that he would understand them. "Your wife, unfortunately, is dead."

Chapter Six

I

In the morning Mullane saw to the organization of the camp before he left for the climb up to the cargo cult village. Vokes, told to be as quick as possible, set off to walk back to the main supply dump, taking Mariba and eleven carriers with him. Mullane kept back Silas and three others to accompany himself. Buka, Yali, still nursing his broken arm, and the two young mission boys were to remain in camp with Ruth, Scheer and General Nara.

Mullane went to see Nara, sat down on the ground beside the Japanese who was now propped up in the rough bed that had been made for him. Ruth had given him a further transfusion during the night; he still looked pale and drawn, almost fragile. Someone had put his gold watch on his remaining wrist; the gold band was too big and it dangled like a heavy bangle on the heel of his hand. Mullane noticed that the watch had stopped, but if Nara no longer cared about time he could not be blamed.

"I'm leaving you in Miss Riddle's tender care, General. She has my permission to shoot you if you try to escape."

Nara looked at Ruth, who sat on a kerosene tin at the foot of his bed. "If I had the strength to get up from here, Miss Riddle, I'd give you every opportunity to do just that."

"I may turn out to be a bad shot, General. I might only wound you instead of killing you. Then you'd be even more uncomfortable than you are now."

Nara turned back to Mullane. "Why don't you give the gun to the Bishop? Germans understand the honour in suicide."

Mullane ignored the suggestion. "How's your arm?"

Nara shrugged the shoulder above his stump, winced a little. His army career was finished, indeed his whole life; it did not

149

matter that they had cut off his saluting arm. He thought sadly of his wife: they had also cut off his loving hand. During the night, fully conscious at last, he had thought of ripping out the stitches and hoping that he would have bled to death before they found him in the morning. But it seemed an ignoble way to commit suicide; what was worse, he really did not want to die by his own hand. He would prefer to be murdered.

"It is going to be all right," said Ruth. "The Bishop did an excellent job."

"Console yourself, General." Mullane stood up. "When you Japanese have lost the war, there'll be others to blame more than you."

"Your optimism, Mr Mullane, is admirable but foolish."

But he wondered at the brittle condition of his own optimism. Though he had not belonged to *Hokushin-pa*, the Strike-North faction, he had supported its aims: after all, Russia was the real enemy of the future. But when *Nampo-ha*, the Strike-South group, had prevailed, he, being a good soldier, had done his best in that direction. There was merit to their objective of expansion into South-east Asia and the East Indies. Those lands were rich in rubber, timber and oil and they offered room for colonists from the overcrowded homeland; and they were all dominated by the Western imperialists, who had no rightful place in the East. Everything had gone well as far as the East Indies; but there, he felt, they should have stopped. He was not convinced that there was much to be gained by the conquest of the South Pacific islands and Australia. The Imperial forces were being extended too far, they were like a *kendo* expert trying to hold his staff with his fingertips. And what would they do with all the Australians if they should be fortunate enough to take that continent? How did one tame seven-and-a-half million barbarians?

"If you were at West Point, General, you must have learned about us Americans. Optimism is as important to us as pasteurized milk. Are you an optimist, Miss Riddle?"

"I'd better be," said Ruth. "Considering my companions."

As she and Mullane left the hut she said, "You be careful of that leg. It's nowhere near as good as you're trying to make out."

"I appreciate your concern for me – "

"I mean it, Con."

"I know you do." He put a hand on her shoulder and squeezed it; it was almost as if he had kissed her and she blinked at the sudden intimacy. "I'll take care, Ruth. You do the same."

Then he called to Silas and the three other carriers and left the camp. He did not force the pace as they climbed, intent on favouring his leg. It was still stiff and sore and there was an irritating itch under the bandage and also under the tape Ruth had placed over the wound below his ribs; but worse afflictions might be ahead in the weeks to come. So far he had kept his malaria in check; he had not had dysentery; he had suffered no tropical ulcers. And he still had both arms, more than Nara had.

They climbed for an hour before they came to the vegetable gardens outside the village. Women, naked but for a pad of woven grass worn as a pubic covering, were at work among the taro, yam and native cabbage plantings. They looked up as Mullane and his carriers stepped out of the jungle into the cleared area; then they rushed together in silent terror and stood in a bunch clutching each other tightly. Mullane told Silas to tell them not to be afraid, then led his party on down the track and into the village.

It lay in a hollow that had been cleared of trees. Mullane knew it must have been clearly visible from the air, but no one had bothered to mark it on any of the maps he had been given; it was not and never would be a military target and there was no point in wasting ink on it. But the men who suddenly appeared at the edge of the village were martial enough; Mullane found himself facing a battery of spears. He called a halt to Silas and the other carriers, held up his hands in what he hoped would be taken as a gesture of peace. For all his languages he was still illiterate and dumb in certain areas of communication. He held the Thompson gun in one hand, but he was certain that these natives would not know what it was or what it could do. Unless Kutari, with his magic machine, had shown them gangster movies. He could only hope that Edward G. Robinson and Jack La Rue had not got here first.

151

"Tell them we come in peace, Silas."

Silas cleared his throat nervously, spoke in dialect. The villagers did not lower their spears, just continued to look threatening. Then behind them Mullane saw Kutari. He came down the cleared strip between the two lines of huts, barefoot but dressed in white shirt and shorts, his thick lime-bleached hair bright in the sun; he came towards Mullane with an arrogant dignity and the American was reminded of certain upstart colonial administrators he had met, small kings in tiny domains. The spear-carriers parted like a Praetorian Guard and Kutari stepped through.

"Sir? What brings you here?"

I've had an attack of fever, Mullane thought, this is an hallucination. I've heard this voice before, but where? "Kutari, I am Mullane. From Kiogo."

"I know it. I worked there when I was a very young man. Won't you come into my village?" He said something in dialect and the villagers lowered their spears.

Mullane followed Kutari up between the huts to a larger hut, more like a house, built on stilts and facing down towards the rest of the village. The two men went up the rickety steps to the narrow veranda and Kutari gestured to Mullane to sit down. The American lowered himself into the canvas chair, re-inforced with strips of bamboo, that threatened to collapse at any moment. The villagers congregated around the foot of the steps, Silas and the three carriers, all apprehensive, pushed to the front. Mullane, images now tumbling into his mind like a movie montage, recognized the scene. Kutari was playing a role, he was the *kiap*, the administrator, of this community.

The cult leader shouted an order and two women brought some wild oranges split into quarters. "I am sorry I cannot offer you gin-and-bitters, Mr Mullane."

The voice, cultured and so pleasant on the ear, was farcical coming out of the betel-stained mouth. "You speak English very well, Kutari. Where did you learn it?"

"I was seven years in Brisbane with my late master, Mr Benjamin. He liked moving pictures very much and he used to take me with him, twice a week, to see them. He would joke that he was in love with Miss Greta Garbo, but I was not to

152

tell Mrs Benjamin. I also have my own moving pictures with talkies. Mr Ronald Colman's *A Tale of Two Cities*."

Mullane knew that anything was possible in this part of the world. But he had never expected to be sitting on a veranda in a wild mountain village listening to a henna-haired brown man talking to him with the voice of Ronald Colman. "Do you run your movie very often?"

"Every night, Mr Mullane. My people love it. It is very old, of course, and is in pieces. Would you know how to fix it, Mr Mullane?"

He could imagine how the film must be: split and scratched, the reels probably broken into dozens of strips. If Kutari had to run the film every night . . . "Is that how you keep your hold on your people?"

The brown man's affable face abruptly changed, hardened into suspicion and threat. He stared at Mullane, then he barked an order at the crowd gathered below the veranda. The villagers looked hurt at being dismissed; but they broke up and drifted back towards their huts. They stood there, the men still holding their spears, the women and children huddled together in the doorways of the huts. Silas and the three carriers looked at Mullane.

"Get the things out, Silas." They had brought a bag of salt, half a dozen knives and some beads and other trinkets with them for trading. Mullane also had money in his pocket, but he did not want to waste it here where all trade might be in barter. "But keep an eye on them."

"What have you come to trade?" Kutari asked.

"That's all the magic you have, is it? Your talking film?"

"I take care of my people." Kutari sat tensed in his chair, a king afraid of being deposed. He carried no weapon, but Mullane knew that a call from him would bring the villagers back with their spears. He, with his Thompson, might manage to escape, but Silas and the carriers might be killed before he could help them. "I have taught them things I learned in Brisbane. Our gardens are better than other people's gardens. And soon the aeroplanes that fly in the sky will bring things for my people. My people believe in me."

"It is a far, far better thing that I do . . ."

153

Kutari looked almost affable again for the moment. "You have seen Mr Ronald Colman's moving picture?"

"No, but I've read Mr Charles Dickens."

Kutari added a frown to all the other lines in his rugged face. "I do not know Mr Charles Dickens."

So much for writers: here on a jungle mountain-top a movie star was the culture hero. "The aeroplanes, Kutari, are going to bring your people nothing. You know that as well as I do. If they bring anything it will only be bombs."

The cult leader looked blank: he knew about tumbrils and the guillotine but he knew nothing about bombers and bombs. He said stubbornly, "The aeroplanes will bring the goods. The white men do not own the world."

Ah, Ronald Colman, if you could only hear the arguments being put in your voice. "The yellow men down on the coast say that, too. What happens if they win the war?"

"War? We have no war."

Mullane shifted carefully in his chair, easing his behind on the bamboo rods. He heard a tearing sound behind him, felt the canvas strip across the back give way. He had noticed that Kutari also sat carefully in his chair; he had also remarked that the brown man's white shirt and shorts, though clean, were threadbare, ready to split and fall off their wearer if he expanded a muscle. Mullane guessed he must have donned the shirt and shorts as soon as he had got word that a white stranger was coming into his village.

"There is a war between the yellow men and the white men." The isolation of this mountain village was untouched; all at once he envied them their ignorance. "Haven't your people been down to the sea and come back to tell you of the men there?"

"My people do not leave the village."

"You mean you don't allow them to leave here?"

"They do not want to leave." The cultured English voice was roughening.

Mullane saw that he had to be more direct. He eased himself out of the chair, heard the canvas tear again. "Kutari, I want to buy your engine."

Kutari was more adept at getting out of a rotting canvas chair; there was no tearing sound as he stood up. He was not a

154

tall man; he stretched himself in an effort to look eye to eye with the American. But his eyes came only to the level of Mullane's breast pocket. His face hardened into belligerence again, but there was also a nervousness to him now.

"My engine is not for buying." Ronald Colman was slipping away, a dying echo. "You better go quick, Mr Mullane. My people do not like white men."

"Is that something else you've taught them? If your people don't leave the viilage, what would they know about white men? I want that engine, Kutari." Christ, he thought, I'm being just the sort of white bastard these people could learn to hate. Whom Kutari, for reasons of his own, had already learned to hate. "I'll give you a bag of salt and six knives for it. And some beads."

"No. The engine is no good any more. It will work again when the aeroplane brings the water in tins."

"You mean you have no gasoline?" Mullane restrained the desire to laugh. He did not ask where Kutari had got the gasoline in the past; possibly he had gone to Rabaul, but dared not go there now the Japanese were in occupation. "Kutari, when did you last show your moving pictures?"

"You go quick or I call my people!" Ronald Colman had faded away completely; the voice was rough with all its primitive hatred. "They believe me – "

Mullane went down the steps, looked around. He saw a bundle of wild sugarcane stacked against one of the stilts that held up the veranda. He took aim with the Thompson, fired a short burst. The sugarcane bundle burst apart, splinters flew off the veranda stilt. There was a yell of terror from the villagers and they ran away down to the end of the village, where they huddled in a tight, fear-stricken bunch. Mullane looked up at Kutari.

"Your people don't know what this is. But you have seen a gun before. You know it can kill a man as well as a pig or a bird."

"Kill me and my people will kill you."

Mullane had to admire the villain's courage. Or maybe he was not a villain at all. Only God knew what laws Kutari ruled by in his domain, but the villagers looked none the worse for

155

them. Leaders who made suckers of the natives were not necessarily villains. Not to anyone who had once said New York was his favourite city, who had dined with Jimmy Walker and laughed at the Mayor's wisecracks and turned a deaf ear to all the rumours of His Honour's peccadilloes.

"I shan't kill you, Kutari. Your engine is no good and you know the aeroplanes won't bring the water in tins. Let me see it." The brown man shook his head and Mullane brought his gun up. "Let me see it, Kutari! I shan't kill you, but I shall shoot your leg off. People never believe in a one-legged king." That sounded like an Irish argument.

Kutari hesitated, then he nodded. Mullane went back up the steps and followed him into the house. Here, behind the thatched walls, there was no attempt to ape the white administrator. This was a native's hut: the bed mat, the smooth log-pillow, the bow and arrows in a corner, the flat heap of stones in the centre of the room that was the fireplace beneath the chimney-hole in the roof. A dance mask hung on one wall, a devil's head in bark; beside it were some possum skins. Only in one corner was the white man's magic: a rusted movie projector, two corroded batteries, a battered amplifier, a grey-white sheet wrapped round two poles, several rusted film cans. And the petrol engine.

Mullane had his own arrogance. He brushed past Kutari, as if this were not the latter's house, and inspected the engine. As far as he could see it was still functional; all that was missing was the gasoline to drive it. Then he looked at the projector, the sound-equipment and the batteries. The latter were useless; and several parts of the projector would never work again. Kutari's magic was finished.

Mullane picked up the cans of film. There were five reels of *A Tale of Two Cities*; from what he remembered there were usually eight reels in a full-length movie. He wondered what parts of the life of Sidney Carton had been lost; perhaps the villagers thought the story had a happy ending. There were two other cans of film: Fox Movietone News and a short from the *Crime Does Not Pay* series. Maybe the villagers had learned something from the latter; or maybe they had thought it was a comedy and laughed their heads off. He looked at the date on the newsreel can: 17 July 1939. The world had still been at peace and only God would remember what hopes and promises had existed then.

"Kutari, all this is no good. Finished. You know that as well as I do."

"The aeroplanes will come – " He sounded pathetic now, a man of promises who looked for his own salvation.

"No, Kutari, they won't come. Sell me the machine. I'll give you the bag of salt and the knives."

"It is not enough. I could have my people kill you and I would take the salt and knives."

"I have this – " Mullane held up the Thompson; but he knew he could never use it against men armed with just spears and bows and arrows. Reluctantly he took the roll of notes from his pocket; he had hoped he would not have to offer money. "I'll give you ten pounds."

Kutari snorted. "It is too little. Mr Benjamin gave me much more than that when he died in Brisbane." So that was how the movie projector and the rest of the equipment had been bought; Mullane cursed the philanthropic Mr Benjamin. "One hundred pounds and you can have the engine."

Mullane swore under his breath. A little civilization was a dangerous thing: Kutari had learned enough to be a damned nuisance. Against all his natural feeling Mullane was thinking like so many of the Islanders he despised. He despised himself; but he went ahead with his hypocrisy. He felt still worse that the money he would pay to Kutari would be worth even less than the salt and the knives. The Australian money was valueless until and if the Japanese were driven out of this region.

"I have only – " He counted the money quickly; he had stuffed the rubber-banded roll into his pocket without looking at it. "Seventy pounds. You can have that and the salt and the knives. Take it or – " He held up the Thompson. "Or I take the engine and pay you nothing."

Kutari held out his hand, took the money, laboriously counted it like a child in first grade. "Seventy, seventy-one – there is too much." He handed back a one-pound note, making a display of his magnanimity and Mullane's poor arithmetic.

Ronald Colman came back: "I am an honest man, Mr Mullane. You may have the engine."

Five minutes later, with the engine slung on poles and carried by Silas and the other three carriers, Mullane was ready to leave. There was a muttering among the villagers as they saw the engine being carried away; the sunlight shone on nervous spear-tips. Mullane wondered what argument Kutari would use to placate them, what other magic he would call on. Jesus, he thought, I've killed him just as effectively as if I'd gunned him down with bullets.

"Don't promise them too much, Kutari."

He looked around at the short, muscular tribesmen, their healthy-looking women, the plump children. Kutari might be a scoundrel, but, unlike so many of the cult leaders, he had fed his people on more than just promises. The village and the gardens were as well kept as any Mullane had seen down on the coast in Administration days. Kutari might see himself as king, chief, District Commissioner: whatever image he had of himself he had not neglected his people. He had promised them gifts from heaven, but in the meantime he had seen that they got the best they could from the earth around them.

"They believe me, Mr Mullane. The aeroplanes will come some day," said Ronald Colman's voice.

He believes it himself; or tries to. "Good luck, Kutari. Just hope that the men down by the sea do not get here first."

At the end of the gardens, before he entered the forest again, Mullane looked back. Kutari stood among the closed crowd of his people, his bright henna-coloured hair shining in the sun above them like a smuggler's false beacon.

II

By the time he got back to camp Mullane's leg was sore and bleeding again. He sat down on his camp stretcher and Ruth came into the hut to attend to him. He had taken off his trousers and was sitting in his shirt, unwrapping the bandage.

"I saw the way you were limping when you came into camp."

"We can't go on meeting like this. Me without my pants."

"You're safe. I took a double dose of bromide."

He was enjoying the sexual banter, but he couldn't see that it would lead anywhere. He looked down at his leg. "What do you think?"

"It could be better. Stay off your leg today."

"I'll do that tomorrow," he promised. "I've got to get that engine working. I want to go on the air this evening. Did you have any trouble with the General?"

She shook her head. "The Bishop has been with him all day. They're like old friends now."

"Both ends of the Axis – that's what I've been afraid of. Do you want to keep that pistol?"

"Do you trust me with it?"

He got to his feet, began to pull on his trousers. "I trust you in a situation like this. Why not with a gun?"

"Mr Mullane, you have all the charm I've dreamed about in a man."

"My pleasure, Miss Riddle."

While he worked on the engine he thought about Ruth. Twice he found himself looking along the ridge towards where she sat reading a book in the afternoon sun. It was not only that she attracted him physically; there was a warmth to her under her cool competence. She in no way resembled Mieko, but he was beginning to feel the same ease with her as he had felt with his late wife. Or perhaps it was just that she was the first woman since Mieko with whom he had allowed himself to be in close contact. But, he chided himself, this was no place even to be thinking of any sort of alliance, no matter how brief. He shifted his position, turning his back on her, and worked on the rust-glued parts of the old engine.

The sun had gone down and dusk was taking the colour from the jungle and the sea before he finished working on the engine. Then he called to Buka to bring him some petrol. Ruth and the Bishop came to watch as he primed the engine, spun the fly-wheel with a length of string and hoped for the best. Nothing happened.

"A few prayers, Bishop. Don't just stand there."

Scheer took a safety-pin from his cassock, pricked the

carburettor, then stood back. "A little mechanical aptitude is often as good as a prayer, Mr Mullane. God helps those who help themselves."

"You see?" Mullane said to Ruth. "That's how they produced the Zeppelin and the Daimler-Benz, with a safety-pin."

He spun the wheel again, there was a cough, then the engine roared into life. It shivered and shuddered on its base; but it worked. Everyone stood round it and admired it as if it were a new-born baby. In the last of the fading light Mullane connected it to the charger and set up the batteries. Then they all went to supper while the engine hummed away in the darkness, sometimes missing a beat but never stopping.

Mullane was about to sit down beside Ruth when he saw Scheer, with two plates, going into the hut where Nara still lay on his rough bed. Mullane excused himself from Ruth and followed the German into the hut.

"You don't mind if I join you, gentlemen?"

In the glow of the candle stuck in an empty bully-beef can he saw Scheer and Nara exchange glances. Careful still of his leg, he lowered himself on to the small log that Scheer had obviously intended as his own seat. The German looked around, then sat down on the ground. The tableau was exactly as Mullane wanted it, with the other two having to look up at him when he spoke.

"I have to watch you two gentlemen," he said amiably. "After all, you are the enemy."

The candlelight flickered on the walls of the hut. Nara threw only a small shadow; the hulking shadow of Mullane loomed over him. The three men and their dark images crowded the tiny hut, creating an intimacy that none of them really felt. Nara went on eating the rice and shredded meat that Ruth had made for him; she had told Mullane that in his weakened condition the Japanese should not be forced to eat a diet he wasn't accustomed to. Mullane and Scheer were eating bully-beef stew and tinned vegetables. Scheer once stopped to hold the Japanese's plate as Nara, hampered by having only one hand, awkwardly scooped up the food with his spoon.

Mullane watched the two men with what seemed on the surface to be nothing more than good humour. But he was alert to any silent rapport between them; and both Nara and Scheer were aware of it. Tension stretched between the three of them like binding cables that threatened to snap.

Scheer had been cautious in his approach to Nara during the day. The isolation in this part of the world had eroded the sophistication he had once felt about world affairs; he now found it hard to believe that Germany and Japan, enemies in the Great War, were allies in this one. He still thought of the 1914–18 conflict as *his* war; he had that in common with Vokes' father, though it would never have occurred to him to discuss it with Vokes. Those years had been painful, especially the defeat at the end of them. He did not really understand this war and the alliances, some of them already broken, that had been made in its name. He had not gone home in 1936 when he had been offered leave; if he had, perhaps he might have been able to identify himself with what the Nazis were aiming for. His only identity, other than as a man of the Church, was as a German. And, when he had first started to talk to Nara this morning, he had not been confident that that would be enough to interest the Japanese.

Nara, for his part, was totally committed to the war. He was a professional soldier whose purpose was to fight; his only doubt was whether his country had chosen to fight the right enemy. He would have preferred that America had not been brought into the war; that country had been caught napping in its preparations but he had no illusions about its potential to recover. If the war in the Pacific was to be won it had to be won quickly, within the next few weeks if possible. He ached with another pain, that he had not managed to get to Rabaul and would miss out on the final assault on Guadalcanal.

Sometimes a side of him, like an unwelcome cousin, tried to intrude, suggesting scruples that puzzled his military character. He had been disturbed today to find himself listening attentively and with growing sympathy to the German who had his own doubts. He had decided that he must escape from this environment before the worms of heresy ate him hollow. A major worry was that the priest wanted to go with him and he had no faith in Scheer's ability to sneak out of the camp undetected; the priest had an open honesty about him, even of his doubts, that promised to make him awkward in any attempt to escape. Yet, failing all else, Nara knew he would need the support of the German in any march down to the coast.

"I'm going on the air tonight to ask them again to come in and take you off my hands," Mullane said.

Scheer looked at Nara, who remained silent. Then the German said, "Anything would be better than this limbo."

"Don't denigrate limbo, Bishop. Isn't it one of the havens of the Church? I don't see either of you as lost souls. You'll survive, both of you. Maybe you'll be grateful to me one day for getting you out of the war."

"Not when we win it, Mr Mullane." Scheer was surprised by his own words; he had been infected by Nara's apparent confidence.

"You're starting to think better of Hitler?"

He wasn't prepared to go that far. "I know what my countrymen are capable of. Our generals have always been the best."

"Did your father tell you that? Maybe General Nara would disagree with you."

Nara recognized that the American was trying to divide him and the Bishop: good military tactics. But it wouldn't work, even though he had little respect for the Germans. Any generals who had allowed themselves to be talked into attacking the Russians, creating another front on their own rear, were not to be admired.

"We can't really be judged, Mr Mullane, till the war is over. Then we professionals will judge each other."

"But never let the poor guys in the trenches know, eh?" Mullane stood up, looked at Scheer. "Stick to religion, Bishop. There's a little less callousness there than among the military."

He went out of the hut and Nara said, "Give me liberty or give me death . . . It never occurs to Americans that other nationalities might believe in that principle."

"I gave up thoughts of dying for my country twenty-five years ago," said the Bishop. "My patriotism is different from yours, General."

"You are fortunate," said the General and was glad he was far from any informers.

By nine o'clock the batteries were charged. Mullane set up

the radio, had young Luke run up a tree and hang out the aerial; then he started tapping on the Morse key. Moresby answered at once, almost cutting in on him, as if the operator there had been waiting on the edge of his seat for some signal. Mullane told them only that he had been unable to transmit earlier because of battery trouble; they did not have to be informed of Vokes' carelessness. Then Townsville, through Moresby, asked the question he had been expecting.

Are you on way to King's Cross?

There was one advantage to coding and decoding messages: it gave you time to think about lying. He wasn't on his way to Rabaul; but he was certainly closer to it than he had been when he had last been on the air: *Yes. But still saddled with Top Jockey and other baggage. Are we expected to take them into King's Cross? Would appreciate little contribution your end.*

He wondered how his sarcasm would go down in Townsville. The reply came back: *Are still seeking evacuation means. Expected means now delayed by engine trouble.*

That meant a submarine or Catalina had been promised, at least. But how long before it would arrive? He uttered an obscenity and behind him Ruth said, "I came at the wrong time. Sorry."

He apologized, handed her the flashlight. "Hold this, please. They never allow any leeway in a code for four-letter words."

The Morse key was a good brake on one's temper and language. *GHQ better accept quid pro quo. Cannot enter King's Cross carrying Top Jockey. Put that in GOC's corncob.*

There was silence for a long time; it was impossible to tell whether it was due to shock or otherwise. Ruth switched off the flashlight and the two of them sat in the darkness of the hut. She was pleased that Mullane had not asked her what she was doing here, had taken her coming for granted.

He was glad of her company. He rubbed citronella on his face and hands, a deterrent to romance as well as mosquitoes. But he said, "I'm glad you came along with us."

"I'm glad I let you persuade me."

He smiled, put out his hand, then changed its direction as the key began to stutter again. Ruth, who had seen his hand coming towards her, relaxed again; she had not been afraid of his touch but had wondered what would follow. She switched on the torch, relieved and yet irritated by Moresby's interruption.

Your quid pro quo accepted. Will have evacuation effected soon as possible. Believe corncob full other bulldust.

He laughed aloud at the final sentence; that would be an addendum not written on any official message form. He had no idea what sort of reception General MacArthur was getting from the Australians, but it seemed that someone in Moresby or Townsville was not impressed by the Supreme Commander.

"So we just sit and wait again?" Ruth said.

He repacked the radio, went outside, hauled down the aerial, came back into the hut. Ruth had not moved, still sat on his camp stretcher.

He paused, then took the flashlight from her and snapped it off. He pulled her to her feet. They stood close together in the darkness, each of them alertly aware of the other's body. It seemed a long moment before he pulled her into him and kissed her. It was years since he had felt a woman against him: the softness of the breasts, the curve of the belly, the buttocks against his hands. She kissed him without restraint and each could feel the trembling in the other.

Then he said reluctantly, "I don't think we'd better."

She held his face in her hands but made no move. "You're probably right."

They both spoke matter-of-factly, like two people debating whether it was the right time to go shopping. Each of them was surprised at their own control. But knew it was necessary.

He felt something pressing into him, remembered an old Mae West line: "Is that your gun or are you just glad to see me?"

"I should be asking you that." She knew the joke; he wondered what man had told it to her and felt a spasm of jealousy. "I think I'd better go back to my hut."

"I shan't walk you home. Just in case . . ." He lifted her hand and kissed her knuckles; it was the sort of gentle intimacy she had never experienced with any other man. "I'm sorry, Ruth. Some other time, some other place, maybe."

"Maybe. Good night."

In the morning she came along to see him. He was washing himself, stripped to the waist, in the canvas basin Silas had brought him. "I had a bad night," she said.

"Me, too." He splashed water into his face.

"I think we'd better not even shake hands from now on."

He dried his face, combed his beard and hair. "I was going to ask if you'd trim my beard and give me a haircut. What about my leg and my ribs? Do I do my own dressings from now on?"

"I can do that for you. But – " She kept looking around, not wanting to look him directly in the eye. "If we start anything, Con, I'm not interested in one-night flings."

"I think I better tell you something," he said carefully. "I hope to get word in tonight on when you and the General and the Bishop can be taken off."

She had known that eventually she would have to be evacuated; and had not minded. But now, somehow, it was as if he personally had told her he did not want her around. And that hurt, now that she was falling in love with him.

In love: it was something she had lain awake all night pondering: "What if I refuse to?"

"You mightn't have any say in it."

"I could go part of the way to Rabaul with you. I could stay with the wireless while you and Frank go in – "

"No!"

Then he heard Silas shout and he hurried out of the hut. A small dark cloud of planes was heading south. Mullane adjusted his glasses, started to count. The planes were too far away for him to hear the sound of their engines; but their silent passage south somehow made them more sinister and threatening. He finished counting them: 64 bombers, more than he had ever seen before.

He went back into the hut, sent out the warning in clear; information like this did not have to be kept from the Japanese. But Moresby came back in code: *Number of raids and planes increasing. Our photo recce unable detect source extra squadrons. Appreciate information this point when you in King's Cross.*

Will do, he replied. Then he sat back and looked at Ruth

standing in the doorway.

"What do you feel when you send out those messages about the bombers?"

"I'm not sure. I don't even know if they're headed where I think they are. I send the same message all the time: *Bombers headed your way*. All I change are the figures. Then I count them when they come back. What's happened in between I can only guess at. But I've never seen a bomb dropped, I don't know how many men it can kill or how much damage it can do. It's the same with the planes that we send over Rabaul. The war's going on in half a dozen places, I suppose thousands of people are dying every day, and I don't know as much as some little old lady sitting in a newsreel theatre in Tulsa, Oklahoma, or some bush town in Australia. It's a hell of a private way of being involved in a war."

"Does that disturb you?"

"Yes. Goddamit, yes!" He stood up quickly, winced as the wound in his leg bit. "I'm beginning to wish I'd gone home right after Pearl Harbor. Maybe with what I knew I should have gone home earlier – "

"What did you know?"

He winced again as he moved; but with a wound of memory as much as from pain in his leg. "I knew Japan was going to war against America. I turned my back on it all and I shouldn't have."

She waited for him to go on, but he brushed by her and went out of the hut. She hesitated, then followed him, hoping he would confide more in her. She wanted to know more (no, *everything*) about him. It struck her that she knew as little about him as he seemed to know about the current events of the war; she wondered if there was some woman somewhere who was the equivalent of the little old lady in the newsreel theatre in wherever-it-was. She wondered what had happened to the Japanese girl who had been his wife.

"Are you going to let me stay with you and Frank?"

He shook his head, said brusquely, "Let's go look at your patient."

She fell back into her role as nurse, led the way back along the ridge. The weather was beautiful, the only good thing

166

about the morning so far. She loved the Tropics, felt at home in the climate and surroundings of these islands; in her heart she wondered if she could ever be really happy away from them. But there had been another climate, of men and women, in which she had never been allowed to feel at home.

Mullane led the way into the hut where Bishop Scheer sat on the log beside the General's bed. Each time he found the two men together now he sensed conspiracy. "How is he, Bishop?"

"The General has remarkable powers of recovery. Another week or two . . ."

In another week or two, if I have my way, he'll be in a POW hospital in Australia. "It's the story of his country, Bishop. They have always recovered quickly from their disasters."

"Including allowing Commodore Perry to have his way," said Nara. He had recovered some of his strength during the night. He still felt weak physically, but mentally he was fully alert again. There was the occasional shock when he would look down at the stump of his arm; he had tried keeping his eyes averted, but it had been like trying to shut his eyes against the daylight. He had decided now against suicide, either directly by his own hand or indirectly through another's; he was going to escape and get to Rabaul. He would not be the first one-armed officer to lead an army. "I am beginning to remember you, Mr Mullane. Though that was not your name when you lived in Japan, was it?"

"No, it was McArdle." Mullane felt Ruth's interest quicken, but he did not look at her.

Nara nodded. "He was a famous baseball player, Bishop. He came to my country in – when was it, Mr McArdle? 1934?"

"That was my first visit." He was telling Ruth something about himself; maybe this was the easiest way. "I was with the Exhibition All Stars. Babe Ruth, Jimmy Foxx, Lou Gehrig, Moe Berg – you wouldn't remember them. Or were you a baseball fan? Somehow you don't strike me that way."

"No, I wasn't. But I saw the crowd that welcomed the American baseballers the day they arrived in Tokyo. Over a million people cheering some American sportsmen. I was riding in a car with another officer, one who out-ranked me – I was not a general then. He looked out of the car and I remember his saying, 'Look at them – a million traitors!' The general had a stroke and had to retire from the army. It was too much for him."

"I have never understood this canonization of sportsmen," said the Bishop.

"I went to the Meiji Shrine Stadium," said Nara. "It had never held so many people. When the American, Baby Ruth – "

"*Babe* Ruth."

"Sorry, Mr Mullane. One should always get the names of heroes correct. When he came out to take up his position with the bat the whole stadium stood up. It was as if the Emperor Meiji himself had been resurrected. I cannot remember if they shouted *Banzai* for you, Mr McArdle."

"I didn't play in that first game."

"What does *Banzai* mean?" asked Scheer.

"May you live ten thousand years. Do you wish to live that long, Mr McArdle?'

But Mullane had not heard the last question. He had stiffened, head cocked. Then he was on his feet, at the door and yelling, "Everybody stay out of sight!"

The other two men and Ruth had heard the light single-engine sound of the scout plane. It went over not more than two hundred feet above the ridge. Nara sat up in his bed and Mullane looked back at him.

"So near and yet so far, General. Don't try anything or I'll break your other arm. And you keep still too, Bishop."

The German and the Japanese exchanged glances, then Scheer shrugged. "I was never a hero, General. Not even in *my* war."

"One has to be practical, Bishop." There was no condemnation in Nara's voice; but he ached with the urge to attract the scouting pilot's attention. "Mr McArdle is bigger and stronger than both of us."

"Mullane," said the American. "McArdle would have killed you long ago, General."

The plane came back, lower this time. It ran the length of the ridge just above the tree-tops; leaves came floating down as from a storm. Mullane, standing back away from the door-way of the hut, was still able to see along the ridge. And saw with horror that he had forgotten to take down the aerial from the tree above his own hut. It hung down from the tree like a vine – but the vine went in through the doorway of his hut. He had forgotten it in his preoccupation with Ruth.

He heard the plane climbing up the slope of the mountain, then it banked and was coming back. Something had aroused the pilot's suspicions. Had he seen the aerial? Or was he suspicious because the huts showed no sign of life about them?

Suddenly he yelled again in pidgin: "Silas – get outside! You and the other boys – the kids, too! Wave to the big bird! Quick!"

There was no movement in the camp; the plane was almost upon it. Then Silas and the three other carriers, pushing young Luke and Mark ahead of them, ventured out into an open patch among the trees. The plane swept over, the roar of its engine and the wind of its passing pressing Silas and the others down into a terrified crouch; Luke and Mark were panic-stricken, but Silas held tightly to them. The plane went up in a steep bank, turned to come back once more.

"Wave to him!" Mullane yelled; and prayed to Christ that the pilot would not gun them down as the Zero pilot had done down at Kiogo.

"Shall I go out and wave too?" said Nara, resigned now, able to indulge himself in sardonic amusement. "Or shout *Banzai*?"

Scheer laughed: the Axis partners, if these two were partners, sat there and shared their joke. Mullane, without looking back at them, now only concerned for his natives, said savagely, "Shut up, both of you!"

The plane came back and out in the open patch Silas and the others waved frantically; they looked comical to Mullane, but they were not professional greeters. The plane swung up, returned yet again, waggled its wings, then went on in a wide sweep across the slope of the mountain. Mullane moved out of the doorway, put his binoculars on the plane. He waited for it to swing down to Noku and the Japanese camped there on the beach; that would surely mean it would drop a message to the soldiers to come up and inspect the huts. But it headed west, then swung north and disappeared over a shoulder of the mountain.

He felt the tension run out of him. He leaned against a post, stared up the mountain at the empty sky.

Ruth, close by him, said, "Is it all right to go out now?"

"We're safe. For a while, anyway." He looked back at Scheer and Nara. "Bad luck, General. I think they've given up hope that you're still alive."

"Perhaps." Nara eased himself down in his bed again. "Why did you say you would have killed me if you were still McArdle?"

It surprised Mullane that Nara should pick up the conversation at the point where it had been interrupted; it was not a polite question and not something he would have expected of a man of Nara's obvious breeding. But these were not polite circumstances. He said nothing for a while, then mentally shrugged. What did it all matter now? His small private war, which he had never really declared, had been engulfed in this far greater one. Eventually all the poisonous hatred he had felt over Mieko's death would have to come out of him; the commitment to go into Rabaul had been the beginning of the blood-letting. But even that would be too remote a revenge. Perhaps something would be gained by letting some of it out now, to this enemy. Ruth could hear it, too: he did not think he would ever want to talk about it alone with her.

"On a certain day in 1937, 2 April to be exact, I would have killed every Japanese in uniform that I could lay my hands on. I went to *kempei* headquarters and there I met a Major Yorida." He caught the slightest flicker of interest in Nara's eyes. "You know him?"

"I know him. He was in Manchukuo with General Nakajima. At Nanking."

"They sent him there after he killed my wife."

III

McArdle had leaned against the cold green-painted wall and stared dazedly at Yorida. He knew he had heard every word distinctly; but it was as if he no longer understood the language. He could feel himself trembling and he was afraid he was going to collapse and slide down the wall.

"It was a most unfortunate occurrence." Yorida had a quiet

voice, but there was no soft quality to it; there was no hint of sympathy in it. "We did not expect her to commit suicide."

"How?" McArdle had to force the word, like a gob of phlegm, out of his throat.

"She fell from a window two floors up. She died instantly, that is the only consolation."

McArdle stood stock-still against the wall, gathering his strength. Then he launched himself at Yorida, hands aimed at the high-collared throat. But Yorida stepped neatly, almost gracefully aside. The door swung open and three guards burst in. They grabbed McArdle and flung him face first into a second wall. He struggled to free himself, but abruptly froze when the bayonet was pushed into his back.

"Be still, Mr McArdle," said Yorida. "We do not want a double tragedy."

"We are only on the first floor." McArdle drew a deep breath, struggled for some sort of composure. "It would be difficult to commit suicide out of a window at ground level."

The bayonet was taken away from his back and he was turned round. A chair was pushed towards him and he sank on to it. Yorida gazed at him for a moment, then nodded to the guards, who left the room and closed the door behind them.

"Do not attempt to be foolish again, Mr McArdle." He went round behind a desk and sat down. The room was sparsely furnished, the walls bare of any pictures or notices, a room stripped of any identification, ideal for interrogation. All that was missing, McArdle thought, was the light blazing into one's eyes. "We know what you have been doing."

"Coaching and managing a baseball team. What else do you think I've been doing?"

"You have also been engaged in spying on our military installations."

McArdle made an effort at a laugh; but how could one laugh with one's wife lying dead somewhere in this building? It came out as a hacking sound.

Yorida said, "We have had you under surveillance for some time, Mr McArdle. You and others."

What others? Kister, probably. And Johnson, the German, who said he was an American? Was he a spy, too, or had he

171

been the one who had kept him under surveillance? McArdle racked his memory, but could not remember anyone's watching him. There had been dangerous moments in getting close enough to the installations to take photographs and notes, but he always thought he had been unobserved.

He decided neither to confirm nor deny any of Yorida's accusations. "Why did you bring my – my wife here?"

"Because she must have connived in your activities. She had Western sympathies."

"How do you know that?"

"She married you."

He wanted to laugh; but it came out like a moan of pain this time. "There were other reasons we married, Major. Love was the main reason, but you wouldn't understand that."

Yorida made no comment on the last remark. "Her father is also a Western sympathizer. He has a traitor's respect for your culture."

Christ, thought McArdle, how they can add it all up. "My wife was a Japanese patriot. So is her father." Then it burst out of him: "What did you do to her? She knew nothing – " Too late he realized he had said too much.

"Knew nothing about your spying? We don't believe that."

"I don't believe she would have committed suicide. I want to see her!"

Yorida stood up. To McArdle, a turmoil of emotion now, the man seemed without any emotion at all. He said, "Do you have a wife, Major?"

"Yes." He could have been answering that yes, he had an automobile. "This way."

They went out of the room and down a corridor. Twice men opened doors to come out of side rooms, saw Yorida and McArdle and closed the doors again; as if they did not want to be identified with what went on in this building. With each step McArdle felt the nervousness and fear taking hold of him. He wanted to turn round, run away from what was going to be shown to him.

Mieko lay on a table in a room at the far end of the corridor. The guard on the door saluted Yorida, let them into the room but did not follow them. A sheet covered the body; Yorida pulled it back. Mieko was naked but for the silk knickers she always wore. McArdle retched, but did not turn away, forcing himself to look at the broken bloodied body. Forcing himself to look for evidence.

"What are those weals across her stomach? And those marks on her breasts?"

Yorida pulled the sheet back over the body; his expression had not changed. "That probably happened when she was being brought in. She resisted the arresting officers. They are immaterial. She died after jumping from a window. That will be our report."

McArdle leaned on the end of the table. He put a hand on one of the small feet sticking up under the sheet; then he began to weep, grief washing out anger for the moment. Yorida stood watching, still expressionless. Perhaps, McArdle thought with bitter concession, it was the best face for the job.

"Here is your wife's handbag. Nothing has been taken."

Automatically Mullane took the handbag, opened it. There was very little in it: a handkerchief, still unused; a small compact of powder; a small wallet; some keys. And his lucky silver dollar, which he had given her as a wedding present. *Because I'll never be so lucky again*, he had said.

He tossed the coin in his hand. "A piece of silver, Major. But you are wrong – my wife would not have sold her country for thirty pieces of it."

Yorida looked at the coin, showed some expression for the first time: he frowned. Then Mullane realized he would know nothing of the Biblical story. "A Western legend, Major. I don't believe even my wife knew of it."

Then, his fingers still nervous, he dropped the coin. Yorida picked it up, looked at it, then handed it back. "American. It will be worth nothing some day."

Mullane drew himself together, almost literally: his joints creaked. "I'll take my wife with me. My car is outside."

"That is not possible. The body will be released to you to-morrow. In the meantime you will remain here for questioning."

"I am an American citizen. I want to see someone from our embassy."

"Tomorrow."

"No – tonight! I deny that I'm a spy! I took photographs – I admit that. But they were the sort of photographs any tourist might take – "

Yorida actually smiled this time. "You are not a tourist. You live here – you have a two-year contract with your baseball club. Tourists take photographs of Fujiyama or our cherry trees or our geishas – they do not take photographs of railroad yards and warships and military aerodromes. Whom are you working for? For Lieutenant Kister at your embassy? We know he is an intelligence agent."

"I know Lieutenant Kister casually, but I don't know what he does."

He could taste the lie on his tongue; he could not bear to look down at the sheet-covered corpse on the table. He wondered what Mieko's thoughts about him had been as Yorida and the other interrogators had flung their questions at her, had tortured her in trying to get her to admit to something she knew nothing about. Had she believed what they had said about him? If she had believed them, had she been angry and hurt because he had not confided in her?

"Mr McArdle – " Yorida almost succeeded in putting a note of patience into his voice. "You are finished here in Japan. You can tell us what you have been doing or you can choose not to – it does not matter. Your baseball club will be informed through the Foreign Office that your contract is to be terminated immediately. You will make no public statement – the newspapers will be forbidden to print anything you may say. Your baseball club will issue a statement that, due to the tragic death of your wife from illness, you are returning to America. You will be on a ship by the end of the week. We shall arrange for your ticket."

"You haven't made all these plans on the spur of the moment – "

"No, Mr McArdle. They were made while we were waiting for Lieutenant Fukisawa to bring you here."

He abruptly went out of the room and McArdle was left with the body of his wife. He looked at it and felt his legs trembling again, but there was no chair on which to sink. The room was bare of all furniture but the table; the sheet-covered corpse looked out of place, like some macabre decoration. He moved slowly round it, once touching the sheet but not removing it; he could not bear to look at what they had done to Mieko in his name. He looked at the formless shape, white and small and almost amorphous in the bright white light of the white-walled room (was this the room where they brought all the corpses of witnesses who had nothing to tell?) and thought of what Liam had said: *There'll be no danger*. Not to Liam, sitting back there in the solid building on Constitution Avenue, safe behind his appointments secretary. Suddenly his anger was directed as much at Liam as at Yorida and the *kempei*. What right had Liam and the Navy and the U.S. government had to call on him to do what he had been doing? Spies were the least noble of patriots.

Yorida came back into the room, leaving the door slightly ajar. From somewhere down the corridor there came a laugh, a good-humoured pleasant sound as if someone was enjoying a good joke. Yorida looked over his shoulder, then closed the door.

"You may go, Mr McArdle. Come back in the morning and you may take your wife's body. The *Empress of Japan* sails on Saturday. We shall book passage for you, first class."

McArdle looked at the table, resisted again the temptation to lift the sheet for one last look at Mieko.

"You haven't heard the end of this," he said to Yorida, but he knew the threat was empty, no more than a spiteful jibe because he could think of nothing else to say.

He went out to his car, drove at once to the home of his father-in-law. In his driving mirror he saw the small car following him; the two plainclothes policemen would stay with him till he sailed on the Saturday. A servant opened the door of Tanaka's house and he was shown straight into the main room, the ten-mat room. He stood in his stockinged feet on the *tatami* mats, all at once feeling more foreign than he had ever felt, isolated, completely without anything to hold on to. He had the sudden fantasy that he was floating in space, in a void where he had been stripped of identity, nationality, reason for being.

175

As soon as Tanaka came into the room McArdle knew that the older man knew what had happened. "They took Asako with them when they took Mieko. Then they let Asako go – " The older man's voice faltered. "Asako came here. She was afraid to go home to your house."

McArdle shook his head, not in denial of anything but like a man trying to shake a jumble of thoughts into some sort of pattern. "I'm sorry, sir. They are releasing Mieko's body in the morning."

"Why did they do it? Just because you are a foreigner?"

He had to keep lying: the words were like bitter aloes in his mouth. "They suspect me of being a spy. I told them the charges were ridiculous, but they won't believe me. I have to leave Japan by Saturday."

"Is it true – that you are a spy?"

They were speaking in English: it was so much easier to lie in one's own tongue. "No. But you know what the *kempei* are like. They hate all foreigners, we're all suspect. That's what I'll never forget – that they took Mieko instead of me – "

"Our country has a poison running through it. Only the gods know where it will take us . . ." He put out a thin strong hand. "Stay here in my house till you have to leave on Saturday. You should not go back to your own empty house. We shall bury Mieko together."

They went next morning to collect the body. McArdle did not see Yorida, had no wish to see him; he was afraid that, then and there, he might try to kill him. And that might then have involved Tanaka. He had already brought enough tragedy to the family.

The funeral was quiet, only himself, Tanaka and Asako there as mourners; and the two policemen standing at a distance outside the crematorium. Later he went to the ball park and only the president of the club was there to wish him farewell.

"We shall handle the matter discreetly." Ugaki Osamu owned a publishing empire as well as the main interest in the ball club. He was stout, with a big yellow sun of a face that was forever smiling and a nature that could fire a man at a moment's notice and then next day send him a year's salary as penance;

176

but he had never been known to take a man back once he had fired him. "Nobody but I knows why you have been asked to leave the country. A high official in the Foreign Office has been to see me. Were you a spy, Mr McArdle?"

"No."

"Good. We shall print a small piece in my newspapers regretting your departure. We shall, of course, pay you the rest of your salary."

"There's no need for that – "

"No, we shall honour the contract. It is not being broken by either you or us. Perhaps I should send a bill to the Foreign Office." He smiled, his big face glowing with humour; then the smile abruptly faded and he shook his head. "I should not be joking. Forgive me."

"Would you like me to recommend another manager? I can put out some feelers when I get back to the States – "

"I do not think it would be advisable. You understand?"

Ugaki's face was full of all the shrewdness that had made him what he was. He knows the truth of what I've been doing, McArdle thought. "No, perhaps not."

He went back to the United States, keeping to himself on the ship. Other passengers, American and Japanese, recognized his name and tried to engage him in conversation about baseball, but he avoided them. From Vancouver he took the train to Seattle and from there several other trains across the country to Washington. By the time he arrived in the capital he was concerned only with the personal tragedy that had happened. The end of his career as a spy meant nothing.

"I want an official protest from the State Department to their Foreign Office. Mieko was a Japanese national but she was my wife."

"Con, no one was more distressed than I when Kister sent us the news from Tokyo." Liam showed genuine concern for his brother. "But a protest would do no good at all. It might even do harm."

"Harm? For Christ's sake, what more harm could it do than has been done? Jesus God Almighty, they murdered my wife! What more harm can they do to me than that?"

"I wasn't thinking of harm to you." Liam looked awkward

177

and uncomfortable, unaccustomed to having to show sympathy in such circumstances. He might have done better if he had not been in his office. The trappings made him ill at ease: behind him a small flag on a desk standard hung as limp as wet washing, FDR watched him from a silver frame. "I was thinking of our Intelligence set-up. There are certain rules . . . If we protested, the Japanese might put it out that you were spying for us. The damage would be done, whether we denied it or not – "

"What the hell would that matter? The damage has been done – they killed my wife!"

"There are others in the field beside you, Con. Spies can't afford to retaliate. Believe me, on a personal level, I couldn't be more sorry for what has been done to you – and to Mieko. But . . ."

And *But* . . . it had been. McArdle left Washington that evening and went back to Rochester. He spent five days there with his father in the big empty house, listening to the old man's sympathy but feeling no better for it. Bitterness gripped him like an incurable illness; he had once been a fair-minded man but now there was only one yardstick for values, the loss of Mieko. He did not even attempt to be objective: Washington, and Liam in particular, became as guilty in his mind as Tokyo and Major Yorida. He left Rochester on a wet Sunday morning, walking out of the house while his father was at Mass. He drove west across the country, trying to put as much of America between him and Washington as possible. When he reached San Francisco the bitterness was still heavy in him and he continued west, taking a Matson ship to Honolulu. Once there he stayed on the ship when he learned it was going to Sydney. He reached that city and after a few days there wondered why he had come to it. He headed north, still drifting. In Brisbane, another town that held no appeal for him after a couple of days, he idly picked up a magazine, the *Pacific Islands Monthly*, in the lobby of Lennons Hotel. One of its advertisements offered a copra plantation in New Britain for sale.

Two weeks later he was in Rabaul. A month later he bought Kiogo.

When Mullane and Ruth left the hut Nara and Scheer looked at each other. Then Scheer, uneasy at the question, asked, "Could it be true? That this – Major Yorida? – might have killed his wife?"

"It might well be true." Nara was one of those who had never accepted *kempei* officers as belonging to his class; one did not have to defend them. "They are no better than your Gestapo."

"Not mine. Those are the sort of things that trouble me – "

"You will have to make up your mind, Bishop." They were speaking in English, the language of the enemy; but it was their only common tongue. "If you are to come with me when I leave here, you will then have to go on back to Germany. I shall guarantee your repatriation to your country. But I can't allow you to stay in Rabaul."

Scheer was dubious. "I don't know if our plan will succeed. Neither of us could move far – "

"Do not worry, Bishop. We shall be carried out of here."

"I wish there were some other way but having to depend on – "

"No names, please. We have learned what we know only by listening to other people talk – we don't want anyone to overhear us. Have no fear, Bishop. Bribery is the second oldest form of seduction. You should know that, with your Christian fetish for cataloguing sin."

The rest of the day passed quietly. Mullane stayed off his leg as much as possible, resting it and giving it a chance to recover before he had to test it again; he knew this camp would have to be struck soon and another trek begun. The movement of General Nara and the other evacuees down to the coast would not be easy; but that journey would be the least of his difficulties. He was still pondering the hazards of a forced march into Rabaul and out again.

He spent most of the day sitting under the rain tree at the end of the ridge, occasionally raising his binoculars to look down at Noku and see if the Japanese were making any sort of movement up towards the camp. But they were lolling on the beach, some of them now and again going into the water to cool off. Behind them in the plantation the natives worked lethargically, tending a crop that, as far as he could see, would never reach a market; but Lee Chin, loyal to Burns Philp, was keeping things going. The war in this tiny part of the world was in the doldrums. But he found it impossible to put out of his mind the thought of Rabaul and what might be going on there. While he sat here in this enforced waiting, the end of the war in the Pacific could be starting just fifty miles north of him.

He eased himself off one buttock, feeling something rubbing against him. He put his hand to his hip pocket, took out Sister Brigid's rosary beads. He was wearing a clean pair of trousers and he guessed that Luke or Mark, who did the laundry, rough as it was, had put the beads back in the pocket after the trousers had been washed. He looked at them, was tempted to throw them away; but the old superstition was too strong. His mother had been a great one for the rosary, saying the Mysteries every night. He put the beads into his shirt pocket, but he knew he would never use them.

Ruth brought him his lunch. "Stew and rice again, I'm afraid. I wish I could get us some fish. What are you reading?"

"*The Roman Legions.*" He closed the book, took the plate from her.

"More war? Why are men always so interested in war? You're fighting one – why spend your time reading about another?"

"You hope to learn something that might help you correct your mistakes."

"Generals might do that. Not plain ordinary Coastwatchers."

"You have a talent for cutting a man down to size. The first talent of a successful wife."

"You want to try your luck as a husband?"

"Heaven forfend!"

She had already eaten, so she sat down beside him. She wanted to ask him about his wife, but she sensed that was a delicate area into which he might never want her to intrude. "I don't know anything about American sportsmen, but are they all as educated as you?"

He swallowed a mouthful of rice. "When I was playing, most of them had never gone further than high school and a lot of them never got that far. But there were some who'd been to college. There was one, Moe Berg, who made me look like an illiterate oaf."

He knew that Moe Berg had made at least two trips to Japan and he sometimes wondered if Berg, too, had ever been enlisted as a spy. It was Berg who, on the 1934 trip, had given him his first lessons in the Japanese language.

"I can't imagine the world you lived in." She was the last person he had expected to sound wistful. "It must have been marvellous."

It had been: or nostalgia had made it so. More and more he had begun to think about the years before he had gone to Japan. "If you had a little money and you knew the right people . . ."

She picked up his book, but didn't open it: Rome was as distant as the farthest star, she had never studied history. "What books do you read about peace-time? What are you going to do after you and your legions have won the war? Stay here or go home to America and play baseball again?"

He laughed. "Baseball is a game for young men. No, I'll take up shuffleboard – " He thought of the old men, bending their creaking knees, whom he had seen on the bowling rinks in Brisbane and Sydney. "Or golf. Or I may just sit on park benches and look at the pretty girls. When a man passes a certain age he has to look for sports appropriate to his years."

"Sitting and watching pretty girls – that's not a very active sport."

"It is if you raise your hat and follow them home."

"Ah," she said, wistful again. "I wish I'd known you in your youth, Mr Mullane."

"You'd have enjoyed me," he said, wistful himself.

Then she said, having skirted the subject too long, "I'm sorry you lost your wife that way. You must really hate the Japs."

"Not all of them. But the military – yes."

"Then you must have felt like killing General Nara?"

"I think I might have if he hadn't been a general." Then he

said, "Some day I may tell you more about my wife. But not now."

"I don't know that I'm a good listener," she said with a smile; but was afraid he would tell her more than she now realized she wanted to know. She was suddenly jealous of his dead wife.

"Ah, don't you know that's what a man wants most in a woman?"

"You could have fooled me." She handed him the book again and as she did so a photograph fell out. She picked it up. "You?"

"One of my few mementoes. My last game for the Yankees before I retired."

She looked at the tall clean-shaven man in the baseball uniform. He held his cap in his hand and bright sun shone on the neat, slicked-down hair. "I'd never have recognized you."

"The same man is still here under this beard."

"Let me shave it off."

"When I come out of Rabaul, I'll ask for a few days' leave in Townsville. If you're there, you can indulge yourself with razor and scissors. It'll be my pleasure."

"Mine, too."

She took his plate and went back towards the cook-hut. She had never felt so – so *satisfied* in the company of a man; yet not completely so, because that would not be till he had also satisfied her sexually. She was not totally at ease with him; she was too far down the slopes of education for that. But he gave her more, with his presence and tolerance and humour, even his tongue-in-cheek arrogance, than any man had ever given her before.

Mullane looked after her, at the swing of her hips, the rise and fall of her buttocks under the trousers she now wore; but there was more to her than those attributes. She was offering him comfort, more than he had experienced or sought since Mieko's death. But he believed in love and he wasn't sure that she was offering him that. Or that he could offer it to her.

She came to his hut that evening when he set up the radio. Moresby was waiting on his call, gave him the answer he was waiting for: *US submarine will rendezvous south end Smokey Bay 2400 hours day after tomorrow. Confirm OK.*

The message had come in Champion code, but it took him only a minute or two to decode it. "Two more nights. I hope Frank gets back tomorrow afternoon. We have about an eight-mile hike up to Smokey Bay."

He sent back confirmation of the rendezvous. Then he went out of the hut, pulled down the aerial, came back and re-packed the radio. It was dark now and Ruth had lit the oil lamp. She looked up at him, but he did not return her gaze.

"Let's do the rounds," he said.

She sighed, but it was so soft that he did not hear it. She stood up and followed him back along the ridge. The moon was not yet up and when she stumbled in the shadows he put back a hand and took hers. But, she noticed, sensitive now to everything about him, it was only a helping hand and nothing more.

They checked first on the natives, then finished at the hut where Bishop Scheer and General Nara, the latter now sitting up, were playing chess.

"Where did you get your chess set?" Mullane said in surprise. It only occurred to him then that he had never thought of searching the Bishop's bed-roll and suitcase. What if he carried a gun?

"I carry it in my suitcase, with my missal and what I need for Mass. I read my missal for spiritual comfort, then play chess, if I can find an opponent, to sharpen my wits."

"Then you should always be both pious and perky. I can't say that is the way you are, though."

"True enough." Scheer nodded. "I'm not very perky, as you call it, tonight. The General must be a grandmaster at chess."

"I was always good at tactics and strategy." The gold watch on Nara's wrist glistened as he moved a knight on the board. It had been a present from his father when he had graduated from the military academy back in – it seemed so long ago now, he had almost forgotten the year. "At least in the classroom and on the chessboard."

"I'm sure you were good in the field," said Mullane. "The Japanese Army, unlike our side, doesn't promote incompetents to the rank of general."

Nara bowed his head. "Thank you for the compliment. But, as I said before, you seem to know so much about us Japanese.

No wonder Major Yorida was so interested in you."

The atmosphere in the hut suddenly changed. Ruth and Scheer, the bystanders, were as still as the ivory figurines on the board. Mullane himself was the only one who looked relaxed; but inwardly he had tensed. He was all at once reminded that Nara, for all his affability and good manners, was still the enemy, still with a mind perky with tactics.

He abruptly said good night, left the hut. Ruth, embarrassed at the rudeness of his departure, said an awkward good night and went out into the darkness. Mullane had gone and she could hear him stumbling back towards his own hut. She stood irresolute, wanting to comfort him, to be with him, but afraid of intruding.

Mullane, cursing, sucking his knuckles where he had skinned them on a tree-trunk, stalked into his hut and sat down heavily on his camp bed. He wished to Christ that he had not mentioned Yorida to Nara. He would never forget the *kempei* officer and what he had done to Mieko; but he had succeeded, though it had taken him till this year, in putting the manner of Mieko's death to the far back of his mind. He had been able to think of her without thinking of the way she had died; there had no longer been any anger or even grief, but just memories of their life together that had brought a sweet pain that was almost a happiness. And now he himself had brought up the ghost of Yorida and Nara was not going to let it lie.

He heard a rustle and looked up, half-expecting to see Nara standing there. But it was Ruth, looking for the first time hesitant and almost shy.

"If you want to be alone, I'll go back to my hut."

It was his turn to hesitate, then he gestured to the bed beside him. She sat down, the stretcher bending under their combined weight. She looked sideways at him, saw that he was studying her, then she smiled, her lips only slightly parting.

"Tomorrow night Frank will be back in here."

"Exactly what I was thinking."

"The night after that we'll be down on the beach at Smokey Bay waiting for the submarine."

"Again exactly what I was thinking." He felt no disloyalty to Mieko: that part of his life was over but for the memories.

184

"Well?"

"Well, Miss Riddle, I think we're both talking too much."

"Exactly what I was thinking."

He turned out the oil lamp. "I've never liked making love in the dark, but I don't want one of the boys to wander by outside and see what's going on."

"We can't go any further on this bed. It wasn't meant for this sort of thing."

They moved the bed, spread out his ground-sheet and blanket on the ground and crawled back under his mosquito net. "We should have rubbed ourselves with citronella," she said.

"Too risky. Too many sensitive spots exposed." He had almost forgotten the pleasure of a full breast against his face.

A little while later she said, "That damned beard. It's been all over me like a woolly dog. No, don't stop . . ."

They didn't rush, but when he thought she was ready he found her wriggling out of his arms. "What are you doing?"

"On this hard ground I'm not making love missionary style. Your back is tougher than mine. Roll over."

"You're a remarkable girl, Miss Riddle. I'm glad you're no missionary. Oh Jesus!"

They made love without restraint, except that love was never mentioned. But it was in the mind of each when they fell asleep.

Chapter Seven

I

Frank Vokes returned to camp in the middle of the afternoon of the next day, too late for Mullane to break camp and begin the move to Smokey Bay.

"I brought you these, Con. I couldn't manage the case you asked for – I didn't have enough boys." He took four bottles of Chivas Regal from his pack. "Notice they're not broken. No accidents this time."

"I'll recommend you for promotion in the Navy. How did the trip go? I hoped you'd be back this morning."

Vokes sat down, took off his boots and socks. "I had a bit of trouble with that bastard Mariba. He wanted to go back to Kiogo – tried to take some of the other boys with him."

"How'd you persuade him not to?"

"I told him I'd follow him and blow his bloody head off. I think I might've, too." Vokes looked rueful, as if not quite believing his own threat. But he knew that, if there had been no alternative, he would have shot Mariba. He had had no training for war, but he was learning that a certain callousness was needed for survival.

"Do you want me to talk to him?"

"No, I think I got him straightened out. But once we get Ruthie and the others away tomorrow night, we're going to have to do something about him. He's a real bloody stirrer, you know what I mean? Maybe we should put him aboard the sub and let them take him back to Aussie."

"Those feet of yours could do with some treatment." Vokes' feet were blotched with ugly red patches of dermatitis. "How's your ankle?"

"Sore." Vokes rubbed it, grinned and shook his head.

"Twenty-two years old and I feel like a bloody old man."

He hobbled away along the ridge towards Ruth and her medical kit. Mullane called Buka, told him not to unpack the supplies but to keep them ready for departure at first light in the morning. Then he waited for the return of the bombers that, regular as mailmen, had gone south this morning. Bishop Scheer came to join him.

"My last smoke." The German tamped down tobacco in his pipe. "My last indulgence, you might say."

"They'll give you tobacco when you get to Townsville."

Scheer puffed on his pipe. "I am not looking forward to internment. I have always made my own decisions up till now. I should still rather be free to choose to go back to Germany or not."

"You're wrong, Bishop – you haven't been free to make your own decisions since you joined the Church. We all have much less free will than we think we do."

The bombers were returning; he counted the planes as they trailed across the eastern sky. Six missing. He lowered the glasses, feeling a certain satisfaction.

"I should imagine you're a free man, Mr Mullane. You're not in the army or navy. As I understand it, you could come out with us on that submarine – "

"How do you know it's going to be a submarine?"

The Bishop shrugged. "It doesn't really matter. I wish you'd believe me, that all I wish to be is neutral. It is the only role for the Church in a war such as this."

"Don't hide behind your cassock. You're as much a German as you are a Catholic."

"In a war, is there a place for a private conscience?" His pipe went out, but he did not relight it. "I really don't know. I envy you your commitment, Mr Mullane. You have no decisions to make."

"You don't believe that, Bishop. I could decide to be a coward, a very natural decision, and go out with you on the submarine."

Mullane turned away, put the binoculars to his eyes and watched a lone speck heading north through the eastern sky. Even as he watched it he saw the bomber seem to come to a stop in the air; then its nose dipped and it went down in a long slide. The small speck fell steeply across his vision; he could imagine the crew trapped in the bomber and he wondered if they would die stoically or, as he knew he would, protesting against fate. The plane hit the water, there was a tiny white eruption, then there was nothing but the blue sea, calm and unshattered. It was the first time he had seen a Japanese plane go down, the first direct evidence that he was not wasting his time and effort staying on here as a Coastwatcher.

The crash was too far away for Scheer to have seen with the naked eye. "Another successful raid?"

"For the Japs? I guess so. But we're whittling away at them."

Scheer shook his head. "It may not be enough. The General is certain that the Japanese will win the war."

"And the Germans?"

The Bishop hesitated, then said honestly, "He is not so optimistic. He thinks Herr Hitler has made too many mistakes."

Then Vokes came along to join them. "The wireless is set up, Con." He looked around him, at the mountains, then down the green slope of jungle to the distant beach at Noku. "Pity we've got to leave here. I'd just like to settle down in one place for a while. How's it going, Bishop? Looking forward to internment?"

"You have a sardonic sense of humour, Mr Vokes."

Vokes slapped his arms awkwardly. "I wasn't slinging off at you. I just thought you'd be glad to get out of here."

"Why should I? I've always enjoyed these Islands. I sometimes think the Lord allowed Himself to be a little pagan when He created them."

"Let's go get on the air," said Mullane. "We'll – "

Then looking back along the ridge he saw General Nara coming out of his hut supported by Mariba. He hobbled off at a run, not knowing why he did so; it was a matter of instinct at seeing the two least trustworthy people in the camp so close together. But after a few yards his leg forced him to slow and he finished up limping towards the Japanese and the native.

"Where do you think you're going?"

Nara stopped, took his arm from round Mariba's shoulder

but continued to lean against the native. "Mr Mullane, why are you so upset? I am going into the bush to relieve myself. Miss Riddle gave me something last night for my bowels. I have been constipated ever since the aeroplane crashed."

"Okay." Mullane felt foolish; and also angry when he saw the barely concealed smile on Mariba's face. "But in future when you want to go to the latrine, call me or Frank Vokes. You don't have the freedom of the camp, General."

"I should not have thought a visit to the latrine was a privilege. But if that is what you wish, I shan't relieve myself in future without reference to you or Mr Vokes. Even in the middle of the night."

He went on with Mariba, his thin weak legs stumbling once so that the native had to lift him up. Mullane watched them go into the bush. Then he saw Ruth coming towards him.

"You're edgy – you've been like that all day. Is it because of what happened last night?"

They had not avoided each other during the day, but they had been so circumspect that it would not have surprised either of them if someone had commented on what was going on between them. Though neither Nara nor Scheer was the sort of man who would make such a comment.

"Of course not."

She, more than their actual love-making, had been on his mind all day. He was cautious about a declaration of love, even to himself. The dozens of girls before Mieko had never been told that he loved them.

"I'm glad," Ruth said. "I have no regrets."

She loved him without question: that much she knew. But she could wait till he declared himself first; she was still conditioned by her experiences with other men. Being truly in love for the first time in her life had made her wary and sensitive. She was afraid of what a rebuff would do to her.

He squeezed her hand; back along the ridge Vokes was watching them but all at once he didn't care. "My only regret will be if I've made you pregnant."

"I shan't even mind that." There, dammit, she'd as much as told him she loved him.

And he knew it; but still held back. "It's going to be a long

189

war. We could be saying good-bye tomorrow night, for God knows how long."

"I'll have regrets about *that*."

"So shall I." Which was as close as he could bring himself to telling her how he felt.

A little later he and Vokes went on the air to report the number of aircraft returning from the raid and to reconfirm the rendezvous tomorrow night. Moresby, in reply, relayed the message from Townsville: *GHQ still on our backs re King's Cross. Want fullest sit report 72 hours outside.*

Mullane fairly banged the Morse key, as if banging the words against GHQ's wooden head: *Tell GHQ if do not like our progress get off asses and take our place.*

"That's telling them," said Vokes. "But there goes my badges of rank."

The reply came in: Mullane recognized the sense of humour that gave Townsville patience: *Will give GHQ your message end of war. Good luck.*

After supper Mullane, taking his mosquito net, a blanket and a bottle of whisky, went along to Scheer and Nara's hut. He went in, sat down on the ground with his back to the central roof pole and poured three nips.

"A nightcap, gentlemen. You're both going to sleep early tonight because you have a long day ahead of you tomorrow."

"Are you going to spend the night with us?" Scheer savoured the first sip of his whisky. "We'll be a little crowded."

"It's all in the cause of seeing that you two gentlemen arrive safely and in good health in Australia."

Nara tasted his whisky, nodded appreciatively. "I should hate this to be known in Tokyo, but I prefer whisky to *sake*. One of the best spoils of war from our victory in Singapore was a hundred cases of Scotch whisky."

There was something slightly odd about Nara that worried Mullane, but he could not pin down what it was. Ruth had been right, he *was* edgy. The Japanese's composure was proving more unsettling than if he had been so uncontrollable that he had to be tied up all the time.

Nara sipped his whisky again, then said casually, "Are you

coming out with us tomorrow night or are you still going into Rabaul?"

"I'm going into Rabaul."

"You're a brave man." Another sip, then just as casually, "Colonel Yorida is there."

"*Colonel* Yorida?" Mullane suddenly could not taste the whisky.

"His promotion has been slow, but there are limited opportunities in the *kempei*."

"You mean he's in Rabaul?" Mullane kept his voice steady, his composure equalling that of Nara.

"He is the chief of field security. He would have been one of my senior staff officers. I wonder if he still thinks about what happened to your wife?"

"Probably not." Mullane finished his drink, recorked the bottle. There was a fluttering in his chest, but his hands were steady and there was only the slightest edge to his voice. "He's killed too many to be able to remember one from another."

"Not necessarily." Nara put down his empty mug, put his arm and hand back under the blanket away from the bite of any marauding mosquito. "A soldier or a policeman may not remember the names, but a professional would remember the circumstances. Colonel Yorida is a professional, Mr McArdle."

Mullane slapped a mosquito that settled on the back of his hand, took the bottle of citronella that Scheer passed him. "I think you better go to sleep, General. You too, Bishop."

Scheer had been watching both men closely. He knew that Nara had been baiting the American and he was shocked at the callousness of it; but he guessed that the Japanese had his reasons and he had made no protest. Nara was not a malicious man, the Bishop was certain of that: if the mention of the killing of Mullane's wife had been nothing more than malice, then Scheer would have spoken out strongly. But he had placed his escape in Nara's hands, or hand (the joke had sickened him, but it had been Nara who had made it this afternoon); the baiting of Mullane must be part of the General's plan. It was difficult to tell, however, what effect it had had on Mullane. The American, in his own way, could be as impassive and

191

composed, at least on the surface, as the Japanese.

The three men settled down for the night as Mullane turned down the oil lamp to a low glow. Scheer crawled in under his mosquito net and Mullane arranged the net over Nara. For a moment, before he let the net drop, the eyes of the two men met in a hard gaze.

"Good night, General," Mullane said softly. "Just keep it in mind – you're not going to tempt me to kill you. You're going back to Australia as a prisoner-of-war."

Then he sat back against the roof-pole, draped his net about him and sat staring into the shadows of the hut and the past. He had to condition himself to the thought that the murderer of his wife could be no more than fifty miles away. That is, if General Nara, the tactician, was telling the truth.

II

Mullane and Vokes took turns in three-hour stretches, each of them having difficulty in staying awake at times. If the General and the Bishop had any trouble in sleeping, it was not apparent to the two watchmen; beneath their nets the Japanese and the German appeared to sleep soundly. But behind their closed lids both men were awake for a long time before falling asleep, each of them wondering about his trust in the other and in the third person Nara had enlisted.

Shortly before six o'clock Mullane woke the entire camp. "We'll be on our way in an hour. Frank, stash what's left of the supplies – we'll have to come back for them. Buka, detail four boys to carry General Nara, two at a time – ".

"Boss, I can't find Mariba. He look like he go home."

"The bastard!" said Vokes. "I bloody knew it – Didn't I tell you?"

Mullane didn't answer. He went striding across to where Scheer was helping Nara out of the hut. "The General wants to go to the latrine – "

"You better hang on to your bowels a little longer, General." Mullane grabbed the Japanese's hand, held up the skinny wrist. He knew now what had looked odd about Nara last night. "Where's your gold watch?"

192

Nara said nothing. He stood leaning against the Bishop, his arm still held high, like that of an exhausted runner, by Mullane. Then the latter flung the arm down and Scheer had to grab at the Japanese to hold him up.

"You son-of-a-bitch! You've paid Mariba – where's he gone?"

Again Nara said nothing, just stared back at the American.

Mullane shot out his hand again, but this time he grabbed the Bishop by the throat. "I need him, Bishop, but I don't need you! Tell me where Mariba's gone or I'll choke you to death!"

No one else said a word: Ruth, Vokes, all the natives just stood and stared, watching Mullane's big left hand tighten on Scheer's throat. The German let go of Nara, put up both hands to pull Mullane's fingers away; Nara fell against him, slid to the ground. But still no one interfered.

"Tell me, God damn you! Tell me – where's he sent Mariba?"

Then Nara, still on the ground, said weakly, "Let him go, Mr Mullane. I have sent Mariba down to Noku."

Mullane let go of Scheer and the German fell back but managed to stay on his feet.

"Sorry, Bishop." He moved his hand, flexing and unflexing his fingers; it was an old habit, something he had done when he had to pitch too many innings. But the tension in his fingers was far different from anything he had felt in the old days: it shocked him to realize how close he had come to killing Scheer. He was learning the ways of war far quicker than he wished. "You almost got to heaven that time."

The Bishop was massaging his throat, staring at Mullane as if he could not believe what the American had done. He turned away and went into his hut. Mullane looked down at Nara, still slumped on the ground, then he nodded at Buka.

"Take the General to the latrine, Buka. And don't take your eyes off him."

Buka picked up the Japanese as if he were a child, put an arm round him and half-carried him into the bush. The other natives melted away to their tasks, disappointed that the drama was over: none of them had ever seen one white man kill another. The two boys, Luke and Mark, remained staring at

Mullane till Ruth snapped at them and then they fled away to help with the packing.

Silas came forward. "We pull the huts down, boss? Might come in handy, we come back here."

If we ever come back . . . "Leave them, Silas. We've got to be out of here in fifteen minutes. Mariba may be back any time with the Japs."

"Him bad bugger, that feller. Buka and me, we kill him some time, boss, don't worry."

No conscience there, no lily-livered sense of guilt: the good old pay-back system. "We'll talk about it, Silas."

They were ready to leave in ten minutes. Mullane went out to the end of the ridge and looked down towards Noku. Thick morning mist, like a tropical glacier, hid the narrow river valley and the plantation. There was nothing to be seen. Any sort of terror could be going on under that white cloud; he wondered what sort of interrogation Lee Chin was undergoing right now. He could only hope that the Chinese would not suffer too much for his loyalty to Burns Philp and the Allied cause.

Then far away there was the drone of engines. He swung his glasses to the east, counted the bombers heading south: forty-eight of them this morning. He yelled to Vokes to set up the radio again, ran back along the ridge. He wanted as much of a head-start as he could manage on the Japanese who would soon be on their way up from Noku; but he and Vokes were Coast-watchers and their first duty lay with the American forces down in the Solomons. He sent the party on its way with Vokes leading it, keeping only the carriers he would need to carry the radio.

He sent the message in clear: *48 bombers heading south. Am moving immediately.* He gave Moresby no time to reply; he was repacking the set the moment he lifted his hand from the key. They were on their way in less than five minutes and he had done all that he and Vokes were asked to do. But the bigger flights every day meant that the Japanese were now putting the pressure on. The war down on Guadalcanal must be coming to the crunch point.

There was only one track heading east and he and his carriers soon caught up with Vokes and the others.

"How about that bugger Mariba, eh? If he's with them when they catch us up, I'm going to – "

"Forget it, Frank. He doesn't owe us anything." But he was only acting in his effort to sound fair and impartial: he thirsted for Mariba's blood as much as Vokes did.

They had been tramping for two hours, stopping twice for a short rest, when they came to the beech forest. The track abruptly ran out, coming to a dead end in a thick carpet of undergrowth as if the men who had made the track had suddenly been swallowed up. The ground sloped away, a smooth green mat out of which the trees grew tall and straight, shutting out the sun.

"Better find another way, boss," said Buka.

Mullane knew what he meant. Once before, tramping into the hills behind Kiogo, he had walked into a native beech forest. At first the ground cover had been no more than spongy as if one were walking on an extra-thick carpet. Then suddenly he had plunged through a weak spot and found himself up to his shoulders in soft rotting undergrowth. The floor of any native beech forest, covered with years of fallen leaves and vines, could be as treacherous as any swamp.

"Okay, Buka, scout around – "

Then they heard the plane. It came in from behind them, as if the pilot had been following the track they had traversed. It was a two-seater scout plane; it went overhead so low that they could see the pilot and the observer looking down at them. Then they heard the rising note of the engine as the plane went up in a steep turn to come back at them.

"Into the trees!" Mullane yelled.

There was momentary confusion as everyone, with no track to follow, suddenly took his own way into the forest. Mullane plunged ahead, leading the way. Fifty yards into the trees he yelled for everyone to halt. They all stood, faces turned up towards the glimmer of sunlight, like patches of yellow stars, showing through the thick green ceiling. They heard the plane go over, climb steeply and come back. But this time it was at least a hundred yards away and Mullane knew at once that the Japanese had lost sight of them.

"Everyone spread out – don't bunch up!"

"Where do we go from here?" said Vokes.

"We've got no choice. We go straight on through this forest. If we stay spread out, maybe they won't spot us again. You take one flank, Buka will take the other and I'll keep an eye on the middle. Just make sure everyone watches his step. We don't want to have to dig someone out of six feet of muck."

They moved on with everyone spread out on a long thin front, like a line of beaters ready to flush out game for an invisible party of sporting guns. It was not easy going; even Luke and Mark, light as they were, sank up to their ankles in the soft green mat. The carriers, weighed down by their loads, sank almost to their knees with each step they took. The plane came over once more; then again and again. Then they heard it climbing and after a while they could hear it droning above them as it circled like a bird of prey.

The air down on the forest floor was hot and foetid. The smell of decay was thick in the nostrils; sweat streamed down into the eyes. Spiders, lizards, once a large snake, slithered away as a foot came down through the thick green mush. A soft green-gold light filtered down through the foliage overhead; lawyer vines shimmered in it like reeds in water. A large flock of lorikeets whistled overhead, a swift rainbow come and gone in a moment. Butterflies floated in slow motion like charred-edged scraps of bright emerald paper. But Mullane and the others, blinded by sweat, saw no beauty; they stumbled on, dragging their feet out of the green trap, lost in a daze where their only alert sense was their hearing. They could still hear the Japanese plane circling high above them, out of sight but so much a presence.

Suddenly there was a scream. Mullane swung round to see Ruth disappearing into the forest floor. He stumbled towards her, fell on his knees and reached down to grab her upstretched hand, all that showed of her. He had a sharp, horrifying memory of Sister Brigid's dead hand showing above the surface of the bloodstained water. Ruth's fingers clutched at him like claws, her panic jolting into him like an electric shock.

She had gone right through the soft mulch of leaves, vines and creepers. Mullane felt the undergrowth bending beneath his weight; he was going to slide in after her. There was no way of knowing how much rotting foliage lay beneath Ruth; she could be standing only inches above a deep swampy hole. He could feel her still sliding down, dragging him with her; they could both slip down into the green muck, be smothered as quickly as if they had sunk into quicksand, before anyone could drag them out. He yelled for Silas and another carrier to grab his belt and hold him.

Ruth's hand was clawing at his; slippery with sweat, it began to slip away. He made a desperate grab with his other hand as Silas and the second carrier grabbed, not his belt but his feet. His own face was now down into the muck; he turned his head, gasping for air. He could feel Ruth jerking convulsively at the other end of her arm; she was going to jerk herself right out of his grasp. Then slowly he felt himself being drawn backwards; he tightened his grip on Ruth's hand and wrist. Silas and the carrier pulled him back and Ruth, covered in green muck, came up out of the forest floor like some monster rising from a primeval swamp. She and Mullane were pulled back on to firmer ground and at once the forest floor closed in again on itself, only a slight dip showing where Ruth had gone in. Mullane rolled over, lay on his back gasping. He turned his head, saw Ruth weakly wiping the muck from her face, her mouth open in great, animal gasps. Her whole body was twitching and then he started to tremble himself at the thought of how close she had come to death.

It took her fifteen minutes to recover. The Bishop attended to her, made her lie still till she had recovered from her shock. Mullane came back to her again and again between checking on the carriers. He had ordered a rest and told Vokes to dole out some food. He stood once and listened, aware for the first time of the silence overhead.

"He's probably gone back to refuel," said Vokes. "How you feeling? That was close – I thought Ruthie was a goner then."

Mullane nodded. "We better be more careful from now on."

General Nara, on his stretcher, and Ruth lay side by side; Bishop Scheer sat between them like a priest ready to administer the last rites. Silas came up with some food; Ruth shook her head, but Scheer insisted she ate at least a couple of biscuits and drank some water. She looked at Mullane and he nodded.

"Do what the Bishop says."

She stared at him, saw the concern for her in his face; then, satisfied, she began to eat a biscuit. She knew now that he loved her and there was no better resuscitation than that. Mullane sat down near her, began to munch on a banana. They all sat there in the green-gold gloom as on a picnic: a picnic, thought Mullane, painted by Goya rather than Watteau or one of the other Romantics.

"You should not be subjecting yourself to this, Mr Mullane," said Nara. "You could have waited at the edge of this forest and spared yourself all this exhaustion – and spared Miss Riddle her ordeal. You will be caught eventually, you must know that."

"Maybe not, General. I still hold one card – your men from Noku don't know where we're going to be picked up. There are a dozen bays between here and Rabaul. They won't be able to patrol all of them, not at night."

"Your optimism is pathetic, Mr Mullane. Still, you'll have the satisfaction of seeing Colonel Yorida again. You won't be able to do much – "

"Did you send him a message that I'm here?"

Nara's face became expressionless. "That's for you to worry about, Mr Mullane. It is an old chess principle – keep your opponent guessing."

Scheer had said nothing, chewing on a biscuit as on a cud. Tonight would be his moment of truth; he felt as he had felt all those years ago when he had had to decide if he had a true vocation as a priest. What would he find if he did return to Germany? His parents were long since dead; his brother was a cautious supporter of Hitler; his two sisters were always politically non-committal in their letters. The estate outside Kahla in Thueringia, they had written him, had been taken over by the Wehrmacht; he wondered what Goethe and the other poets would think of what had happened to the Green Heart of Germany. He loved these islands in the South Seas, had a warm affection for the people; but he knew in his heart that his work amongst them was finished, that by the time the war was over he would be too old and weak to continue. Retirement to the Fatherland was a magnet that constantly drew him; but what had been done to Germany in his long absence? He would only know by going home and he was afraid of what he might find.

"Bishop – "

"Yes?" He looked up, lost for the moment. His gaze was still full of long vistas, of rolling hills and castles against the skyline; one never got such panoramic views here in these jungle-tangled hills. Mullane was standing over him, head cocked to one side. "Yes, what is it?"

"On your feet. We're moving on." The party had already begun to move off. "How's your throat?"

Scheer got slowly to his feet, feeling his joints creak. "I feel that your fingermarks are still there."

"They are. I'm sorry, Bishop. Do you want me to do penance?"

Scheer managed a smile: absolution, he thought, was more difficult when you had to forgive a sin against yourself. "A decade of Sister Brigid's rosary."

Mullane also smiled, knew he had been forgiven. "You know how to rub it in, Bishop." Then, the smile gone, he said, "Did the General give Mariba any message about me for Colonel Yorida?"

The rest of the party had moved on; only Ruth was close by. She was still weak from shock, but she had her senses about her. She waited on Scheer's answer.

"I don't know, Mr Mullane." The Bishop was glad that he did not have to lie; his loyalty lay with the General, but, despite what he had done to him, the American was not really his enemy. "We had no paper or pencil to write a message. Mariba speaks only pidgin – the verbal message had to be very simple."

"You must have heard what was said."

"No. The General gave him the message some time yesterday when I was out of the hut. Possibly when I was talking to you."

"Okay." But Mullane was not satisfied. He itched to see Yorida again, but he knew that if ever he did he would be in the position of loser. "Better get going, Bishop."

The Bishop moved off, stepping cautiously across the forest

floor. Mullane turned to Ruth. "Do you feel up to it?"

"What?"

He grinned. "Not sex, Miss Riddle." Then he said seriously, "You are all right, aren't you? Don't try putting on a brave face, please."

She took his hand. "I'm all right. A little shaky, but I'll get over it."

Then they heard the plane, a deeper sound this time than the single engine of the scout plane. It was somewhere down the slope, between them and the coast.

Up ahead Vokes yelled back at Mullane, "That's the Kawanisi again! He can fly for bloody hours – they're going to hang around up there till we come out in the open!"

They could not see the flying-boat, but for the next hour, as they moved on down through the beech forest, feeling their way cautiously across the treacherous floor, they could hear it. The sound of its engines came and went as it moved back and forth on its patrol. Then abruptly the beech forest ended and the trees started to thin out.

Buka found a track and they started down it, the party well spaced out now. The trees here were a mixed lot: the *erima* and the eucalyptus-like *kamerere*, both of them tall trees with their foliage right at the top, obscuring little of the sky; a few thick-trunked walnuts; and several clumps of pandanus palms. The Kawanisi came back up the slope and the small groups stood stock-still close to the trees while it went overhead.

The next three hours was a cat-and-mouse game; or an eagle-and-lamb game. The flying-boat seemed to run on tracks round the sky, hardly varying its routine, as if its crew was certain that its prey had to come out into the open eventually. Mullane knew the safest policy would be to stay put and not to move at all, but he had no idea how much rugged country lay between them and Smokey Bay and he had to be within sight of the bay before darkness fell.

He looked back over his shoulder and at once let out a yell. "For Christ's sake, put down that umbrella!"

He stormed back along the track, grabbed the umbrella from the startled Scheer and was about to snap its ferrule in two when the German, recovering, grabbed at it.

"No!"

Mullane, set back by the fierceness of the Bishop's attack, let go of the umbrella. Scheer closed it, furled it with shaking hands. The mud-stained, frayed-edged sunshade had become important to him; he had no other bishop's staff than this. He had had it for more years than he could remember; a Chinese tailor in Rabaul had re-covered it for him two or three times. It was a memento, something that had to be taken with him to-night. To open it in another clime some time in the future would be like opening up memory itself.

"I did not put it up to attract attention." His voice was trembling; he had not believed he was still capable of such passion. "I did it without thinking – the sun was scorching my head – "

Mullane was looking at him closely: the elderly German was on the very edge of his nerves. He put out a hand, gently touched the Bishop's shoulder.

"I believe you. Just don't do it again. Because if these fellers in that flying-boat see us, there's no guarantee they won't start shooting at us. You don't know how much value they place on the General. Maybe they'd rather kill him than let us send him out to Australia. If they do start shooting, they're not going to be selective, Bishop."

The Bishop stood very still for a long moment, then he nodded.

On his way back to the head of the line Mullane stopped by Nara's stretcher. The Kawanisi came overhead, but the party was spread out beneath a screen of palms. "I thought for a moment you'd put the Bishop up to that little trick."

"You're too suspicious, Mr Mullane. But I do wish you'd give up. I'm losing patience with you."

The laughter burst out of Mullane. "Jesus, you're a marvel, General! You're the prisoner here, not me!"

The flying-boat went by overhead, its shadow flitting down between the trees. "Do you think so?" said Nara.

"I *know* so!"

But Mullane wondered if he was shouting into the wind.

It was late in the afternoon when they reached the final ridge above the sea. The Kawanisi was still with them, but they knew it would soon have to return to its base. It came up along the coast from the direction of Noku as Mullane led the party up to the top of a ridge and saw the sea only a mile or so below them. The flying-boat kept going, heading north, and Mullane knew then that it was going back to its base at Rabaul or Kavieng.

Smokey Bay lay below, the small volcano at its northern end sending up a thin drift of smoke that gave the inlet its name. A shallow curve of black sand ran round to the steep southern headland. A narrow river ran into the sea at the southern end through a swamp of mangroves. At the northern end there was a small overgrown plantation below the long brown scar that ran down the side of the volcano. At the edge of the beach a flame tree blazed like a pool of still-glowing lava.

It took them three-quarters of an hour to make their way down to the beach. Mullane followed the overgrown track that Buka had found; they crossed the river high up, where it was no more than a shallow ripple above rocks, and managed to keep away from the mangroves. Mullane wanted no more encounters with crocodiles.

"I hope that bloody volcano doesn't take it into its head to blow up," said Vokes.

"Don't think about it."

They came into the plantation, under the scraggly coconut palms and past the neglected cocoa trees; rotting coconuts lay about like corroded cannonballs. Some of the trees were black and scarred and there was other evidence of the last eruption of the volcano. The plantation house had collapsed under the weight of ash and pumice rock and the vegetation that had grown over it; the peak of the roof stuck up like the prow of a ship sunk amongst frozen green waves. A sense of death hung over the place and Mullane, the Celt in him stirring, hoped that it was not an omen.

"A bloke named Wagner lived here," said Vokes. "He and his wife and kids all died when the volcano blew out, oh, ten or fifteen years ago. He was a German. They told me about it up in Rabaul. Nobody would ever take over the plantation again. They said it's loaded down with bad luck."

"Someone back in Townsville has a macabre sense of humour," said Mullane. "They nominated this rendezvous."

"Maybe they're hoping the bad-luck story will keep the Nips away."

Mullane looked at Nara, who had now got off his stretcher and was testing his weak legs. "Are you superstitious, General?"

"I'm fatalistic, Mr Mullane. But also optimistic."

The cook-boy lit a fire behind the house and a meal was prepared. In the meantime Mullane and Vokes had some of the natives gather wood for two large heaps at opposite ends of the beach. Mullane could not be sure there would be any glow from the volcano's crater at night and the submarine would need beacons to guide it into the bay.

"I don't like the look of those breakers," said Vokes.

He and Mullane had taken off their boots and socks before they had come on to the sand and now they stood at the water's edge cooling their chafed and sweating feet. Vokes had rolled up his trousers and was letting the white cream of water swirl round the sores on his legs.

A breeze, freshening into a light wind, was blowing up from the south; the surf was rising, long ranks of white combers breaking on the black sand. If it kept up, the boats coming ashore from the submarine would have difficulty in putting out again.

"There's nothing we can do about it, unless you want to play King Canute."

Vokes shook his head. "It's ironical, you know what I mean? Back home I'd go down to the beach Saturdays, Sundays, and I'd be praying for the big ones to come rolling in. But now – " His arms went up, then dropped in exasperation.

"Did you have a good life before the war, Frank?"

Vokes stared out to sea, surprised by the question; Mullane had shown no interest in him or his life up till now. But he sensed that Mullane felt the bond, as much as he did, that had grown between them.

"I enjoyed it. But I guess you'd have thought it pretty – I dunno, *dull*. But I keep thinking about it, you know what I mean?"

"I keep thinking about what I used to do."

"What was it like, Con? To most Aussies America's always been full of glamour. The films did that to us, I suppose . . .

What did you do, I mean besides play baseball?"

"When I think about it, I guess it was all pretty empty. I'd go to Broadway shows, I'd date some of the chorus girls, I'd go to the fights with Jack Dempsey after he retired – "

"You know *Jack Dempsey*?"

Mullane smiled. "I'm sorry, *mate*. I'm name-dropping – "

"Drop some more."

"Well – " The life may have been empty but suddenly he was warmed by memories of it. "Did you ever hear of Helen Morgan?"

"No."

"She was a singer, one of the best. Tommy Dorsey introduced me to her – "

"Tommy Dorsey! I had practically all his records – " He sang a few bars of 'Marie' in a surprisingly pleasant voice. Then he stopped and stared out to sea again. "Christ, what a life! And you've finished up here!"

What he meant was: *I've finished up here*. Mullane, in the past few days, had opened up a whole new world to him. Suddenly all the things he remembered with nostalgia had no meaning, were – well, *dull*.

"Frank – " Mullane could see the effect his few words had had. "I was one of the lucky ones. There's no more glamour in America for most Americans than there is for Aussies back where you come from. Maybe you have better lives back there. Better, I'd say, than people on New York's Lower East Side or up in Harlem."

"Maybe," said Vokes. "But any bloke who personally knew Tommy Dorsey – don't try to tell me not to envy you, Con."

He abruptly went off along the beach. Mullane looked after him, suddenly wishing he had not started the conversation. He had made the original remark – "Did you have a good life before the war?" – out of a sense of sympathy, of, yes, affection for the boy. And all he had succeeded in doing was making Vokes dissatisfied with what he had probably once thought was a good life.

He went back into the plantation, sat down amidst the crotons and hibiscus, grown wild, and Ruth brought him his meal. She sat down beside him, uncaring now as to whether the others noticed a deepening in her relationship with him. She had the aching, sickening thought that she might not see him again after tonight.

She looked down towards the beach where a pair of hornbills had just settled on a branch of a casuarina tree. "Those birds mate for life, did you know that?"

"Yes."

"Don't be on the defensive, Con. It was just an idle remark." But it had not been.

"You're not eating."

"I'm not hungry." She set down her plate. "Are you coming with us or staying on here?"

"You know I'm staying. We have to."

Vokes had now come back from along the beach and was sitting near them.

"Why can't your people back in Townsville get all they want from the General?" Ruth said. "He would know everything they would want to know."

"He'd never talk. I know him and his kind too well."

"They could get it out of him – torture him if they had to – "

He was shocked at her practical callousness; Vokes sat still with a forkful of food halfway to his mouth. "You don't mean that – "

"I do mean it! You keep telling me we're at war – What's decent and honourable and civilized about war?"

"The female of the species – " Mullane looked at Vokes, trying to turn the topic aside with a light remark.

But Ruth said, "Don't be so bloody patronizing!"

"I think she's got something," Vokes said quietly.

"Frank, it wouldn't work. They'd never get a word out of Nara – he'd almost welcome anything they did to him. He believes in bushido – people like him aren't afraid of death – "

"Everyone's afraid of it," Vokes said stubbornly, deathly afraid of it himself.

"If our people did resort to torture – I hate to think of the possibility, it puts us on the lowest level." He waited for them to agree with him, but they said nothing. "Frank, for Christ's sake, how would you feel if they did torture him?"

"If I didn't know about it, it wouldn't worry me. And they're not going to tell a nobody like me what they do."

"I can't believe it – you two sound so goddam callous!"

"Like Ruthie said, it's war. All I'm thinking about is my own neck."

"I'm thinking about yours, Con," said Ruth. "I don't want to lose you. I love him, Frank."

"Good on you," said Vokes. "He wants his bloody head read if he turns his back on you."

Mullane abruptly stood up. "I'm going into Rabaul. If you're so concerned for your goddam neck, Frank, you can go out on the sub tonight. Maybe they'll let you help interrogate the General!"

He left them, walked round the house and down to the beach. And saw the Japanese patrol boat come round the point below the volcano.

III

He ran back behind the house, yelling for the cook-boy to throw earth and palm fronds on the fire. In less than a minute there was no sign of the fire. All the gear was gathered up and Mullane herded the party back up through the coconut groves towards the jungle at the rear of the plantation.

"I'll stay down here and keep nit." Vokes checked the magazine of his rifle; he had put out of his mind the argument of a moment ago. "Maybe the buggers will go right on past. They could be on their way down to Noku."

"Don't take any pot-shots at them. If they come ashore, get the hell out of here and we'll go back up into the hills."

Vokes went round to the front of the house, lay down in thick grass behind a screen of crotons. He was trembling a little with apprehension; he was still new to danger, to the thought that in another few minutes he might be dead. He fingered the trigger of his rifle nervously, wondering how steady his hands would be if he did have to fire on the Japanese. He had talked calmly about letting the people back home torture Nara if they had to, but that had not been difficult. Out of sight, out of mind made certain things easy. He just wondered

206

how he would feel when he had a Japanese, a man like himself, lined up in his sights and was about to pull the trigger.

Mullane was hurrying the party ahead of him, keeping both Nara and Scheer close to him. "No tricks, General, or I'll tie you to that stretcher again."

The Japanese made no reply, just trotted on unsteady legs up through the long grass. He had not yet become accustomed to the loss of the weight of his right arm and he was having to adjust his balance. Beside him the Bishop did his best to keep up with the pace Mullane was imposing, holding up his cassock so that he would not trip on it. Ruth was up ahead with the carriers, already disappearing into the bush.

Two hundred yards behind the plantation the ground sloped up to a small ridge. Mullane called a halt and everyone, exhausted by the sudden exertion, sank down in the undergrowth. Mullane, with Buka beside him, adjusted his binoculars and looked down over the plantation to the beach.

The sun had gone down behind the mountains and the air was blue with dusk. It would be dark in another half-hour; perhaps the approaching evening would dissuade the Japanese boat from coming into the uninhabited bay. But even as he focused his glasses on the boat he saw it turn in towards the beach. It stopped about a hundred yards off-shore, beyond the first swell of breakers, and he saw the soldiers, about twenty of them, lining the rail on the narrow deck.

Mullane looked back over his shoulder. General Nara sat with his back against the rough bark of a *taun* tree, his hand absently stroking the stump of his arm. He looked calm and – and Jesus, Mullane thought, so goddam *confident*. He caught Mullane's eye and smiled.

"Why don't you surrender, Mr Mullane? I shall personally guarantee that no harm will come to you."

"Don't be stupid, General." Ruth's voice was quiet but there was acid in it. "He's like you – he's never going to surrender."

Then Buka said, "Boss – "

Two rubber rafts were coming in from the patrol boat, each of them carrying half a dozen men. They came bouncing in through the surf, the soldiers clinging desperately to the rafts' ropes. They hit the beach, one of them spinning high and turning over to spill out its passengers. Then Vokes came running up through the plantation.

"They'll know we've been here! We forgot – our bloody footprints are all up and down the beach!"

"Relax," said Mullane, but he was more worried than he sounded. "You and I had our boots off. It could have been some boys from up in the hills."

"What about the firewood we've set?"

Mullane nodded, on edge again. He had forgotten all about the heaps of wood at either end of the beach, the most obvious clues that a rendezvous had been arranged.

"I really do think you should surrender, Mr Mullane," said Nara. "If you don't walk down there with me now, those soldiers will follow you and they'll start shooting before I can stop them. A lot of you may be killed. Including Miss Riddle."

You son-of-a-bitch, Mullane thought, you never miss a trick.

"Leave us here," said Scheer. "The General and I – let us go down to the beach. The General will let you and the others escape back into the hills – "

Mullane, torn between the choices, looked at Nara. "Would you strike a bargain like that, General?"

"No," said Nara quietly; he still sat with his back to the tree, in command of the situation. "Your work with Mr Vokes is too valuable to be allowed to continue. I'm sorry, but you have to be stopped, Mr Mullane. Either by surrendering or being killed."

Scheer looked at him, frowning in puzzlement as if Nara had all at once turned into a stranger. "General, you promised – "

"Bishop, forgive me. But promises when one is at war – " He spread his only hand. "Don't be naive, Bishop. Lies are just another weapon."

"You don't use them against a friend – an ally!"

"You are not an ally, Bishop. You haven't made up your mind whether you are a priest or a German."

Then Mullane snapped, "Okay, that's it. Get moving, everyone!"

Vokes led off and everyone fell in behind him. But Scheer

grabbed Mullane's arm. "Mr Mullane – please listen to me! Let me go down there to the beach – I can tell the Japanese you are back in the hills, heading for the north coast. Once they see those heaps of firewood, they'll know you've been here – they'll come looking for you and they'll find you. The General is right – they'll start shooting, people will be killed – "

"They might kill him, too – "

"Please, Herr Mullane, let me go down there – " Scheer suddenly spoke in German; he was desperate, he could not think in the other language. "I'll convince them – "

"Bishop, I can't afford to trust you – "

"I can't go on – I'm worn out – "

"You're coming with us. You could go down there and the Japs could kill you and still come after us. I don't want that to happen to you – "

He pushed Scheer ahead of him up the track, turned for a last look down at the beach. Through his glasses he saw the Japanese still in the surf, still trying to bring ashore the cap-sized raft. Then he heard the crashing through the bushes and spun round.

The Bishop was running at an angle down through the bushes into the plantation, stumbling on his old legs, crashing down but picking himself up at once, running, Mullane thought later, with the crazed faith of a martyr, the last thing the Bishop had ever wanted to be.

IV

Scheer stumbled into the plantation, pulled up and leaned against a coconut tree. His breath came out of him in long searing gasps; his heart felt ready to stop at any moment. There were scratches on his arms and face and a long tear in his cassock. Blood was running from a cut on his cheek and his right ankle, which he had turned as he had fallen, was swelling painfully. He leaned against the tree and wanted to weep, suddenly feeling helpless and hopeless.

"God, please help me – "

He stared down between the long lines of trees, waiting for the Japanese to come round the ruined house and open fire on him at sight. But they were still down on the beach, out of his view. He straightened up, looked at the umbrella he still held. Then he opened it and with the spreading of the small white canopy he seemed to gather strength. It had sheltered him for seventeen years against the sun and tropical rain; it had been his mark of identification, even more than his gold cross, amongst the souls he had dedicated himself to.

He marched down through the plantation, something of the soldier that his father had been in the straightness of his spine; he had been a humble man all his priestly life but something told him more than humility would be needed down on the beach. He could feel the fear building up inside him as he neared the ruins of the house, skirted it and came out through the tangled crotons and hibiscus within sight of the Japanese. *Lord, be at my side . . .*

The soldiers, both rafts now drawn up on the sand, looked up as he stepped on to the black beach and walked down towards them. A battery of guns came up and he waited for the bullets to thud into him, wondered how much pain he would feel before he died. Then someone barked an order and the soldiers, guns still aimed at him, moved up the beach.

He went down towards them, umbrella held above him against a sun that had already disappeared, that he might never see again after today. He paused only ten yards from them, took a deep breath, tried to stop the trembling that shook him like an attack of malaria. *I'm no hero or martyr*: he suddenly wished for the safety of the hills and of Mullane's party, no matter how temporary it might have been.

"*Sprechen sie deutsch?*" There was a certain, if brittle, security in his native tongue.

Two officers, one middle-aged and the other little more than a boy, stepped forward. The young officer said something in Japanese; but Scheer shook his head. Suddenly he knew he was not going to be able to communicate at all with these soldiers. They would kill him and his coming down here would have achieved nothing.

Then the older officer said, "I speak German, not very well. Who are you?"

"I am the Roman Catholic Bishop of Waku, Friedrich von Scheer." He stiffened, clicked his heels and bowed. Suddenly he was pragmatic: he was right, the humility of a priest would not be recognized here. "I am German and I wish to give myself up and be taken to Rabaul to your commander."

The officer looked up towards the ruins of the house, then back at Scheer. "You are alone? Where are the Australian spies? And General Nara?"

So Mariba had got down to Noku with Nara's message. "They have gone over the mountains, they are to be picked up by submarine on the north coast."

"How did you come here?"

"I escaped last night – General Nara helped me. He was too ill to come with me – he asked me to try to get to Rabaul for help when the Coastwatchers changed their plans." He was surprised at how easily the lies were coming; it was a luxury to lie to such purpose without a feeling of sin. "They are heading for – " he tried desperately to see the map of the north coast in his mind; he had never been there, it had not been part of his diocese – "for Open Bay – "

"When are they to be picked up?"

"Tonight, at midnight. There will be a submarine – " In the deepening dusk the Bishop could not see the heaps of firewood at the ends of the beach, but he was aware of them as if they were already blazing beacons. He must see that the Japanese did not start scouting around. "You must hurry – do you have a radio on your boat?"

"I am Colonel Yorida. How am I to know you are telling the truth?"

The shock of the name unnerved Scheer. What was this man doing here? Had General Nara somehow managed to get his message across to Mariba that Colonel Yorida was to be told that his old American enemy, the spy named McArdle, was here on New Britain?

"I am a priest – " The umbrella shivered above him, as if about to engulf him. His voice trailed off.

Yorida took out his pistol, held it at the German's head. "Everyone can tell lies, even priests. Do you swear by your

God that what you say is the truth?"

Lord, forgive me . . . "I swear it is the truth. They are heading for Open Bay."

On a ridge well behind the plantation Mullane, glasses to his eyes, peered through the dusk at the tiny figures on the beach. He had called a halt after the quick climb up the track; the strain of the trek was beginning to tell, even Buka looked exhausted. Vokes leaned against a nearby tree and Ruth sat on a log. Nara, more exhausted than any of them, lay flat on the ground.

"We should've gone after him," said Vokes. "He's on their side – he'll dob us in, I'll bet – "

"No," said Ruth. "You've got to trust him."

"They're leaving!"

Mullane could feel his hands shaking as he held the binoculars. All at once he was emotional with gratitude and admiration for the Bishop. The old German had sacrificed himself; Mullane could not believe that he had faith in the future of his Fatherland under Hitler. He was like Sister Brigid had been, lost without the opportunity to practise his vocation.

Down on the beach the two rafts put out into the surf, noses riding high into the waves as if they were going to be flung back on the sand. But the rafts rode the breakers and a moment later Mullane saw them moving steadily out towards the waiting patrol boat. The Bishop had put down his umbrella and Mullane could not pick him out amongst the soldiers in the two small boats.

V

"Another half-hour," said Vokes. "I'd better send Buka and Silas along to the fires, get them to stand by. You think the sub will come?"

Mullane looked up at the moon, noticed for the first time the star shining dimly in its glow. He remembered the sailor's superstition about a star-dogged moon, wondered if it was an omen. But it was too late now for doubts; the submarine, if indeed it was coming, was probably already standing offshore, still submerged but with its periscope scanning the black coast for the warning fires. There was no discernible glow from the volcano.

"It'll come."

"I wish you'd come with us," said Ruth.

Mullane felt for her hand in the darkness. The party was congregated at the edge of the sand where it merged into the long grass that had once been the front lawn of the plantation house. The breeze had dropped and the surf had flattened out; the low waves came in and slapped the sand with a tired sound. The scent of frangipani was a mocking perfume, too romantically sweet for the occasion.

"They'll relieve me soon." There had been no declared truce after their argument of this afternoon; Ruth had accepted the inevitable and he did not want to argue further with her. "They're not going to keep me here forever."

"If the Japs catch you, you'll be here forever. Buried."

"Don't talk like that, Ruthie." Vokes stirred uncomfortably in the grass. "We'll be all right. I think my luck is starting to turn – "

"I thought you said you were coming out with me – "

"No, I didn't say that. I thought about it, yes. But I couldn't leave Con to go in there on his own . . . You know what I mean, Con." He couldn't bring himself to say anything about duty. And he hoped Con wouldn't try to explain to Ruthie that he had to go along to show his Old Man back in Manly that all the patriotism didn't belong to the Old Soldiers of the last war. "I'll be going with you."

"You'll be welcome, Frank," said Mullane.

General Nara listened to the conversation but without any real interest. He had not said a word for the past two hours. Despair had taken hold of him, had weakened him till he felt as he had felt immediately after the plane had crashed and he had known he was helpless. He had placed so much faith in the certainty of his being rescued, in the competence of his forces to find him once he had sent Mariba down with the necessary information, that he had not even allowed himself to think what would happen if everything failed. He had told the American that he was both fatalistic and optimistic. He had lied, to himself as well as to the American; he was a fool whose

213

faith was as stupid as that of the German priest. His mind had begun to wander, seeking comfort in the past, shutting out the present and the future. At one point he had imagined himself back at the military academy. The image had been so clear he had heard the shouts and the clatter of staves as, dressed in his blue smock, face masked, hands awkward in their thick gloves, he had practised *kendo* with the instructors. He had been good at it; but later he had wondered if it had helped him. It did not win wars, not modern wars. He had come back to the present, looked at the stump of his arm and his shrunken body, wept for the boy he had once been, the youth with hopes and faith. Perhaps he might be more fatalistic now if the *kendo* staves had knocked some of the optimism out of him.

Then Vokes, who had been staring at the dark sea, shouted. "There it is! Down there off the southern point!"

Everyone was on his feet at once. Vokes sprinted off to the southern end of the beach; Luke and Mark, on an order from Mullane, raced to the northern end to tell Silas to light the fire there.

Mullane pulled Nara upright. The Japanese leaned against him and he could feel the exhaustion, of spirit as well as of body, in the small man. He knew how the General felt, how centuries of tradition would have conditioned him to view defeat and capture as the ultimate shame. He knew enough not to try to comfort the Japanese at this moment, but he felt sorry for him, even though he was the enemy.

He heard himself say, "I'm sorry it has to end this way for you, General."

"Give me a knife, please – or my gun – "

"No, General. I'm afraid your honour isn't that valuable – not to us – "

Then Nara suddenly slipped out of his arms, fell on to the sand and grabbed the rifle, Vokes' .303, lying there. The Australian, in his haste to get the fire lighted at the southern end of the beach, had raced off without it. Nara picked up the rifle, whimpering with pain as he brought up his stump to hold the gun steady, aimed at Mullane. Somehow he managed to slam back the bolt without dropping the rifle; then his finger was on the trigger.

"It is not going to end your way, Mr Mullane – "

"You'll never get away, General. They'll be ashore here in a few minutes – they'll hunt you down – "

"I'll be dead before then, Mr Mullane. So will you – and Mr Vokes, too. When he comes back I am going to shoot you both. I am sorry, but it has to be done – "

Mullane let out a long nervous sigh. He wanted to curse Vokes for his carelessness; but how could he blame the Australian? He had been just as careless for not having seen the rifle before Nara had.

Then there was a shot and Nara suddenly sat down; the .303 went off but the bullet went wide of Mullane. Ruth looked at the pistol in her hand, Nara's own gun, then she dropped it in the sand and looked at Mullane. At that moment, at both ends of the beach, the fires flared up.

Mullane stepped forward, leaned over the dead Japanese. He took the rifle, snapped on the safety catch and straightened up again.

"I had to do it, Con. Just as he said – but for the opposite reason – "

"It's all right." He put his arm round her.

"He would have killed you – "

"I know that."

Then Vokes came running back along the beach, followed by Buka. Silas and the young boys came running from the northern end. In a moment there was a milling group around Mullane, Ruth and the dead Nara.

"I heard the shots – " Then Vokes looked down at Nara's body. "Did he shoot himself? Where'd he get the gun – Oh Jesus, no!"

Mullane handed him the Lee-Enfield. "Take better care of it from now on, Frank. No, he didn't use it on himself. Ruth shot him. He was going to kill you and me."

Vokes slammed a fist savagely against his hip. "Jesus, I'm sorry, Con. I'm so bloody stupid – " Then he looked at Ruth. "Thanks, Ruth."

She remarked that he called her *Ruth*. But she said nothing, just put out a hand and touched his arm.

Then Buka said, "Boss, here come the boats!"

215

The two canvas pinnaces came gliding in through the flat surf, ran up on to the middle of the beach. There were two men in each boat, one of them a lieutenant.

"I'm Joe Pilowski. Lieutenant-Commander Berry sends his compliments, says he'd like to get us out of here as quickly as possible. There are patrol boats all up and down this stretch of coast. How many passengers do we have, Mr Mullane?"

"Just three. A woman and two native kids."

"*Three?* We were supposed to be coming in here for a German bishop and some Jap colonel or something – "

"He was a general – he's up there, dead. And the Japs took the bishop away this afternoon."

"Begging your pardon, Mullane, but we've come a hell of a way – "

"For just a woman and a couple of kids? I'm sorry about that. Maybe if they'd sent you in when I first asked, you'd have a full cargo. Here's my report." Mullane handed over the six-page report he had scribbled out by torchlight earlier in the evening. "It's all in there, except about the Jap general being shot. That happened only a while ago. Tell them he had to be shot. Miss Riddle will explain it all to them back in Moresby or Townsville."

"Well, okay – " Pilowski sounded disappointed, put out. "We brought you some supplies. Can you get your fellers to unload them? We don't want to hang around here."

The three sailors who had come in with Pilowski were already lifting boxes out of the boats. Mullane felt a sudden welling of feeling, of comfort and relief, at the sound of the American voices. He all at once wanted to go home; but then these Navy men and the submarine were not going home. America was a world away.

He went back up the beach to where Ruth stood waiting. "Would you mail these letters for me?"

He had written them yesterday while waiting for Vokes to return to the camp: one to his father, one to Liam. He wondered what Liam would think when he read the enclosure in the letter to him: the last will and testament of Cornelius James McArdle, in which everything he owned or might inherit was bequeathed to Ruth Riddle, care of Coastwatching Service, Townsville,

Queensland. He also wondered what Ruth would think of it if she knew of it. He had no idea how much he was worth, but he knew his father had set up a family trust and his share of it would not be inconsiderable. Whatever it was, it would be more than Ruth had ever dreamed of possessing.

"I hope some day you'll write to me – "

"I will, I promise." He held her by the arms, kissed her gently on the lips. "I'll take care, Ruth. I love you."

She said nothing, just clung to him with a fierce passion that did not need words, then she broke from him and went down to the boats. He followed her, picked her up and set her down in one of the boats.

He gave the boat a shove and it rose up over a small wave, then was gliding out towards the dim shape of the submarine some distance off-shore. The fires at the ends of the beach had already been doused with sand. Ruth, sitting in the forward boat, looked back at the beach. But it was indistinguishable against the black bulk of the mountains behind it. She looked in vain for a last sight of the man she loved and hoped she had not lost. But all she saw was the dark silhouette of the mountains under the death's-head moon, the wild hills where Mullane and Frank Vokes would continue to fight their very small and private war.

Chapter Eight

At first light in the morning Mullane paid off all the natives with the exception of Buka. As he handed out the money, paying each of them a bonus, he once more felt a hypocrite, but excused himself with the hope that the money would some day have value again. If he did not believe that, then he and Vokes might just as well have gone out last night with Ruth and sat the war out in Australia waiting for the eventual Japanese victory.

"Silas, take the boys back to Kiogo. You are to tell the Japanese, if they are still there, that Boss Vokes and I went off last night in the boat that goes under the sea. I trust you, Silas. Tell the boys I trust them, too. Tell them not to be like Mariba." He looked at Yali, arm still in a sling, standing near-by.

"If Mariba come back to Kiogo, I kill him," said Silas matter-of-factly. "He plenty bad, that feller. You want us again, boss, you send Buka with message. We come."

"I'll need you again," said Mullane and made himself sound as confident as possible.

When Silas and the carriers had gone, Mullane, Vokes and Buka took the radio, the batteries and the engine up into the bush behind the plantation and hid them; they also hid what supplies had been left behind. Mullane felt he could trust the natives, but there was no point in taking chances. He did not want to come back here and find all the gear stolen by some native suddenly ambitious to be a cargo cult leader.

He and Vokes and Buka gathered their packs and guns. He had not asked Buka if he wanted to go back to Kiogo, certain that the big native would have refused. Mullane checked their ammunition, knowing that they were more likely now to have to use their guns.

"I think we better test our guns. My Thompson is okay, but you and Buka had better try your rifles."

Buka lay down on the sand, aimed the Japanese 6.5 mm at a small rock farther along the beach. He took his time, squeezed the trigger and hit the rock high to the right. "Good enough," said Mullane. "Try yours, Frank."

Vokes lay down, aimed the .303 and fired at the same rock. The shot went wide; he tried another with the same result. "It pulls a bit to the right. And I'm not very good anyway, like I told you."

Mullane took the rifle, lay down and sighted along the barrel. He remembered the Winchester he had owned, the hunting in the fall months in the Maine woods; he had been a good marksman and he had enjoyed the pleasure of a shot on target. He took aim, allowed for the pull to the right and hit the rock dead centre. Then he took aim again, this time at a thick coconut tree some distance beyond the rock.

"What's the distance accuracy on this?"

"They said it should be accurate up to a thousand yards, but it was safer to think about eight hundred. I've never had a crack at anything over three hundred."

"Let me have that telescope."

He fitted the telescopic sight, chose another tree beyond the one he had been sighting on. It was at the far end of the beach, an isolated coconut palm growing at the edge of the mangrove swamp; he estimated the distance as seven hundred yards from where he lay. He took careful aim, squeezed the trigger; took aim again and fired a second shot. He stood up, unclipped the sight and handed the rifle back to Vokes.

"Now let's see how accurate it is."

They walked down the beach to the coconut palm. There was a fresh scar on the right-hand side of the trunk where the bullet had clipped it; the other bullet was embedded in the middle of the trunk.

"You're not bad," said Vokes admiringly. "Could you throw a baseball as accurately as that?"

"Not that distance," Mullane said with a grin. He knew there had been a degree of luck in the accuracy of the two shots, as there always was in a good accurate pitch, but he felt a certain satisfaction.

They went back along the beach, pulled on their packs, slung their guns over their shoulders and started up through the plantation. When they came to the spot where they had cached the radio and the supplies Mullane paused.

"I wonder if I shouldn't swap these Jap grenades for a bottle of Scotch." The four grenades were in a native string-bag tied to the top of his pack.

"Let's leave it, Con. If we get back, I'll get drunk with you, even though I don't like whisky."

"If . . . You're not feeling confident?"

"Righto. *When* we get back . . . But don't ask me that question again, Con. I'm no bloody hero."

"Nor am I." But he knew that he could not have gone out in last night's submarine with Ruth.

They moved up the slope. They were heading almost due north and would be out of sight of the coast all the way. They were a mile inland when they heard the Kawanisi flying-boat coming up behind them from the direction of Smokey Bay. It went directly over them as the three men paused beneath a screen of trees and disappeared behind the mountains ahead.

"It looks as if it's heading for the north coast," Vokes said. "I wonder what the Bishop told them?"

"I'm not even guessing. I just hope he's still alive."

"Yeah." Vokes was abruptly sober. "He wasn't a bad sort, you know what I mean? I've always felt uncomfortable with priests and parsons, but I was coming to like him. Do you think they might try working him over?"

"I hope not." But he feared for the Bishop if he should be taken before Yorida and interrogated by him.

They covered only ten miles that day. Buka had found a path, but it wound up and down ridges that seemed never-ending. They crossed a river, stripping off and crossing it with their gear held as high as possible out of the water; they went across in turn, with two of them remaining on the bank with their guns at the ready in case a crocodile should appear. They camped that night on a high ridge, undisturbed except by mosquitoes trying to get at them through their nets; they could have been light-years away from any war, it was difficult to conjure up what lay ahead of them in Rabaul. Mullane, lying awake, thinking of tomorrow (if there should be a tomorrow), saw the flying-foxes scrape a dark line across the moon, heard the call of a night-bird, felt the urge to stay here and let the war take care of itself. He slipped into the womb of sleep pursued by devils of fear.

They woke in the morning to a world of white mist. There was no point in trying to move on till the mist lifted; visibility went no more than ten or fifteen yards. At last the mist lifted, coming up out of the valleys as slowly-swirling wraiths dying under the sun's attack. The forest came alive; a cloud of cockatoos, whiter than the mist, came up out of a valley in a screaming chorus. The men moved on, part of the jungle, not even looked upon as intruders by the rest of the wildlife. Men, even natives, were so rare in this region of the hills that the birds seemed unafraid of the strangers.

It was midday before they caught sight of the first village. It stood on the next ridge ahead of them, a small collection of grass huts and a burned-off strip of land where a garden had been planted.

"We in Baining land, boss," said Buka. "They bad buggers. People say they still eat long pig."

"Jesus, I hope not!" said Vokes. *Long pig* was the native term for human flesh.

"They could be. Especially if the Japs have cut off their usual food supplies. Do you fancy being a bit of gourmet's delight?"

"I'd do my best to poison any bastard who took a bite out of me."

"I think you better find us another track, Buka. Mr Vokes wants to remain intact."

Buka grinned, not understanding all the banter but understanding that both the bosses still had their sense of humour. He was in high good humour himself, felt that he was on equal terms with the bosses. He patted his rifle, hoped he would get a chance to use it.

He found another track and led them round the base of the

ridge and below the village. They saw three other villages in the next four hours and skirted those, too. In the late afternoon they came upon their first Japanese.

The hills and ridges had flattened out and they were moving through forest over a plateau that rose and fell like a gentle sea. They were coming down through a thick stand of *erima* trees when they heard the sound of a motor-cycle, then that of two trucks. They moved on cautiously through the trees, came out behind a pile of huge limestone boulders. Straight ahead and below them was a dirt road and the motor-cycle and trucks were bowling along it, spinning out a thick train of dust behind them.

Mullane waited till the tiny convoy had gone past and the dust had settled. Then he looked up and down the road; he could see it winding among the trees for half a mile in either direction. There was no sign of any road-blocks or patrols.

"This must be the perimeter road," said Vokes. "They're pretty cocky. No sentries out, nothing."

"Why shouldn't they feel cocky? They know there are none of our troops on the island. And none of the natives are going to attack them."

"This feller would," said Buka, grinning broadly, betel stain looking like blood on his lips.

"How many would you get to help you? Let's face it. This island, or anyway the Gazelle peninsula, belongs to the Japs and they know it. That's the one thing we have going for us. They're not going to be looking for someone trying to get inside their perimeter."

They crossed the road and kept on through the forest. They went round several villages – "Tolais," said Mullane. "At least the Tolais don't eat you. Not any more."

"My father's father, he ate long pig," said Buka. "He live a long time. Must be good for the belly."

"Cut it out," said Vokes. "You're making me feel like a Christmas turkey."

They came to a second road and paused while half a dozen trucks went by, each separated from the one in front of it by fifty yards and each trailing its own thick wake of grey dust.

When the dust cleared Mullane saw the guard-post two

hundred yards down the road to the left. A hundred yards away in the other direction were three soldiers, so coated in dust that they looked like mummies; they were smacking the dust from themselves, but were making no attempt to move on. Mullane crept out to the edge of the timber, raised his glasses and looked down to where the road dipped into a hollow. He could see a small Chinese trading store with some trucks pulled up outside it and a dozen or more Japanese standing around drinking from bottles. Back in the other direction, beyond the guard-post, there was a small bridge with sentries posted at either end of it.

Vokes and Buka came forward to join him, lay in the long grass amongst a bright red pool of flowers from the flame tree above them. Vokes said, "We're not going to make it to Taluka before dark, not if we have to make a detour. That means we lose another day holed up in the bush."

Taluka, some eight or ten miles south of the township of Rabaul, was one of the two main Japanese airstrips; there was a third one farther west at Keravat. An appreciation of the Japanese locations at Taluka was the first task Mullane had set himself.

"We wait till the next convoy comes along. Then we cross the road, one by one, through the dust each truck kicks up."

"Jesus, you come up with some bloody great ideas."

"Higher education. Only a Yale man would think of it."

"Up Yale," said Vokes, gesturing with his thumb. "We showed more sense at Manly High."

"Good idea, boss." Buka loved being with these two men, was enjoying himself more and more. "You make bloody good kanaka."

"A kanaka from Yale. I must write the Dean."

The banter meant nothing; it was only a way of easing their nerves. They had had an easy time getting this far, except for the physical toil of the hard trekking; there had been no danger. But from here on they would be in constant danger and they all knew it.

They had to wait another twenty minutes before they heard the sound of engines again. Then, through his binoculars, Mullane saw the convoy of six trucks, four of them petrol tankers, coming over the bridge beyond the guard-post.

"This is it. There are four tankers, all of them between the first and last truck. There'll be no one riding on the backs of those, so that'll give us a blind side – you can go right through behind the tanker as it comes along. You go first, Frank – take the first tanker. Then you, Buka, behind the next one. Then I'll come. Keep going into that timber on the other side."

They watched the six trucks come up the road. The surface of the road was volcanic soil, which did not provide stable traction for the vehicles' wheels. The road obviously had a lot of traffic and the surface had been ground into a fine grey dust. The leading truck slewed once as it came up past the guard-post and dust rolled back along both sides of the road. It was now impossible to see the following tankers and Mullane could imagine their drivers struggling to peer ahead through the thick grey murk.

The leading truck went past, there was a gap, then the first tanker rumbled by. Vokes, crouched over, sprinted out like the rugby half-back he had once been; he ran blindly through the choking dust, came out on the other side and plunged into the thick bush that came right to the road's edge. The second tanker came by and Buka, running with the high knee-action peculiar to the natives, went through the dust like a black spirit. Then it was Mullane's turn. He had no idea whether Vokes and Buka had made the other side; they could be lying there in the swirl of dust. The roadway now was nothing but a thick grey fog.

The trucks were barely discernible; he heard rather than saw the third tanker coming. He tensed himself, saw the dust thicken again, and launched himself out and across the road. He almost hit the back of the tanker; he had to sidestep and he went by its tail with only inches to spare. The pack on his back slipped, pulling him sideways and he went down on his knees, losing the Thompson gun. Frantically he felt for it, unable to see anything even an inch from his face; then the gun was under his blind hand, he grabbed it, tried to get to his feet. He heard the next tanker coming at him through the thick dust; the roar of its engine seemed almost on top of him. He flung himself forward and the tanker went by right above him, its front wheel actually brushing the heel of his boot. He lay there while the rear wheel rolled by, holding his breath against the choking dust, his eyes shut tight so that he would not be blinded. Then he was on his feet, had plunged straight ahead into the bush that he couldn't see and heard the fourth tanker and then the last truck rumble by behind him. He picked himself up and ran into the forest, seeing Vokes and Buka waiting up ahead for him.

Taluka could not be more than two or three miles from here.

II

"How's your ankle?"

"A bit sore," said Vokes. "It's my boots that are worrying me – they're starting to rot. I look like walking out of here barefoot."

Mullane looked down at his own boots, covered in mud and with a gap starting to show in the seam of the toe-cap. It was the one item of equipment he had forgotten to order in the last supply drop and he wondered if Vokes would be right and they could indeed go out of here barefoot. If this rain kept up it was more than possible.

It had started to rain, steadily and heavily, when they were no more than a quarter of an hour into the forest after they had crossed the road. Luck had been with them; the road was now probably a quagmire and if they had been half an hour later there would have been no dust to obscure them. The rain had slowed them but at the same time it was helping them. In such a downpour there were few Japanese or natives likely to be moving around. The trio went round a village that suddenly appeared ahead of them on the track they were following; they halted behind some thick lantana while four Japanese, heads bent, plodded by. They crossed another road, this one little more than a flooded bush track, and then came to the outer edge of the timber. Ahead of them lay a field of tall kunai grass, a slope dotted with trees and scrub and, at the crest of the hill, appearing out of the easing rain, a thick wall of banyan-like ficus trees.

Then they saw the small scout plane come over the hill and,

225

wobbling as the pilot tried to keep his line down through the rain, go down beyond the field of kunai.

"That's it!" Vokes said. "That's Taluka!"

But from where they stood they could see nothing of the airstrip or what surrounded it. From the line of the plane's approach Mullane guessed that the strip must run on a north-south axis. He looked towards the tree-crested hill, barely visible through the rain, at the southern end; he estimated it would be no more than half a mile from the end of the strip. It would be an ideal observation point.

"When it's dark we'll head for that hill. We'll hide in those trees at the top."

They stayed in the forest till darkness fell. Each of them had wrapped himself in a ground-sheet and sat down; but the rain and the dampness seeped into them. Mullane began to imagine that not only his boots but his whole being was beginning to rot. He ate a banana and munched on some biscuits and, to distract himself, thought of an old German legend he had read when he had been studying German.

It concerned itself with a marvellous country called Schlaraffenland. To enter this magical land one had to eat one's way through a wall of porridge; but after that everything was lushly laid on. Trees were weighed down with candied fruits. Braised pigeons, breast brown and juicy, flapped about on medium-rare wings, cooing to be eaten. Pigs, covered in crackling, ambled about with knives and forks already sticking out of their meat. Beautiful girls, with golden goblets, sat by streams of red wine. Mullane, mouth slobbering at the dream, turned his face up to the less-than-intoxicating rain. He wondered if Bishop Scheer, the priest who saw no sin in the good life, had ever heard of Schlaraffenland.

They moved off as soon as it was dark. The rain was still falling and they were halfway up the slope of the hill, slipping and sliding in the mud, before it ceased. They saw a light over to their left, but in the black night they could not make out what surrounded it. At last they reached the long line of ficus trees, a huge wall of timber that loomed over them like the battlements of a castle.

Mullane had seen several stands of these trees in the Rabaul district when he had come up to the town for supplies. They had been planted as windbreaks by German plantation owners before the Great War, some as long ago as the 1890s. They were now a hundred feet high, with as many trunks as a banyan tree; he had once seen a tree whose intertwined trunks had covered more than an acre of ground. There were six trees in this stand, their roots and trunks long interlinked in twisted patterns that suggested Nature's nightmares. Their foliage at the top was thick and massive, ideal for hiding in.

Buka went up first, being the expert climber of the three. Vokes followed, then Mullane. It was not easy climbing, with the trunks wet and slimy from the rain, but there were plenty of footholds. At last they were high among the top branches, under a canopy of thick leaves. Then suddenly there was a great commotion right above them and Vokes almost fell out of the tree in fright.

"Bloody things!"

The flying-foxes, dozens of them, streamed away in a great cloud, a black mass against the stars that were now beginning to show through. They left behind them a disturbing smell and Vokes gingerly felt about him in the darkness.

"They've probably shit all over the tree. Geez, if I don't get the Victoria Cross for this little trip – "

"Better try for some sleep. Wedge yourself in somewhere and tie yourself to something."

Despite his advice to Vokes, it took Mullane himself some time to fall asleep. The flying-foxes came back in the middle of the night, brushed through the foliage above, found their home was still invaded and went off again on wings that seemed to creak in protest. All three men woke at the disturbance, but soon fell asleep again. When Mullane woke at first light he was shivering and he wondered if he was going to come down with malaria. He took an extra tablet of atebrin, then ate some cold Spam, some biscuits and a wild orange. Then he stood up on his perch and relieved himself. Vokes and Buka did the same.

"I wish a cousin of mine was down there below," said Vokes. "He's such an uppity bastard I've always wanted to piss on him from a great height."

Mullane smiled, glad of the younger man's spirits. Several

times yesterday he had wondered if Vokes was losing his willingness for this expedition; the boy had at times been unnaturally quiet, as if racked by doubt. But now they had arrived at Taluka, were safe, at least for the moment, his spirits seemed to have revived.

"This is a great spot, Con. We can see everything."

The strip was plainly evident, a long white patch of mist stretching away to the north, a wide swathe cut through kunai grass. Parking bays were at either side of the runway, all of them covered with camouflage netting; mist filtered out of them like smoke from burning caverns. There were several low buildings set back against some trees on the western side of the strip and there were cleared areas at the southern end where petrol tankers and other trucks were parked. A hundred yards to the east of the strip, beyond a stretch of kunai through which tracks had been cut, was a coconut plantation. But, except for the planes parked one to a bay, there was no sign of the squadrons Mullane had expected to see.

"Twelve planes," said Vokes. "There should be more than that. Double, treble. Where the hell have all those bombers been coming from?"

Mullane knew that aerial reconnaissance had given a fair appreciation of the plane strength at the other strips, Vunakanau and Keravat. "I don't know. They must be flying at least another four or five squadrons out of somewhere in this area."

Halfway down the slope towards the strip was the source of the light they had seen last night, a small radar post, the cup of its antenna turning slowly in the morning light like a cold steel eye. Some men had come out of the hut and were washing themselves in a basin; others were going into the kunai to a rough latrine. A night picquet, stretching his arms, came up the slope towards the hut, unslung his rifle and slumped down in a canvas chair.

"You want me to go down, look around, boss?" Buka, the native, the one who could merge with the landscape, was eager to prove he had not come along just for the walk.

"Be careful, Buka. Try talking to some of the villagers, find out if anything special is going on. They may be using more boys to load supplies or something."

Buka, leaving his Japanese rifle and his pack, disappeared down into the depths of the tree. Mullane couldn't see which way he went once he reached the ground; he'd had the good sense not to walk out directly from beneath the tree. It was now broad daylight, the ground mist beginning to rise, and Mullane could see each way along the stand of tall trees. It was almost as if he and Vokes were hidden in a high green bank; the trunks and foliage beneath them were as impenetrable to anyone's gaze as solid earth. If they did not move around they were as safe in these upper galleries of the trees as they had been miles back in the jungle.

Then the mist lifted and the airfield came alive. Trucks started up, came out of the parking area and rolled down towards the parking bays. Aircraft were pushed out to the sides of the runway and were fuelled by the tankers. Mullane counted them: an even dozen, as Vokes had said.

Then Vokes let out a stifled yelp. "Over to the right! The plantation!"

Mullane swung his glasses. The plantation was perhaps two hundred yards long by about a hundred wide, an estate of mature coconut palms. But as he focused his glasses he saw several of the boundary trees being *drawn aside*.

"Holy Jesus!" said Vokes. "The whole bloody plantation is camouflage!"

Mullane gazed carefully at what was being exposed, amazed by and admiring of the Japanese ingenuity. Actual trees had been left standing at intervals of perhaps a hundred feet, wide enough for a bomber to be manoeuvred between them. Wires were strung between the trees; netting hung from the wires, painted with fake trunks. Sections of the netting had been pulled, like curtains being opened to the morning sun; in the shadows beyond Mullane could see planes parked and tree-trunks rising above them. The top of the plantation, hundreds of palm fronds spread out like umbrellas, was nothing more than one huge camouflage net hung across supporting trees and carrying the tops of the trees that had been cut down to make room for the bombers. From the air the estate would have looked like a plantation still in production. The dead, camouflaging palm tops looked as if they had been sprayed with paint to help the illusion that they were still the tops of thriving trees. Black-and-white aerial photographs must not have picked up the deception.

"Is that a Burns Philp plantation?"

"No," said Vokes. "I'm trying to remember who it belonged to. He was a German who'd stayed on here, I can't remember his name. Geez, what a job they've done!"

Planes were being pushed out through the opening in the curtained wall and rolled down two of the wide tracks through the kunai grass to the strip. In the next twenty minutes twenty bombers, Mitsubishi G4Ms, Bettys, came out of the plantation hangar and were moved down to the landing strip. Then, for the first time, Mullane saw the half a dozen Zeros high in the sky on patrol. The Japanese seemed to have thought of everything: if any reconnaissance plane should come over while the bombers were being moved out from their cover, the Zeros would be there to shoot it down.

When all the bombers were down on the strip gangs of natives appeared, began sweeping the two tracks and laying palm fronds; from the air, Mullane guessed, it would appear that the Japanese had laid a palm cover over soft ground to prevent their trucks from sinking into the mud. There was no sign that something as heavy as a bomber had passed down the tracks.

Five minutes later the first bomber took off, racing down the strip towards the hill where Mullane and Vokes were hidden. Its nose came up gently and it rushed at them and went over with a thunderous roar. They crouched down, making themselves as small as possible. The noise was deafening each time a plane passed over. Mullane counted them: 32; but the number was academic. They would link up with other bombers from the other strips and the mass of them would head south for another heavy raid. He could only hope that the Coastwatchers down in the Solomons were back on the air and able to alert the fighters waiting to take off from Guadalcanal. He itched to get to a Morse key, excited by their discovery. But there was more to be learnt and it might be another three or four days before he or Vokes could get back to the radio and pass the information to Moresby and Townsville.

The rest of the day passed slowly and uncomfortably. The two men took it in turns to doze off, knowing that there would be little sleep for them tonight when they moved on to Rabaul itself. The weather, ironically, had now cleared: it would have been a splendid day for aerial reconnaissance over Simpson Harbour and maybe Mullane and Vokes would not have had to move in further. But there was no sign of any planes coming in high from the west.

The sun poured down out of the almost cloudless sky. The flying-fox droppings, now clearly visible on the branches and leaves, began to smell. Rotten fruit from the tree itself had fallen into crevices in the trunks and they gave off their own sickening sweet stink. Birds approached the tree, sensed it was already occupied and swung away to settle in branches farther along the stand of timber. During the morning planes came and went: some Zero fighters, two scout planes, a couple of big transports. By late afternoon Mullane and Vokes knew all they wanted to know about the Taluka airstrip and they looked forward to darkness and the opportunity to escape from what had become their stinking prison.

Buka came back in the late afternoon, an hour after the last bomber had returned. There had been no missing planes, a bad sign; it suggested that the Coastwatchers down in the Solomons had still not been able to get back on the air. Mullane wondered if the posts had been overrun, the men captured and, probably, executed, or had they had the same bad luck as himself and Vokes and lost the use of their radios? The loss of a radio only emphasized the isolation of all Coast-watchers.

Buka came up out of the twisted depths of the tree as if he were emerging from the bowels of the earth. He wrinkled his nose at the smell, but made no comment on it.

"I found a police boy worked with me one time. He work for Jap now, he got job working on roads. He say plenty things going on, lots more Jap come here. Jap took him and other boys down to Rabaul yesterday in truck. Plenty ships in harbour. But he dunno where they going or when. He just think plenty soon."

They climbed down out of the tree as soon as darkness fell.

The sky was still clear and Mullane set a course by the stars.

"A bloody navigator, too," said Vokes. "With all your study, when did you get time to play baseball?"

"I never believed that maxim about a little knowledge being a dangerous thing. Bits and pieces and lots of confidence and you can pass for a genius."

"In other words, bullshit. I always knew you Yanks were full of it."

"Vulgarity fits you like a glove, Frank. As it does most Aussies."

Again they were letting out their tension chaffing each other. The insults at each other's national faults were only gently satirical and each of them knew it. They were now a team and each of them knew that, too.

They had only about six or seven miles to go to come out on the cliffs above Simpson Harbour at Rabaul. They passed through some cultivated land and several plantations, by-passed a couple of villages, crossed a sparsely-travelled main road, then were in thickly-wooded hills that fell steeply towards Blanche Bay, the outer bay covering the harbour. They kept to the top of connecting ridges and made good progress. But Mullane's and Vokes' boots were beginning to crack and Vokes' remark about leaving here barefoot no longer sounded like a joke.

It was midnight when they came out on top of the cliffs that ran above the Kokopo road that skirted the western shore of the harbour. They had passed several Japanese guard-posts, but these were in cleared areas and easily visible. There were native gardens that were well-tended and obviously enlarged since the Japanese occupation; once, when they passed too close to a garden, a dog barked at them but no one came out of the near-by huts to see what had disturbed the animal. Once again Mullane was grateful for the Japanese complacency; except for the occasional Allied air raid they believed the war was a long way from Rabaul. The Japanese were safer here, he sur-mised, than the Germans were in any of the occupied European countries. They knew they did not have to worry about any resistance movement among the native population.

Not all the cliff-top had been cleared. The early German

settlers had known the value of windbreaks and here again they had planted ficus trees to protect their plantations. Mullane and the others came to a thick stand of ten or twelve trees that blocked their path as effectively as if it were another cliff face rising above the natural rock one. They climbed into the end tree, disturbing another flock of flying-foxes. Vokes swore softly, cursing at another day to be spent among the smell of dung and rotting fruit.

The moon was still high, a bomber's moon, and Mullane was able to pick out identifiable landmarks. Immediately to their right was the 600-foot high Vulcan Crater, the volcano that had come up out of the sea in the eruption of 1937. The harbour itself was a flooded crater of what, before time had begun to be counted, had been a huge volcano. On the eastern side of the harbour three other volcanoes, the Mother and the North and South Daughters, thrust up towards the moon. Out in the harbour itself two peaks of rock showed above the water, the only remaining evidence of the ancient buried crater. On the far side of the palely shining stretch of water, between the Mother and the North Daughter, was Rabaul township.

They could hear traffic passing on the road beneath the cliff but could not see it. They could see the dim shape of ships in the harbour, their lights blacked out, but over in the town the effort at a blackout seemed only casual. Mullane stared across the blue-silver water at the yellow diamonds of light in the darkness below the black hills. Somewhere there Colonel Yorida lay sleeping, probably without an itch on his conscience.

"I wonder if the Bishop is over there?" Vokes said.

"Maybe we can find that out tomorrow." Their voices were mere whispers. Mullane was restless now, wanting to gather all the information they could and be gone, but he knew they would need daylight to get an accurate estimate of how many ships were on hand in the harbour and out in Blanche Bay and to guess at when the Japanese planned their move. "You willing to go into town tomorrow, Buka?"

"Okay, boss. Tomorrow morning."

"Be careful, Buka. Don't take any risks."

"Nobody going to touch me. Them Jap fellers, they all think us kanakas all look the same. The Tolais, they know I'm different, but they ain't going to say nothing."

"Okay, but be careful where you ask your questions. There's a storekeeper in Chinatown named Charlie Hong – you remember him, we used to buy some of our stuff from him. I think he could be trusted. He'd co-operate with the Japs, but he wouldn't be on their side. I know he came from near Nanking, though he wouldn't tell them that."

"Charlie Hong good feller. I talk to him."

"If he's going to a store," said Vokes, "how about buying us some boots? I take a size eight."

"What's he going to buy them with? Charlie Hong's not going to risk taking any Australian money. And I don't want Buka to take any risk – "

"No risk, boss. I get you boots."

"No, Buka. I'd rather walk all the way from here to Gasmata barefoot than have Colonel Yorida and his buddies shoving bayonets in you to find out who the boots were for."

"You want me to ask Charlie Hong anything special?"

"Ask him where Jap headquarters are. If we can pinpoint it, then maybe our planes can drop a bomb or two on it."

"Anything else, boss?"

Mullane hesitated, then said, "Find out where Field Security has its office."

"Oh, for Christ's sake!" said Vokes. "You're not thinking of going over there after that bloke Yorida, are you?"

Mullane was glad of the darkness. "No. But a bomb on *him* would be some satisfaction."

Just before dawn Buka climbed down from the tree, going off once again armed only by the colour of his skin. Day came up out of the east grey and drab; clouds had come over in the shank of the night and there was a touch of rain in the air. At least it promised that the day here in the tree-tops would be more bearable than yesterday.

The harbour and the town were now clearly visible. The two Coastwatchers sat in the dress circle of a theatre of war: a small theatre perhaps but one where all the elements of war were marshalled for a larger performance elsewhere. In the inner harbour there were dozens of ships: tankers, supply ships, transports, destroyers; out at sea on the edge of the big bay were warships, an aircraft carrier and several large cruisers. From his haversack Mullane took out some papers pinned together; they were pages from *Jane's Fighting Ships*. They were yellowed and torn, some of them stuck together with Scotch tape; he had taken them to Japan with him, used them to identify ships in Tokyo Bay and other harbours. He called the types of ships as he identified them and Vokes wrote down the information:

"At least seventy ships this area, tell them. Two Nati first-class cruisers, two Kako first-class cruisers, two Magami second-class cruisers, one Kuma second-class cruiser, one Tanryu second-class cruiser, three sloops, thirty destroyers, two passenger liners, look like 10,000-tonners – all these standing off Blanche Bay. In Simpson Harbour four more destroyers, sixteen freighters, six tankers, one submarine mother ship. And eight Kawanisi flying-boats."

"Christ, that's a regular fleet! Any sign of subs?"

"None."

"When do you reckon the fleet's going to take off?"

"Pretty soon, I'd say. They're not going to keep a build-up like that standing around waiting for our fellers to come and bomb it. They'll be on their way tomorrow at the outside."

"They must be heading for Guadalcanal, you can bet on it." Vokes was doing some quick calculations: "They'd average, what d'you reckon, about twelve knots? No more, not a convoy that size. That's um, er, um, about 270 miles in twenty-four hours. It's about 700 miles down to Guadalcanal – two-and-a-half days' steaming. If we wait here till they start off, we're going to have to get our finger out to get back to the wireless in time. Headquarters will want all the notice they can get."

"You'd better move out right after dark then."

"Me? Why me? What are you planning to do?"

"I'm going back to Taluka." The plan, wild though it might seem, had been taking hold in his restless mind all night. "I'm resigning from the Coastwatchers for a few days. I'll rejoin when I meet you back at Smokey Bay."

Vokes looked carefully at him through the green light under the canopy of leaves. "You still got that bloke Yorida on your mind? Forget him, Con. How the hell are you going to settle anything with him? Not unless you're set on something bloody stupid, like a suicide mission or something?"

"No, nothing like that. I'm going to try and do something about that plantation hangar."

"To *what*? Oh, you're out of your bloody head – Ah, what's the use?"

Mullane looked across the harbour again, as conscious of Yorida's presence as if the man were standing in full view only a hundred yards away down in the plantation between the road and the water's edge. He was surprised at how clearly he remembered the man, after trying so hard to forget him. Then he said, "I'll take your .303 and the telescopic sight. You can have the Tommy gun."

Vokes waved his arms, almost fell off his perch and had to grab at a branch to save himself. Then he looked with disgust at his hands. "Shit!"

Mullane laughed softly. "Find some clean leaves – "

Vokes wiped his hands, scowling at the muck; but really scowling at the thought of Mullane's planned folly. He was not quite sure what the American had in mind, but preferred not to know; whatever it was, he knew he could not talk him out of it. He had developed an affection for Mullane that he would not have believed possible in the time they had been together. He had had mates down in Sydney to whom he had thought he was close; he had been surprised to find that he had hardly missed them in his months up here in the Islands. He had, however, begun to think of Con Mullane as a *friend*, one whom he would miss terribly if something happened to him. The word did not enter his mind, because he was shy of it, suggesting some sort of queerness, but he had begun to love the American.

"I'll be okay, Frank. Really."

Mullane sensed the other's concern for him and was touched by it. He, unlike Vokes, had never had any really close friends. He had always got on well with other men; but when it came to confidences he had always been a loner. He doubted that he would ever exchange close confidences with Frank Vokes; the worlds each of them had left behind were too far apart for that. But he knew that if the Australian should, by chance, be captured or killed he would feel a sense of loss that would remain with him.

236

"Bugger!" Vokes said suddenly. "Look along there!"

Less than two hundred yards away to their left was an anti-aircraft gun emplacement, its crew going about their morning ablutions, cooking breakfast, dragging a camouflage net back over the gun-pit.

Mullane studied them. "We'll be all right if we just sit tight. They're like all the other Japs – they don't think there's anyone like us within miles of them."

"Unless the Bishop told them that you and I were planning to come in here."

"That's a risk we have to take. But those fellers certainly aren't looking for us." From his observations of the Japanese back at Taluka and these men in the gun-pit, he was learning at least one thing, that men in war were rarely, if ever, concerned with anything beyond their immediate task. "We just sit here and wait for dark."

The day dragged on without incident. They saw fighters and small planes come and go on the airstrip south of the town. Barges moved constantly between the ships in the harbour and the shore; other barges chugged out to the larger ships anchored in Blanche Bay. There was the constant hum of traffic on the obscured Kokopo road beneath the cliffs. Once they heard singing and whistling and down on the road they guessed that troops were on the march. The singing and whistling went on for a long time and Mullane wondered how many soldiers were passing by unseen beneath them. An hour later a fleet of barges appeared from somewhere round to the left, all of them packed with troops. They moved out to the transports in the harbour and the outer bay.

"They must be moving out tonight or tomorrow morning," Vokes said. "Jesus, I've got to get moving!"

"You have to wait till dark."

Buka came back with the darkness, climbing out of the depths as he had done at Taluka. He carried a string bag with something wrapped in taro leaves in it. He opened the leaves and in the darkness shoved two pairs of boots at Mullane.

"Jap boots, boss. Dunno if they fit, but they all Charlie Hong had. He pinched them from Jap, say you pay him after war finish."

"Thanks, Buka." Mullane was annoyed at him for taking such a risk; but he could not chide him. "What did you find out?"

"Jap going out, some tonight, some tomorrow night. Charlie not know where they going, but he think Bougainville, Guadalcanal, somewhere down there."

"It's on, then," said Vokes.

"Jap headquarters, it up in New Guinea Club, Charlie say. I couldn't get up that street, they got guards all around it. But Charlie say there is big hole in ground, covered up – "

"A bunker?"

"Yeah, that what he call it. A bunker. It where the Jap big boss is. It just across the road from the New Guinea Club."

Mullane knew the club, had always gone there for a drink whenever he had come up to Rabaul on business. It had always been the bastion of the white man, no kanakas allowed in except as servants; he wondered what the more educated of the natives thought now of its being taken over by their new masters. They probably felt no resentment, were just laughing quietly to themselves at the ironies of history.

"Any damage from our bombing raids on the town?"

"Charlie say not much damage. Worst thing, he say, was bomb on big brothel in Chinatown. It kills girls and Jap, all with pants down." Even in the darkness Mullane imagined he could see Buka's big grin.

"We'd better put in a complaint about that," said Vokes. "That was a good clean brothel. The Air Force ought to be a bit more accurate."

"What about Field Security, Buka?"

"Charlie know all about that. He say feller, Colonel Yorida, he very tough on all Chinamen."

"Where's their headquarters?"

"Charlie say it in police station."

"You hear that, Frank? When you get back to Smokey Bay, make sure you give them those two targets. Tell them I'd particularly appreciate a bomb right on the police station."

"If they're so bloody wide of the mark the best they can do is bomb a brothel – Okay, I'll tell 'em. Well, I'd better start moving."

238

"Do those boots fit you?"

"Too small. Yours are going to be the same. Aren't there any Nips with decent-sized feet?"

Buka grunted with disappointment and Mullane said, "Thanks anyway, Buka. Frank, with a bit of luck you'll be back at Smokey Bay by nightfall the day after tomorrow. That will give Townsville plenty of time to warn them down in the Solomons."

"I'm not going to make it in these boots – they'll fall off my feet before I've gone half a mile. I'm going down to Smokey Bay by boat."

"How do you think you're going to do that, for Christ's sake?"

"Con, look out there. There are boats coming and going all the time, even now – it's like Sydney Harbour on the Anniversary Day regatta. I've been looking down at that plantation on the water there. There are five or six launches and a petrol dump at the end of the jetty. All I'll want is a four-gallon drum on board one of those boats. It's only fifty, maybe sixty miles by sea and that'd get me there. Once I'm out past the headland nobody's going to see me."

"That's going to be the easiest part of it. How are you going to get down there to the plantation and swipe the boat and the gasoline? It'll be much safer to find some Jap, knock him on the head and take his boots."

"What do I do – go looking in the dark for some big-footed Nip? No, I've thought it out, Con. It can be done and I'm going to do it."

"Boss," said Buka, speaking to both of them, "one thing bugger up everything. Down them cliffs, there's big holes. Caves. Jap, he got workshops or something in them."

That silenced Vokes; but only for a moment. "Well, I've just got to be more careful, that's all. But the boat's my only hope. I'm never going to make it barefoot back to Smokey Bay. Pity we didn't teach you, Buka, to work the wireless."

"I stay with Boss," said Buka simply, as if the sending of radio messages was unimportant.

"Well, I'm going to try it anyway. Once I'm on my way, then you two can start off for Taluka – and after what you're planning to do back there, whatever it is, don't talk to me about what I'm going to try."

Mullane saw there was no point in further argument. And the possibility of Vokes' being back at Smokey Bay within a matter of hours had given him a further idea. "If you do get away, you should be down at Smokey Bay in – what – four hours? Five? Send the main message, that's the important one. Then tell them I'd like some Air Force co-operation and this is what I'm planning to do – "

Vokes listened in silence, then said, "You *are* committing suicide, Con. They don't expect something like that from us. What about the Ferdinand principle – ?"

"The hell with Ferdinand. I told you – I've resigned from the Coastwatchers for a few days. Just tell the RAAF – it'll have to be Hudsons coming in at night – that I'll want them over the target area at 0020 hours."

"Righto, I'll tell them. But there's going to be hell to pay when Townsville finds out what you're up to."

"They can't cashier me. I'm still a civilian, remember? The worst they can do is repatriate me back to Australia."

"Well, that'd please Ruthie, if no one else." Vokes fumbled in his pack, then with his shoulders. "You've just reminded me. I've put my tabs up, just in case. There. Pity I can't see them. A bloody sub-lieutenant. An officer and a gentleman – almost."

Mullane made a movement with his hand in the darkness. "I just saluted you."

"Thanks. I hope I can do the same for you some day."

But Vokes could not move immediately. It was another hour before the traffic down on the Kokopo road had thinned out till there was only an occasional truck going past. Then Vokes said, "Well, time I was going. Good luck, Con. You too, Buka. I'll see you back at Smokey Bay in three days' time. Don't try anything too bloody stupid at Taluka."

"I'll come down to the road with you, make sure you get started. Stay here, Buka."

He went down ahead of Vokes, not wanting any argument. He left his pack and the Lee-Enfield in the tree; he had also left his cap, but he did not notice its absence. He was only concerned with seeing that Vokes got off to a safe start.

Vokes came down after him, slithering the last few feet and biting on a curse. "Bloody nail in my boot!"

They looked along towards the gun emplacement, but could see nothing. Buka had told them of a path, close to the line of trees, that led down the cliff. They found it and started down, clinging to rocks and shrubs to prevent themselves sliding down the almost vertical track. It was a path for native's bare feet, not white men's rotting boots.

Then Mullane, leading the way, held up a hand, holding Vokes back. Almost immediately beneath them, no more than twenty feet below, a Japanese came out from a cave in the cliffs and went down between the trees towards the road. Now they saw for the first time the set of rails running up from the road to disappear into the base of the cliff.

Two more Japanese came out of the cave and started down through the trees. Mullane, feeling the beginning of cramp, moved his foot cautiously; but not cautiously enough. His foot slipped and a scatter of small pebbles went sliding down the path. The two Japanese stopped and turned round, but didn't seem startled. Mullane and Vokes flattened themselves against the cliff-face, thankful that they were below the level of the tops of the trees that grew at the base of the cliff; they were in shadow and Mullane knew the Japanese would have to come back to investigate more closely if they were to see him and Vokes. Then he heard one of the Japanese say, "A possum," and the two men went on down through the trees to the road.

Vokes leaned down, breathed into Mullane's ear: "I can't see if they're still down there on the road."

Then luck, the element the generals say should not be trusted in war, struck for them. There was the drone of engines high in the moonlit sky and four RAAF Hudsons, taking advantage of the bomber's moon, came in from the west, flying right over the line of ficus trees.

The anti-aircraft guns along the top of the cliffs opened up before the first bombs were dropped; Mullane hadn't seen the other guns but now it sounded as if the whole of the top of the cliffs was lined with them. The night suddenly exploded with noise and red light. The moon was lost somewhere above the blazing guns. Out on the harbour fans of blue-white water opened up in a ghastly sort of beauty; then there was a brilliant mixture of red, yellow and black as a ship blew up. Vokes could not have wished for a better distraction than this raid.

Mullane went down the remainder of the track in a hurry. He saw the big patch of lantana just in time and fell to one side; but Vokes coming down behind him in a rush didn't miss it. He fell right into it, felt it scratch at him like a clowder of wild-cats. Mullane dragged him out of it and they ran on down through the trees to the road. There Mullane stopped.

"No sign of those Japs – they must have beat it." He clasped Vokes' hand. "Take care, Frank."

"You too, Con."

For a moment Vokes wondered if he would ever see Mullane again; but there was no time for the emotion he suddenly felt well up in him. He ran in a crouch across the road. The bombs were still falling out in the harbour, but he knew the Hudsons would not be around much longer.

He ran down through the plantation, which he now saw was some sort of workshop area; there was a row of five trucks and behind them three tin sheds that he had not been able to see from their tree-top observation post. He suddenly lost heart, knew he had done the wrong thing in attempting such a stupid bloody act as trying to steal a boat; but there was no turning back, he had to keep going. His boot flapped on his foot like a trap; his shirt and trousers had been ripped by the lantana; he was in an awful bloody mess. He almost ran into the Japanese picquet before seeing him, dropped down behind a pile of petrol drums just in time. Then behind him he saw the truck swing in off the road and a dozen soldiers came tumbling out of it and fell into the ground, disappearing from sight. There must be slit trenches all around the area. He was bloody lucky he hadn't fallen into one and broken his leg. But that seemed to be the limit of his luck. He wasn't going to get out of here, not before the bombers had gone.

On the other side of the road, hidden in the trees, Mullane saw the speeding truck come along the road, swing sharply into the plantation right opposite him and skid to a halt. He saw the soldiers fall out of the truck and dive into the ground. One of the bombers came back above this western shore; Mullane looked up and saw it caught for a moment in a searchlight's beam. Then it had disappeared, but a moment later the bomb landed no more than fifty yards away along the road. Something went up with a loud roar, then flames were leaping high from a shed at the road's edge.

Mullane could not see Vokes but he knew it was only a matter of minutes before the Australian would be discovered. He was never going to get away, not unless there was another diversion.

Mullane sighed, not feeling in the least heroic but only disappointed that it should end this way. He patted his right-hand breast pocket: the silver dollar's luck had at last run out. Then his hand strayed, almost of its own accord, to the other pocket and he took out the rosary beads. But not to pray.

He held them while the idea formed in his mind: he had to remember a name. Then he crossed the road on the run, ran into the plantation and stood by the truck. The guns along the cliff-top still barked and thundered; out in the harbour ships were adding their bit to the barrage. It was impossible to hear the bombers; but they were still dropping their bombs. Mullane stepped out into the open, away from the shadow of the truck. Again, for a moment, he had the impression that war was a farce: he stood surrounded by a dozen Japanese and it seemed that none of them was interested in him. Then he saw a head come up out of a slit trench, remain fixed as if its owner could not believe what he saw; then the soldier came upright in the trench and his rifle pointed straight at Mullane. The latter flung his hands in the air, just in time.

The other soldiers sprang out of their trenches, converged on Mullane; for a moment he thought they were going to spear him with their rifle barrels. Arms still above his head, the rosary beads dangling from one hand, he looked around at the puzzled, threatening Japanese.

"I am Father Holtz," he said in German. "A German missionary, from Waku." He straightened his right arm: "Heil Hitler!"

He might just as well have spoken in Sanskrit or Urdu. He had almost to bite his tongue to stop himself from speaking in Japanese.

Then a bomb went off just off-shore and most of the Japanese dived back into their trenches. Two of them, one a corporal, hesitated; then the corporal jabbed his rifle at Mullane and pushed him towards the truck, shouting to the other soldiers to follow him. There was no immediate movement, then reluctantly they came up out of their trenches and ran to the truck.

III

Down behind the petrol drums Vokes saw Mullane being bundled up into the truck. The picquet who had been lying in the trench close by had gone up to the road and was running towards the blazing shed farther along. The truck, lights out but illuminated fitfully by the blazes from the guns up on the cliff, swung out on to the road and started off at speed in the direction that Vokes knew led to the town.

He stood up, sick at the thought of what was going to happen to Mullane. But he knew Mullane had done what he had with a purpose: to make sure that he himself got away. So at least he owed it to Con to get his finger out, to make it back to Smokey Bay.

He ripped back the tarpaulin on the petrol dump (*Jesus, what a place to have picked during an air raid!*) and grabbed two drums. Then, staggering under his load, he stumbled down to the launches, little more than skiffs with inboard motors, drawn up on the beach. The guns were still blasting away at the night sky; he wondered where the bombers were. Then a bomb dropped a hundred yards away along the beach.

He hurriedly inspected the first, the second, then the third boat: no oars in any of them. He gave a yelp of relief when he saw the oars in the fourth launch. He dumped the drums and his gear into the boat, pushed it out into the water. He had to shove with all his strength to get it out of the sand; he dug in his feet to get leverage and cried out as his foot trod on the nail in his ruined boot. Then the boat slowly, reluctantly, as if it had a mind of its own that realized it was being used for the wrong purpose, slid into the water, floated, began to move out ahead of him. He scrambled aboard, whimpering now with pain and exhaustion, grabbed the pair of oars.

He sculled out past the end of the small jetty. He had taken off his broad-brimmed hat and kept low in his seat as he rowed. The bombers came back for one last run and the guns, as if sensing that this was their last chance to down one of them, let go a barrage that seemed to blow the night apart. Suddenly there was an explosion and one of the Hudsons blew up, a giant hibiscus in the night sky; then it came plunging down as a long, broad stream of fire. By the time it hit the water Vokes had rounded the narrow point at the end of the beach.

He fumbled with the starter of the engine. There was a cough, then silence. He tried again: another stuttered cough. On the third attempt the motor caught. He settled back against the tiller and headed the launch at the shadow thrown by the tall cone of Vulcan Crater ahead of him. He had a long, still dangerous way to go, but he knew he was going to make it.

He owed it to Con Mullane.

Chapter Nine

I

By the time the truck was two hundred yards along the road leading to town the surviving three Hudsons were on their way home. The Allied air forces in the Pacific were still woefully short of bombers; with tonight's raid and the loss of one plane there could be no guarantee that planes would be available for what Mullane had suggested for tomorrow night. But it was all academic anyway: he would not be at Taluka to guide the bombers in on target.

The barrage from the anti-aircraft guns died away; out along the southern point a gun gave a last double bark, like an end note. The two ships that had been hit were still burning in the harbour and there were several fires on shore. The truck passed a blazing oil dump and Mullane, sitting in the open back of the truck with the soldiers, could feel the searing heat of the flames. But as they got closer to town he saw that there had been little damage done by past raids. He felt suddenly depressed, beginning to realize that the Japanese might never be driven out of this stronghold.

The road into town was busy with traffic now. Two fire engines, bells ringing, sped by on their way to the oil dump blaze. Troops were standing around in groups beside the road, looking a little bewildered and upset, as if not quite sure why they had been called out now the raid was over.

A soldier in the truck said, "Organized confusion again," and all the others laughed. Mullane was about to smile, more to ease his tension than because he was amused by the remark, then remembered he was supposed to be German. It might not be safe to let them know he spoke Japanese.

It struck him only now that he could be on his way to come

246

face to face with Yorida. Posing as the German missionary had been no more than quick-witted self-protection while creating the diversion for Vokes to escape. To have stepped forward and spoken in his American voice, especially while the Japanese were nervous and jumpy during the raid, might have meant an instant bullet.

He wondered if Vokes had managed to get away; but refused to entertain any thought that he might not have. The Australian *must* have got away; if he hadn't then Mullane had done the wrong thing in giving himself up. Instead of sacrificing himself, he should have sacrificed Vokes, climbed back up the cliff and set off back to Smokey Bay with Buka to send the information they had gathered. He had acted only on a personal level, been concerned only for Vokes and not for the larger, more important issue. He wondered about Buka, still up on the cliff-top, and hoped that he would have the sense to give up and go back to Kiogo. The war now was over for him at least.

The truck turned into the street where the police station was located and Mullane knew now that he was going to meet up once again with Yorida. Would the Japanese recognize him? His hand went up to his beard, then felt the hair curling round his ears and down on his neck; the old McArdle would have looked at his present image and dismissed what he saw as a wino bum or some Greenwich Village poet. *I'd never have recognized you*, Ruth had said, comparing him as Mullane with the old photo of McArdle. But would Yorida, the professional investigator, be sharper-eyed than Ruth, the lover, had been?

The truck pulled up and Mullane was roughly bundled down and marched into the police station. The soldiers did not seem to have any ill-feeling towards him as they might towards an enemy they recognized; rather, they seemed to be eager to be rid of him, as if arresting suspect Europeans was not their job. Mullane, still grasping the rosary beads in his hand, allowed himself to be pushed into the police station.

He remained impassive, doing his best to hide that he understood what was being said, while the corporal explained to the Security sergeant where he had picked up the newcomer. "He must be German, he saluted Hitler. He has those beads – what are they?"

"Rosary beads." The Security sergeant was a young man with a slight cast in one eye that gave his intelligent face an unfortunate look of shiftiness. "He could be a missionary. Leave him with us."

When the corporal and the soldiers had left, the sergeant sat down behind his desk. This main room had been stripped of any identification with its previous tenants, the civil police. Patches showed on the walls where notices had been ripped off; Mullane wondered if all the Wanted men on the notices had been granted a mass amnesty: murder, rape, robbery had perhaps been classified now as only misdemeanours. The government-issue furniture had been retained, however, including the oil lamps burning on each of the three desks. Two electric light bulbs hung from the ceiling: Mullane guessed that the bombing raid must have disrupted the power supply to this section of town.

There were two other Security men in the office besides the sergeant and all three looked at Mullane with enough suspicion to make him uneasy. He decided that for the moment there might be some safety in a lack of communication.

"Do you speak German?" he said. "I am Father Holtz – "

The sergeant shook his head. "You speak Japanese?" Then in English: "Do you speak English?"

Just in time Mullane stopped himself from shaking his head; with an effort he looked blank. "I am German – "

"Try him with that horrible pidgin," said one of the clerks, a plump man who looked as if he would fight the whole war at his desk.

"That's no good for interrogating anyone – it's baby-talk. No, you'd better go and get Colonel Yorida. He speaks German."

Oh Christ, thought Mullane. Would he have an ear for accent? Scheer had complimented Mullane on his fluency in German, but had made no comment on his accent.

"The Colonel isn't going to like being dragged out of bed – "

"He'd have got out of bed as soon as the raid started. You know how scared he is of bombs."

It would never have occurred to Mullane that Yorida would be scared of anything; but he was remembering the Yorida of old, the man secure in *kempei* headquarters in Tokyo. He had a sudden wild wish that a bomb had fallen right beside Yorida's quarters, had scared the hell out of the son-of-a-bitch, so much so that he would be deaf to accent and even blind to features that he might otherwise have recognized. It was a wild ridiculous wish, a fanciful prayer. He looked down at the beads in his hand, found he was running them through his fingers like worry beads.

It was fifteen minutes before Yorida arrived. In the meantime Mullane, seated on a chair the sergeant had pushed towards him, had played the village idiot, smiling inanely each time the sergeant or his colleague looked towards him, remaining blank-faced while the desultory conversation, of which he understood every word, went back and forth past him. Now that he had relaxed on the chair weariness had taken hold of him and he could feel his mind slipping out of gear. He sat upright, trying to make himself alert by making himself uncomfortable.

Yorida came in, didn't look at Mullane but at the oil lamps on the desk, then up at the dead electric light globes. "The power gone again? Every time there is a raid . . ." Then he looked at Mullane, but still spoke to the sergeant: "This could have waited till morning. Why didn't you just lock him up?"

"I am sorry, Colonel. I thought it was important. Two Germans in three days . . . I would have got Captain Mizukami, but he doesn't speak German – "

In five years Yorida had changed. He was even thinner, looked unhealthy; he took off his cap and Mullane saw that he was now almost bald. He wore horn-rimmed glasses and they seemed to accentuate the thinness of his gaunt face. I'd never have recognized him, Mullane thought; but then knew that would only have been if he had passed Yorida in a crowd. There were other, indefinable features about Yorida that he would always remember.

Yorida looked Mullane up and down. The latter wondered if he should smile; then did so. After all, he was supposed to be a missionary, a man of charity. But he could feel the old anger and hatred welling up inside him like a sickness that would vomit out of him at any moment. Five years fell away like an instant and the two of them were back in the harshly-lit bare room with Mieko's body lying on the table between them.

"You are German?" Yorida's accent was bad; his soft voice seemed to have trouble with the gutturals. "You are a Christian missionary? What is your name?"

"Father Gottfried Holtz." He didn't know where the *Gottfried* came from; it just fell on to his tongue. "I am from Waku, west of here, down near Gasmata."

Yorida stared at him and for a moment Mullane thought he saw the dawning of recognition in the Japanese's face. Then Yorida nodded and led the way into an inner room. Mullane hesitated, had a momentary urge to turn and run and hope for some miracle; then he controlled himself and followed Yorida into the room. The Japanese lit the lamp on his desk, gestured to Mullane to sit down on a chair opposite him. Mullane pulled the chair back a little, sat down and hoped that the light from the lamp did not fall directly on his face.

"You should tell me your story, Father Holtz." Yorida sat and waited.

Mullane was still having difficulty in keeping control of himself each time he looked directly at Yorida. He had never believed that confrontation would happen; and now Yorida still held the whip-hand. He looked down at the beads, wondered why he was still holding them (they seemed such a simple, futile disguise), then put them in his shirt pocket. He was aware of the silver dollar in the other pocket and wondered how much luck still remained in it. He applied himself to his story, inventing as he went along but keeping it simple so that he would be able to remember it if questioned again. Face to face with Yorida, his mind had become fully awake.

"My bishop, Bishop von Scheer – " He paused, but there was no expression on Yorida's face. Was Scheer already dead? "My bishop ordered me to leave the island last March with a party of nuns and go to Australia. But I disobeyed him – I went to see some sick natives first and when I got back to the coast the boat had gone. Since then I have been living with the natives in the mountains."

"Why have you come in to Rabaul now?"

"My conscience has been worrying me." His conscience *was*

worrying him, that he should be lying to this killer just to save his own life; he should be avenging the life that had been taken, that of Mieko. "I want to go home to the Fatherland, where I feel I can perhaps do more good."

"As a missionary? From what I hear, Germany needs more than missionaries just now."

"I have heard no news for six months. We are still winning the war, aren't we?"

"*We* are. But Germany – ?" He shrugged. "Waku is a long way from here. Why did you not go down to Gasmata and give yourself up there?"

"I thought about how our Church works. Often it is impossible to get past one's immediate superior." *I'm not only posing as a priest but a rebel one at that, one who criticizes the Church's system.* Perhaps he should have posed as a Lutheran . . . "What if it was like that in the Japanese army? I asked myself. I did not want some junior officer at Gasmata deciding my fate. I decided to come to Rabaul, to the top, as it were."

"The senior officer at Gasmata is of superior rank to myself," said Yorida. "But I'm the one who will decide your fate here."

Mullane resisted the temptation to be too deferential. "With due respect, Colonel Yorida, I demand that I be taken before the General in command."

Yorida smiled. "Would you demand to see the Pope if your bishop refused you something? You will have to be satisfied with me, Father Holtz. I think your story needs to be checked. We seem to be over-run with priests wanting to go home to save their Fatherland." Then he called out in Japanese: "Sergeant, come in here."

The sergeant appeared at the door. "Colonel?"

"Bring the German bishop here at once. But don't tell him why we want him here."

When the sergeant had gone, Yorida looked back at Mullane. He pushed a packet of cigarettes across the desk, but Mullane shook his head. The Japanese lit a cigarette, coughed and sat back in his chair. He looked exhausted and ill and Mullane wondered what had happened to him in the past five years.

"You don't speak Japanese?"

He had spoken in Japanese and once again Mullane was

251

almost trapped. He frowned, trying to look puzzled, said in German, "Please speak German, Colonel. Otherwise I do not understand what you are saying."

"Of course. A slip of the tongue, as they say." But it had not been, Mullane was sure of that. This man's tongue hadn't slipped since he had first learned to speak. "But we shall soon know whether you are telling the truth. Do you respect the truth, Father Holtz?"

"Yes."

Yorida nodded and smiled, as if he doubted that any man had respect for the truth. "Do you have family in Germany?"

"No." The less history one had, the less one had to remember. "They are all dead."

"Killed in the war?"

"No. My parents and my brother died before the war." He could not resist the question he had asked five years ago: it was like a man fascinated by heights walking as close as he dared to the edge of the precipice: "Do you have a family in Japan, Colonel? A wife perhaps?"

"No." He was surprised at the answer. He was further surprised when Yorida offered more information than he had expected: "My wife and children were killed in a bombing raid by the Americans on Tokyo last April."

The bastard's human, Mullane thought. But he could feel no satisfaction at the other man's tragedy; he was glad to discover he was not so mean and malicious as that. But he could not bring himself to offer any sympathy.

He sat there on the uncomfortable chair, thinking about Scheer now, wondering how he was going to enlist the bishop on his side. While he pondered the problem, he looked about him; but there was nothing to catch his interest other than the silent, suddenly morose man on the other side of the desk. This room seemed even barer than the room outside: a desk, two chairs and that was all. He seemed destined to meet Yorida in rooms as stark and unidentifiable as those in hopeless dreams.

Yorida smoked his cigarette, at last put out the butt in a large shell that served as an ash-tray. He sat back again in his chair and seemed to have difficulty in getting his breath. He's dying, thought Mullane; and wondered what disease had got to him. T.B., malaria, typhus, cancer: any of them might have attacked him. He could not bring himself to believe that Yorida was just dying from grief.

It seemed that an hour had passed before there was noise and movement in the outside room; but Mullane knew it could not have been that long. The silence and constant stare of Yorida had just stretched the time.

The sergeant brought Bishop Scheer into the room. Mullane stood up at once, tried to remember whether a priest kissed a bishop's ring or whether that was a deference paid only to cardinals. He decided for the informal, familiar approach.

He grabbed Scheer's hand, said in German, "Your Reverence, how glad I am to see you still alive! When you said to me – Father Holtz, you must leave the island – I should have listened to you. I wanted to come back to the mission – "

"That's enough," snapped Yorida and stood up. He swayed slightly, put his hands on his desk to support himself and leaned forward. "Bishop Scheer, do you know this man?"

Scheer said nothing for almost too long. He's going to give me away, Mullane thought, he's chosen his side. The German no longer wore his tattered cassock; he had been issued with new cotton twill trousers and shirt and rubber-cleated boots; he was clean-shaven and his hair had been cut *en brosse*. He stood much straighter and Mullane couldn't help thinking that he was looking at a military man, not a priest.

Then at last Scheer said, "You always were a stubborn man, Father Holtz. Perhaps that is why you were such a good missionary. Yes, Colonel, I know this man. He was one of my assistants down at Waku. His name is Father Willy Holtz."

Yorida straightened up, looked recovered. "Father *Willy* Holtz? That was not the name he gave me."

Mullane said, almost too quickly, "Willy was my nickname. The natives called me Father Willy. They had trouble saying Father Gottfried."

"First names? You Germans are far too familiar. The natives can have no respect for you."

"We were priests, Colonel, not soldiers," said Scheer.

Obviously Yorida thought that was no excuse. "Father Holtz is like you, Bishop. He wants to go home and fight the war for

253

Herr Hitler. He can join you. You will both sail on the ship leaving tomorrow morning for Singapore. How you get home from there to Germany will be someone else's problem. Good night."

I can't believe it, Mullane thought, after all these years it can't end like this. A formal bow, a polite good night: you didn't say good-bye to your wife's killer like this. But that was how it was. The sergeant stepped aside and Scheer, after a moment's hesitation, took Mullane's arm.

"Let us go, Willy. You look in need of a rest." The grip on Mullane's arm was strong; Scheer was going to get him out of this room before he attempted something stupid and fatal. "We have a lot to talk about."

Mullane allowed himself to be led out of the police station. The sergeant turned him and the Bishop over to two soldiers, said a polite good night to the two prisoners and went back into the station.

"We have some distance to walk," said Scheer. "They have no transport to spare for a couple of unwanted priests. What are you doing in Rabaul?" He saw Mullane glance back enquiringly at the two soldiers close behind them. "Don't worry, I know these two. They don't speak German. They don't speak very good Japanese either, I gather. They are Formosans."

Mullane, knowing now that the German could be trusted, told him everything. "But I don't know if Frank Vokes got away. I just hope so."

"What about Buka?"

"If he had any sense he's headed back home."

"What made you decide to pose as Father Holtz?"

Mullane grinned, took out the rosary beads. "Inspiration, I guess. Sister Brigid must have put a ghostly hand on my shoulder."

Scheer smiled. "I've always been a poor priest – I've always had difficulty believing in miracles. But who would have expected one from Sister Brigid?"

"I'm still a sceptic, Bishop. Her intervention, if that was what it was, hasn't really solved my problem. If anything, she

254

has got me in deeper. But that may be what they call Irish Lend-Lease."

"You can still joke, Mr Mullane."

"It's an effort, Bishop."

Scheer was being held in a house south of Chinatown and down on the beach, a good twenty minutes' walk. They passed groups of soldiers, some natives and, once, half a dozen Chinese standing outside a store. Mullane wondered if any of the Chinese would recognize him; then once more he placed his trust in his beard and longer hair. The last time he had been in Rabaul in January he had been clean-shaven and crew-cut.

The action and the confusion following the air raid had subsided and the town was settling down again. Out on the harbour the two ships were still burning and across the water the oil dump was still blazing. But traffic out on the harbour had started up again and barges were moving out from the wharves towards the transports and supply ships.

"Have you heard anything of what's going on?" Mullane said.

"The convoys start moving out tomorrow for Guadalcanal. I've got that from the native boy they sent to look after me. He's a mission boy from here in town. Is that what you came to Rabaul to find out?"

"Yes. But if Frank got away, they'll know down in Guadalcanal. Let's hope they're well enough prepared to stop them."

"Well, that's something you can think about on our way to Singapore."

They turned down a side street, then followed a path that led along the narrow strip of beach towards the house on the point. They had almost reached the house when they saw the outboard launch coming in. It ran up on to the beach and four soldiers jumped out. They fumbled in the bottom of the boat, then lifted out what looked to be a body.

Scheer paused, looked at the two guards, gestured down at the group carrying the corpse and made the sign of the cross. The two soldiers looked at each other, puzzled; then one of them shrugged and led the way down to the water's edge. The body was laid on the sand, a boy in khaki shirt and trousers, a helmet with the ear-plugs still dangling from it like a growth, and the harness of a parachute but no parachute. There was no sign of any wound and Mullane wondered how the airman had not been burned in the plane that had gone down into the harbour in flames. Perhaps he had jumped out of the plane on its way down, preferring to die hitting the water than being burned to death.

"An Australian flying-officer," he said, recognizing the rank-badges on the boy's shoulders. All he knew about the RAAF he had got from magazines: he was, in a way, one of the RAAF's principal watch-dogs but he had to inform himself about the service that depended so much on him. Christ, he thought, we're still fighting this war as amateurs.

The Bishop said a prayer, while the soldiers waited impatiently. Then he turned away and led the way up to the house, while the four soldiers picked up the corpse and carried it up the beach towards a truck parked in the shadow of some trees.

"He's the first one I've ever seen," said Mullane. "I work for them, I help them all I can, and he's the first one I've ever seen. And he was dead. I'm beginning to wonder how much I belong to this war!"

"Don't be too depressed, Mr Mullane."

"Oh, for Christ's sake – sorry. I suppose you do everything for His sake?"

"I try. I don't always succeed. At least you still have more hope than that poor boy."

They went into the house, leaving the two soldiers to sit down on the veranda, where they instantly lit up cigarettes and relaxed. Inside the house, which was built of fibro and consisted, as far as Mullane could guess, of no more than four small rooms, Scheer led the way into a bedroom. A single iron-framed bed stood against a wall; a wardrobe with a full-length mirror in it stood against the opposite wall; there was nothing else in the room but a straight-backed, rush-bottomed chair. Mullane wondered who had been kicked out of his home to make way for a German priest whom the Japanese did not want but were unsure how to treat.

"You had better sleep here," said Scheer. "My room is

opposite. They are calling us early. Our ship sails at six o'clock in the morning."

"Bishop, I'm not going anywhere on that damned ship!"

"Mr Mullane, what's the alternative? Suicide? I don't think that is in your nature, any more than it is in mine. Perhaps even less – I am so much older than you."

"How long do you think I can keep up this pretence of being a German?"

The Bishop sighed. "Who knows? But so long as you can, you will remain alive. There may be Germans in Singapore – I don't know. We may never even reach Germany. We may spend the rest of the war together as guests of the Japanese. The prospect doesn't appeal to me . . ." His voice trailed off: he sounded as he had when Mullane had first met him that morning by the river – a week, a month, a year ago?

"Nor to me, Bishop. Either as a German or an American. I'm not going on board that ship in the morning. If you hear any sort of disturbance during the night, just stay in your room."

"If you get away, what shall I tell Colonel Yorida? That you had changed your mind about fighting for Herr Hitler?" Scheer went to the window, looked out through the rattan blind. There was no light in the room and he pulled the blind slightly aside. "There are those two guards out front. There are also two more out in the road at the back. I was flattered that Colonel Yorida thought I was worthy of such surveillance, till I realized he really doesn't trust me. He thinks I am potentially dangerous – " He laughed softly; but only for a moment. "They will shoot you, Mr Mullane, as soon as you make a move. Catholic priests, genuine or otherwise, aren't held in much regard by Colonel Yorida. I'm sure he has given orders for them to shoot without asking questions if either of us attempts anything suspicious. Why should he worry about us? We're just a nuisance."

"I should have told him who I was, got it over and done with."

"What would that have achieved? I am concerned for you, Con." It was the first time he had used the name. "I don't

257

want to have to say the last rites over you as I did over that poor boy down on the beach."

"I'm concerned for you too, Bishop. If I do get away it will make things awkward for you – Yorida may not believe that you did not help me. But I have to try. I may be too young for suicide but I'm not old enough for surrender."

It seemed that Scheer winced. "You did not have to say that, even if it's true. Well, I suppose it is good-bye again." He put out his hand. "I'll pray for you."

Mullane pressed the thin bony hand. "Take care. And don't be too disappointed when you get home to Germany. Try and survive."

"That's all there is left to do."

Scheer went quickly out of the room, afraid that emotion would crumble him. Mullane felt the same weakness in himself, cursed the circumstances that had brought them together; he wished that he had met the German in another time and another clime. For a moment he lost the resolve to escape: he could not leave the Bishop to his fate at Yorida's hands. Scheer would fare no better than Mieko had.

He lay down on the bed, tried to put his mind in some sort of order. He put aside the thought of what would happen to Scheer: that would have to be left to God's grace and he hoped the Bishop's faith would not let him down. But what about the two soldiers out in front of the house and the other two in back? He had no weapon, nothing but his bare hands. The men were not going to present themselves individually and alone so that he could strangle them. And he was not even sure that he could kill a man in such a way. A gun or a knife somehow meant a remove, made the killing a little less direct. Though he knew he was splitting hairs: he thought of Yorida as Mieko's murderer and the colonel probably hadn't laid a hand on her.

Then he heard one of the soldiers on the veranda say something and move away. He sat up, eased himself carefully off the bed and looked out through the rattan blind. The soldier went round the corner of the house, obviously to relieve himself, and the second man stood up, stretched and uttered a loud yawn. He stood there, looking out at the moonlight on the harbour, and Mullane wondered if he could get out of the bedroom and across the veranda and kill him before the first soldier came back. But he knew at once that the attempt would be useless.

Several minutes passed, then the soldier out front looked round, walked to the corner of the house. Mullane, still peering through the blind, could see him looking into the shadows.

"Adachi?"

Then Mullane saw a dark blur hurtle out of the shadows and the soldier went down with a loud gasp. Though he had caught only a glimpse of the figure as it lunged forward out of the darkness, Mullane knew at once that it was Buka. He ran out of the bedroom and on to the veranda as Buka straightened up from above the body of the soldier, a knife in his hand, and grinned up at his boss.

"Boat down on beach, boss. We go across to Kokopo road. Quick!"

"Hold it a moment, Buka."

He turned to go back into the house, but Scheer was blocking the doorway. "I've changed my mind, Mr Mullane. May I come with you?"

Mullane didn't know whether to feel relief or annoyance. At least his conscience would be relieved if he took the German with him; but would Scheer be able to stand up to the long trek back to Smokey Bay? But all he said was, "You're welcome, Bishop. Go down with Buka to that launch. I'll be with you in a moment – first, I've got something to do. Do you have pencil and paper?"

"In my room – I'll get it – "

"No." Mullane pushed him across the veranda and down the steps. "Get down to the boat."

He went through into the Bishop's bedroom, turned up the low-burning oil lamp on the table beside the bed. Scheer had been writing a letter: *My dear Lotte and Ilse. Perhaps I shall reach home before this letter . . .*

He grabbed a clean sheet of paper, wrote his name and a date in bold Japanese characters: McArdle, 2 April, 1937. It was not easy to write the characters with a pencil; he would have been much quicker with a brush. But he knew Yorida would be able to read it and the quality of the calligraphy wouldn't matter. He went back to his own room, laid the note on the bed. Then, as he was about to turn away, he had another thought. He took the silver dollar from his pocket and laid it on the note as a weight. If Yorida could not, by chance, read the message, then maybe he would remember the silver dollar.

He left the house at a run, sped down over the beach and jumped into the launch as Buka pushed it out. Mullane started up the engine, handed over the tiller to Buka and lay down beside Scheer in the bottom of the boat.

"Better that we stay out of sight." Then he pushed the umbrella towards Scheer. "I grabbed that as I came out of your room. Somehow you're not you without it."

"Thank you, Mr Mullane." Scheer lay on the uncomfortable board, his buttocks in a pool of water; he looked up at the night sky, all that he could see above the gunwales of the boat. "Are you wondering why I asked to come with you?"

"Not really, Bishop. I think it's a case of the devil you know and the devil you don't . . . At least you'll be more comfortable in Australia than in Germany."

"What a test of one's patriotism . . . I'll do my best to keep up with you, Mr Mullane. But I don't want you to stop and wait for me."

"No," said Mullane, but wondered what he would do if he was put to the test.

They made their way across the harbour unchallenged, while Buka explained how he had seen Mullane captured and bundled into the truck. "I had to run into town, boss. Long bloody way. I guess they take you to police station. Then I see them bring you out and take you to house. Was easy, then."

Was easy, then: two men knifed to death, his own life risked, all just to save his boss, the man who was going to desert him in a day or two. "Thanks, Buka."

Twice they passed close to barges heavily laden with supplies, but no one seemed to query why a lone native should be moving across the harbour in a launch in the middle of the night. It was obvious that the Japanese had much bigger things on their minds than the breaking of a curfew by one of the locals.

Buka took the launch in to the western shore, switching off the motor and pushing it in with a single oar he took from the seat beside him. He whispered to Mullane, "Nobody along here, boss. But we got to walk mile, half a mile, back along road to them trees on cliff. Our guns and packs still up tree."

Mullane, still lying on the floor of the boat, said to Scheer, "We have something to do on the way back to Smokey Bay, Bishop. There may be some risk. Do you want to go on alone and we'll meet up with you?"

"If you don't mind, I'll stay with you. I may be able to help."

"Sabotage, Bishop?"

"I'll imagine I'm a Crusader. Some of them were excellent saboteurs."

II

They beached the launch and went back along the Kokopo road to the steep path that led up the cliff. They moved cautiously, stepping into the bushes beneath the cliff as trucks came along; but they were not challenged and soon they had reached the bottom of the path. Buka went up first to make sure the way was clear; Mullane, looking up through the trees, saw him outlined against the moonlit sky. He gave a reassuring wave and Mullane and Scheer started up. The Bishop found the going hard; once Mullane had to grab him to prevent him from falling backwards. Twice they had to stop, flattening themselves against the rocks, as Japanese came out of the cave-workshop immediately beneath them. But at last they had reached the top and Mullane and Scheer waited in the long grass while Buka climbed the ficus tree and came down again with the guns and packs.

He pushed something at Mullane in the darkness. "You want this, boss."

It was the Yankees' cap. He put it on and it was almost like slipping on an old identity: for the time he had been there in the police station tonight with Yorida he had been McArdle. Mullane was a *persona* that had no longer become necessary. If he got back to Townsville he would present himself to Ruth as Con McArdle . . .

They set off back along the route they had traversed last night with Scheer this time taking Vokes' place. This time Mullane knew what they had to avoid and they made good time. It was an hour before daylight when they reached the end of the Taluka airstrip. They kept going, up the slope past the radar post, and came once again to the stand of ficus trees. They climbed into the same tree as they had occupied before, with Scheer having to have help from both Mullane and Buka. He was exhausted by the forced march, but he made no complaint and did his best to hide how he felt. Now that he had made his decision to give himself up to internment in Australia he felt stronger, spiritually and emotionally if not physically. He was only ashamed at the thought that he would, in fact, probably be more comfortable in Australia than back home in Germany. His brother and sisters and the rest of his countrymen would be suffering while he, the one whose life was supposed to be dedicated to sacrifice, would be luxuriating (well, comparatively) in safety and comfort.

They made themselves as comfortable as possible and settled down for the night. The flying-foxes, which had been out on their night flight when the three men arrived, came back, found squatters in their home and flapped away again. It was broad daylight when the three men woke, cramped and stiff but at least refreshed by their sleep.

The day was another warm one, humid and, here in the tree-tops, stinking. Once Scheer felt faint and almost fell out of the tree, but Mullane grabbed him and gave him a drink of water.

"Sorry you can't put up your umbrella, Bishop."

Clouds began to build up in the afternoon and by dusk were thick and low. Mullane suddenly felt pessimistic. There had always only been a slight chance that the bombers would come at his request but now his scheme seemed hopeless.

He had told Buka what he had in mind and there had been some small satisfaction when the big native did not question or scoff at the idea. Perhaps an unsophisticated mind was what was needed in such a situation.

But it was Scheer who said, "How are you going to get up those trees? You'll need to start your fire at the top."

Then Buka said, "Maybe we better use arrows."

"Arrows?" Cowboys and Indians: shades of the heroes of

his early youth, of Broncho Billy Anderson and William S. Hart.

"I see it in a fillum, boss, one time over in Rabaul. Fellers shoot arrows with fire on them – "

Hollywood and a simple primitive to the rescue. But why should he shake his head at the source of inspiration? Sennacherib and the Assyrians had used flaming arrows centuries ago: he had not learned enough from his study of military history. "Can you make a bow and some arrows? Won't you need a special wood for the bow?"

"I can find it, boss. I'll be back."

So in mid-afternoon Buka had slipped down out of the tree and disappeared. He came back just after dark with a bow about five feet long and a bark quiver full of arrows.

"Took me long time, boss. I found that police boy I know, he took me to feller out in hills. These Baining bow and arrows. Feller buy them from Bainings, sell 'em to Japs for – what they call 'em?"

"Souvenirs." He and Buka would give the Japs a souvenir tonight that they would remember for a long time. He felt a sudden elation, but it went almost at once as he looked up again into the cloud-filled darkness.

There had been a lot of activity on the airstrip during the day, though no squadrons had taken off on sorties. Just before dusk twenty Mitsubushi Bettys came in from the north, circled the strip and landed, the last putting down just before darkness fell. Mullane peered through the darkness, but he could only guess at what was happening down there. He could see the hooded lights of trucks and from their positions he guessed that the newly arrived bombers had been parked along both sides of the strip. The bombers must have come from some distant base, possibly Manus Island, and were staging here overnight before joining a combined raid tomorrow. They had come in so late in the day so that they would not be detected by some high-flying reconnaissance plane. Mullane guessed that there must now be over fifty bombers down there on the strip and in the camouflaged hangar: sitting ducks waiting to be bombed. The Allied planes *had* to come tonight.

But the night remained black and unpromising. Mullane

became cramped, hungry and miserable. He munched on a banana, once more dreamed of the feasts of Schlaraffenland, but did not mention it to Scheer. If he got back to Australia he would take Ruth, on their first night together, to the best restaurant in town. He wondered what sort of restaurants Townsville had in wartime. They might be on a par with those in Brownsville, Texas, in peacetime.

At last he looked at his watch in the shaded glow of his flashlight. "Time to go. You stay here, Bishop. If Buka and I don't come back, here's my map. I've marked the route we took. It won't be easy, but with a little luck and a lot of prayer you should make it. You can report to Frank whether we succeeded or not."

"Good luck, Con. I'll give you two hours."

"We'll be back before then – I hope."

He and Buka left their rifles and packs stacked in a cleft in the tree, taking only the bow and arrows, their knives and one grenade with them. They would have to get away from the airstrip on the run as soon as their job was done and Mullane did not want either of them hampered by a rifle or pack. The rifles would be of little use, anyway. If they found themselves in a situation where they had to be used, there would be too much firepower against them.

So they took with them only the bare essentials for the job, including Mullane's spare shirt. His leg had stiffened up again, but when he had dressed the wound in the afternoon there had been no sign of bleeding. The stiffness wore off by the time they were halfway down the slope.

They moved in towards the southern end of the strip and had little difficulty in finding their way to where the petrol tankers were parked. The ground was waterlogged and treacherous and several times Mullane slipped, jerking his bad leg. As they came out of the tall kunai grass he looked back; he could barely make out the hill towards which they would have to run. He tried to remember the lie of the land as he had seen it from the top of the ficus tree; there was a narrow track on the far side of this kunai that would probably be the quickest escape route in the darkness. He whispered to Buka to keep close to him and they moved on towards the parking area.

They saw the two picquets when they were less than thirty yards from them. The Japanese were standing beside a tanker; one of them said something and the other laughed. Buka touched Mullane's arm and held up his knife. Mullane knew what the big native was suggesting: that the knife had already proved its value, let it be used again. He took out his own knife, feeling squeamish at the thought of what he was going to do with it in a few moments. I'm not a killer, he thought. But of course he was: given the opportunity he would kill Yorida without a qualm.

He and Buka crept towards the two Japanese. One of them was still talking, the other still laughing at whatever joke he was being told. The humorist died first, with Buka's knife deep in his back. Mullane took the other man, grabbing him round the throat and pulling him backwards. There was a moment's hesitation before he drove the knife home; but he knew it had to be done and so it was done. But he brought the knife round to the front and stabbed the small man in the chest. The Japanese slumped forward and Mullane let him go. He'd got no blood on him and even in that moment he thought what a fastidious killer he was.

Then he and Buka moved quickly. He heard the sound of an engine farther up the strip and saw a pair of shaded headlamps, like hooded eyes, coming down from the far end. But the car or truck suddenly slowed, then swung to the left and went towards the plantation.

It took Mullane a minute or two to find the drainage cock on the tanker. He fumbled with it, managed at last to unscrew it. Petrol spilled out; in a moment the air reeked with the fumes. He raced to the second tanker; then the third; in five minutes he had unscrewed the cocks on all five tankers. He pulled the spare shirt from where he had had it stuck in his belt, soaked it under the spilling cock of the last tanker. By the time he had finished Buka was beside him with the jerry-can he had snatched from the dump at the side of the parking area. They filled the can, then raced up the strip, past the parked bombers, towards the first track that led towards the plantation. They could hear the voices of other picquets farther up the strip and Mullane wondered if they would smell the fumes of the leaking petrol.

The two men were halfway down the track when Mullane saw the hooded headlamps coming towards them through the walls of tall kunai. He dived to one side, felt Buka crash into the grass behind him. They lay flat, only a yard from the track, behind a thin and bent screen of kunai; then the truck rolled by them, skidding in the mud as it slipped off the palm fronds on to the side of the track. Mullane saw it looming over him and for one horrifying moment thought they were going to be crushed; then the truck spun back and went on. They got to their feet and ran on up the track.

They came out from between the kunai on to another track that ran round the perimeter of the plantation. There was no sign of any more picquets, but Mullane knew there would be men on patrol tonight, especially with so many planes on the strip.

Most of the plantation was in darkness; but almost immediately ahead of them and some distance into the huge hangar there was a shaded light. They could see the silhouettes of three or four mechanics working on an aircraft. They could also see the dim shapes of planes parked wing-tip to wing-tip; coconut palms stood amongst the planes, supporting the roof of netting and palm-tops. The walls of the hangar were loosely-knitted netting, the fake trunks painted on it. At this distance, even in the dark, the camouflage was obvious; but Mullane could guess how successful it must have been viewed from the air. The Japanese must have learned a great deal about camouflage during their war in China.

He could not see his watch in the darkness and he dared not use his flashlight. He touched Buka's arm and they moved down the edge of the kunai, following the plantation to its southern end. They had almost reached the end when the two picquets came round the corner. Buka acted on the instant.

He dropped the jerry-can and raced at the two Japanese. Perhaps they had not been alert; perhaps in the darkness they did not see the dark figure till the last moment. With two swift stabs of his knife he killed them both. He shoved the knife into his belt, grabbed the men by their collars and dragged them into the kunai.

"Okay, boss." Mullane could imagine him grinning. "Everything all right now."

They moved deeper into the kunai, to give Buka a better angle for firing the bow. Mullane ripped the shirt into six strips, tied each strip to an arrow. Then he doused the pieces of cloth in petrol from the can. At last he straightened up, stood waiting and listening and hoping.

He had no idea how long it was before he heard the faint drone of an aircraft engine. Two more picquets had come down the side of the plantation, paused as if they had expected to meet the two already-dead picquets, then turned and strolled slowly back to disappear into the darkness. Then the plane came. It was over to the west, too far to the west; he wondered if it might be a single Japanese plane making a late flight into Vunakanau or Keravat, though he knew from experience that the Japanese did not fly at night in these islands unless absolutely necessary. Then he heard the other engines: five, six, he couldn't guess how many. And these were closer.

"Ready!"

He splashed the arrows once again with petrol, handed the first to Buka. He felt rather than saw the big man fit the arrow into the bow.

"Right, boss!"

He felt his way up Buka's arm to the cloth-wrapped arrow-tip. Then he struck a match and held it to the arrow. The cloth flared up at once and a moment later, with a twang of the bow-string, shot up into the air and looped towards the roof of the plantation-hangar. A second and a third arrow followed; but nothing was happening up on the netting roof. Then suddenly flames flared up and in seconds the netting and dead palm leaves began to burn. The last three arrows were shot straight into the wall of netting; it, too, flared up. Then it was time to run.

The safest route was through the tall kunai; but Mullane had reckoned that would take them too long. They raced back to the track up which they had come, turned down it and had almost reached the end of it when they heard the trucks racing down the strip itself. They plunged off the track into the kunai, fighting their way through it. Once Mullane glanced back, saw above the tall grass the glow of the growing blaze as the whole of the roof of the plantation took fire. But there was still no sign of the bombers.

Then he and Buka came out of the kunai, were at the southern end of the strip less than fifty yards from the petrol tankers. They raced between the tankers; then Mullane abruptly pulled up. Not too high above them he could hear the drone of aircraft. He wrenched the grenade from his pocket, pulled out the pin.

"Run, Buka!"

Then he hurled the grenade. It was a toss rather than a pitch, but he had never thrown a ball with as much satisfaction as he did that grenade. He dropped flat as the grenade went off, then he was on his feet, running after Buka. The big native was looking back over his shoulder, grinning broadly in the glare of the huge blaze behind them. He did not see the picquet who rose up right in front of him and fired at him point-blank.

Buka, running at full speed, went over like a hurdler who had clipped a hurdle. He went straight into the soldier who had shot him and the two went down in a tumbling heap. Mullane, following on fast, went over the top of Buka and drove his knife into the chest of the Japanese as he tried to get up. Then he rolled off the dead man and crawled towards Buka, who lay face down, arms spread wide.

One look was enough: Buka was dead. He let out a terrible cry of anguish, but it was lost in the roar of the first bomb as it landed. He saw the plantation, a mass of flames, heave outwards as the bomb landed dead-centre amongst the hidden Japanese bombers. Then a second bomb landed on the runway and one of the bombers parked there went up in an explosion of flame. Mullane turned Buka's head, but the big dark eyes saw nothing of the destruction he had helped cause.

Sobbing with grief, Mullane got to his feet and started running again.

III

"I just wish I could have buried him, that's all. Christ knows what they'll do to him when they find him."

"If he is so close to those petrol tankers, perhaps he will be cremated."

"I hope so. I didn't think – that's what I should have done, dragged him back there so that he would be cremated."

Mullane had got back to the ficus tree, climbed up it and slumped into a cleft amongst the branches. It had taken him several minutes to recover enough to tell Scheer what had happened. The German at first had been almost youthful in his excitement, but had quickly subsided when he had realized Buka was not with Mullane. Then, when told the tragic news, he had done his best to comfort the still grieving Mullane.

"I think we should leave now, Con. You can't stay here and watch all that – " The Allied bombers had gone, but the airstrip and plantation was still a mass of wrecked and blazing aircraft. "It's not going to compensate for Buka's death or make you feel any better."

"I'm not leaving yet, Bishop. I still have something else to do." He didn't attempt to explain; he was in no mood to be dissuaded. "Here's my compass. Keep heading west till you cross the outer of the two perimeter roads. Wait for me just beyond that – " He closed his eyes, tried to remember the countryside he, Vokes and Buka had passed through. "About fifteen minutes' walk beyond it you'll come to a small limestone escarpment. The track goes up it, past a big clump of pandanus. Wait for me there. If I'm coming, I'll be there no later than mid-morning. If I'm not there by then, head for Smokey Bay. Give my regards to Frank and tell him everything went off as planned. Well, nearly everything."

Scheer said nothing, just slung Buka's pack on to his back and grasped his umbrella. "I have an idea what you're planning, Con, but I'm not going to voice it. Good luck."

Then he disappeared down into the darkness and Mullane was left alone to stare down at the brightly blazing night half a mile away and the memory of Buka's last big smile before he died.

IV

Colonel Yorida knew he should not have trusted the German bishop. He had never been a religious man himself and he had had little respects for priests. They were as capable of lies as the sinners they professed to be saving; and the German priest had been a double liar. It only proved something that Yorida had always believed, that no one had any real respect for truth.

He hoped the bishop had gone to the hell he believed in and no doubt feared. He had lied about the Australian spies' heading for the north coast to be picked up. As soon as he had got back on board the patrol boat at Smokey Bay Yorida had radioed to Rabaul and since then there had been a constant patrol of planes and boats along the north and north-west coasts from Ataliklikun Bay right round to Open Bay. Nothing had been sighted: no party, no submarine, no flying-boat coming in at night. The party, with General Nara still held prisoner, must still be on the island.

The bishop should never have been allowed to get away with his second lie, that the American McArdle was Father Holtz. Yorida stiffened with fury each time he thought how easily he had been fooled. He could not believe it when he had been wakened for the second time during the night to be told by his sergeant that the German priests had escaped; his disbelief had increased when the sergeant had produced the piece of paper with the pencilled characters on it and the American silver dollar. How could he have not recognized the American, even with his beard and long hair? He knew he himself was not the man he had once been; he had advanced tuberculosis, the doctors had told him, and he was to be repatriated as soon as the impending big campaign got under way. He was not as alert as he had once been and he tired easily. But he should have remembered the American. If he had, last night's sabotage out at Taluka would not have occurred.

The piece of paper and the silver dollar were in his pocket. He had told the sergeant he would write the report himself; but nothing would be mentioned of the paper and the coin. If they were going to retire him, he wanted to retire with honour.

He sat in the back of the staff car, with his aide Captain Mizukami up front with the driver, pondering whether he should send parties out searching for the American and the German. If they were caught, the American would talk and the truth would come out. And this time the truth would be dangerous, to himself. He would be blamed, even if only indirectly, for last night's catastrophe. He stiffened again with fury at how the American had got his revenge for what had happened in Tokyo five years ago. The death of the woman, the American's wife, had been a mistake, the result of too much zeal on the part of two of his men; she had obviously known nothing of her husband's espionage work. He had failed to get any information from the woman and he had failed in not being able to detain McArdle; but last night's failure had been the worst of all. He took the coin out of his pocket, looked at it, then closed his hand on it. Was it some sort of unlucky charm?

"Shall I organize search parties, Colonel?" Captain Mizukami, eager, youthful, ambition written all over him like eczema, turned round in the front seat. "The Germans, I mean. They must still be in the area."

"I doubt it," said Yorida. "I think this was well organized. The Germans have a talent for organization. You can be sure they had their escape well planned. They probably headed back down to the bay and took a boat down the coast. A flying-boat probably came in and picked them up."

"But why would the Germans . . .? And priests, at that?"

"All priests are renegades, Captain. That's why they turn their backs on our world, the real world."

Captain Mizukami looked dubious; he had no experience of priests, still respected them as his parents had taught him to do. "I still don't understand them, Colonel. Especially the Bishop – he seemed a gentle man, a pacifist. What was the other one like?"

"He seemed to be the same." Yorida was on the defensive; he would have to see the subject was dropped very soon. "Which shows that in our job one cannot go on appearances."

It was seven o'clock when their car reached the airstrip at Taluka. As the car drove down beside the long strip he could see the havoc that had been caused. Work gangs were busy trying to clear the strip for the few undamaged aircraft to take off in case there should be another raid. Yorida knew that, despite what had happened here, bombers were taking off from Keravat and Vunakanau to head south; the undamaged planes here at Taluka would be expected to join them as in the original plan. As the staff car went down beside the strip the first bomber started up its engines and moved down to the end of the runway.

Right at the southern end of the strip Yorida could see the black wrecks of the petrol tankers. Some staff cars were parked there, a group of officers standing beside them, and he instructed his driver to drive down to them.

He got out of the car, walked across to the Commanding Officer and saluted. It was not a crisp salute; he had forgotten the silver dollar still clutched in his hand. He dropped his arm, fumbled to put the coin away, couldn't open the flap of his pocket and held on to the coin.

"A bad business, Colonel Yorida." The CO was about Yorida's age, but came of another class. He had known Yorida in Nanking and Singapore, but he had never been able to bring himself to be anything more than formally polite to the Security chief. "I cannot believe it was the work of natives. You are not going to order reprisals against them, I hope."

"No, Colonel Toyama." He looked up and down the strip, then south to the hill some distance away where he could see a line of thick trees. "I'm sure it was not the work of natives."

He was facing south, head-on to the distant hill and the line of ficus trees, when the first bomber roared by on take-off.

In the tree Mullane was firmly settled, the Lee-Enfield .303 with the telescopic sight affixed resting on a thick, unmoving branch. He had been watching the airstrip since daybreak, waiting for Yorida to come. He had not allowed himself to think that the Field Security chief would not put in an appearance; he *had* to come. No Security chief, unless he was seriously ill (dear Christ, I know he's ill, but please let him be hale and hearty and ready for death) would send out a subordinate to report on such a major disaster as last night's.

Through his binoculars he had seen the staff car coming down the strip and he had known Yorida would be in it. There had been no surprise when he saw the tall thin figure step out of the car; there equally was no surprise when he saw the bomber racing down the strip and knew that in a few moments its roar as it passed overhead would drown out the sound of his shot. He knew now that luck was going to be with him all the way.

He drew a deep breath and steadied himself. He put out of his mind how long he had waited for this moment; till a day or two ago he had never dreamed he would ever see Yorida again. Through his telescopic sight he saw Yorida face him. The range, he guessed, was just over 800 yards; he hoped the rifle was as accurate as Vokes had been told. He shut out all distraction: the sudden swoop of lorikeets immediately above him, the roar of the bomber as it came up towards him, rising steadily from the end of the strip. He was deaf; and all he could see was Yorida in the centre of his sights. He allowed for the slight pull to the right, then squeezed the trigger.

Yorida had a moment of bewilderment before he died. The first bullet hit him in the chest; the second in the top of the head as he bent over as if to look at what had hit him. His hand tightened on the silver dollar; then opened and the coin fell to the ground. He knew who had shot him: the American. He knew he was going to die and he could not believe it. But it was the truth.

V

Mullane, rifle slung over his shoulder, slid down the tangled trunk of the tree at a dangerous speed and hit the ground running. He slung on his pack, then he was running through the tall kunai heading for the shelter of the nearest forest almost half a mile away. He knew the sound of the shots would have been lost in the sound of the already disappeared bomber and it would be a few minutes before those on the airstrip near Yorida worked out where the shots had come from.

He was in fair condition, but he had not run half a mile in more years than he could remember; certainly he had not run it with a pack and rifle bouncing on his back and in boots that threatened to fall off his feet at every pounding step. He

273

went down into a dip, ploughed through some watery mud, scrambled up the other side and kept going.

Then suddenly, so suddenly that it was almost as if the forest had come forward to meet him, he ran in under the blessed, sheltering screen of trees. Twenty yards into the forest he fell against a tree, let it support him while he tried to mend his bursting lungs and turn the water in his legs back into bone and muscle. Then he drew himself together, stood listening for a moment, heard nothing but the sounds of the forest. Then he moved on, no longer running but walking fast, feeling luck was still with him.

He should catch up with the Bishop long before mid-morning.

Chapter Ten

Ruth sat on the veranda of the house on the hill outside Townsville and watched the big man in the white shirt and shorts, his Navy officer's cap pushed back on his head, come up the street. She knew he was bringing bad news and she wondered how she was going to accept it.

Lieutenant Blomfield had come up here four days ago to tell her they had had word from Frank Vokes. Blomfield had said that Vokes had made no mention of Con Mullane, but she had had the feeling he was lying. She had gone down each morning and afternoon to Coastwatchers' headquarters and each time Blomfield, who had appointed himself her protector, had told her there had been no further news from Vokes.

And now Blomfield was coming in the gate and up the steps to the veranda. It was he who had got her a billet here with a woman whose husband was on service in New Guinea; the woman, after some demur, had agreed to Luke and Mark's being allowed to sleep in the laundry beneath the stilt-raised house. She had been a bit upset to find that Ruth herself was not all-white, but she was a kindly woman and her prejudices had soon evaporated. Now Ruth felt at ease here in the house. Or as nearly at ease as she could feel while still racked with worry for Con Mullane.

She stood up, steeling herself; she wondered where she would go, what she would do without Con. Then she saw that Blomfield was smiling. He took off his glasses, wiped the fog from them and put them back on. He was hot and flushed from the walk up the hill; maybe he was too old for this war after all. But the news he had to tell her made him feel young and worthwhile.

"We've heard," he said. "They came on the air this afternoon."

"Both of them? Con Mullane, too?"

"Both of them."

She wanted to weep and to laugh; but succeeded in doing neither. In a dry voice that hurt her throat she said, "Is he all right?"

"Con? I gather so. But he's asked us to bring them out and we're going to do that. He brought the German bishop – Bishop Scheer? – out of Rabaul with him."

"The Bishop – alive? How did he do that?"

"God knows. He's been doing more than he was supposed to – we're going to have a little trouble playing down what he's done. Anyhow, a Catalina is going in tonight to bring them out."

"Did they get all the information you wanted?"

"More than we expected. Marvellous stuff. I shouldn't tell you this, but you're privileged company, I suppose. You were part of the operation in a way. Yes, they got everything we needed and more. It'll be released to the press tomorrow or the day after. There's been a big battle in the Solomons and the Japs have been pushed back. It's still going on, but the Japs have obviously failed. Con's and Frank's information, plus what we got from our chaps at the top end of the Solomons when they got back on the air – their radios had gone on the blink – all that info had the Yanks waiting when the Japs arrived. I gather it was one hell of a battle," he said wistfully, wishing he were still at sea.

"Will Con and the others be mentioned in the press report?"

"Afraid not. Nobody is supposed to know we exist. We just run our own private little war."

"Will you want them to go back?"

"Afraid so. The chief has said they can have two weeks' leave, then he wants them back on New Britain. The war is a long way from over, girl. We're just at the corner, we haven't turned it yet. What will you do?"

"Wait for Con. After that . . ."

But she couldn't think about it. She could not think about anything but tomorrow.